All Trivia

ALL TRIVIA
浮生琐记

［英国］洛根·波绍尔·史密斯 / 著 朱纯深 / 译

Logan Pearsall Smith

译林出版社

序
译笔点开的琐事

人之缘，书之缘

一个开放的人生，应该是一个不断与自己与世界对话的人生。在这对话中，人一遍遍地以一种孩儿般的目光看着世界的“陌生”，领略这陌生中的“新奇”，领受自身一次次的顿悟，以及顿悟中“自我”的重生。也许，一个人一辈子都在学着如何开放自己与之对话，开放自己与世界对话吧。回首当年上山下乡，自己是如何见识了十指抠泥的——literally and physically——汗与血的生存状态，是如何以风霜磨砺出的执拗背着人暗夜里挑灯自学，像儿童般在山野阡陌中领受了一次次的顿悟与重生。到1977级上了大学，连老师朗读英文时双下巴随着音调节奏的颤动也逃不过那双重新认识世界的童眼而印入脑际，在上个世纪七八十年代之交的校园绿荫中由此诞生成长起又一个新的自我。八九十年代之交，负笈英伦，一个全方位的文化冲击给了当时已经是大学老师的我一双新的童眼，带着黄泥汗血和闽地南风的基因，在异国的校园和街巷中再次成长起一个新的自我。

把这些自我的重生串在一起的，是一种缘分，人之缘分，书之缘分。有说和一个人相遇是一种缘分，那么与一个人相知而相交，更要一点灵犀相通。邂逅一本书，同样也是一种缘分，与一本书相知相交，同样也需要灵犀相通的那一点。教育，不就是师缘书缘结出的善果吗？让我与《浮生琐记》(*All Trivia*)结缘的，是诺丁汉大学的艾伦(Dr. Allan Rodway, 1919—2008)。与艾伦认识是在1988年，我在诺丁汉大学英文系访学的第一年。那时他已经退休几年了，系上专门聘请回来给来自中国的访问学者开英国文学的研讨课。一年过去，我转读博士，虽然艾伦不再继续上课，却与我成了忘年之交，成了课堂之外我随时可以请益的“私人”导师和家庭朋友。能与这一位既倔强又可爱的老先生结缘，除了共同的文学追求，还有共同的乒乓球爱好，更有他对我打的太极拳的兴趣。他七十岁那一年，在自己足球、网球等的长年爱好之外，还跟我学起了太极拳。后来我还知道，他的大学前经历，竟与我们这上山下乡的知青一代有类似之处。上世纪30年代，出身劳动阶级家庭的他十五岁辍学，找到一份打扫仓库的工作，每周挣五十便士，后来谋得一份保险公司的工作。聊天时他不止一次说过，当年要是在保险公司干下来会赚很多钱的，但他更喜欢的是读书，是语言和文学。“二战”爆发时，他因为登记为“良心拒服兵役者”被送到湖区务农，遇上跟他情况相似的一些知识分子，用知青的话说是“一道修理地球”的。战后他想圆自己的大学梦，可惜没有中学毕业资历，面对的竞争却是战时积存的六届毕业生申请读大学排的长队；无奈只能去拼公开奖学金，尽管希望渺茫。于是乎，在湖区一处农舍的角落，艾伦开始秘密地准备剑桥大学的公开奖学金考试，晚上挑灯夜读，白天复习偷读藏在身上的笔记。终于他成功考上剑桥读英文，从此在一片新天新地中获得了一次重生，毕业后来到刚于1948年升格独立的诺丁汉大学读博。

相隔有四十年，应无逻辑又不无逻辑地，英文系毕业的最早一个博士和招收的第一个来自中国的博士生走到一起，两人通常是每周一约，单对单地练太极拳，有时还来一场乒乓球。但最重要的是，艾伦会带我读一些英语诗文名篇，还一个一个音节纠正发音调整节奏，一个一个词语讨论文本阐发意义；在选读《浮生琐记》篇章时，还说这是他见过的最美的英文。的确，从人缘到书缘，第一篇《幸福》（“Happiness”）马上就在我心中勾起一种宋词般的意境，还让桃花源带上了一种异国情调。缘分所至，便动了翻译这本书的念头。那是1992年的事了。

作者与原作

《浮生琐记》作者洛根·波绍尔·史密斯（1865—1946）是一位批评家、散文家及传记作家，还是研究17世纪神祇信仰的专家，“嗜文如命”，对英文写作可说是个精益求精的完美主义者，如他借别人之口说的，不怕“一个劲儿地精雕细琢，到头来什么都抠没了”（《前言》）。他生于美国新泽西州米尔维尔一个富裕的玻璃瓶制造商家庭，受过哈佛教育，本来可以活成个美国富豪，却无意接手家族生意，拿到两万五千美元的补偿金之后跑到英国入读牛津大学，1891年毕业了便定居下来，1913

年干脆入籍为英国公民。此后一生中大部分时间都在英国及欧洲大陆度过，从事古典学研究，钻研英语语言文学，追寻他心仪的简·奥斯丁（Jane Austen，1775—1817）小说世界，“把数不清的牧师女儿从封面追到封底”（《乐园复得》）。史密斯一生广交文人名士，在大西洋两岸可谓是谈笑有鸿儒（当然是洋儒啦）。早在费城家中，常客就有名作家亨利·詹姆斯的哥哥哲学家威廉·詹姆斯（William James，1842—1910）、诗人沃尔特·惠特曼（Walt Whitman，1819—1892）；并与哲学家伯特兰·罗素（Bertrand Russell，1872—1970）、美国艺术史学家伯纳德·贝伦森（Bernard Berenson，1865—1959）是姻亲；伦敦时的好友包括当时最重要的文学和戏剧评论家德斯蒙德·麦卡西（Desmond MacCarthy，1877—1952）和作家罗斯·麦考利（Rose Macaulay，1881—1958），1913年他还参与创办了“纯粹英语学会”（the Society for Pure English），一个由一些名作家、名教授组成的旨在维护“纯正英语”的象牙塔社团。

史密斯工于格言警句式的极短篇章，讽喻、悲哀、幽默、愤世嫉俗，兼而有之，曾因其精美灵秀的文字、洗练的文笔和渊博睿智的观察评说，在大西洋两岸享有盛名。对语言表达的苛求简直同苦吟的贾岛和“信达雅”的严复有得一比。如果严复是“一名之立旬月踟蹰”，那他为“一句之立”可以数日推敲。继1912年的《英语》（*The English Language*）之后，1925年出版的《词与语》（*Words and Idioms*）一书更令他成为当时英语正确用法的权威。

原作书名是*All Trivia*：“所有的琐事”；内容是一系列极短

篇散文随笔和隽语警句。第一部分*Trivia*发表于1902年，很受好评。作者当时三十七岁；近二十年之后于1921年续上一集*More Trivia*；到1931年发表*Afterthoughts*时，史密斯已经六十六岁了。三年之后，全部内容结集于1934年问世，此时作者按中国人的说法已届古稀之年，加进*Last Words*作结也就顺理成章了。整个集子前前后后，无论是鞭辟入里的幽默，还是哀而不伤的怀旧，都以一种举重若轻的言辞含而蓄之，既集中体现了作者的文体追求，又历时地记录了作者三十多年最旺盛的人生经历中灵光乍现的思绪见解，漫步于伦敦街头巷尾所领略的大大小小的顿悟与重生。

开篇的《作者》即标新立异，几笔下来，借达尔文进化论激起的余波，活灵活现地描绘出一幅超现实的自画像：

> 亲爱的读者，写这些道德文章的，是一头硕大的食肉哺乳动物，属于动物界的一个亚目，该亚目还包括红毛猩猩、有獠牙的大猩猩、屁股大红大紫的狒狒，以及温文尔雅的黑猩猩。

如此先声夺人，定下的自嘲与低调陈述（understatement）作为基调贯穿全书，作者对世态人情再怎么调侃揶揄，也显出一种谑而不虐、讥而不刺的跳脱。这不愠不怒的跳脱，让作者能以嬉笑怒骂皆成文章的机锋游走于各种意识形态设下的价值框架之外，从自己的角度透视生活与人性的本真。但他似乎也知道自己的文字不拘一格，在同代人当中觅得理想读者并非易事——“他们是谁呢？到底在哪儿，在什么天堂或殿堂，我找得着他们？”（《他们》）：

> 他们品味精妙高雅，住在意大利新古典风格的侯门巨宅里，他们的天地由琳琅满目的象牙和古瓷装点，由古砖墙和石壁柱围护。在白色的起居室里，或者在莺歌燕舞的青草地上，我看见他们。他们在愉快地谈论着我，眼睛望着我。从世界的镜子把我照成的那个萎顿可笑的影像我掉开头，转而去看在这些眼睛那善良的镜子中照出的我的形象，从中寻找安慰和幸福。
>
> 他们是谁呢？到底在哪儿，在什么天堂或殿堂，我找得着他们？我可以踏遍大街小巷，按遍天下门铃，却永远也找不到他们。然而，我别无所求，除了他们有如冠冕的嘉许。为了他们的到来——他们永远不会来的——我修建种植；只为了他们，我暗暗写了这本书，他们永远不会读的。

“他们”似乎找不到，作者把眼光投向未来，想象那“跨越时间的巨大鸿沟”的“后人”（《跋》）：

> “你们穿的大衣多滑稽啊，亲爱的读者！还有戴的帽子！一想到你们的帽子我真就忍不住要笑，另外我觉得你们的各种性爱理论很是吓人。”
>
> 就这样，跨越时间的巨大鸿沟我挥一挥手，送去一声问候，给那些古怪的人，我们称之为后人的那些人；我，一如其

> 他大作家，认他们为我的读者——催他们快点，快点出生，好有幸读读这琐事琐思，这闪现于巷陌间的特丽维亚。

这种独怆然般的嗟叹背后，似乎是作者以对"知音"的期许"告慰自己"(《奇想一则》)，暗合了"生有闻于当时，死有传于后世"(王安石《祭欧阳文忠公文》)的文人心意：

> 能在我葬礼之后，还活在一句完美的话语中。(《成就》)

也许，这就是字斟句酌所文的心、要雕的龙吧——"成就某种精妙且经久不衰的东西，一种有幸赢得宇宙最高权威们赞许的东西"(《成就》)？

我们，又是什么意义上的读者呢？能否哪怕一时间悬置身外的羁绊，在作者笔下百年前的英伦风情中流连一番，像朱光潜先生引阿尔卑斯山路上的标语所说的那样，将自己的人生艺术化——"慢慢走，欣赏啊！"——慢慢地，在语言的精妙中追索心中的灵犀之龙？

译者与翻译

这读者之问，首先是关于译者之问。

我是1993年离开英国到新加坡国立大学任教的，次年艾伦夫妇从澳大利亚旅行回英国路过狮城勾留数日，应我所托带来了原作，但要到1997年5月开始我才认真动笔翻译了一小部分。

1998年7月续译，但是9月便从新加坡转赴香港城市大学执教，于1999年3月重提译笔。可惜因为大学教授的职业逻辑和其间不时冒出的学术研究课题，令《浮生琐记》成了"琐译"，在身外羁绊与内心向往的拔河中时断时续。2017年夏自香港城大退休，携余热不必取长途地来到香港中文大学（深圳）接受再循环，当年秋季刚鼓起余勇接着往下翻译，没承想因为其他写作计划打断又停到了2020年末，终于借深居简出的环境要求，在完成一本英文专著之后四鼓作气译完初稿审定终稿。这已经是2021年10月底了。

从当初起意翻译到如今完稿，*All Trivia*耐心地等待着我断断续续的译笔，陪着我穿过三十年最充实的学术生涯，为我的大学教授那刻板的学术岁月缀上一串"艺术"的流苏，延续着一份跨越百年的书缘。虽然无法一鼓而作气，但每次开卷，浏览数篇，往往有一种童眼看世界的新奇，不管是心灵小确幸还是见识大醒觉带来的重生之感，都含蓄在译作这一原作的后续生命中。作者那看似琐屑的精微、看似信马由缰的洒脱往往令原作的文字变得非常微妙；或经或典，信手拈来，无不涉笔成趣，如此积淀的文本层次如何在新的语言和语境中呈现，处处都是对译者的考验。从全书最重要也最"琐碎"的一个词，标题中的trivia，就可以看出原作含义的多重性和——有些论者一定会说——不可译性。

单词trivia作"琐屑"解是指无关宏旨的细枝末节，这个用法可以追溯到莎士比亚创作于16世纪90年代早期的《亨利六世》（第二部分第三幕）。然而，与英语中意思相似的其他"小词”不同，它出身拉丁语，原来的意思是“三岔路口”，也是掌管着天下岔路的月神的名字：“特丽维亚”；词义还从“三岔路口”延伸为“空阔的地方”或“公共场所”。到了英国诗人和剧作家约翰·格伊（John Gay，1685—1732）笔下，在他于1716年发表的千行长诗《特丽维亚：或，闲步伦敦街头之艺术》(*Trivia: or, the Art of Walking the Streets of London*)开头一节，Trivia的管辖权更扩大为统管街巷和道路的女神：

> Thou, Trivia, Goddess, aid my song,
> Thro' spacious streets conduct thy bard along.

于是原作中所有提及trivia的地方，便有了除“琐屑”之外更深厚的意涵。史密斯也在自传中说了以Trivia作书名是受了格伊的影响。书中第一部分*Trivia*卷二的开篇诗句引的正是格伊的这句诗，译文循此加上“巷陌”点出含义，这句诗便成了：

> 你啊，特丽维亚，巷陌之女神，助我歌兴，
> 以宽阔的街道引你的诗人且吟且行。

这个特丽维亚，在《跋》的引题诗句中再次出现，那是出自意大利诗人但丁（Dante Alighieri，1265—1321）《神曲·天堂篇》第二十三首的一句，因为与格伊的诗句意涵不尽相同，译文不再以“巷陌”定义特丽维亚，但希望有心的读者能将前后两句诗关联解读：

犹如夜空清澈月轮正满，

特丽维亚微笑于永恒的林泽仙女间——

此处的特丽维亚一般都注为月神的别称。放在但丁原诗全文看，这显然言之成理。但既然脱离了原诗单独引出，又放在这新的语境中成为承接全书领起后跋的关节，特丽维亚似乎还可以另有所指。的确，作为单独一句看，上一行已经说了“月轮正满”，第二行如果再度指涉“月神”便显得有点多余；联想到格伊的特丽维亚，不知能不能也让但丁的特丽维亚在这里当一回“(岔)路之神”，从而读出这么一幅景象：月明之夜，林下水边的小路在永远是豆蔻妙龄、永远裸着双足的希腊仙女们欢舞嬉闹的脚下荡起盈盈笑意？

因此，trivia的翻译，就平衡在“琐屑”“街路”“神灵”的三重关涉之上，以及由这三重关涉牵出来的那一点拉丁的显赫、但丁的诗意，以及格伊的灵气。格伊的Goddess译为“巷陌之女神”，既在于点题又希望给但丁的特丽维亚做个铺垫。原作《跋》中结束全书的最后一个词TRIVIA，通过整词大写强调，似乎也是在提醒读者留心；译作将其多重含义展开成“琐事琐思”和“闪现于巷陌间的特丽维亚”，以自己的方式为全书作结，再次点题之余也算是给读者追加一个提醒吧。

循此思路，书中主要部分的标题在译文中也以“巷陌”和“记”串联呼应：第一部分的*Trivia*加“巷陌”为“巷陌琐记”，相连的第二部分*More Trivia*就成了“巷陌续记”，再接下来的*Afterthoughts*延续而成为“追记”。巧的是，中文里的“街路”意象，既可以在白话口语中隐含“琐屑”和“不重要”的意思——比如“大路货”“街头小食”等，更有源自古文的经典语汇——比如“市井”“闾巷”“道听途说”“街谈巷议”等。用“巷陌”一词，也希望能和trivia一样，带点低调的奢华串起作者“琐屑地记下”的伦敦那城中街巷郊外阡陌的百景图、众生相，及其观察内省带来的一次次“琐屑”的神思与感悟。至于这些“琐事”集腋成裘聚成了的*All Trivia*，如前所说涵盖了作者最丰盛的一段生命旅程，便因袭其低调陈述的文风（“读着读着，梦掉了自己的人生”，《乐园复得》）加了“浮生”一词总括，遥接李白“逆旅”和“浮生若梦”（《春夜宴从弟桃花园序》）的比喻；而以《浮生琐记》为书题，又暗暗与沈复《浮生六记》的节奏照应。

说到节奏，其基础在于选词和造句。选用类似“浮生六记”的四字格，也许还能引起译文读者在自己语言里的互文联想呢。对于“自己的语言”，中英文有个非常亲切非常贴切的共同称呼：母语，既是母亲的语言，更是母亲一样的语言。按照“母亲”的隐喻，每个人都是这一语言的孩子。海德格尔还把语言称为人类的家园。于是乎，以母语思考、言说、写作，便是在母亲的花园中游戏，向她讨要材料和工具制作各种我们称之为话语或者作品的玩具。作为语言，这母亲有她的规矩——我们姑且称之为语法吧——划下的园地界限，在这些规矩的约束下她的孩子即使能玩得别出心裁也无法随心所欲地逾矩。作为母亲，语言对自己的孩子又是慷慨宽容的，让她的规矩在稳定中保持着动态，与制作各种新玩具的需要相调适，在规矩划下的园地边缘给创意留下了空间——且看她的那些宠儿，历代那些诗人作家是怎样讨要到材料工具制作了无数别出心裁的玩具的。翻译人也许是语言母亲最调皮的孩子，他们跑到邻居的花园中玩游戏，看上了邻家小孩的一个玩具，便跑回家中也向母亲讨要材料和工具，按心中勾画的设计图来制作一个我们称之为译作的“新”玩具。由于各家有各家的规矩，这份设计图比照的不可能也不应该是邻家的规矩，而更应该是这些规矩形成的信息呈现次序，照着这个次序的构图，译者向自己的语言母亲讨要材料和工具，编排出一个可比的信息呈现次序作为新玩具的骨架。其间少不得还要与语言母亲在规矩上商量，在边缘地带探索，看看最终可以让自己多么“随心所欲不逾矩”地接近原作；因为毕竟不是技术上的规矩，而是先说什么后说什么以及怎么说产生的效果，才让译者看上了原作这个语言玩具。

邻居玩具的形态功能和自家规矩的刚柔尺度，两相携手在翻译中跳的探戈，也许从以下句子及其翻译可见一斑：

> From the bright, unbookish constellations my thoughts float back to the dim-lit reading-room of this circulating library, the earth.

照语法规矩看，原文是表领有关系的of短语后置修饰语加同位语并置，形成了reading-room—library—the earth这一从小到大的信息呈现次序，将reading-room隶属于library中，而以circulating勾连，“巡回”图书馆在最后的焦点位置同位并列带出“地球”，在宇宙中巡回运转的一个星球。按这个次序，整个句子，像苏轼的中秋词一样，完成了从天（constellations）到人（地）再回到天的大节奏。翻译成中文时，如果比照的是语法规矩，那么领有关系of短语后置的修饰语library及其同位的the earth就要置于reading-room之前。信息总量似乎不变，但可惜这不是信封地址的英译中，可以把由小到大的罗列"本地化"地改为由大到小。如果前置，那在这句话中造成的差别之大，犹如将苏轼"人有悲欢离合，月有阴晴圆缺"那从人到天的浩叹颠倒成了"月有阴晴圆缺，人有悲欢离合"的自怜。

超脱了语法的领属关系，可以看到信息次序所呈现的天—人—天节奏，但是描述这空间关系中的流转所需要的介词结构又是矛盾的：可以说"在图书馆里"，一旦比成地球又只能是"在地球上"。介词不可用又无得商量，只好继续搜索古今词汇；终于讨到了一个于今口语不常用的谦词"厕身"，从领有的"的"跨过介词的"在"，以一个动词串成并列句，低调地避开了"里""上"之争：

> **从那些明亮、没有书卷气的星座，我的思绪飘回这间灯光昏暗的阅览室，厕身这座巡回图书馆，这颗地球。**

如果说我们每一个人都是自己母语的孩子，那么每个人都从这语言母亲领得了一份属于自己的语言馈赠。依原作之图创作一个译作，是译者开放自己的语言份额领受更多馈赠的经历；而画原作之图，则是一个把自己的生命对原作中的生命开放的经历。因此，每一次翻译，说到底都是一次语言的试验，一次面对作者呕心沥血的文字，带着童眼开放自己语言开放自己内心的历练，是一次因为开放而升华的涤荡，一次因为升华而谦卑的背伪归真。这种开放、升华与谦卑，沿着语言的街路引领译者走进前人作者的生命，且吟且行，把那个通过原作对他们开放的生命化成译作的文字，让语言的岔路之神在一个个语词仙女般的欢歌曼舞中微笑，让新的文本在新的语境中对更多的生命开放。

翻译的这种种道理，中文一字以蔽之曰“譯”。一个“言”字旁，点明了翻译的言说本质；一旁的“睪”，说是声旁但本身却是个多音字，因此若将声旁的定论悬置而集各家训诂所见，则活脱脱是一个关于翻译的故事。“睪”者，可以是横目伺视罪人，一如严复“我罪我知”的自我审视；可以是携矢射目，堪比翻译中的举笔瞄向标的，亦即属意的target text；还可以通“择”通“宰”，提示着锤炼译文时对“言”的斟酌与掌控。“睪”者，还可以是“败”——言有不逮的“罪过”和潦草从事的“冒犯”都是“败笔”——但也可以是“引”、是“给”、是“绘”、是“生”、是“乐”、是“好”：翻译之乐、翻译之功不就在引出译语词句，从而生出、给出一个新的文本，以新的文字描绘出原作中呈现的世界图景吗？“譯”中乾坤，更包含了翻译在功罪与悲喜的工具伦理之上所具有的人文意义：“幸”可以不是罪人的“㚔”而是“吉而免凶”的“幸”，“睪”成了“目察幽微”而得吉免凶之福——“譯”，难道不就是通过观察入微之后的转述而令“四夷之言”相通，让世界“免凶”的吗？因此“譯”中之目所见证的，更应该是言之幸。一个语言能在翻译中对另外一个语言开放，这难道不是语言的幸运和福分吗？一个译者能见到自己的心在翻译中对他者之心开放，这难道不是一份值得感恩的缘分与幸福吗？

邂逅《浮生琐记》，是与一段三十多年的生命印迹结缘，它来自一个如木心说的从前慢的世界。阅读《浮生琐记》，是分享那段生命在三十多年的“慢”中品出的生活厚度，和它托付文字穿过时空距离传来的于“琐屑”中探出的人生启迪。翻译《浮生琐记》，则是努力用中文捕捉和重现沉潜于水静流深的文字中的隽永机警那或明或暗的意义涟漪。这何尝又不是一种欣赏，一种透过文字、隔着距离，反观自己语言与内心的精神行旅呢？三十年来断断续续的翻译，追求的何尝不是一种开放的荡涤、一种自省、一种在追寻意义中体验的升华呢？

当年离开诺丁汉临行之际，艾伦将他于1970年出版的*The Truths of Fiction*最后一本作者样书送我，题赠词中说这是一个小小的memento，以资纪念相处的“英伦岁月”。刚开始翻译《浮生琐记》时碰到困难，少不得与艾伦书信往来向他请教；他去世之后，幸好网上参考资料日趋丰富成熟，后期翻译中许多背景介绍和注释的准备便不至于太困难。在这期间，书缘又续上人缘，得同样是几十年来亦师亦友的叶步青博士相助，就一些篇章警句的译文表达一起推敲，时不时逼出了连我自己都觉得惊奇的译文。《浮生琐记》得以与读者见面，还要感谢译林出版社从刘锋先生到陈叶、於梅、姚燚等各位编辑朋友。而这，又是一份延续了二十多年的友谊和缘分。当然，作为译者，翻译中的任何疏漏错误，责任在我。

希望这小小的一本译作，会是一个targeted text，“草船借箭”般地得到各路同好的批评指正，一道开发中文的言说能量，让翻译作为艺术精益求精；也希望这些文字能够成为一个memento，成为这跨国跨代的书缘人缘及其背后那份学术真诚的一个纪念，成为对实体和虚拟世界中有名无名的英雄筑起的文献宝库、对文字的有限与知识的无垠、对读者吹毛求疵的关爱的一次谦卑的礼敬。也许因为这一点幽思，完稿之际，竟有一丝不舍。

我是不是说得太多了？阅读当如星月对望，本不该被这些云影遮隔的。

朱纯深
2021年10月27日
于香港火炭有天台的村屋家中

译献给依然的心情

The Author

These pieces of moral prose have been written, dear Reader, by a large Carnivorous Mammal, belonging to that sub-order of the Animal Kingdom which includes also the Orang-outang, the tusked Gorilla, the Baboon with his bright blue and scarlet bottom, and the gentle Chimpanzee.

作者

亲爱的读者，写这些道德文章的，是一头硕大的食肉哺乳动物，属于动物界的一个亚目，该亚目还包括红毛猩猩、有獠牙的大猩猩、屁股大红大紫的狒狒，以及温文尔雅的黑猩猩。

LIST OF CONTENTS

目录

TRIVIA

巷陌琐记

BOOK I

'How blest my lot, in these sweet fields assign'd
Where Peace and Leisure soothe the tuneful mind.'

SCOTT, of Amwell, *Moral Eclogues* (1773).

卷一

“我的福分多大啊，在这上苍赐予的田园美景中
让宁静和悠闲抚慰着歌调谐和的心。”

阿姆维尔的司各特，《道德牧歌》（1773 年）

Preface

'You must beware of thinking too much about Style,' said my kindly adviser, 'or you will become like those fastidious people who polish and polish until there is nothing left.'

'Then there really are such people?' I asked eagerly. But the well-informed lady could give me no precise information about them.

I often hear of them in this tantalizing manner, and perhaps one of these days I shall have the luck to come across them.

前言

“您应该注意，别把太多心思花在风格上，”有人好心劝我，“要不然会像那些个抠字眼儿的人，一个劲儿地精雕细琢，到头来什么都抠没了。”

“当真有这样的人吗？”我热切地问道。可是那位见多识广的女士没能给我有关这种人的确切见识。

常常听人如此吊胃口地谈起他们，也许这几天我有幸会碰到他们。

Happiness

Cricketers on village greens, hay-makers in the evening sunshine, small boats that sail before the wind—all these create in me the illusion of Happiness, as if a land of cloudless pleasure, a piece of the old Golden World, were hidden, not (as poets have fancied) in far seas or beyond inaccessible mountains, but here close at hand, if one could find it, in some undiscovered valley. Certain grassy lanes seem to lead through the copses thither; the wild pigeons talk of it behind the woods.

To-day

I woke this morning out of dreams into what we call Reality, into the daylight, the furniture of my familiar bedroom—in fact into the well-known, often-discussed, but, to my mind, as yet unexplained Universe.

Then I, who came out of the eternal silence and seem to be on my way thither, got up and spent the day as I usually spend it. I read, I pottered, I complained, and took exercise; and I sat punctually down to eat the cooked meals that appeared at regular intervals.

幸福

村边草地上玩板球的人们，夕阳中晒着干草的农夫，河面上小船鼓着帆款款而行——这一切在我心中唤起了幸福的幻想，犹如一片晴空万里的福地，一隅往日的黄金世界，并不像诗人们想象的那样藏匿于遥远的海外，或者隔着高不可攀的崇山峻岭，而就在这儿，咫尺之遥，如果找得到的话，就在某一条不被外人发现的河谷中。有几条绿草如茵的小巷似乎穿过那边的矮树林，野鸽子们在树林后正谈论着呢。

今天

我今早醒来，从梦中醒到了我们所称的现实中，醒到了白天，醒到了我卧室中熟悉的家具中来——事实上是到了那个人人知道、常常讨论，而我觉得尚未得到解释的宇宙中来。

然后，我这个从永恒的静寂中出来，似乎又在向那里走去的人，起床了，像通常度日那样度过这一天。读读书、溜达溜达、发发牢骚、做做运动；而后正点入座，受用那煮好了的、有规律地出现在桌上的三餐。

The Afternoon Post

The village Post Office, with its clock and letter-box, its postmistress lost in the heartless seductions of the Aristocracy and tales of coroneted woe, and the sallow-faced grocer watching from his window opposite, is the scene of a daily crisis in my life, when every afternoon I walk there: through the country lanes and ask that well-read young lady for my letters. I always expect good news and cheques; and then, of course, there is the magical Fortune which is coming, and word of it may reach me any day. What it is, this strange Felicity, or whence it shall arrive, I have no notion; but I hurry down in the morning to find the news on the breakfast table, open telegrams in delighted panic, and cry 'Here it comes!' when in the night-silence I hear wheels approaching along the road. So, happy in the hope of Happiness, and not greatly concerned with any other interest or ambition, I live on in my quiet, ordered house; and so I shall live perhaps until the end. Is it merely the last great summons and revelation for which I am waiting?

The Busy Bees

Sitting for hours idle in the shade of an apple tree, near the garden-hives, and under the aerial thoroughfares of those honey-merchants, —sometimes when the noonday heat is loud with

午后邮件

村里的邮局，摆着时钟和信箱，有女局长埋头于贵族的偷香窃玉和王室的伤心故事，有那个脸色灰黄的杂货店老板从路对面玻璃窗望过来，在这里我每天都会经历生活中一个揪心的时刻——每天下午我穿过乡村小巷走来，问那位书读得很多的少妇有没有我的信。我总是期盼着好消息和支票；接着，当然了，是那正在到来的命中奇迹，谁知哪一天就有话传来了呢。到底是什么，这奇妙的好运气，会从何处降临呢？我一无所知。但我清晨会匆匆赶来找早餐桌上的新闻，又喜又怕地打开电报，夜深人静时听到路上过来的车轮声便大叫“来了！”。就这样，怀着幸福的希望幸福着，其他任何兴趣和志向都不大放心上，我在我宁静整洁的房子里过着日子；也许会这样终老。是不是就为了那最后的伟大召唤和启示我在等待着？

蜜蜂营营

几个小时地闲坐在一棵苹果树的绿荫下，不远处是园里的蜂房，头顶上是那些贩蜜者来回的空中大道——有时，当正午的热

their minute industry, or when they fall in crowds out of the late sun to their night-long labours, —I have sought instruction from the Bees, and tried to appropriate to myself the old industrious lesson.

And yet, hang it all, who by rights should be the teacher and who the learners? For those peevish, over-toiled, utilitarian insects, was there no lesson to be derived from the spectacle of Me? Gazing out at me with myriad eyes, from their joyless factories, might they not learn at last—could I not finally teach them—a wiser and more generous-hearted way to improve the shining hours?

The Wheat

The Vicar, whom I met once or twice in my walks about the fields, told me that he was glad that I was taking an interest in farming. Only my feeling about wheat, he said, puzzled him.

Now the feeling in regard to wheat which I had not been able to make clear to the Vicar, was simply one of amazement. Walking one day into a field that I had watched yellowing beyond the trees, I was dazzled by the glow and great expanse of gold. I bathed myself in the intense yellow under the intense blue sky; how it dimmed the oak trees and copses and all the rest of the English landscape! I had not remembered the glory of the Wheat; nor imagined in my reading that in a country so

气里营营响着它们那纤毫不漏的勤勉，或者当它们成群从暮色中降落开始彻夜的劳作——我便向蜜蜂们讨教，努力要把那古老的勤奋功课学过来。

且慢，谁天生就该当老师，谁天生又该当学生？那些个脾气乖张、操劳过度、营营役役的昆虫，难道我的做派就没有它们可学之处？从它们那没有欢乐的工厂里，拿无数的复眼瞪着我，难道它们不可能最终学会——难道我不能最终教给它们——一种更具智慧、更见豪爽的处世之道，让阳光灿烂的时辰更加美好？

麦子

教区牧师有一两次碰见我在田野里散步，跟我说他很高兴我会对农事感兴趣。只是我对麦子的感受，他说，令他不解。

而我当时无法向牧师讲得清的那种对于麦子的感受，只不过是一种惊叹之感。有一天我走进一片看着它在树那边渐熟渐黄的田野，不禁为那片炫目的辉光，那广袤的金黄而惊诧。我在浓酽的蓝天下沐浴着这浓酽的黄；这色泽又是怎样令橡树林和灌木丛，以及英格兰风光中其他的一切黯然失色啊！我本来已不记得麦子的辉煌，阅读中也没能想象到一个离太阳如此遥远的国度，

far from the Sun, there could be anything so rich, so prodigal, so reckless, as this opulence of ruddy gold, bursting out from the cracked earth as from some fiery vein beneath. I remembered how for thousands of years Wheat had been the staple of wealth, the hoarded wealth of famous cities and empires; I thought of the processes of corn-growing, the white oxen ploughing, the great barns, the winnowing fans, the mills with the splash of their wheels, or arms slow-turning in the wind; of cornfields at harvest-time, with shocks and sheaves in the glow of sunset, or under the sickle moon; what beauty it brought into the northern landscape, the antique, passionate, Biblical beauty of the South!

The Coming of Fate

When I seek out the sources of my thoughts, I find they had their beginning in fragile Chance; were born of little moments that shine for me curiously in the past. Slight the impulse that made me take this turning at the crossroads, trivial and fortuitous the meeting, and light as gossamer the thread that first knit me to my friend. These are full of wonder; more mysterious are the moments that must have brushed me with their wings and passed me by: when Fate beckoned and I did not see it, when new Life trembled for a second on the threshold; but the word was not spoken, the hand was not held out, and the Might-have-been shivered and vanished, dim as a dream, into the

居然会有什么能如此的丰富，如此的恢宏，如此的忘情，像是来自地底下哪条怒张的血脉，穿透皲裂的地表，喷涌而出。我记起了千百年来麦子是怎样贵为财富的基石，为显赫的名城帝国所聚敛囤积；我想到了麦子的种植过程、耕牛的劳作、巨大的仓房、扬谷的风扇、磨坊边哗哗的水轮或悠悠的风车；我想到了收获季节的田野，成堆的麦秸辉映着西沉的落日，或者顶着一钩镰刀般的弯月。它带给北地景观的是怎样一种美啊，那古远的、激情充盈的、圣经般的南国之美！

机缘

我在探求我各种思绪的源头时，发现它们都始自稍纵即逝的机遇，生于过去那些莫名其妙为我乍现灵光的刹那。是小小的冲动让我在十字路口转这边而不转那边，不期然的小小幸会让人得以见面，细如游丝的那根线把我和朋友拉到一起。这一切自是充满奇妙；更神秘的是那些如羽翼轻拂、过而无痕的时刻：命运召唤了我，我却视而不见，新的生活在门槛上倏忽一闪；但没等话说出口，没等手伸出来，那个“也许可能”就颤悠悠地不见了，如梦

waste realms of non-existence.

So I never lose a sense of the whimsical and perilous charm of daily life, with its meetings and words and accidents. Why, to-day, perhaps, or next week, I may hear a voice, and, packing up my Gladstone bag, follow it to the ends of the world.

My Speech

'Ladies and Gentlemen,' I began—

The Vicar was in the chair; Mrs. La Mountain and her daughters sat facing us; and in the little schoolroom, with its maps and large Scripture prints, its blackboard with the day's sums still visible on it, were assembled the labourers of the villages, the old family coachman and his wife, the one-eyed postman, and the gardeners and boys from the Hall. Having culled from the newspapers a few phrases, I had composed a speech which I delivered with a spirit and eloquence surprising even to myself. The Vicar cried 'Hear, Hear!' the Vicar's wife pounded her umbrella with such emphasis, and the villagers cheered so heartily, that my heart was warmed. I began to feel the meaning of my own words; I beamed on the audience, felt that they were all my brothers, all wished well to the Republic; and it seemed to me an occasion to divulge my real ideas and hopes for the Commonwealth.

Brushing therefore to one side, and indeed quite forgetting

如幻，没入荒凉的乌有之境。

因此我永远不会失去一种对日常生活的意识，来感受它那飘忽不定、凶吉难卜的魅力：那些个相逢相聚、话长话短，那些个意外和偶然。嗯，今天，也许吧，或者下星期，我说不定就听到一个声音，便收拾好我的行囊，跟着它到地角天边。

我的讲话

“女士们先生们，”我开始讲——

牧师坐在主持人座上，牧师太太和她的女儿们坐在我们对面。这间小小的学校教室，墙上挂着地图和大幅《圣经》语录，黑板上当天的加法算题还依稀可见，聚集着附近几个村里干力气活的人、老车夫和他的妻子、独眼邮差、庄园那边来的园丁和男仆。我从报纸上寻章摘句写了篇讲稿，便在这儿说开了，那口若悬河的激昂劲头连我自己也吃惊。牧师高呼“说得好，说得好”，牧师太太拿雨伞尖在地板上用力敲重点，村民们衷心欢呼。这让我心中一阵阵发热，开始感觉到自己话语的意义，欣欣然望着我的听众，觉得他们全是我的弟兄，全都希望共和国好；我觉得似乎可以借此机会透露我对联邦的真实想法和希望。

于是将我的安全原则放在一旁，其实是忘得差不多了，我

my safe principles, I began to refashion and new-model the State. Most existing institutions were soon abolished; and then, on their ruins, I proceeded to build up the bright walls and palaces of the City within me—the City I had read of in Plato. With enthusiasm, and, I flatter myself, with eloquence, I described it all—the Warriors, that race of golden youth bred from the State-ordered embraces of the brave and fair; those philosophic Guardians, who, being ever accustomed to the highest and most extensive views, and thence contracting an habitual greatness, possessed the truest fortitude, looking down indeed with a kind of disregard on human life and death. And then, declaring that the pattern of this City was laid up in Heaven, I sat down, amid the cheers of the uncomprehending little audience.

And afterward, in my rides about the country, when I saw on walls and the doors of barns, among advertisements of sales, or regulations about birds' eggs or the movements of swine, little weather-beaten, old-looking notices on which it was stated that I would address the meeting, I remembered how the walls and towers of the City I built up in that little schoolroom had shone with no heavenly light in the eyes of the Vicar's party.

Stonehenge

There they sit for ever around the horizon of my mind, that Stonehenge circle of elderly disapproving Faces—Faces of the

开始重新构思规划国家的结构。现存的机构大部分很快就取消了；接着，在这废墟上我着手建起我心中之城那明亮的围墙和宫殿——我从柏拉图那里读来的心中之城。我怀着热情（还有，自夸一下），施展辩才，把我的城和盘托出——这里有勇敢的战士，这些金色青年是由国家指令的勇与美交合育出的人种；这里有哲理深邃的守护人，他们从来就具备最为高远的目光，因此自然就带上伟人风范，具有最坚忍不拔的精神，的的确确怀着一种不屑俯视人的生死。接着，在宣称这城的规划由上天设定之后，我坐了下来，身边响起似懂非懂的几个听众的欢呼声。

后来，我骑车在乡间游逛时，看到在墙壁和谷仓门上贴着的减价广告或有关禽蛋和猪群活动的规定布告当中，有那些风吹雨淋、斑驳老旧的小告示，上面写着我将在聚会上讲话，便记起了自己那天在小教室里建的那座城池的围墙和高楼，在牧师那班人眼里一点也没闪耀出什么上天的光芒。

巨石阵[1]

在那儿，它们永远围坐在我内心的地平线上，那些年长的、什么都看不顺眼的脸庞摆成的巨石阵——有叔伯们的，有校长们

Uncles, and Schoolmasters and the Tutors who frowned on my youth.

In the bright centre and sunlight I leap, I caper, I dance my dance; but when I look up, I see they are not deceived. For nothing ever placates them, nothing ever moves to a look of approval that ring of bleak, old, contemptuous Faces.

My Portrait

But after all I am no amoeba, no mere sack and stomach; I am capable of discourse, can ride a bicycle, look up trains in Bradshaw; in fact I am and calmly boast myself a Human Being—that Masterpiece of Nature, and noblest fruit of time—I am a rational, polite, meat-eating Man.

What stellar collisions and conflagrations, what floods and slaughters and enormous efforts has it not cost the Universe to make me—of what astral periods and cosmic processes am I not the crown, the wonder?

Where, then, is the Esplanade or world-dominating Terrace for my sublime Statue; the landscape of palaces and triumphal arches for the background of my Portrait; stairs of marble, flung against the sunset, not too narrow and ignoble for me to pause with ample gesture on their balustraded flights?

的，有老师们的，一张张脸都冲着我的青少年时代皱过眉头。

在巨石阵明亮的中心，在阳光中我蹦跳，我雀跃，我跳着自己的舞；但等我朝上一看，就明白这一切骗不过它们。从来没有什么能使它们消气，从来没有什么能令这一圈黯淡的、倚老卖老的脸庞露出一丝赞许的表情。

我的肖像

可我到底不是阿米巴虫，不光是个胃囊是副皮囊；我能说会写，会骑单车，会看全国的火车时刻表定班次；事实上我是，而且也心安理得地自诩为人类一名——天地之杰作，岁月之正果——我是一个有理性的、懂礼貌的、吃肉的人。

有什么星球碰撞、水火劫难、伤生害命的代价，有什么惊天动地的努力宇宙没有付出过，这才造出了我？——有什么星辰升降宇宙演化，不以我为冠冕、为奇迹？

那么，何处才是通衢大道的广场，或雄视万物的高台，足以摆放我崇高的塑像？何处才有一座座宫殿一道道凯旋门，足以充作我肖像的背景？何处才有玉石台阶，迎着夕照拔地而起，不会太窄，也不会显得小气，让我在拾级而上时，气气派派地驻足凭栏？

Complex Questions

The Age, the Vicar would remark, was a serious one; Englishmen were met face to face with complex questions. But the questions that had an interest for me at that time, would no doubt have seemed to the Vicar, many of them, old and imaginary. I was too often occupied, I am afraid, with the complexities of my own thoughts; their odd travels and changes; their way of peopling English forests with wood-nymphs, or transforming English orchards—seen perhaps at dawn or in the late sunshine—into Hesperian gardens. Sometimes it was merely names that filled my mind: 'Magalat, Galgalat, Saraïm,' I syllabled to myself; were these the names of the Magi of the East; or Atos, Satos, Paratoras? What were the names of the nymphs Actaeon surprised bathing with Diana? The names of the hounds that hunted to his death that rash intruder; Ladon, Harpyia, Laelaps, Oresitrophos, as some call them; or, as they are given in other authentic books, Boreas, Omelampus, Agreus, Aretusa, Gorgo?

Silvia Doria

Beyond the blue hills, within riding distance, there is a country of parks and beeches, with views of the faded, far-off sea. I remember in one of my rides coming on the place which

难题

这年头，牧师会这么说，是个不能掉以轻心的时代；英国人正面临着许多难题。可那时我觉得感兴趣的问题，要是在牧师看来，有许多无疑是子虚乌有的老问题。恐怕我是太经常耽于自己纷繁的思绪了，各种念头离奇地游走嬗变，让英国的树林住进希腊的林中仙女，或者把英国的果园——大概是黎明或黄昏时看到的果园——变成了神话中的金苹果园。有时只是些名字塞满心中："玛伽拉、伽伽拉、萨拉姆。"我一字一顿地自言自语。这些是不是那东方三博士[2]的名字？或者是艾托斯、萨托斯、帕拉托拉斯？那些同月神狄安娜共浴、被亚克托安[3]吓着了的仙女们叫什么名字？那些把这个鲁莽的不速之客追着咬死的猎犬又叫什么名字？拉顿、哈皮亚、雷拉波斯、奥列西托洛弗斯，有些人这么叫它们；或者，就像其他一些权威著作中写的那样，叫波利亚斯、奥米兰普斯、阿格列斯、阿列图沙、果戈？

希尔维亚·多丽亚

青青的小山那边，在骑车可及的那一带，是一片有公园和山毛榉树林的乡野，望得见远处淡淡的海洋。记得有一次我骑车到

was the scene of the pretty, old-fashioned story of Silvia Doria. Through the gates, with fine gate-posts, on which heraldic beasts, fierce and fastidious, were upholding coroneted shields, I could see, at the end of the avenue, the facade of the House, with its stone pilasters, and its balustrade on the steep roof.

More than one hundred years ago, in that Park, with its Italianized house, and level gardens adorned with statues and garden temples, there lived, they say, an old Lord with his two handsome sons. The old Lord had never ceased mourning for his Lady, though she had died a good many years before; there were no neighbours he visited, and few strangers came inside the great Park walls. One day in Spring, however, just when the apple trees had burst into blossom, the gilded gates were thrown open, and a London chariot with prancing horses drove up the Avenue. And in the chariot, smiling and gay, and indeed very beautiful in her dress of yellow silk, and her great Spanish hat with drooping feathers, sat Silvia Doria, come on a visit to her cousin, the old Lord.

It was her father who had sent her—that he might be more free, some said, to pursue his own wicked courses, —while others declared that he intended her to marry the old Lord's eldest son.

However this might be, Silvia Doria came like the Spring, like the sunlight, into the lonely place. Even the old Lord felt himself curiously happy when he heard her voice singing about the house; as for Henry and Francis, it was heaven for them just to walk by her side down the garden alleys.

了那地方，那个有关希尔维亚·多丽亚的好听又老套的传说的发生地。庭园大门口立着精美的门柱，上面的纹章兽凶巴巴一丝不苟地擎着贵族的徽盾。我朝门里望去，看得见林荫道尽头大楼的正面，其上嵌着石头壁柱，陡峭的屋顶上有圈栏。

一百多年前，在这座公园里，在那意大利风格的宅第中，在装点着雕像和花园神殿的那些平整的庭园间，他们说，住着一位老勋爵和他两个英俊的儿子。老勋爵无时不在为他死去的夫人伤心，尽管他夫人去世已经很有些年头了。他不造访邻居，也鲜有生人踏足高墙围着的大庄园。然而，在一个春日里，正是苹果花怒放的时节，镀金的园门推开了，一部伦敦来的双轮马车腾腾腾跑上了林荫道。马车上，一袭黄色丝裙，一顶垂着羽毛的、宽大的西班牙帽子，喜笑吟吟地坐着希尔维亚·多丽亚，真是美丽非常；她这是拜访她的表哥老勋爵来了。

是她父亲要她来的——有人说，这样那老头就能更自由地去胡作非为了，也有人声称她父亲是要让她嫁给老勋爵的大儿子。

不管怎样，希尔维亚·多丽亚就像春天，就像阳光，来到了这孤寂的地方。就连老勋爵，听到宅院四处响着她曼妙的声音，也会觉得自己莫名其妙地高兴起来；至于亨利和弗兰西斯，只要能同她并肩走在花园小径上，便飘飘欲仙了。

And Silvia Doria, though hitherto she had been but cold toward the London gallants who had courted her, found, little by little, that her heart was not untouched.

But, in spite of her father, and her own girlish love of gold and rank, it was not for Henry that she cared, not for the old Lord, but for Francis, the younger son. Did Francis know of this? They were secretly lovers, the old scandal reported; and the scandal, it may be, had reached her father's ears.

For one day a coach with foaming horses, and the wicked face of an old man at its window, galloped up the avenue; and soon afterwards, when the coach drove away, Silvia Doria was sitting by the old man's side, sobbing bitterly.

And after she had gone, a long time, many of the eighteenth-century years went by without change. And then Henry, the elder son, was killed in hunting; and the old Lord dying a few years later, the titles and the great house and all the land and gold came to Francis, the younger son. But after his father's death he was but seldom there; having, as it seemed, no love for the place, and living for the most part abroad and alone, for he never married.

And again, many years went by. The trees grew taller and darker about the house; the yew hedges, unclipped now, hung their branches over the shadowy paths; ivy almost smothered the statues; and the plaster fell away in great patches from the discoloured garden temples.

But at last one day a chariot drove up to the gates; a

希尔维亚·多丽亚呢，虽然迄今为止对伦敦那些追着她献殷勤的风流哥儿们爱理不理，却渐渐地，发觉自己并非毫不动心。

但是，不管她父亲旨意如何，也抛开她自己那份女孩子家对金钱地位的喜爱不论，她所属意的，不是亨利，也不是老勋爵，而是弗兰西斯，那个小儿子。弗兰西斯知道吗？他们暗中相爱，当时传言是这么说的；而这传言，也许吧，就传到了她父亲耳朵里。

因为有一天来了一部四轮马车，车前马喷白沫，车内露出恶狠狠的一张老人脸，那车呼呼呼跑上了林荫道。过不久马车离开时，希尔维亚·多丽亚就坐在老头身旁，伤心地啜泣。

她走了，之后好久好久，十八世纪的好多个年头过去了，一切不变。然后，亨利，那个大儿子，打猎出事死了；几年后老勋爵也死了，爵位、巨宅、所有的田园和钱财就都传给了小儿子弗兰西斯。可是自从他父亲去世后，他很少在那儿居留；似乎对那地方毫无眷恋之情，大部分时间他都住在国外，单身一人，从未娶妻。

就这样，又过去了好多年。楼四周树木长得更高，树荫遮得更暗了。紫杉树篱长年未修，枝条垂遍了树影森森的小路；常青藤几乎窒息了那尊尊雕像；黯然失色的花园神殿，泥灰大块大块剥落。

但是终于有一天，一部双轮马车来到了大门前。一名男仆拉

footman pulled at the crazy bell, telling the gate-keeper that his mistress wished to visit the Park. So the gates creaked open, the chariot glittered up the avenue to the deserted place; and a lady stepped out, went into the garden, and walked among its moss-grown paths and statues. As the chariot drove out again, 'Tell your Lord,' the lady said, smiling, to the lodge-keeper, 'that Silvia Doria came back.'

Bligh House

To the West, in riding past the walls of Bligh, I remembered an incident in the well-known siege of that house, during the Civil Wars: How, among Waller's invading Roundhead troops, there happened to be a young scholar, a poet, and lover of the Muses, fighting for the cause, as he thought, of ancient Freedom, who, one day, when the siege was being more hotly urged, pressing forward and climbing a wall, suddenly found himself in a quiet garden by the house. And here, for a time forgetting, as it would seem, the battle, and heedless of the bullets that now and then flew past him like peevish wasps, the young Officer stayed, gathering roses—old-fashioned damask roses, streaked with red and white—which, for the sake of a Court Beauty, there besieged with her father, he carried to the house; falling, however, struck by a chance bullet, or shot perhaps by one of his own party. A few of the young Officer's verses, written in the stilted fashion

响摇摇欲坠的门铃，告诉守门人他的女主人想看看这庭园。于是大门吱吱呀呀地打开了，马车亮晃晃地跑上了林荫道，来到那空无一人的大楼前。只见一位女士步出车外，走进花园，在苔痕斑斑的小路和雕像间徜徉。马车驶出门离开时，“告诉你们勋爵，”那女士微笑着对守宅的人说，“希尔维亚·多丽亚回来了。”

柏莱大楼

往西骑着车路过柏莱大楼墙外时，我记起了一段历史旧事，发生在内战时期有名的围攻这座大宅的战斗[4]中：在入侵的沃勒圆颅党军队里，刚好有一位年轻的学者，是个诗人，一个钟情于缪斯的青年，在为，他自己认为，在为古老的自由理想而战。有一天，战事愈趋激烈，他往前冲，翻过一道围墙，发现自己落在一个安静的花园里，就在大楼旁边。在这儿，似乎一时忘了身边的战况，也不顾子弹不时像愤怒的黄蜂一般呼啸而过，年轻的军官停下来，俯身采摘园中的玫瑰——老式的、红白二色的大马士革玫瑰——为了一位与父亲一起身陷重围的宫廷美人，他揣着这些玫瑰向大楼走去；但是，一颗流弹飞过，他中弹倒下，也可能是被自己人射杀了。这位年轻军官有几句诗，以当时虚饰的风格写的，

of the time, and almost unreadable now, have been preserved. The lady's portrait hangs in the white drawing-room at Bligh; a simpering, faded figure, with ringlets and drop-pearls, and a dress of amber-coloured silk.

The Stars

Battling my way homeward one dark night against the wind and rain, a sudden gust, stronger than the others, drove me back into the shelter of a tree. But soon the Western sky broke open; the illumination of the Stars poured down from behind the dispersing clouds.

I was astonished at their brightness, to see how they filled the night with their lustre. So I went my way accompanied by them; Arcturus followed me, and becoming entangled in a leafy tree, shone by glimpses, and then emerged triumphant, Lord of the Western sky. Moving along the road in my waterproof and goloshes, my thoughts were among the Constellations. I too was one of the Princes of the starry Universe; in me also there was something that blazed, that glittered.

In Church

'For the Pen,' said the Vicar; and in the sententious pause

如今几乎难以卒读，留存了下来。那女郎的画像挂在柏莱大楼白色的客厅里，一副黯淡造作的模样，垂着鬈发，挂着珍珠，身着一袭琥珀色丝绸礼服。

星星

一个暗夜里我顶风冒雨往家里走，半路上突然刮起一阵风，特别猛，刮得我只好退到一棵树下躲避。可是不一会儿，只见西边云破天开，一片星光从四散的乌云间倾泻而下。

我不禁惊诧于这满天星辉，看繁星是怎样让夜色充满了自己的璀璨。于是我有它们陪着往家走；大角星跟着我，过一棵树时缠在了茂密的树叶间，一瞥一闪地亮着，过后又胜利地重现天穹，到底是西天的主宰。我披着雨衣套着雨靴前行，思绪在星座间漫游。我也是啊，宇宙星空中的一个王子；我心中也有东西在燃烧，在闪光呢。

教堂礼拜

“因为笔——”牧师说道；接着是一个句间停顿，这时我觉得

which followed I felt that I would offer any gifts of gold to avert or postpone the solemn, inevitable, and yet, as it seemed to me, perfectly appalling statement that 'the Pen is mightier than the Sword.'

Parsons

All the same I like Parsons; they think nobly of the Universe, and believe in Souls and Eternal Happiness. And some of them, I am told, believe in Angels—that there are Angels who guide our footsteps, and flit to and fro unseen on errands in the air about us.

The Sound of a Voice

As the thoughtful Baronet talked, as his voice went on sawing in my ears, all the light of desire, and of the sun, faded from the Earth; I saw the vast landscape of the world, dim, as in an eclipse; its populations eating their bread with tears, its rich men sitting listless in their palaces, and aged Kings crying 'Vanity, Vanity, all is Vanity!' lugubriously from their thrones.

我愿以一切金银财宝作为献礼来挡住、来延缓那庄严的、肯定要说的，然而我觉得根本是耸人听闻的一句话：“笔比刀剑更强大。”

牧师

不管怎样我还是喜欢牧师。他们对宇宙怀着高尚的情怀，相信灵魂及永恒的幸福。而且他们中还有些人，我听说，信奉天使——认为有天使在指引我们的脚步，在我们周围振翼轻飞，人看不见地东奔西忙。

谈吐之声

那位满脸沉思的准男爵开口说话，他的声音拉锯似的在我耳朵里响着，这时候，一切希冀之光，太阳之光，都从地球上消失了；我看到世界上茫茫山水全暗了，犹如日食；天下万民就着眼泪吃面包，富人无精打采地坐在他们的豪宅广厦中，年迈的国王在他们的宝座上凄惨地叫着“虚空啊虚空，一切全是虚空！”

What Happens

'Yes,' said Sir Thomas, speaking of a modern novel, 'it certainly does seem strange; but the novelist was right. Such things do happen.'

'But, my dear Sir,' I burst out, in the rudest manner, 'think what life is—just think what really happens! Why people suddenly swell up and turn dark purple; they hang themselves on meat-hooks; they are drowned in horse-ponds, are run over by butchers' carts, and are burnt alive—cooked like mutton chops!'

Luton

In a field of that distant, half-neglected farm, I found an avenue of great elms leading to nothing. But I could see where the wheat-bearing earth had been levelled into a terrace; and in one corner there were broken, overgrown, gateposts, almost hid among great straggling trees of box.

This, then, was the place I had come to see. Here had stood the great house or palace, with its terraces, and gardens, and artificial waters; this field had once been the favourite resort of Eighteenth-century Fashion; the Duchesses and Beauties had driven hither in their gilt coaches, and the Beaux and Wits of that golden time of English Society. And although the house had long since vanished, and the plough had gone over its pleasant

发生的事

“没错，”托马斯爵士说道，他讲的是一部现代小说，“的确显得奇怪；可那作家是对的。像这样的事的确会发生。”

“可是，我亲爱的爵士，”我脱口而出，口吻极为粗鲁，“想想生活是什么——只消想想真正发生的是什么！为什么人会突然肿胀，全身黑紫；他们为什么把自己悬吊在挂肉的钩子上；为什么被放在洗马池内溺死，被屠夫们的大车碾过，被活活烧死——就像煮羊排那样！”

卢顿[5]

在那偏远的、半抛荒的农场里，我在一片田野中找到了一条林荫路，夹道长着高大的榆树，道路所通，尽头什么也没有。可是我看得出那片长着麦子的田地过去曾被平整为露天平台；一个角落里立着爬满青藤的残门断柱，几乎被零零落落的一些大黄杨树遮住了。

那么，这就是我要来看的地方了。这里曾经矗立着那座华屋或宫殿，一层层高台一个个花园，还有人工开凿的湖泊喷泉。这片田野，曾经是十八世纪上流社会的乐园胜地，贵族夫人、佳丽美妇乘着镀金马车赶来赴会，英国社会鼎盛时期的名流佳媛齐聚一堂。虽然屋宇楼台早已荡然无存，安乐乡也已付诸犁耙，可是有

places, yet for a moment I seemed to see this fine company under the green and gold of that great avenue; seemed to hear the gossip of their uncharitable voices as they passed on into the shadows.

A Precaution

The folio gave at length philosophic consolations for all the misadventures said by the author to be inseparable from human existence—Poverty, Shipwrecks, Plagues, Famines, Flights of Locusts, Love-Deceptions, Inundations. Against these antique Disasters I armed my soul; and I thought it as well to prepare myself against the calamity called 'Cornutation,' or by other less learned names. How Philosophy taught that after all it was but a pain founded on conceit, a blow that hurt not; the reply of the Cynic philosopher to one who reproached him, 'Is it my fault or hers?' how Nevisanus advises the sufferer to ask himself if he have not offended; Jerome declares it impossible to prevent; how few or none are safe, and the inhabitants of some countries, especially parts of Africa, consider it the usual and natural thing; how Caesar, Pompey, Augustus, Agamemnon, Menelaus, Marcus Aurelius, and many other great Kings and Princes had all worn Actaeon's badge; and how Philip turned it to a jest, Pertinax the Emperor made no reckoning of it; Erasmus declared it was best winked at, there being no remedy but patience, *Dies*

一瞬间我似乎在那条金光翠色的大道上看见了这群绅士淑女，似乎听到了一片尖刻的流言蜚语，随他们错身而过没入阴影中。

有备无患

这大部头对开本[6]中洋洋洒洒介绍了为所有天灾人祸准备的富有哲学意味的劝导之词，据作者说这些灾祸与人的存在不可分离——贫穷、海难、瘟疫、饥荒、蝗灾、情变、洪水。为对付这些古来有之的厄难，我将灵魂武装停当；而且我觉得还要准备好应对被称作“戴绿头巾”的灾难，或者也叫别的一些比较直白的名称。且听哲学是怎么开导我们的：这毕竟只是一种面子之痛，一种即使挨了一记也不疼的打击；那位犬儒派哲学家在有人责备他时回复道：“错在我还是在她？”尼维桑诺斯要戴绿头巾者扪心自问，是否自己无错；哲罗姆声称此等事无可避免；幸免于此的人简直太少，简直没有，而在有些国家，特别是有些非洲地方，那里的人认为这种事平常又自然；看恺撒、庞贝、奥古斯都、阿伽门农、墨涅拉俄斯、马尔库斯·奥勒利乌斯，还有许多伟大的国君王子，他们都戴过绿头巾；腓力把它当成笑话一个，皇帝伯丁那克斯对此置若罔闻，伊拉斯谟则宣布睁一只眼闭一只眼最好，因为除了忍耐别无良策，如拉丁谚语*Dies dolorem minuit*所云，时光冲淡伤痛；

dolorem minuit; Time, Age must mend it; and how, according to the authorities, bars, bolts, oaken doors, and towers of brass, are all in vain. 'She is a woman,' as the old Pedant wrote to a fellow Philosopher ...

The Great Work

Sitting, pen in hand, alone in the stillness of the library, with flies droning behind the sunny blinds, I considered in my thoughts what should be the subject of my great Work. Should I complain against the mutability of Fortune, and impugn Fate and the Stars; or should I reprehend the never-satisfied heart of querulous Man, drawing elegant contrasts between the unsullied snow of mountains, the serene shining of the planets, and our hot, feverish lives and foolish repinings? Or should I confine myself to denouncing, like Juvenal or Jeremiah, contemporary Vices, crying 'Fie!' on the Age with Hamlet, sternly unmasking its hypocrisies, and riddling through and through its too-comfortable Optimisms?

Or with Job, should I question the Universe, and puzzle my sad brains about Life—the meaning of Life on this apple-shaped Planet?

时间、年岁必定令创伤愈合；而且，据权威人士称，高楼重门、铁窗铜锁，又是如何无济于事。“她是一个女人”，就像那老学究在给一个同行哲学家的信中说的……

大作

坐着，手握着笔，一个人在死寂的图书室里，只有苍蝇在映着阳光的百叶窗后嗡嗡作响，我心中转着念头，我的大作到底该写什么主题好。是控诉钱财的流散不居，声讨命运和星宿呢，还是斥责人的牢骚太盛、欲壑难填，优雅地把高山上的晶莹白雪、长空中的宁谧星光，同我们这火烧火燎的日子、怨天尤人的愚蠢，做一番对比？或者，我应该像古罗马的讽刺诗人尤维纳利斯和《圣经》中的先知耶利米一样，专注于对当前罪恶的谴责，同哈姆雷特一起对时世喊一声“呸！”，不留情地撕下它种种虚伪的面具，把它各种太过安逸的乐观主义驳得体无完肤？

或者，我应该同约伯[7]一道，叩问苍天，让悲哀的心为生命而困惑，为生命在这颗苹果状星球上的意义而百思不解？

My Mission

But when in modern books, reviews, and thoughtful magazines I read about the Needs of the Age, its Complex Questions, its Dismays, Doubts, and Spiritual Agonies, I feel an impulse to go out and comfort that bewildered Epoch, to wipe away its tears, still its cries, and speak edifying words of Consolation to it.

The Birds

But how can one toil at the great task with this hurry of birds just outside the open window? I hear the Thrush, and the Blackbird, that romantic liar; then the delicate cadence, the wiry descending scale of the Willow-wren, or the Blackcap's stave of mellow music. All these are familiar; —but what is that unknown voice, that thrilling note? I hurry out; the voice flees and I follow; and when I return and sit down again to my task, the Yellowhammer trills his sleepy song in the noonday heat; the drone of the Greenfinch lulls me into dreamy meditations. Then suddenly from his tree-trunks and forest recesses comes the Green Woodpecker, to mock at me with an impudent voice full of liberty and laughter.

Why should all the birds of the air conspire against me? My concern is with our own sad Species, with lapsed and erroneous

我的使命

但是，当我在现今的书籍、评论以及严肃的刊物上，读到关于时代的需要，它面临的难题，它的失望、困惑、精神上的痛苦时，我便感到一股冲动，要走出去抚慰这无所适从的时世，抹去它的眼泪，止住它的哭喊，给它说些启迪心智的安慰话。

鸟语

这教人如何能埋头处理大事呢——就在开着的窗外，鸟踪雀影一片声的熙熙攘攘？我听见画眉，还有燕八哥那浪漫的谎言；接着是柳莺纤巧的韵律，宛如弦上一跌而下的滑奏；还有黄莺圆润丰美的乐音。这些全是旧相识了；——但那一个不知名的声音，那令人怦然心动的调门，又是谁的？我赶出屋外；那声音逃走了，我跟了过去；等我回来又坐下来做我的大事时，只听金翼啄木鸟在午间的热气中鸣啭着它那昏昏欲睡的曲子，翠羽雀单调的啼鸣又令我掉进了梦般的冥想之中。接着，突然从树林深处的树干间，传来绿色啄木鸟的声音，嘲弄着我，放浪的嗓门透着满满的潇洒与笑意。

为什么空中所有的鸟雀要共谋来与我作对呢？我关心的是我们自己这个哀伤的物种，这份堕落荒谬的人性；而非那个不近

Humanity; not with that inconsiderate, wandering, feather-headed race.

High Life

Although that immense Country House was empty and for sale, and I had got an order to view it, I needed all my courage to walk through the lordly gates, and up the avenue, and then to ring the door-bell. And when I was ushered in, and the shutters were removed to let the daylight into those vast apartments, I sneaked through them, cursing the dishonest curiosity which had brought me into a place where I had no business. But I was treated with such deference, and so plainly regarded as a possible purchaser, that I soon began to believe in the opulence imputed to me. From all the novels describing the mysterious and glittering life of the Great which I had read (and I have read thousands), there came to me the vision of my own existence in this Palace. I filled those vast halls with the shine of jewels and stir of voices; I saw a vision of ladies sweeping in their tiaras down the splendid stairs.

But my Soul, in her swell of pride, soon outgrew these paltry limits. Oh no! Never could I box up and house under that roof the Pomp, the Ostentation of which I was capable.

Then for one thing there was stabling for only forty horses; and this, of course, as I told them, would never do.

人情、游荡不居、毛毛糙糙的属类。

奢侈生活

尽管那座巨大的乡村豪宅空置待售，自己又是按约前去看房，我还是得鼓足十二分勇气才敢迈进那巍峨的大门，沿那条林荫道走上前，拉响门铃。有人领我进去，百叶窗打开了，让光线照进那些空荡荡的大套间，我蹑手蹑脚地穿过这些房间，暗地里骂自己那份不老实的好奇心，把我带到这个与我毫不相干的地方。可人家是如此恭敬有加地待我，明摆着把我看作可能的买主，使我不久也把这误置于我的富翁形象信以为真了。从看过的那些描写大富大贵人家生活如何光怪陆离的小说中（我看过的这类小说数以千计），冒出我自己在这宫殿般的豪宅中生活的情形。我将让那些空旷的大厅填满珠光宝气、声色音容；我看到了一幅头饰如冠的仕女们长裙曳地，沿着华美的楼梯走下来的景象。

但我的灵魂，傲气上来，很快就超越了这不足挂齿的局限。不能啊！我绝不能把我能达致的奢华和气派装箱库存于这屋顶之下。

那么就说一点，马厩只能养四十匹马；而这个，当然了，我告诉他们，是绝对不行的。

Empty Shells

They lie like empty sea-shells on the shores of Time, the old worlds which the spirit of man once built for his habitation, and then abandoned. Those little earth-centred, heaven-encrusted universes of the Greeks and Hebrews seem quaint enough to us, who have formed, thought by thought from within, the immense modern Cosmos in which we live—the great Creation of granite, planned in such immeasurable proportions, and moved by so pitiless a mechanism, that it sometimes appals even its own creators. The rush of the great rotating Sun daunts us; to think to the distance of the fixed stars cracks our brains.

But if the ephemeral Being who has imagined these eternal spheres and spaces must dwell almost as an alien in their icy vastness, yet what a splendour lights up for him and dazzles in those great halls! Anything less limitless would be now a prison; and he even dares to think beyond their boundaries, to surmise that he may one day outgrow this Mausoleum, and cast from him the material Creation as an integument too narrow for his insolent Mind.

At the Window

But then I drew up the curtain and looked out of the window. Yes, there it still was, the old External World, still

空空的贝壳

它们像空空的贝壳一样躺在时间的岸边，那些旧日的世界，人类的精神曾经为自己建造的一个个家园，过后又将它们抛弃。希腊人和希伯来人的那些小小的、以地为心以天为壳的宇宙，对我们来说似乎够古色古香古怪了——我们以出自内心的一个接一个的思想，建构了我们所居住的浩瀚的现代宇宙——这花岗岩的伟大作品，规划的比例之大无法丈量，驱动的机制如此无情，有时就连创作的人自己都吓坏了。巨大的太阳旋转着，行色匆匆地令我们害怕；那些恒星的距离又让我们想破了脑袋。

但假如那个短暂的生命，既想象出这些永恒的天穹和太空却又必须在这冰冷的广漠中流寓客居几如外人，则又有怎样的一份辉煌为他照明，在那些个浩大的殿堂里闪耀啊！任何东西如果没有这么无垠无限，如今都会成为牢笼；他甚至敢于让思想越出这些疆界，想象着有一天将可以突破这陵墓，扬弃这物质的创造，就像蜕出一个已盛不下他桀骜之心的躯壳一样。

临窗眺望

但我接着拉起窗帘望出去。是的，还在那儿呢，那个原来的外部世界，还是一副对它自己的无存不甚了了的样子。在它面

apparently quite unaware of its own non-existence. I felt helpless, small-boyish before it: I couldn't pooh-pooh it away.

How it Happened

This vision or blur bubbled up, the Buddhists believe, from some unaccountable agitation beneath the eternal serene of Nirvana; but the naked Thinkers of the Ganges look upon it as an optical delusion of Brahma's, when he slipped up and grew giddy a moment, and put his foot, so to speak, into this Misapprehension.

But we in the West believe that God created the world in the pure caprice of his superabundant omnipotence; that He clapped his hands when He finished it, and declared that it was very good, and just what He wanted.

Vertigo

Still, I don't like it; I can't approve of it; I have always thought it most regrettable that serious and ethical Thinkers like ourselves should go scuttling through space in this undignified manner. Is it seemly that I, at my age, should be hurled with my books of reference, and bed-clothes, and hot-water bottle, across the sky at the unthinkable rate of nineteen miles a second? As I

前，我觉得很无奈，像个小男孩似的：没法啐啐两声就把它赶走。

此事怎讲

这个景象或者这片模糊冒了上来，佛教徒相信，那是来自极乐世界永恒的宁静之下某种说不清的躁动；但是恒河边赤着身子的思想家却把它看作是创造之神梵天的一个视觉幻象，他滑了一下，一时头晕，比方说，一脚就踩进了这错觉之中。

但是在西方我们相信，上帝创造世界纯粹是一时起兴于那多得无处体现的全知全能；造好了，拍拍手，宣布造得很好，想要的就是这个样子。

惧高症

这样的事，我还是不喜欢，觉得不可取；我向来认为令人遗憾不过的是德高望重思想精湛如我等，还要这么不雅观地在空中穿来穿去。这合适吗——我到了这年纪，还要连参考书带被单、热水瓶地，在空中以每秒十九英里这难以想象的速度被抛来抛去？

say, I don't at all like it. This universe of astronomical whirligigs makes me a little giddy.

That God should spend His eternity—which might be so much better employed—in spinning countless Solar Systems, and skylarking, like a great child, with tops and teetotums—is not this a serious scandal? I wonder what all our circumgyrating Monotheists really do think of it?

The Evil Eye

Drawn by the unfelt wind in my little sail over the shallow estuary, I lay in my boat, lost in the dream of mere existence. The cool water glided through my trailing fingers; and leaning over, I watched the sands that slid beneath me, the weeds that languidly swayed with the boat's motion. I was the cool water, I was the gliding sand and the swaying weed, I was the sea and sky and sun, I was the whole vast Universe.

Then between my eyes and the sandy bottom a mirrored face looked up at me, floating on the smooth film of water over which I glided. At one look from that too familiar, and yet how sinister and goblin a face, my immeasurable soul collapsed like a wrecked balloon; I shrank sadly back into my named personality, and sat there, shabby, hot, and very much bored with myself in my little boat.

我说了，我一点都不喜欢这样。宇宙的这种天文意义上的起落回旋，让我感到有点头晕。

上帝竟然把他永恒的精力——本来完全可以派上更好的用场——用于旋转无数的太阳系，还上上下下折腾取乐，活像个巨大的孩子在玩陀螺——这岂不是个非同小可的丑闻？不知我们旋游中的一神论者们对此到底做何感想？

恶眼一瞥

感觉不到的风牵着我的一帆小船，漂泛在浅浅的小海湾上，我躺在船中，陷入此身何身的遐思，随船任清凉的水从手指间流过。探出船帮，我看着底下黄沙向后滑去，水草跟着船身的浮动懒洋洋地飘悠。我是这清凉的水，我是这滑动的沙、这飘悠的水草；我是大海、天空和太阳，我就是浩浩邈邈的整个宇宙。

然后，在我眼睛和水底黄沙之间，倒映出一张脸，浮在我飘摇而过的平静的水面，朝上看着我。就看我一眼，这张太熟悉，然而又多么邪恶如鬼的脸马上令我那高远无比的灵魂瘪得像戳破的气球一样；人也凄凄惨惨地缩回到那个标了姓名的自己中去，坐在那儿，邋里邋遢，浑身燥热，对自己烦不胜烦地待在我的小船里。

Dissatisfaction

For one thing I hate spiders: I hate most kinds of insects. Their cold intelligence, their stereotyped, unremitting industry repel me. And I am not altogether happy about the future of the human race. When I think of the earth's refrigeration, and the ultimate collapse of our Solar System, I have grave misgivings. And all the books I have read and forgotten—the thought that my mind is really nothing but an empty sieve—often this, too, disconcerts me.

Self-Control

Still I am not a pessimist, nor misanthrope, nor grumbler; I bear it all, the burden of Public Affairs, the immensity of Space, the brevity of Life, and the thought of the all-swallowing Grave; —all this I put up with without impatience. I accept the common lot. And if now and then for a moment it seems too much; if I get my feet wet, or have to wait too long for tea, and my soul in these wanes of the moon cries out in French *C'est fini!* I always answer *Pazienza!* in Italian—*abbia la santa Pazienza!*

不如意

我讨厌蜘蛛，一个理由就是：大部分昆虫我都讨厌。它们那冷漠的智力，那如出一辙、不屈不挠的勤奋，令我反感。而对人类的将来我也不能完全高枕无忧。想到地球冷却，太阳系终有一天要坍塌，我便忧心忡忡。还有那一本本我读过又忘了的书——一想到我的头脑真不过是个空筛子罢了——这一点，也常常让我心神不宁。

自制

可我还不是一个悲观的人，也不是一个遁世者，也不是个好发牢骚的家伙；什么我都忍受着，公务的繁重，宇宙的茫茫，生命的短暂，还有想到那吞噬一切的坟墓；——这些我全都不气不急地忍耐着。我听天由命。假如时不时有哪一刻事情似乎弄过了头；假如我湿了脚，或者等茶等太久，我的灵魂在这些残月时光便用法语嚷道：*C'est fini!* 完蛋了！我总会用意大利语回答：忍一忍！——*abbia la santa Pazienza!*

A Fancy

More than once, too, I have pleased myself with the notion that somewhere there is good Company which will like this small uncontemporaneous Book—these Thoughts (if I may call them so) dipped up from that phantasmagoria or phosphorescence which, by some unexplained process of combustion, flickers over the lump of gray soft matter in the bowl of my skull.

They

Their taste is exquisite; They live in Palladian houses, in a world of ivory and precious china, of old brickwork and stone pilasters. In white drawing-rooms I see Them, or on blue, bird-haunted lawns. They talk pleasantly of me, and Their eyes watch me. From the diminished, ridiculous picture of myself which the glass of the world gives me, I turn for comfort, for happiness to my image in the kindly mirror of those eyes.

Who are They? Where, in what paradise or palace, shall I ever find Them? I may walk all the streets, ring all the door-bells of the World, but I shall never find Them. Yet nothing has value for me save in the crown of Their approval; for Their coming—which will never be—I build and plant, and for Them alone I secretly write this Book, which They will never read.

奇想一则

不止一次，我也以这个念头来告慰自己：知音就在哪个地方，他们会喜欢这本已是时过境迁的小书——这些想法（如果我能称它们为想法的话）出自那一片幻影或者磷火，也不知是什么烧出来的，在我硕大的头颅内那一团软绵绵的灰色物质上忽闪忽闪地飘来飘去。

他们

他们品味精妙高雅，住在意大利新古典风格的侯门巨宅里，他们的天地由琳琅满目的象牙和古瓷装点，由古砖墙和石壁柱围护。在白色的起居室里，或者在莺歌燕舞的青草地上，我看见他们。他们在愉快地谈论着我，眼睛望着我。从世界的镜子把我照成的那个萎顿可笑的影像我掉开头，转而去看在这些眼睛那善良的镜子中照出的我的形象，从中寻找安慰和幸福。

他们是谁呢？到底在哪儿，在什么天堂或殿堂，我找得着他们？我可以踏遍大街小巷，按遍天下门铃，却永远也找不到他们。然而，我别无所求，除了他们有如冠冕的嘉许。为了他们的到来——他们永远不会来的——我修建种植；只为了他们，我暗暗写了这本书，他们永远不会读的。

In the Pulpit

The Vicar had certain literary tastes; in his youth he had written an *Ode to the Moon*; and he would speak of the difficulty he found in composing his sermons, week after week.

Now I felt that if I composed and preached sermons, I would by no means confine myself to the Vicar's threadbare subjects—I would preach the Wrath of God, and sound the Last Trump in the ears of my Hell-doomed congregation, cracking the heavens and dissolving the earth with the Thunders and eclipses of the great Day of Judgement. Then I might refresh them with high and incomprehensible Doctrines, beyond the reach of Reason—Predestination, Election, Reprobation, the Co-existences and Co-eternities of the undemonstrable Triad. And with what a holy vehemence would I exclaim and cry out against all forms of doctrinal Error—all the execrable hypotheses of the great Heresiarchs! Then there would be many ancient, learned and out of the way Iniquities to denounce, and splendid, neglected Virtues to inculcate—Apostolic Poverty, and Virginity, that precious jewel, that fair garland, so prized in Heaven, but so rare, it is said, on earth.

For in the range of creeds and morals it is the highest peaks that shine for me with a certain splendour: Ah! It's towards those radiant Alps, that, if I were a Clergyman, I would lead my flocks to pasture.

布道坛上

牧师有一定的文学修养，年轻时写过一篇《月亮颂》；他会讲他撰写布道词时遇到的困难，讲了一礼拜又一礼拜。

我于是觉得，假如要我写稿讲道，我绝不会局限于牧师的那些干巴巴的老生常谈——我会讲上帝的愤怒，会把末日的号声在我那些注定下地狱的会众耳边吹响，用最后审判的雷霆和黑暗劈开天穹瓦解大地。然后我可以用高深莫测的教义使他们振作，超越理性之外——宿命、神的选择与摒弃、无以展示的三位一体的共存与永在。我又会以怎样一种神圣的怒火声讨各式各样教义上的谬误——异教祖师们一切可诅咒的假设！还有许多古老的、博学的、行于偏僻处的不义需要谴责，许多被人忽视的煌煌美德需要苦口训诲——安贫乐道、守身如玉，这无价的宝石，这美丽的花环，上天是如此珍重，然而在地上，据说又是如此稀缺。

因为在信条与道德的群山之中，是最高的山峰为我闪耀着某种辉光：啊！正是那些辉煌的阿尔卑斯山巅峰，假如我是牧师的话，我要领我的羊群上去放牧。

Caravans

Always over the horizon of the Sahara move those soundless caravans of camels, swaying with their padded feet across the desert, till in the remoteness of my mind they fade away, and vanish.

Human Ends

I really was impressed, as we paced up and down the avenue, by the Vicar's words, and weighty, weighed advice. He spoke of the various professions; mentioned contemporaries of his own who had achieved success: how one had a Seat in Parliament, would be given a Seat in the Cabinet when his party next came in; another was a Bishop with a Seat in the House of Lords; a third was a Barrister who was soon, it was said, to be raised to the Bench.

But in spite of my good intentions, my real wish to find, before it is too late, some career or other for myself (and the question is getting serious), I am far too much at the mercy of ludicrous images. Front Seats, Episcopal, Judicial, Parliamentary Benches—were all the ends then, I asked myself, of serious, middle-aged ambition only things to sit on?

旅队

在撒哈拉大漠的地平线上总是无声地走着一队队商旅，骆驼多肉的脚掌踏过片片黄沙，一摇一晃地，一直到我心中辽远的一角，他们渐渐淡去，消失了。

人心所求

我们沿着林荫道来回踱着，牧师的话，那一席语重又心长的忠告，的确让我动心。他谈到许多专业；谈到他自己那些事业有成的同辈：有一个如何拿到了国会议席，他的党下次当选便会进入内阁；另一个是位主教，在上议院有个席位；第三个是位律师，说是不久就要升迁，坐上法官的交椅。

但是尽管我意愿良好，真心希望在还来得及的时候为自己谋份或此或彼的职业（这问题越发紧要了），我还是太受一些滑稽的形象所左右。内阁席位，还有教堂、法庭、议院里的席次——难道人到中年后的雄心，我问自己，认认真真求的只是些能坐的东西？

Where?

I, who move and breathe and place one foot before the other, who watch the Moon wax and wane, and put off answering my letters, where shall I find the Bliss which dreams and blackbirds' voices promise, of which the waves whisper, and hand-organs in streets near Paddington faintly sing?

Does it dwell in some island of the South Seas, or far oasis among deserts and gaunt mountains; or only in those immortal gardens pictured by Chinese poets beyond the great, cold palaces of the Moon?

Lord Arden

'If I were Lord Arden,' said the Vicar, 'I would shut up that great House; it's too big—what can a young unmarried man ...?'

'If I were Lord Arden,' said the Vicar's wife (and Mrs. La Mountain's tone showed how much she disapproved of that young nobleman), 'if I were Lord Arden, I would live there, and do my duty to my tenants and neighbours.'

'If I were Lord Arden,' I said; but then it flashed vividly into my mind, suppose I really were this Sardanapalian young Lord? I quite forgot to whom I was talking; the Moralist within ceased to function; my memory was full with the names of people who had been famous for their enormous pleasures; who had filled

在哪儿呢?

我，一个会动弹有声息、走路先迈一只脚的人，一个看着月亮阴晴圆缺、回信能拖就拖的人，会在哪儿找着那份幸福呢？那份梦境和鸟鸣所应许的、浪花悄悄细语着的、伦敦西区帕丁顿街边手风琴隐隐约约唱着的幸福?

是不是在南洋的哪个岛上？是不是在沙漠荒山远远的哪片绿洲上？或者只是在中国诗人描画的广漠寒冷的月宫更远处那些神仙花园中?

亚登勋爵

“我要是亚登勋爵，”牧师说道，“我会关了那座大房子；太大了——干吗一个未成家的年轻人……”

“我要是亚登勋爵，”牧师太太说道（拉·姆汀太太的口气显出她对那位年轻的贵族是多么反感），“我要是亚登勋爵，我会住在那儿，为佃户和邻居尽我的责任。”

“我要是亚登勋爵——”我说道。可这时活脱脱在我心中闪现的是，假如我真的是这位穷奢极侈的年轻勋爵，又会怎样？我真忘得差不多自己是在跟谁说话，心中那个道德家不管用了，脑海里浮现的全是那些以尽享荣华富贵而闻名的人物。他们令宫

their palaces with guilty revels, and built Pyramids, Obelisks, and half-acre Tombs, to soothe their Pride. My mind kindled at the thought of these Audacities. 'If I were Lord Arden!' I shouted ....

The Starry Heaven

'But what are they really? What do they say they are?' the small young lady asked me. We were looking up at the Stars, which were quivering that night in splendid hierarchies above the lawns and trees.

So I tried to explain some of the views that have been held about the stars. How people first of all had thought them mere candles set in the sky, to guide their own footsteps when the Sun was gone; till wise men, sitting on the Chaldean plains, and watching them with aged eyes, became impressed with the solemn view that those still and shining lights were the executioners of God's decrees, and irresistible instruments of His Wrath; and that they moved fatally among their celestial Houses to ordain and set out the fortunes and misfortunes of each race of newborn mortals. And so it was believed that every man or woman had, from the cradle, fighting for or against him or her, some great Star, Formalhaut, perhaps, Aldebaran, Altaïr: while great Heroes and Princes were more splendidly attended, and marched out to their forgotten battles with troops and armies of heavenly Constellations.

廷充斥着罪恶的宴饮狂欢，他们建造金字塔、纪念碑、延绵数亩的陵墓，来骄纵一己之傲气。我的心被这种种寡廉鲜耻的行径点燃。“如果我是亚登勋爵！”我高喊道……

望星空

“可它们到底是什么呢？人们说那到底是什么呢？”这位小个子的年轻女士问我。我们正望着天上的星星，看它们那天晚上层层叠叠在草地和树梢的上空闪烁着。

于是我就试着跟她解释关于星星曾经都有些什么观点。最初人们是怎样认为星星无非是蜡烛插在天上，在太阳下山后为自己照路；后来又有智者坐在古巴比伦的迦勒底平原上，老眼观星，心之所动便庄严地认为，那些凝然又灿然的光是上帝旨意的执行者，是他愤怒所向不可抵挡的利器；它们巡行于天庭间，生杀予夺地为每个种族新生的凡胎厘定悲欢祸福。因此人们相信男男女女，每一个从一生下来，或者为他或她征战，或者跟他或她作对的，便有哪一颗伟大的星星，北落师门也许吧，或者是毕宿五、牵牛星。而大英雄和王子们的随从就更其壮观，整军整团的星座陪同出征，打他们那些已被人遗忘了的战役。

But this noble old view was not believed in now; the Stars were no longer regarded as malignant or beneficent Powers; and I explained how most serious people thought that somewhere—though just where they could not say—above the vault of Sky, was to be found the final home of earnest men and women, where, as a reward for their right views and conduct, they were to rejoice forever, wearing those diamonds of the starry night arranged in glorious crowns. This notion, however, had been disputed by Poets and Lovers: it was Love, according to these young astronomers, that moved the Sun and other Stars; the Constellations being heavenly palaces, where people who had adored each other were to meet and live always together after Death.

Then I spoke of the modern immensity of the unimaginable Skies. But suddenly the vast meaning of my words rushed into my mind; I felt myself dwindling, falling through the blue. And yet, in that pause of acquiescence in the universal scheme of things there thrilled through me no chill of death or nothingness, but the taste and joy of this Earth, this orchard-plot of earth, floating unknown, and very far away with her Moon and her meadows.

My Map

The 'Known World' I called the map, which I amused

但是这一高古的观点而今没人相信了；不再有谁把星星看作是主吉凶的力量；我解释说大多数认真的人是怎样认为在哪个地方——虽然到底在哪儿他们也说不出——天穹之上吧，虔诚的男女会找到他们最后的家园，作为对他们观点、行为正确的报答，他们在那里永远喜乐，头上戴着那些星夜之钻编就的辉煌的冠冕。然而这个看法又受到诗人和情侣们反驳：是爱情，据这些年轻的天文学家所说，驱动着太阳和其他星星；星座乃天上宫阙，让有情人死后得以相会，永不分离。

接着，我讲到难以想象的天宇到了现代所展现的浩大。可是突然间我话里的深远意义涌上心头；我感到自己在缩小，在从蓝天里坠落。然而，就在那默然认命的一刻停顿中，透心而过的不是死亡和虚空的寒意，而是这个地球的况味和喜悦，这一小片果园似的人间，无人知晓地飘浮着，飘得很远很远，带着她的月亮和她的青草地。

我的地图

“已知的世界”，我这么称呼自己画着玩让孩子们挂在教室的

myself making for the children's schoolroom. It included France, England, Italy, Greece, and all the old shores of the Mediterranean; but the rest I marked 'Unknown'; sketching into the East the doubtful realms of Ninus and Semiramis; changing back Germany into the Hercynian Forest; and drawing pictures of the supposed inhabitants of these unexploited regions, Dog-Apes, Satyrs, Cannibals, and Misanthropes, Cimmerians involved in darkness, Amazons, and Headless Men. And all around the Map I, coiled the coils, and curled the curling waves of the great Sea Oceanus, with the bursting cheeks of the four Winds, blowing from the four hinges of the World.

The Full Moon

And then one night, low above the trees, we saw the great, amorous, unabashed face of the full moon. It was an exhibition that made me blush, feel that I had no right to be there. 'After all these millions of years, she ought to be ashamed of herself!' I cried.

The Snob

As I paced in fine company on that terrace, I felt chosen, exempt, and curiously happy. There was a glamour in the air, a

地图。这包括法国、英国、意大利、希腊，以及地中海所有那些古老的海岸；但其余部分我标为“未知”；向东描到了古亚述的尼努斯王和赛米勒米斯女王那可疑的疆域中；把德国变回莽莽苍苍的海西尼亚森林；还画了认为住在这些未开化区域的居民，狗猿、人身羊形的树神、食人族和厌人族、永远住在黑暗中的辛梅里安人[8]、亚马孙族的女斗士，还有无头人。围着地图，我用笔该弯的弯，该卷的卷，掀起大洋的滔滔浪花，召来四位风神鼓起腮帮，从张挂世界的四个方位紧吹着。

满月

接着有一天晚上，低垂于树梢之上，我们看到满月那秋波脉脉、不知害臊的一张大脸。如此的展露令我脸红，觉得自己无权在那儿。“都这么千百万年了，她也应该感到羞愧才是！”我嚷道。

自我感觉良好

我在那露天平台上信步闲行，有嘉朋好友相伴，感到自己得上苍垂青与眷顾，莫名其妙地觉得高兴。空气中迷漫着一种曼

something in the special flavour of that moment that was like the consciousness of Salvation, or the smell of ripe peaches on a sunny wall.

I know what you're going to call me, Reader; but I am not to be bullied by words. And, after all, why not let oneself be dazzled and enchanted? Are not illusions pleasant, and is this a world in which Romance hangs, so to speak, on every tree?

And how about your own life? Is that, then, so full of golden visions?

Companions

Dearest, prettiest, and sweetest of my retinue, who gather with delicate industry bits of silk and down from the bleak world to make the soft nest of my fatuous repose; who ever whisper honied words in my ear, or trip before me holding up deceiving mirrors—is it Hope, or is it not rather Vanity, that I love the best?

Desires

These exquisite and absurd fancies of mine—little curiosities, and greedinesses, and impulses to kiss and touch and snatch, and all the vanities and artless desires that nest and sing

妙，一种此时此刻别具风味的什么，犹如获得救赎的意识，或者阳光中探出墙头的桃子那成熟的醇香。

我知道您要说我什么了，读者先生；但我是不会向人言低头的。况且，说到底，为什么不让自己神魂颠倒一下呢？难道幻觉不令人愉快吗？难道在这个世界上，浪漫，比方说，不就在每棵树上挂着吗？

而您自己的生活呢？是不是也如此充满了金灿灿的愿景？

良伴

随我左右最亲最美最甜蜜的良伴，你们从那凄凉的世界兢兢业业地拣来片片丝绸绒羽，筑出温软的窝让我昏昏安眠；你们总在我耳畔轻声说着蜜糖般的细语，或者走在我前头高擎一面面惑人眼目的镜子——告诉我，是希望，抑或虚荣，是我的最爱？

欲望

我的这些精致又荒唐的奇想——小小的好奇、贪念、想亲想碰想夺的冲动，以及所有那些虚荣和直白的欲望，在我心中筑巢

in my heart like birds in a bush—all these, we are now told, are an inheritance from our pre-human past, and were hatched long ago in very ancient swamps and forests. But what of that? I like to share in the dumb delights of birds and animals, to feel my life drawing its sap from roots deep in the soil of Nature. I am proud of those bright-eyed, furry, four-footed or scaly progenitors, and not at all ashamed of my cousins, the Apes and Peacocks and streaked Tigers.

Edification

'I must really improve my mind,' I tell myself, and once more begin to patch and repair that crazy structure. So I toil and toil on at the vain task of edification, though the wind tears off the tiles, the floors give way, the ceilings fall, strange birds build untidy nests in the rafters, and owls hoot and laugh in the tumbling chimneys.

The Rose

The old lady had always been proud of the great rose-tree in her garden, and was fond of telling how it had grown from a cutting she had brought years before from Italy, when she was first married. She and her husband had been travelling back in

唱歌就像灌木丛中的小鸟一样——这一切，如今有人告诉我们，都承袭自我们在人类形成之前的遗传，很久以前便在那非常古老的沼泽和森林中孵化出来了。但那又有什么呢？我愿意分享鸟兽那无言的欢娱，愿意感受自己的生命从大自然土壤深处的根须汲取汁液。我为那些目光敏锐、毛茸茸、四条腿或者披鳞挂甲的祖先感到自豪，而且一点也不觉得羞愧，表亲中有猿猴、孔雀和条纹斑斑的老虎。

心智建设

“我的心智真应该改善改善了。”我告诉自己，说着便再一次着手来修补这个拉杂拼成的架构。于是乎，我苦苦努力瞎忙着加固我心智的大厦，尽管风刮掉屋顶的瓦片，地板下陷，天花板坍塌，陌生的鸟儿在梁上乱糟糟做了许多窝，猫头鹰在摇摇欲坠的烟囱中叫着笑着。

玫瑰

老太太向来为她花园中那棵很大的玫瑰树感到自豪，总是喜欢向人说起，这玫瑰是怎样从多年前她由意大利带回来的一段插枝，长到现在这模样的。那时，她才结婚不久，正和先生从那不勒

their carriage from Naples (it was before the time of railways), and on a bad piece of road south of Sienna they had broken down, and had been forced to pass the night in a little house by the roadside. The accommodation was wretched of course; she had spent a sleepless night, and rising early had stood, wrapped up, at her window, with the cool air blowing on her face, to watch the dawn. She could still, after all these years, remember the blue mountains with the bright moon above them, and how a far-off town on one of the peaks had gradually grown whiter and whiter, till the moon faded, the mountains were touched with the pink of the rising sun, and suddenly the town was lit as by an illumination, one window after another catching and reflecting the sun's beams, till at last the whole little city twinkled and sparkled up in the sky like a nest of stars.

Finding they would have to wait while their carriage was being repaired, they had driven that morning, in a local conveyance, up to the city on the mountain, where they had been told they would find better quarters; and there they had stayed two or three days. It was one of the miniature Italian cities with a high church, a pretentious piazza, a few narrow streets and little palaces, perched, all compact and complete, on the top of a mountain, within an enclosure of walls hardly larger than an English kitchen garden. But it was full of life and noise, echoing all day and all night with the sounds of feet and voices.

The Café of the simple inn where they stayed was the meeting-place of the notabilities of the little city; the *Sindaco*,

斯乘马车（当时火车尚未问世呢）回国。途中锡耶纳南边的一段路不好，马车坏了，他们被迫只好在路边的一所小房子过夜。境况当然是糟透了；她彻夜未眠，早早便下了床，裹了条毯子，站在窗前，任清凉的晓风吹在脸上，眺望着曙色渐开。这么多年过去了，她还记得明月下那一片蓝色的山峦，远远的一座山峰上有座小城是怎样越变越白，直到月亮隐去，晨曦的一抹粉红点染了道道峰峦，突然间那个小镇就像亮灯似的，一个又一个窗户接着太阳的光芒交相辉映，直到最后整个小城在天空中闪闪烁烁的，宛如一窝星星。

他们发现要等马车修好了才能继续上路，那天上午就搭当地的车去了山顶上的小城，人们说那边找得到好一些的住处；他们在那城里待了两三天。这城是意大利的一座迷你小城，有一所高高的教堂、一个煞有介事的广场、几条窄窄的街道、几处小小的豪宅，一应俱全，小而精地高踞于一座山峰之巅，四周一溜城墙，地盘比英国的家庭菜园大不了多少。可是城里充满了生机和喧闹，整日整夜回荡着脚步声和人声。

他们落脚的这个简朴的小旅馆有个咖啡厅，是小城里显贵们的聚会之所，镇长、律师、医生，还有其他人等。他们注意到其中

the *avvocato*, the doctor, and a few others; and among them they noticed a beautiful, slim, talkative old man, with bright black eyes and snow-white hair—tall and straight and still with the figure of a youth, although the waiter told them with pride that the *Conte* was *molto vecchio*—would in fact be eighty in the following year. He was the last of his family, the waiter added—they had once been great and rich people—but he had no descendants; in fact the waiter mentioned with complacency, as if it were a story on which the locality prided itself, that the *Conte* had been unfortunate in love, and had never married.

The old gentleman, however, seemed cheerful enough; and it was plain that he took an interest in the strangers, and wished to make their acquaintance. This was soon effected by the friendly waiter; and after a little talk the old man invited them to visit his villa and garden which were just outside the walls of the town. So the next afternoon, when the sun began to descend, and they saw in glimpses through doorways and windows blue shadows spreading over the brown mountains, they went to pay their visit. It was not much of a place, a small, modernized, stucco villa, with a hot pebbly garden, and in it a stone basin with torpid gold fish, and a statue of Diana and her hounds against the wall. But what gave a glory to it was a gigantic rose-tree which clambered over the house, almost smothering the windows, and filling the air with the perfume of its sweetness. Yes, it was a fine rose, the *Conte* said proudly when they praised it, and he would tell the Signora about it. And as they sat there, drinking the wine he offered them, he

有位美男子模样、瘦削健谈的老人，两眼乌黑明亮，一头雪一样的白发——修长挺拔，仍旧是一副年轻人的身材，虽然侍者得意地告诉他们，伯爵已经*molto vecchio*，很老了——实际上明年就八十岁了。他是家族的最后一个成员，侍者又说——他们曾经是个有钱有地位的家族——可是伯爵没有子嗣；那侍者真还得意地说了，好像这是当地引以为荣的一个故事似的，伯爵曾经在爱情上不幸，从未结过婚。

然而老先生自己却够乐天的；显然对陌生的客人产生了兴趣，希望同他们认识认识。很快，热心的侍者从中成全；聊了几句后老人便邀请他们到他的别墅和花园做客，就在城墙外。于是第二天下午，太阳开始西斜，透过一个个门廊和窗口可以瞥见褐色的群山上蓝色的日影在蔓延时，他们就过去登门造访。地方并不大，一座现代风格、灰泥粉饰的小别墅，有个卵石铺地、热腾腾的花园，园中有个石盆，养着懒懒散散的几条金鱼，靠着墙边是一尊猎神狄安娜和她的猎犬的雕像。但是让这一切生色增辉的是一株巨大的玫瑰，爬满了整座房子，简直把窗户都给掩捂住了，空气中充满了它甜蜜的芬芳。是的，很好的一株玫瑰，当他们称赞时伯爵自豪地附和道，他还会给夫人讲这玫瑰的事呢。他们坐在那儿，喝着老人招待他们的葡萄酒，听他以上了年纪的那种乐呵呵

alluded with the cheerful indifference of old age to his love affair, as though he took for granted that they had heard of it already.

'The lady lived across the valley there beyond that hill. I was a young man then, for it was many years ago. I used to ride over to see her; it was a long way, but I rode fast, for young men, as no doubt the Signora knows, are impatient. But the lady was not kind, she would keep me waiting, oh, for hours; and one day when I had waited very long I grew very angry, and as I walked up and down in the garden where she had told me she would see me, I broke one of her roses, broke a branch from it; and when I saw what I had done, I hid it inside my coat—so—; and when I came home I planted it, and the Signora sees how it has grown. If the Signora admires it, I must give her a cutting to plant also in her garden; I am told the English have beautiful gardens that are green, and not burnt with the sun like ours.'

The next day, when their mended carriage had come up to fetch them, and they were just starting to drive away from the inn, the *Conte*'s old servant appeared with the rose-cutting neatly wrapped up, and the compliments and wishes for a *buon viaggio* from her master. The town collected to see them depart, and the children ran after their carriage through the gate of the little city. They heard a rush of feet behind them for a few moments, but soon they were far down toward the valley; the little town with all its noise and life was high above them on its mountain peak.

She had planted the rose at home, where it had grown and flourished in a wonderful manner; and every June the great mass

的淡然婉言暗指他的爱情故事，似乎想当然地认为这事他们已经听说过了。

“那女的住在山谷那边的那座山外。我那时年轻，许多年前的事了。我常骑马过去看她；路远着呢，可我骑得快，年轻人嘛，夫人肯定懂得的，就是性子急。可那女的不好，她会让我等，噢，一等就是几个钟头。有一天我等了好久好久，非常生气，就在她说要来见我的花园里来来回回走着，没想到把她的一株玫瑰弄断了，一根枝条折了；当我看到自己惹下了什么事，就把那枝条藏在上衣里边——于是——回到家后我把那枝条栽下，夫人看它长成了这个样子。如果夫人喜欢，我一定要送她一枝，回去也种在花园里。我听说英国人的花园绿油油的很美，不像我们的都让太阳晒焦了。”

第二天，他们的马车修好后上来接人，他们从旅馆里出来刚要上路时，伯爵的老仆人来了，带着包得整整齐齐的玫瑰插枝，还有她主人的美言和“一路顺风”的祝词。镇上的人都聚拢来送行，小孩子还跟着马车追出了小城的城门外。他们听到急急的脚步声在后面响了一阵，但不一会儿他们就远远地下了山谷；身后的小城带着那一派喧闹和人气，留在了它高高的山巅上。

她把那玫瑰栽在家中花园，在这儿它长得枝繁叶茂，生机盎然；年年六月照样从团团新蕊嫩芽怒放成夺目的深红和如醉如痴

of leaves and shoots still broke out into a passionate splendour of scent and crimson colour, as if in its root and fibres there still burnt the anger and thwarted desire of that Italian lover. Of course, said the old lady (who had outlived sixty generations of these roses), the old *Conte* must have died long ago; she had forgotten his name, and had even forgotten the name of the mountain city that she had stayed in, after first seeing it twinkling at dawn in the sky, like a nest of stars.

Tu Quoque Fontium——

Just to sit in the Sun, to bask like an animal in its heat—this is one of my country recreations. And often I reflect what a thing after all it is, still to be alive and sitting here, above all the buried people of the world, in the kind and famous sunshine.

Beyond the orchard there is a place where the stream, hurrying out from under a bridge, makes for itself a quiet pool. A beech-tree upholds its green light over the blue water; and there, when I have grown weary of the sun, the great glaring undiscriminating Sun, I can shade myself and read my book. And listening to this water's pretty voices I invent for it exquisite epithets, calling it *silver-clean* or *moss-margined* or *nymph-frequented*, and idly promise to place it among the learned fountains and pools of the world, making of it a cool green thought for English exiles in the glare of Eastern deserts.

的清香，似乎它的根茎叶脉里还燃烧着那位意大利情人的怒火和被挫辱了的渴念。当然了，老太太说（她已经历了六十代的花开花落），老伯爵一定早就去世了；她也忘了他的姓名，甚至她小住过的那座山城的名字；那城，她当初曾望着它在黎明的天空中闪闪烁烁，宛如一窝星星。

你也会是一眼源泉[9]

就这么坐在太阳底下，像一头动物似的沐浴着热烘烘的阳光——这是我的乡村消闲方式之一。我常常心中思忖，毕竟难得啊，还活在世上还坐在这儿，在所有长眠地下的世人之上，在和颜悦色、遐迩闻名的阳光之中。

在果园过去那一边有个地方，溪流从一座桥下匆匆而过，给自己聚了一汪静悄悄的池塘。一株山毛榉在碧蓝的池水上撑起它绿色的光彩；那地方，等我晒腻了太阳，那咄咄逼人不解炎凉的伟大太阳，便是我遮阴读书的好去处。听着这悦耳的叮咚流水，我为它编造了许多美妙好词，说它是“清净如银”、“水痕苔色”或者“仙踪倩影”，闲情所至还答应要让它跻身天下文名昭著的源泉湖潭之列，让它成为东方沙漠烈日下英国流亡者心头一缕沁凉的绿色思绪。

The Spider

What shall I compare it to, this fantastic thing I call my Mind? To a waste-paper basket, to a sieve choked with sediment, or to a barrel full of floating froth and refuse?

No, what it is really most like is a spider's web, insecurely hung on leaves and twigs, quivering in every wind, and sprinkled with dewdrops and dead flies. And at its geometric centre, pondering for ever the Problem of Existence, sits motionless and spider-like the uncanny Soul.

The Age

Again, as the train drew out of the station, the old gentleman pulled out of his pocket his great shining watch; and for the fifth, or as it seemed to me, the five hundredth, time, he said (we were in the carriage alone together) 'To the minute, to the very minute! It's a marvellous thing, the railway; a wonderful age!'

Now I had been long annoyed by the old gentleman's smiling face, platitudes, and piles of newspapers; I had no love for the Age; and Satan put it into my heart to denounce it.

'Allow me to tell you,' I said, 'that I consider it a wretched, an ignoble age. Where's the greatness of Life, where's dignity, leisure, stateliness; where's Art and Eloquence? Where are your

蜘蛛

我该将它比成什么呢，我称作我心的这个神妙的东西？比成一个废纸篓、一只筛眼被堵住的筛子，还是一口大桶，漂浮着渣沫和垃圾？

不，它真正最像的是一面蜘蛛网，在枝叶树杈间战战兢兢地张着，每一阵风过都令它颤抖不已，上面挂着露珠和死苍蝇。而在它几何图形的中心，永远在沉思着生存问题的，是那个动也不动坐着像蜘蛛似的诡怪灵魂。

时代

火车离站时，老先生又一次从衣袋里掏出他那锃亮的大怀表；第五次，在我看似乎是第五百次了，开口说道（车厢里就我们两人）："正点，一分不差的正点！这物神哪，火车铁路；真是个神奇的时代！"

我早被老先生的那副笑脸、那腔陈词滥调、那堆报纸弄得心烦；对这个时代我可没那么一往情深，邪火一上来就开口数落。

"恕我直言，"我说，"我觉得这是一个糟糕的、低俗的时代。敢问先生，今时今世，生命的伟大哪儿去了？尊严、淡泊、庄重呢？艺术与文采哪儿去了？你们的大学者、大政治家哪儿去了？"

great scholars, statesmen? Let me ask you, Sir,' I cried, glaring at him, 'where's your Gibbon, your Burke or Chatham?'

我嚷道，拿眼睛瞪着他，“你们的吉本[10]、你们的伯克[11]，还有查塔姆[12]，都哪儿去了？”

BOOK II

'Thou, Trivia, Goddess, aid my song,

Thro' spacious streets conduct thy bard along.'

Trivia: or, the Art of Walking
the Streets of London. By MR. GAY.

卷二

“你啊，特丽维亚，巷陌之女神，助我歌兴，

以宽阔的街道引你的诗人且吟且行。”

引自格伊先生：

《特丽维亚：或，闲步伦敦街头之艺术》

L'Oiseau Bleu

What is it, I have more than once asked myself, what is it that I'm looking for in my walks about London? Sometimes it seems to me as if I were following a Bird, a bright Bird which sings divinely as it floats about from one place to another.

When I find myself, however, among persons of middle age and steady principles, see them moving regularly to their offices—what keeps them going? I wonder. And then I feel ashamed of myself and my Bird.

There is though a Philosophic Doctrine—I studied it at College, and I know that many serious people believe it—which maintains that all men, in spite of appearances and pretensions, all live alike for Pleasure. This theory certainly brings portly, respected persons very near to me. Indeed, sometimes with a sense of low complicity I have watched a Bishop. Was that Divine, too, on the hunt for Pleasure, solemnly pursuing his Bird?

At the Bank

Entering the Bank in a composed manner, I drew a cheque and handed it to the cashier through the grating. Then I eyed him narrowly. Would not that astute official see that I was posing as a Real Person? No; he calmly opened a little drawer, took out

青鸟

是什么呢？我不止一次问自己，我在伦敦城里四处走动，找寻的是什么呢？有时我觉得自己似乎在尾随一只小鸟，一只鲜亮的小鸟，鸣啭如神曲，从一处悠悠转到另一处。

然而，当我发现自己处身于已入中年、守正而不惑的人士之间，看他们按部就班朝他们的办公楼走去——又是什么令他们如此行事呢？我寻思。接着便为我自己和我的小鸟感到羞惭了。

可是有一条哲学大道理——我在大学里研习过，也知道许多正经人都相信——说是天下人，不管其表面的虚实真伪，活着全是为了享乐。这个理论当然就把一班威仪富态的人士拉得跟我非常接近了。的确，有时我会以一种小人之心盯着一个主教看。那侍奉神的人，是否也在寻求欢乐，庄严地追逐着他的小鸟呢？

银行里

走进银行我神态自若地开了一张支票，隔着铁栅窗递给出纳员，接着便仔细观察他。那位精明的职员难道看不出我这是在假冒一个真的人吗？是看不出；只见他不慌不忙地打开一个小抽

some real sovereigns, counted them carefully, and handed them to me in a brass shovel. I went away feeling I had perpetrated a delightful fraud. I had got some of the gold of the actual world!

Yet now and then, at the sight of my name on a visiting card, or of my face photographed in a group among other faces, or when I see a letter addressed in my hand, or catch the sound of my own voice, I grow shy in the presence of a mysterious Person who is myself, is known by my name, and who apparently does exist. Can it be possible that I am as real as anyone, and that all of us—the cashier and banker at the Bank, the King on his throne—all feel ourselves ghost, and goblins in this authentic world?

Mammon

Moralists and Church Fathers have named it the root of all Evil, the begetter of hate and bloodshed, the sure cause of the soul's damnation. It has been called 'trash,' 'muck,' 'dunghill excrement,' by grave authors. The love of it is denounced in all Sacred Writings; we find it reprehended on Chaldean bricks, and in the earliest papyri. Buddha, Confucius, Christ, set their faces against it; and they have been followed in more modern times by beneficed Clergymen, Sunday School Teachers, and the leaders of the Higher Thought. But have all the condemnations of all the Saints and Sages done anything to tarnish that bright lustre?

屉，取出一些真金币，仔细数了数，用一个小铜铲装了递过来给我。离开柜台时我觉得自己很开心地耍了个诈骗妙计，从真实的世界那里弄到手了一些金子！

可不时地，一看到印在名片上的我的名字，或是自己的脸混在别的脸当中拍出的集体照，或是自己亲笔写下姓名地址的信，或者猛地听到自己的声音，我便不好意思起来：怎么有一个神秘人在场，还是我自己，叫的是我的名字，而且看那样子真还存在着呢。有没有可能我和任何人一样真实？有没有可能我们大家——银行里的出纳和行长、宝座上的国王——全都觉得自己是鬼魂，是精灵活在这确确实实的世界上？

金钱[13]

道德家和神父们称它为万恶之源、仇恨与杀戮之根、让灵魂遭贬受罚的不二祸因。正儿八经的文人把它叫作“垃圾”“粪土”“狗屎堆”。爱钱在所有神圣的书文中都受到谴责；在迦勒底人的砖刻文字中、在最早的古埃及人纸莎草纸文稿中，都见到它挨骂。释迦牟尼、孔丘、基督，也不给它好脸色看；他们更为现代的追随者是受圣俸的教士、主日学校的教师、领一代思潮的俊杰。但是所有这些圣人智者的所有这些鞭挞，是否使它的光芒减损分

Men dig ever deeper into the earth's intestines, travel in search of it farther and farther to arctic and unpleasant regions.

In spite of all my moral reading, I must say I do like to have some of this gaudy substance in my pocket. Its presence cheers and comforts me, diffuses a genial warmth through my body. My eyes rejoice in the shine of it; its clinquant sound is musical in my ears. Since I then am in his paid service, and reject none of the doles of his bounty, I too dwell in the House of Mammon. I bow before the Idol, and taste the unhallowed ecstasy.

How many Altars have been thrown down, and how many Theologies and heavenly Dreams have had their bottoms knocked out of them, while He has sat there, a great God, golden and adorned, secure on His unmoved throne?

Appearance and Reality

It is pleasant to saunter out in the morning sun and idle along the summer streets with no purpose.

But is it Right?

I am not really bothered by these Questions—the hoary old puzzles of Ethics and Philosophy, which lurk around the London corners to waylay me. I have got used to them; and the most formidable of all, the biggest bug of Metaphysics, the Problem which nonplusses the wisest heads on this Planet has become quite a familiar companion of mine. What is Reality?

毫？只见人们越挖越深，将地球搜肠刮肚，为找它越探越远，探进了北极和许多穷山恶水之地。

尽管读了这么些道德文章，老实说我还是喜欢有一些这样的闪闪发光物装在自己口袋里。有了它，我便心安心喜，周身舒泰暖和。我眼睛看到那闪光就高兴，那金箔似的声音我耳朵听着如仙乐。既然我这样就是受雇于玛门，对他的恩泽施舍绝不推拒，那也就住到了他的黄金屋里，为那尊偶像折腰，品尝着不圣洁的销魂之乐。

有多少圣坛被推翻了，有多少神学说教、多少超然物外的梦想都被粉碎了，而他却坐在那里，俨然有上帝之尊，金碧辉煌的，端坐在他纹丝不动的宝座上？

表象与真实

很舒服，这么踏着朝阳无所事事地出来闲逛，沿着夏日的街道无为无羁地漫游。

可是这没错吗？

我还真不为这些问题操心呢——管他这些老掉牙的伦理哲学之谜，埋伏在伦敦的边边角角要突袭我。我已经习以为常了；而其中最令人生畏的，最大的形而上学怪题，那个叫天底下最聪明的脑袋搔破头皮的难题，差不多是我的老伙伴了。何谓真实？

I ask myself almost daily: how does the External World exist, materialized in mid-air, apart from my perceptions? This show of streets and skies, of policemen and perambulators and hard pavements, is it nothing more than a mere hypothesis and figment of the Mind, or does it remain there, permanent and imposing, when I stop looking at it?

Often, as I saunter along Piccadilly or Bond Street, I please myself with the Berkeleian notion that Matter has no existence, that this so solid-seeming World is all idea, all appearance—that I am carried soft through space inside an immense Thought-bubble, a floating, diaphanous, opal-tinted Dream.

In the Street

These eye-encounters in the street, little touches of love-liking; faces that ask, as they pass, 'Are you my new lover?' Shall I one day—in Park Lane or Oxford Street perhaps—see the unknown Face I dread and look for?

I See the World

'But you go nowhere, see nothing of the world,' my cousins said.

Now though I do go sometimes to the parties to which I am

我几乎天天问自己：外部世界是如何存在的？在半空中兀自成形，与我的感知无关吗？眼前展现的这一切，街道和天空，警察和行人，还有坚硬的人行道，难道不过是内心的假想和虚构，抑或本来就在，永永远远、堂堂皇皇，我不看它也在？

常常，悠游于名店林立的皮卡迪利或邦德大街时，我以哲人贝克莱[14]的观点自乐：物质没有存在，这看似确凿的世界全是意念，全是表象——我被带着施施然穿过空间，裹着一个巨大的思想泡沫，一个飘浮的、精致透明的、有着蛋白石光泽的梦。

街上

这些街上四目交投的相遇、这些含情带意的轻轻碰触；他们擦肩而过，脸在探询："你是不是我新的爱人？"我会不会有一天——在公园路或牛津街吧大概——看见那张素昧平生的脸，那张我既害怕又在找寻的脸？

见世面

"可你什么地方都不去，一点世面也没见过。"我的表亲们说。

虽然不时有人请我，有时也的确接受邀请赴了餐宴聚会，可

now and then invited, I find, as a matter of fact, that I get really much more pleasure by looking in at windows, and have a way of my own of seeing the World. And of summer evenings, when motors hurry through the late twilight, and the great houses take on airs of inscrutable expectation, I go owling out through the dusk; and wandering toward the West, lose my way in unknown streets—an unknown City of revels. And when a door opens and a bediamonded Lady moves to her motor over carpets unrolled by powdered footmen, I can easily think her some great Courtezan, or some half-believed-in Duchess, hurrying to card-tables and candelabra and strange scenes of joy. I like to see that there are still splendid people on this flat earth; and at dances, standing in the street with the crowd, and stirred by the music, the lights, the rushing sound of voices, I think the Ladies as beautiful as Stars who move up lanes of light into those Palaces; the young men look like Lords in novels; and if (it has once or twice happened) people I know go by me, they strike me as changed and rapt beyond my sphere. And when on hot nights windows are left open, and I can look in at Dinner Parties, as I peer through lace curtains and window-flowers at the silver, the women's shoulders, the shimmer of their jewels, and the divine attitudes of their heads as they lean and listen, I imagine extraordinary intrigues and unheard-of wines and passions.

是我发觉，说实在的，更惬意得多的是隔着窗户朝里望，以一种自己的方式见世面。夏日黄昏，当汽车急急穿过向晚的余晖，华屋豪宅摆出一副叫人莫测高深的期待神情，我便像猫头鹰似的潜行于暮色中；向西区漫游而去，在不熟悉的街巷迷了路——迷失在一座陌生的销金城里。等有扇门开了，看到一位佩戴钻石的妇人踏着脸上施粉的男仆铺开的地毯，朝她的汽车走去，我很容易就能把她想成某个大交际花，或是某个叫人半信半疑的公爵夫人，正匆匆赶赴牌局、烛光晚会、一些寻欢作乐的奇怪去处。我喜欢看到在这平淡的地球上仍有光彩夺目之人；舞会时，我站在街头同人群一道，为音乐、灯光、熙攘的人声所触动，把女士们想成了姣好的星辰，沿着光的街路登上那些宫阙；年轻的男士模样如小说中的王侯；假如（而且也发生过一两次）有认识的人走过，我会突然觉得他们变了个人，心醉神迷得超乎我想象。天热的夜晚，窗户开着，我能看屋里的晚宴，目光透过纱帘和窗台上的花朵，瞥见桌上的银器、女士们的肩膀、她们珠宝的闪光、欠身聆听时那副宛若天仙的神态，我便想象着惊世骇俗的阴谋，还有闻所未闻的佳酿与激情。

Social Success

The servant gave me my coat and hat, and in a glow of self-satisfaction I walked out into the night. 'A delightful evening,' I reflected, 'the nicest kind of people. What I said about finance and philosophy impressed them; and how they laughed when I imitated a pig squealing.'

But soon after, 'God, it's awful,' I muttered, 'I wish I was dead.'

Apotheosis

But oh, those heavenly moments when I feel this three-dimensional universe too small to contain my Attributes; when a sense of the divine Ipseity invades me; when I know that my voice is the voice of Truth, and my umbrella God's umbrella!

The Goat

In the midst of my anecdote a sudden misgiving chilled me—had I told them about this Goat before? And then as I talked there gaped upon me—abyss opening beneath abyss—a darker speculation: when goats are mentioned, do I automatically and always tell this story about the Goat at Portsmouth?

社交成功

侍者递上来大衣和帽子，我扬扬自得地步入外边的夜色。“一个愉快的晚上，”我心想，“碰上了最好的一些人。我谈到金融和哲学的那些话让他们印象深刻；学猪叫时他们又笑成那个样子。”

可过了不一会儿，“天哪，糟透了，”我喃喃自语，“我真还不如死了的好。”

超凡入圣

但是啊，那是些飘飘欲仙的时刻：一时间，我感到这个三维宇宙，其大盛不下我的才性；舍我其谁的神圣之感侵入我心；我知道我的声音乃真理之声，我的雨伞即上帝之伞！

山羊

趣闻讲了一半，我突然心头一凉——是不是以前也给他们讲过这头山羊？接着我一边讲一边心里就冒出了——如深渊套着深渊——一个更为不祥的疑虑：说到山羊时，我是否总是自发自动讲起这个关于朴次茅斯山羊的故事？

Longevity

'But when you are as old as I am!' I said to the young lady in pink satin.

'But I don't know how old you are,' the young lady in pink answered almost archly. We were getting on quite nicely.

'Oh, I'm endlessly old; my memory goes back almost for ever. I come out of the Middle Ages. I am the primitive savage we are all descended from; I believe in Devil-worship and the power of the Stars; I dance under the new Moon, naked and tattooed and holy. I am a Cave-dweller, a contemporary of Mastodons and Mammoths; I am pleistocene and eolithic, and full of the lusts and terrors of the great pre-glacial forests. But that's nothing; I am millions of years older; I am an arboreal Ape, an aged Baboon, with all its instincts; I am a pre-simian quadruped, I have great claws, eyes that see in the dark, and a long prehensile tail.'

'Good gracious!' said the terrified young lady in pink satin. Then she turned and talked in a hushed voice with her other neighbour.

In the Bus

As I sat inside that crowded bus, so sad, so incredible and sordid seemed the fat face of the woman opposite me, that I

长寿

“但等您到了我这个年纪！”我对那位身着粉红色缎料衣服的年轻女子说。

“可我并不知道您多大年纪了。”那位穿粉红色衣服的女士几乎是俏皮地回了我一句。我们谈得挺愉快的。

“哦，说多大有多大；我的记忆简直没个尽头。我出自中世纪。我是原始野人，是我们大家的共同祖先；我信魔鬼崇拜、星宿的神力；我在新月下起舞，身体赤裸有文身，虔诚又圣洁。我是个穴居人，与乳齿象和猛犸象同代；我是更新世、原始石器时代人，充满了大冰川期之前莽莽丛林中的欲望与恐惧。可这都算不了什么；我还要再老上数百万岁；是一头树栖猿猴，一头老年狒狒，各项本能一应俱全；是一头比类人猿更早的四足动物，长着大脚爪，眼睛夜里看得见，一条长尾巴能抓能握。”

“天哪！”穿着粉红色缎料衣服的年轻女士吓坏了，说着便转头压低声音，同另一边的邻座说起话来。

公共汽车上

我坐在那拥挤的公共汽车上，如此凄凉、如此令人不可思议、如此惨不忍睹的，是坐在对面的女子那张胖脸的模样，我只好加

interposed the thought of Kilimanjaro, that highest mountain of Africa, between us; the grassy slopes and green Arcadian realms of negro kings from which its dark cone rises; the immense, dim, elephant-haunted forests which clothe its flanks, and above, the white crown of snow, freezing in eternal isolation over the palm trees and desert of the African Equator.

Daydream

In the cold and malicious society in which I live, I must never mention the Soul, nor speak of my aspirations. If I ever once let these people get a glimpse of the higher side of my nature, they would tear me in pieces.

I wish I had soulful friends—refined Maiden Ladies with ideals and long noses, who live at Hampstead or Putney, and play Chopin with passion. On sad autumn afternoons I would go and have tea with them, and talk of the spiritual meaning of Beethoven's late Sonatas; or discuss in the twilight the pathos of life and the Larger Hope.

Providence

But God sees me; He knows my beautiful nature, and how pure I keep amid all sorts of quite horrible temptations. And

插进来去想乞力马扎罗山，非洲最高的那座山，来隔开我们俩；绿草满坡，黑人头领们的田园属地上方高耸着它深色的锥形山体；莽莽苍苍、野象出没的森林围在山边，而峰顶上，则是那白雪的冠冕，冻住了一份永恒的孤绝，俯瞰着棕榈树和非洲赤道的茫茫沙漠。

白日遐思

生活在这个冷漠恶毒的社会，我绝不能提灵魂二字，也不能谈到我的志向抱负。只消有一次让这些人窥见我本性高尚的一面，他们便会把我撕成碎片。

但愿我能有灵魂充实的朋友——优雅的淑女，有理想鼻梁又高，住在汉普斯特或普特尼区，弹奏起肖邦来激情荡漾。在凄清的秋日下午，我会过去同她们一道喝茶，谈论贝多芬后期奏鸣曲的精神意义，或者在暮色中讨论人生的凄凉和超越一己的希望。

天意

但是上帝看得见我；他知道我美好的天性，知道我在各色各样很是可怕的诱惑之中如何洁身自好。这就是为什么，我刻骨铭

that is why, as I feel in my bones, there is a special Providence watching over me; an Angel sent expressly from heaven to guide my footsteps from harm. For I never trip up or fall downstairs like other people; I am not run over by cabs and buses at street-crossings; in the worst wind my hat never blows off.

And if ever any of the great cosmic processes or powers threaten me, I believe that God sees it: 'Stop it!' He shouts from His ineffable Throne, 'Don't you touch my Chosen One, my Pet Lamb, my Beloved. Leave him alone, I tell you!'

The Saying of a Persian Poet

All this hurry to dress and go out, these journeys in taxicabs, or in trains with my packed bag from big railway stations—what keeps me going, I sometimes ask myself; and I remember how, in his 'Masnavi I Ma'navi' or, 'Spiritual Couplets,' Jalalu 'D-Din Muhammad Rumi tells us that the swarm of gaudy Thoughts we pursue and follow are short-lived like summer insects, and must all be killed before long by the winter of age.

Monotony

Oh to be becalmed on a sea of glass all day; to listen all day to rain on the roof, or the wind in pine trees; to sit all day by

心地觉得，有一份特别的天意在看顾我；有一位天使专门从天上派来引领我的脚步以避开祸端。因为我从来没有像其他人那样绊过跤，或滚下过楼梯，穿越马路也没被小车或大车撞倒过，即使风再猛头上的帽子也从未被刮掉。

倘若浩大的宇宙真有什么运作或什么力量威胁到我，我相信上帝看得到的："停下！"他从他那非你我所能言表的神圣宝座上喝令，"别碰我所拣选的这个，我的小羊羔，我所疼爱之人。别碰他，我告诉你！"

波斯诗人语

如此急急地穿衣出门，或搭的士或行囊鼓鼓奔大车站搭火车出行——是什么令我行迹匆匆呢？我有时间自己；我想起了波斯诗人鲁米[15]在他的《玛斯纳维》也即《训言诗》中，是怎么告诉我们的，我们所追求、所跟从的那群俗艳的念想，就像夏天的昆虫一样短命，必定会很快被年岁的冬季除灭净尽。

单调

啊，心无挂碍地整日待在明镜似的海上；整日里听着屋顶的雨声或松间的风声；整日里坐在一挂瀑布边读着斯宾塞的寓言

a waterfall reading the 'Faerie Queene,' or exquisite, artificial, monotonous Persian poems about an oasis garden where it is always spring—where roses bloom, and lovers sigh, and nightingales lament without ceasing, and groups of white-robed figures sit by the running water and discuss all day, and day after day, the Meaning of Life.

The Spring in London

London seemed last winter like an underground city; as if its low sky were the roof of a cave, and its murky day a light such as one reads of in countries beneath the earth.

And yet the natural sunlight sometimes shone there; unenduring clouds whitened the blue sky; the interminable multitudes of roofs were washed with silver by the Moon, or mantled in snow. And the coming of Spring to London was not unlike the descent of the maiden-goddess into Death's Kingdoms, when pink almond blossoms blew about her in the gloom, and those shadowy people were stirred with faint longings for meadows and the shepherd's life. Nor is there anything more virginal and fresh in wood or orchard, than the shimmer of young foliage, which, in May, dims with delicate green all the smoke-blackened London trees.

诗《仙后》[16]，或者一些精妙做作又单调的波斯诗歌，诗中写着一座绿洲花园，那里春光永驻——玫瑰盛开、情侣叹息、夜莺悲鸣不止，还有身穿白色长袍的人，三五成群坐在流水边，整日地、日复一日地，讨论着生命的意义。

伦敦之春

伦敦去年冬天似乎像是座地下城；低低的天空宛如山洞的洞顶，灰蒙蒙的白天好似书上读到的地府中的一片光。

但自然的阳光有时也出来照照；不会久留的云块令蓝天泛白；一望无际、鳞次栉比的屋顶或因月色银装如洗，或因落雪一片素裹。等春到伦敦，则无异于天上仙女降临死神的国度，阴郁中有粉红的杏花纷飞簇拥着她，那些影影绰绰的人也受到触动，隐隐兴起了对草地牧歌和田园生活的向往。没有什么能比树林和果园中闪闪烁烁的新叶更鲜美如处子了，到了五月，那娇嫩的翠绿便会让所有被烟熏黑的伦敦树黯然失色。

Fashion Plates

I like loitering at the bookstalls, looking in at the windows of print-shops, and romancing over the pictures I see of shepherdesses and old-fashioned Beauties. Tall and slim and crowned with plumes in one period, in another these Ladies become as wide-winged as butterflies, or float, large, balloon-like visions, down summer streets. And yet in all shapes they have always (I tell myself) created thrilling effects of beauty, and wakened in the breasts of modish young men ever the same charming Emotion.

But then I have questioned this. Is the emotion always precisely the same? Can one truly say that the human heart remains quite unchanged beneath all the ever-changing fashions of frills and ruffles? In this elegant and cruel Sentiment, I rather fancy that colour and shape do make a difference. I have a notion that about 1840 was the Zenith, the Meridian Hour, the Golden Age of the Passion. Those tight-waisted, whiskered Beaux, those crinolined Beauties, must have adored one another, I believe, with a leisure, a refinement, and dismay not quite attainable at other dates.

Mental Vice

There are certain hackneyed Thoughts that will force

时装图片

我喜欢漫步于报摊之间，望进书画店的橱窗，让心在看到的那些牧羊女和老式美女的画像上浪着漫着。亭亭玉立、羽冠如簇是一时期之风，换一个时期这些女郎又变成广袖如蝶，或气球般宽宽大大载浮载沉地飘过夏日街市的一幅幅图景。然而尽其千姿百态，她们总是（我对自己说）生发出令人怦然心动的美之效果，在时髦的年轻男士心中引动那份从未改变的旖旎情怀。

但我又心生疑问。那份情怀真的就丝毫不变？真就可以说，在那短长宽瘦无时不在变的时尚底下，人的心还能一点不变吗？怀着这份优雅又残忍的情致，我倒喜欢那形形色色的消长真能带来变化。我有个看法，激情这东西，大约1840年达到高峰，那是它如日中天的黄金时代。那些瘦腰美髯的时髦男士、那些身套衬裙的美女，必定相互倾慕，我相信，带着一种闲情、一种意趣、一种愁绪，那是别的时代不太能有的况味。

思想之恶

有某些迂腐的念头会硬钻进我的脑海；我发现自己，特别是

themselves on me; I find my mind, especially in hot weather, buzzed about by moral Platitudes. 'That shows—' I say to myself, or, 'How true it is—' or, 'I really ought to have known!' The sight of a large clock sets me off into musings on the flight of Time; a steamer on the Thames or lines of telegraph inevitably suggest the benefits of Civilization, man's triumph over Nature, the heroism of Inventors, the courage amid ridicule and poverty, of Stephenson and Watt. Like faint, rather unpleasant smells, these thoughts lurk about railway stations. I can hardly post a letter without marvelling at the excellence and accuracy of the Postal System.

Then the pride in the British Constitution and British Freedom, which comes over me when I see, even in the distance, the Towers of Westminster Palace—it is not much comfort that this should be chastened, as I walk down the Embankment, by the sight of Cleopatra's Needle, and the Thought that it will no doubt witness the Fall of the British, as it has that of other Empires, remaining to point its Moral, as old as Egypt, to Antipodeans musing on the dilapidated bridges.

I am sometimes afraid of finding that there is a moral for everything; that the whole great frame of the Universe has a key, like a box; has been contrived and set going by a well-meaning but humdrum Eighteenth-century Creator. It would be a kind of Hell, surely, a world in which everything could be at once explained, shown to be obvious and useful. I am sated with Lesson and Allegory; weary of monitory ants, industrious bees,

天气热时，会让道德的陈言老套弄得头昏脑胀。“那说明了——”我自言自语道，或者“这真不假——”或者“这我真该知道才是！”看到一个大时钟便沉思起时间的流逝；泰晤士河上的一艘火轮、手里的几行电报，也免不了提示我文明的好处、人战胜自然的业绩、发明家的英雄气概、在贫穷与讥笑中奋起的斯蒂芬孙[17]和瓦特[18]的勇气。就像隐隐约约、颇令人不快的气味似的，这些念头在火车站四处躲着。差不多每投一次信，我都忍不住赞叹一番邮电系统的优越与精确。

接着是我引以为傲的不列颠宪法、不列颠自由，看到威斯敏斯特宫的高塔，甚至只远远望见，那份自豪便冲涌上来——让人心里不太舒服的是，这份自豪感，在我沿着泰晤士河堤行走时，要被映入眼帘的克娄巴特拉方尖碑[19]泼一下冷水；恼人的还有那个念头，觉得那方尖碑无疑将目睹不列颠王国的没落，一如它所目睹过的其他帝国的没落，自己则留着继续将其寓意，那古老如埃及的寓意，指点给在破败的桥两边栏杆上相对而立沉思着的人像。

我有时会怕发现每件事都有寓意；发现宇宙整个的大框架有一把钥匙，就像一口箱子那样；由一个好心但乏味的十八世纪造物者设计启动。那会是一种地狱，肯定是的，要是世界上一切都解释得了，都能显示得明明白白、各有用处。我听腻了寓言训喻；看烦了警诫世人的蚂蚁、兢兢业业的蜜蜂，以及说教连篇的动

and preaching animals. The benefits of Civilization cloy me. I have seen enough shining of the didactic Sun.

So gazing up on hot summer nights at the London stars, I cool my thoughts with a vision of the giddy, infinite, meaningless waste of Creation, the blazing Suns, the Planets and frozen Moons, all crashing blindly for ever across the void of space.

Loneliness

Is there, then, no friend? No one who hates Ibsen and problem plays, and the Supernatural, and Switzerland and Adultery as much as I do? Must I live all my life as mute as a mackerel, companionless and uninvited, and never tell anyone what I think of my famous contemporaries? Must I plough always a solitary furrow, and tread the winepress alone?

The Organ of Life

Almost always in London—in the congregated uproar of streets, or in the noise that drifts through walls and windows—you can hear the hackneyed melancholy of street-music; a music which sounds like the actual voice of the human Heart, singing the lost joys, the regrets, the loveless lives of the people who blacken the pavements, or jolt along on the buses.

物们。文明的好处叫我倒胃口。我领受够了好为人师的太阳的光芒。

于是乎，在燠热的夏夜抬眼眺望伦敦的星空，我用来冷却自己心绪的，是那一片令人眩晕的景象，那幅无边无际也无意义、枉费造化之功的创作，看炽热的恒星，还有行星和冷冻的卫星，一个个跌跌撞撞、漫无目的、无休止地穿行于汗漫太空。

孤独

这么说来，就没有朋友了？没有哪个人像我这么讨厌易卜生[20]和问题剧，以及超自然异象，还有瑞士和通奸？难道我就得一辈子不吱声地像一条鲭鱼，无人做伴也没人相邀，永远告诉不了任何人自己对同代那些名人的看法？难道我永远就得形单影只地扶犁而耕，孤身一人地踩葡萄榨汁酿酒？

生活的风琴

在伦敦——在街头人群的呼叫声中、在穿墙过户飘荡着的嘈杂声中——你几乎永远听得到俗套忧郁的街头音乐；那音乐，就像发自人心深处真切的声音，吟唱着失去的欢乐，倾吐着悔恨，以及那些黑压压在人行道上涌动、在巴士车上颠簸的人们无爱的生活。

'Speak to me kindly,' the hand-organ implores; 'I'm all alone!' it screams amid the throng; 'thy Vows are all broken,' it laments in dingy courtyards, 'And light is thy Fame.' And of hot summer afternoons, the Cry for Courage to Remember, or Calmness to Forget, floats in with the smell of paint and asphalt through open office windows.

Humiliation

'My own view is,' I began, but no one listened. At the next pause, 'I always say,' I remarked, but again the loud talk went on. Someone told a story. When the laughter had ended, 'I often think——'; but looking around the table I could catch no friendly, no attentive eye. It was humiliating, but more humiliating the thought that Sophocles and Goethe would have always commanded attention, while the lack of it would not have troubled Spinoza, nor Abraham Lincoln.

Green Ivory

What a bore it is, waking up in the morning always the same person. I wish I were unflinching and emphatic, and had big, bushy eyebrows and a Message for the Age. I wish I were a deep Thinker, or a great Ventriloquist.

“好好对我说话吧，”手风琴在哀求，“我孤苦伶仃！”它在人流中呼号；“山盟海誓君皆忘，”它在昏暗的庭院里悲鸣，“君之名轻薄如飘絮。”而在夏天燠热的午后，它又呼唤重拾记忆的勇气，诉说忘却过去的冷静；一声声，和着油漆与柏油的气味，飘进了开着窗的办公室。

羞辱

“本人观点是——”我开口说道，可是没人听。在下一个停顿处，“我从来都认为——”我说，可周遭依旧是很响的谈话声。有人讲了个什么故事。等笑声停歇，“我常常想——”；可四下里望去，整桌人当中看不到一个友善的眼神、一丝专注的目光。这很让人觉得受辱，但更令人觉得无地自容的是想到换成索福克勒斯[21]和歌德便总会捉住人们的注意力，要是人们不理不睬，也惹不恼斯宾诺莎[22]，或者亚伯拉罕・林肯。

绿象牙

太没意思了，每天早上醒来总是同一个人。我希望自己坚韧不拔、令人刮目相看，有两道浓浓的眉毛还有一个讯息要带给这时代。我希望自己是个深邃的思想家，或者一个了不起的腹语演员。

I should like to be refined-looking and melancholy, the victim of a hopeless passion; to love in the old, stilted way, with impossible Adoration and Despair under the pale-faced Moon.

I wish I could get up; I wish I were the world's greatest living Violinist. I wish I had lots of silver, and first Editions, and green ivory.

The Correct

I am sometimes visited by a suspicion that everything isn't quite all right with the Righteous; that the Moral Law speaks in equivocal tones to those who listen most scrupulously for its dictates. I feel sure I have detected a look of misgiving in the eyes of its earnest upholders.

But there is no such shadow or cloud on the faces in Club windows, or in the eyes of drivers of four-in-hands, or of fashionable young men walking down Piccadilly. For these live by a Rule which has not been drawn down from questionable skies, and needs no sanction. What they do is Correct, and that is all. Correctly dressed from head to foot, they pass, with correct thought and gestures, exchanging correct remarks, across the roundness of the Earth.

我会喜欢自己仪表优雅、性情忧郁，为一份毫无希望的激情所累；以旧日那夸张于言表的方式去恋爱，怀着无人可说的倾慕和绝望对着一轮脸色苍白的月亮。

但愿我能出人头地；但愿我是当今世界最伟大的小提琴家。但愿我有很多银器，很多初版书，还有绿象牙。

正确

我心中有时会冒出个疑惑，觉得对正人君子而言，并非一切都那么方方正正；道德律法讲的，碰到那些最一丝不苟来听它规矩的人，口气就模棱两可了。我敢肯定我在那些最循规蹈矩的人眼中见过一种无所适从的无奈神情。

可是，这样的暗影和疑云一点也不会出现在那些映在俱乐部窗口的脸庞上，或者马车夫的眼睛里，或皮卡迪利大街上那些衣装入时的年轻人眼里。因为这些人的生活遵照的规矩并非从那可疑的天上而降，就不需要谁的认可。只要做得正确，就行了。衣着从头到脚正确，想法姿势正确，谈吐正确，他们如此这般，在圆圆的地球上行过。

'Where do I Come In?'

When I read in the *Times* about India and all its problems and populations; when I look at the letters in large type of important personages, and find myself face to face with the Questions, Movements, and great Activities of the Age, 'Where do I come in?' I ask uneasily.

Then in the great *Times*-reflected world I find the corner where I play my humble but necessary part. For I am one of the unpraised, unrewarded millions without whom Statistics would be a bankrupt science. It is we who are born, who marry, who die, in constant ratios; who regularly lose so many umbrellas, post just so many unaddressed letters every year. And there are enthusiasts among us, Heroes who, without the least thought of their own convenience, allow omnibuses to run over them, or throw themselves month by month, in fixed numbers, from the London bridges.

Microbes

But how is one to keep free from those mental microbes that worm-eat people's brains—those Theories and Diets and Enthusiasms and infectious Doctrines that we catch from what seem the most innocuous contacts? People go about laden with germs; they breathe creeds and convictions on you whenever they

“我能做什么？”

当我读着《泰晤士报》关于印度及其所有问题与人口的报道，当我看着用大号字母印着的重要人物的名字，发现自己与当今世界各种问题、运动和重大活动直面相对，这时我便不安地自问：“我能做什么？”

然后，在这个由《泰晤士报》反映的大世界里，我找到了自己的角落，我在这里出着一份绵薄但必要的力量。因为我是那成千上万得不到赞扬、拿不到奖赏的芸芸众生中的一员，没有这些人，统计的科学便要破产。是我们，出生、婚嫁、老死，比率稳定；每年固定要丢失这么多雨伞、投寄这么多没写地址的信件。我们当中还有忘我之人呢，有英雄置个人方便于不顾，让巴士从自己身上碾过，或者月复一月，人数固定，跳下伦敦那些桥。

病原体

但一个人又该怎样去避开那些蚕食人们头脑的心灵病原体呢？——那些理论、饮食限制、狂热和诱人的教义，那些我们通过似乎是最无伤大雅的接触便染上了的东西？人们带着病菌四处走动，一开口条规信念便朝你喷下来。书籍报章简直爬满了这

open their mouths. Books and newspapers are simply creeping with them—the monthly Reviews seem to have room for little else. Wherewithal then shall a young man cleanse his way; how shall he keep his mind immune to Theosophical speculations, and novel schemes of Salvation? Can he ever be sure that he won't be suddenly struck down by the fever of Funeral or of Spelling Reform, or take to his bed with a new Sex Theory?

But is this struggle for a healthy mind in a maggoty world really after all worth it? Are there not soporific dreams and sweet deliriums more soothing than Reason? If Transmigration can make clear the dark Problem of Evil; if Mrs. Mary Baker Eddy can free us from Death; if the belief that Bacon wrote Shakespeare gives a peace which the world cannot give, why pedantically reject such solace? Why not be led with the others by still waters, be made to lie down in green pastures?

The Quest

'We walk alone in the world,' the Moralist writes in his essay on Ideal Friendship, somewhat sadly. 'Friends such as we desire are dreams and fables.' Yet we never quite give up the hope of finding them. But what awful things happen to us, what snubs, what set-downs we experience, what shames and disillusions. We can never really tell what these new unknown persons may do to us. Sometimes they seem nice, and then begin

些东西——每月评论似乎没空说什么别的。那么年轻人该如何洁净自己的处世之道呢；如何使自己的心灵有免疫力，抗得住神智学的种种揣测和那些得救的新方术？他真能肯定自己不会突然染上葬礼热或者拼写改革的热病，或者带着一个新的性爱理论上床去？

但是，在一个蛆虫遍地的世界上竭力保持心灵康健，这到底值得吗？难道没有昏昏然的梦想和甜蜜的幻觉比理性更舒服吗？假如轮回转生洗刷得清邪恶这一黑暗的罪孽，假如艾娣夫人[23]能让我们摆脱死亡，假如相信是培根[24]写的莎士比亚剧本能给我们这个世界给不了的安宁，那为什么要迂腐地拒绝这样的慰藉呢？为什么不同旁人一道逐静水而居，听从摆布躺卧于绿草场上？

找寻

“我们独自行走在这个世界上，”道德家在论述理想友情的文章中写道，笔触不无伤感，“像我们所希求的朋友只在梦中，只在童话中。”然而我们从未放弃希望要找到他们。但碰到的是多么糟糕的事啊，经历的是怎样的怠慢和奚落、怎样的羞辱和幻灭啊。我们永远也不知道这些不认识的新交会怎样对待我们。有时他们好像很不错，可接着说话就像留声机似的。有时他们会手心湿

to talk like gramophones. Sometimes they grab at us with moist hands, or breathe hotly on our necks, or make awful confidences, or drench us from sentimental slop-pails. And too often, among the thoughts in the loveliest heads, we come on nests of woolly caterpillars.

And yet we brush our hats, pull on our gloves, and go out and ring door-bells.

The Kaleidoscope

I find in my mind, in its miscellany of ideas and musings, a curious collection of little landscapes, shining and fading for no reason. Sometimes they are views in no way remarkable—the corner of a road, a heap of stones, an old gate. But there are many charming pictures too: as I read, between my eyes and book, the Moon washes the harvest-fields with her chill of silver; I see autumnal avenues, with the leaves falling, or swept in heaps; and storms blow among my thoughts, with the rain beating for ever on the fields. Then Winter's upward glare of snow brightens; or the pink and delicate green of Spring in the windy sunshine; or cornfields and green waters, and youths bathing in Summer's golden heats.

And as I walk about, places haunt me; a cathedral rises above a dark blue foreign town, the colour of ivory in the sunset light; now I find myself in a French garden, full of lilacs and

湿地拽住我们，或者往我们脖子上喷热气，或者说些令人心里发毛的悄悄话，或者把自作多情的滥话朝我们浇下来。而且太经常了，在那些可爱之极的脑袋生出来的想法中，我们碰上了一窝窝毛毛虫。

可我们还是拂了拂帽子，拉了拉手套，出外按门铃去了。

万花筒

我发现，在自己心中那杂七杂八的意念思绪之间，莫名其妙收藏着一些小小的景致，或闪现或淡出，毫无道理可言。有时冒出的景象乏善可陈——一处街角、一堆石头、一道旧门廊。但也有许多迷人的画面：在我阅读时，书与眼之间，月亮以其清冷的银辉荡涤着秋收的原野；我看到秋意萧索的林荫道，树叶或飘飘而落，或卷扫成堆；思想之间，风暴刮起，雨点不停歇地敲打着田野。接着，是冬雪反照的耿耿白光；是春色里日影摇风的粉红嫩绿；或者麦田与碧水，有年轻人沐浴在夏日金色的热浪中。

我四处漫步时，许多地方便在我脑海流连；一座大教堂高耸于一处深蓝色的外国小镇上空，落日余晖映着那象牙般的色调；一会儿我发现自己身在一处法国花园，满园的丁香满园的蜜蜂，

bees, and shut-in sunshine, with the Mediterranean lounging outside its walls; now in a little college library, with busts, and the green reflected light of Oxford lawns; —and again I hear the bells, reminding me of the Oxford hours.

The Abbey at Night

And as at night I went past the Abbey, saw its walls towering high and solemn among the Autumn stars, I pictured to myself the white population in the vast darkness of its interior—all that hushed people of Heroes—; not dead, I would think them, but animated with a still kind of life, and at last, after all their intolerable toils, the sounding tumult of battle, and perilous sea-paths, resting there, tranquil and satisfied and glorious, amid the epitaphs and allegorical figures of their tombs; —those high-piled, trophied, shapeless Abbey tombs, that long ago they toiled for, and laid down their gallant lives to win.

Oxford Street

One late winter afternoon in Oxford Street, amid the noise of vehicles and voices that filled that dusky thoroughfare, as I was borne onward with the crowd past the great electric-lighted shops, a holy Indifference filled my thoughts. Illusion had faded

墙锁阳光一片，地中海懒散地在墙外荡漾；一会儿又是个小小的学院图书馆，装点着几尊胸像，透着牛津草坪反光的绿意；——又一次，我听到了钟声，提醒我牛津的时辰。

修道院夜思

晚上路过修道院，看着它的围墙肃穆地高耸于秋夜的星斗间，我自己在心中勾画着在它寂寥幽暗的内厅里的一众白人——一个个不再喧腾的英雄——他们并非死了，我愿这样想，而是以一种静止的生命活跃着，在尝遍常人无法忍受的辛苦、闯过千军万马、历尽惊涛骇浪之后，在此休憩，安详、满足、荣耀，伴着墓头的铭文和富有寓意的一方方丘冢；——那些堆得高高、雕着战利品纪念装饰、形状不一的修道院墓群，那很久以前他们冒着千难万险、献出他们英勇的生命赢得的安息之地。

牛津街

有一个冬日傍晚我走在牛津街上，暮色中大道上车喧人欢，让人流带着前行，经过那电灯照明的大店铺，一种超然物外的圣洁之感充满心间。幻想已逝，什么欲望都撩不动我去向往那金灿

from me; I was not touched by any desire for the goods displayed in those golden windows, nor had I the smallest share in the appetites and fears of all those moving faces. And as I listened with Asiatic detachment to the London traffic, its sound changed into something ancient and dissonant and sad—into the turbid flow of that stream of Craving which sweeps men onward through the meaningless cycles of Existence, blind and enslaved for ever. But I had reached the farther shore, the Harbour of Deliverance, the Holy City; the Great Peace beyond all this turmoil and fret compassed me around. *Om Mani padme hum*—I murmured the sacred syllables, smiling with the pitying smile of the Enlightened One on his heavenly lotus.

Then, in a shop-window, I saw a neatly fitted suit-case. I liked that suit-case; I wanted it. Immediately I was enveloped by the mists of Illusion, chained once more to the Wheel of Existence, whirled onward along Oxford Street in that turbid stream of wrong-belief, and lust, and sorrow, and anger.

Beauty

Among all the ugly mugs of the world we see now and then a face made after the divine pattern. Then, a wonderful thing happens to us; the Blue Bird sings, the golden Splendour shines, and for a queer moment everything seems meaningless save our impulse to follow those fair forms, to follow them to the clear

灿的橱窗里陈列的货品，一点也没沾上走过的那些脸庞所带的物欲和恐惧。我以亚洲人的超脱听着伦敦的车马，那声音变得很古老、刺耳、忧伤——变成了由渴望汇成的浊流，挟卷着人们向前，穿过那没有意义的生存之循环，盲目地、永远地为其所奴役。但我已经渡到了彼岸，驶进了解脱的港湾，到达了得救的圣城，获得了凌驾于周遭的烦恼与躁动之上的大安宁。"唵嘛呢叭咪吽"——我口中念着这佛教密咒的六字真言，与修成正果坐在莲花宝座上悲天悯人的那位一起微笑。

然后，在一个橱窗里，我看到个做工很好的手提箱。我很喜欢，我想要。顷刻间我裹在了幻想的迷雾中，又一次套在了生存之轮上，沿牛津街转着，没入那杂念、欲望、忧伤和愤怒的喧喧浊流中。

美

在世间所有那些丑陋的面孔中时不时我们会看见一张惊为天人的脸型。于是乎，好事临头；耳边青鸟歌唱，眼前金光闪耀，在那奇妙的一瞬间，一切似乎都失去了意义，除了内心的冲动，要

Paradises they promise.

Plato assures us that these moments are not (as we are apt to think them) mere blurs and delusions of the senses, but divine revelations; that in a lovely face we see imaged, as in a mirror, the Absolute Beauty—; it is Reality, flashing on us in the cave where we dwell amid shadows and darkness. Therefore we should follow these fair forms, he says, and their shining footsteps will lead us upward to the highest heaven of Wisdom. The Poets, too, keep chanting this doctrine of Beauty in grave notes to their golden strings. The music floats up through the skies so sweet, so strange, that the very Angels seem to lean from their stars to listen.

But, O Plato, O Shelley, O Angels of Heaven, what scrapes, what scrapes you do get us into!

The Power of Words

I tipped the club porter who helped me into my coat, and stepped out gayly into the vastness of the Night. And as I walked along my eyes were dazzling with the glare behind me; I heard the sound of my speech, the applause and laughter.

And when I looked up at the Stars, the great Stars that bore me company, streaming over the dark houses as I moved, I felt that I was the Lord of Life; the mystery and disquieting meaninglessness of existence—the existence of other people,

追随那优美的形体，要跟着到它们所应许的天国福地去。

柏拉图向我们担保，这些个瞬间并不像我们往往所认为的那样不过是感官的恍惚幻觉，而是神的启示；在一张可爱的脸上我们看到了，如同镜中所见，绝对之美的成像——它是真实，为穴居于阴影与黑暗中的我们一闪而现。所以，我们应该追随这些优美的形体，他说，它们闪光的脚印将引领我们向上，达到智慧的最高天。诗人们也一样，拨动金色的琴弦以庄严的歌调不断吟唱这美的信条。那音乐扶摇而上，冲破云天，是多么甜美，多么奇妙，就连天使似乎都从他们的星星上探身聆听。

可是啊，柏拉图，雪莱，上天的天使们哪，你们可真是把我们带进了多么、多么无地自容的境遇啊！

词语的威力

俱乐部门房帮我穿上大衣，我给了他小费之后，便欢天喜地踏入苍茫的夜色中。走在路上，身后的亮光晃得我眼花；我听到自己演说的声音，还有鼓掌和笑声。

当我抬头看星星，看伟大的星星为我做伴，随我流淌过黑黢黢的屋顶，便觉得自己是人生的主宰；存在的神秘及其令人不安的空虚——别人的存在、我本人的存在，于我已经解决。至于说

and of my own, were solved for me now. As for the Earth, hurrying beneath my feet, how bright was its journey; how shining the goal toward which it went swinging—you might really say leaping—through the sky.

'I must tell the Human Race of this!' I heard my voice; saw my prophetic gestures, as I expounded the ultimate meaning of existence to the white, rapt faces of Humanity. Only to find the words—that troubled me; were there then no words to describe this Vision—divine—intoxicating?

And then the Word struck me; the Word people would use. I stopped in the street; my Soul was silenced like a bell that snarls at a jarring touch. I stood there awhile and meditated on language, its perfidious meanness, the inadequacy, the ignominy of our vocabulary, and how Moralists have spoiled our words by distilling into them, as into little vials of poison, all their hatred of human joy.

Away with that police-force of brutal words which bursts in on our best moments and arrests our finest feelings! This music within me, large, like the song of the stars—like a Glory of Angels singing, — 'No one has any right to say I am drunk!' I shouted.

Self-Analysis

'Yes, aren't they odd, the thoughts that float through one's

地球，在我脚下行色匆匆，它的旅程是多么光明；它穿过天庭晃晃荡荡——你也许真可以说是蹦蹦跳跳——奔向的目标又是多么辉煌啊。

“我一定得把这个告诉人类！”我听见自己的声音在说，看到自己一边摆着预言家的手势，一边把存在的终极意义向人类那些聚精会神的白皮肤脸庞阐述。只是要找到合适的言辞——这令我发愁；难道就没有词语可以描述这个境界——神妙——陶醉？

然后，要的词突然有了；是大家都会用的词。我在街上停住脚，灵魂一下子没声音了，就像一口被乱碰了、低吼着的钟给按停了似的。我站在那里一会儿，思考着语言问题，它那表里不一的低劣、我们词汇的贫乏与无耻，以及道德家们又是如何败坏了我们的词语，就像把毒药灌进小瓶那样，在词语中滴入他们对人类欢乐的全部仇恨。

滚吧，那些像警察一样蛮横的词语，别让它们在我们最好的时光闯进来，把我们最精美的感觉拘捕！我内心的这个音乐，浩浩如星星之歌——煌煌似天使佳音——“谁也没权说我醉了！”我高喊。

自我分析

“没错，难道不奇怪吗，那些莫名其妙就从心中飘过的想法？

mind for no reason? But why not be frank? —I suppose the best of us are shocked at times by the things we find ourselves thinking. Don't you agree,' I went on, not noticing (until it was too late) that all other conversation had ceased, and the whole dinner-party was listening, 'don't you agree that the oddest of all are the bawdy thoughts that come into one's head—the unspeakable words, I mean, and Obscenities?'

When I remember this occasion, I immediately think of Space, and the unimportance in its unmeasured vastness of our toy solar system; I lose myself in speculations on Eternity, reflecting how, at the best, human life on this minute and perishable planet is but a mock episode, as brief as a dream.

The Voice of the World

'And what are you doing now?' The question of these school contemporaries of mine, and their greeting the other day in Piccadilly (I remember how shabby I felt as I stood talking to them)—for a day or two that question haunted me. And behind their well-bred voices I seemed to hear the voice of Schoolmasters and Tutors, of the Professional Classes, and indeed of all the World.

What, as a plain matter of fact, was I doing? how did I spend my days? The life-days which I knew were numbered, and which were described in sermons and on tombstones as so

可为什么不坦诚面对呢？——我想我们当中最好的人也免不了有时被心中油然而生的念头吓着了。你难道不同意吗？”我继续说，没注意到（等注意到已经来不及了）别人的谈话都停止了，整个晚宴的人都在听着，“你不同意吗，最怪的莫过于脑袋中冒出的淫秽念头——那些说不出口的话，我的意思是，还有那些下流的意念？”

每当我记起此时情景，马上就想到宇宙太空，在它无边无际的浩瀚之中我们太阳系玩具似的无足轻重；我陷入对永恒的沉思，思索着人的生命在这细小易坏的行星上，最多也不过是个假戏真做的插曲，短得像一场梦。

世界的声音

“你现在做什么？”当年老同学们的这个问题，那天他们在皮卡迪利广场同我打的招呼（记得站在那里同他们谈话我觉得自己有多寒酸）——有那么一两天在我心头挥之不去。在他们那教养有素的腔调背后我似乎听到校长、导师，还有专业人士阶层的声音，那的确是全世界的声音。

说到底，我在做什么呢？我的一天天又是怎么度过的？我知道命中时日无多，布道会上、墓碑上，到处都说着人生苦短、光阴

irrevocable, so melancholy-brief.

I decided to change my life. I too would be somebody in my time and age; the world should hear of me; my contemporaries should treat me as an important person. I began thinking of my endeavours, my studies by the midnight lamp, my risings at dawn for stolen hours of self-improvement.

But alas, the Day, the little Day, was enough just then. It somehow seemed enough, just to be alive in the Spring, with the young green of the trees, the smell of smoke in the sunshine; I loved the old shops and books, the uproar darkening and brightening in the shabby daylight. Just a run of good-looking faces—for I was always looking for faces—would keep me amused. And London was but a dim-lit stage on which I played the part I liked. I would wake up in the morning like Byron to find myself famous; be drawn like Chatham to St. Paul's, amid the cheers of the Nation, and exclaim with Cromwell, 'Take away that bauble!' as I stalked past the Houses of Parliament.

And Anyhow

And anyhow, soon, so soon (in only two thousand million years or thereabouts, the Encyclopædia said) this Earth would grow cold, all human activities end, and the last wretched mortals close their eyes on the rays of the dying Sun.

去而不返。

我决定改变自己的生活。我也会成为我所处时代的大人物，让世界知道我是谁，让同代人对我刮目相看。我开始想着怎么去努力，半夜挑灯钻研，清晨即起，偷得时间自我提升。

可是天哪，一天，短短的一天，刚刚够我过呢。不知怎么这似乎就够了——只消在春天里活着，看到树木的新绿，闻着阳光中的烟味；我喜欢老商店和书籍，惨淡的白日里忽明忽暗的喧哗。就那一溜而过的俊俏脸蛋——我总爱看人家的脸——便足以让我喜滋滋的。而伦敦不过是个灯光暗淡的舞台，我在上面表演一个自己喜欢的角色罢了。我会像拜伦那样清早起来发现自己一夜成名；像老皮特[25]那样在国人的欢呼中坐车到圣彼得大教堂，会一边同克伦威尔[26]一道高喝“把那玩意儿拿掉！”，一边昂首阔步走过议会上下两院。

不管怎样

不管怎样，很快地，快得很（只要二十亿年光景，百科全书说了），这个地球就会变冷，一切人类活动就会停止，世界上最后那些倒霉的凡胎俗子会盯着渐渐熄灭的太阳闭上眼睛。

Drawbacks

I should be all right ....

If it weren't for these sudden visitations of Happiness, these downpourings of Heaven's blue, little invasions of Paradise, or waftings to the Happy Islands, or whatever you may call these disconcerting Moments, I should be like everybody else; as blameless a ratepayer as any in our Row.

Talk

Once in a while, when doors are closed and curtains drawn on a group of free spirits, the miracle happens, and Good Talk begins. 'Tis a sudden illumination—the glow, it may be, of sanctified tapers, or more likely, the blaze around a cauldron of wicked gossip.

Is there an ecstasy or any intoxication like it? Oh, to talk, to talk people into monsters, and carve them as dishes for the Gods; to talk one's self out of one's clothes, to talk Jehovah from His heaven, to say everything, and turn everything in the world into a bright tissue of phrases!

These Pentecosts and outpourings of the spirit can only occur very rarely, or the Universe itself would be soon talked out of existence.

不是之处

我应该不会有事的……

要不是这些突如其来光顾的幸福、这些蓝天里降下来的滂沱大雨、这些小小的天国入侵，或者随风飘送到快活岛上的造访，或者随你怎么称呼的这些叫人心绪不宁的时刻，要是没有这些不是，我应该同大家一样，同我们这条街上的任何人一样是个无可指摘的纳税人。

人言

偶尔有的时候，门关上，窗帘拉上，一伙口无遮拦的人精聚拢，奇迹出现，畅所欲言开始。那一刻豁然明亮——那光芒，可以是小小的神殿烛光，或者更可能是熊熊烈焰，烧着大铁锅，炮制谗言佞语。

有什么狂喜有什么痴醉可与之相比？说啊，说啊，把人说成妖怪，把他们切成一盘盘祭奠神灵；把自己说得又高又大，把耶和华说得从天堂里下来，什么都说，把世上一切都变成了亮晶晶的一派口舌之言！

这些灵光毕现[27]和精魂的昌言无忌只能鲜少发生，否则天地宇宙自己很快就会被说得不存在了。

The Church of England

I have my Anglican moments; and as I sat there that Sunday afternoon, in the eighteenth-century interior of the London Church, and listened to the unexpressive voice chanting the correct service, I felt a comfortable assurance that we were in no danger of being betrayed into any unseemly manifestations of religious fervour. We had not gathered together at that performance to abase ourselves with furious hosannas before any dark Creator of an untamed Universe, no Deity of freaks and miracles and sinister hocus-pocus; but to pay our duty to a highly respected Anglican First Cause—distinguished, undemonstrative, gentlemanly—whom, without loss of self-respect, we could decorously praise.

Misgiving

We were talking of people, and a name familiar to us all was mentioned. We paused and looked at each other; then soon, by means of anecdotes and clever touches, that Personality was reconstructed, and seemed to appear before us, large, pink, and life-like, and give a comic sketch of itself with characteristic poses.

What fun it was! 'But of course,' I said to myself, 'this sort of thing never happens to me.' For the notion was quite

英国国教

我有我领略英国国教的时候；就在那个礼拜天下午，坐在伦敦教堂十八世纪风格的大厅里，聆听没有表情的声音在吟诵正确无误的礼拜词，我觉得舒服安心，明白绝不会有危险被骗而卷进任何宗教狂热不得体的发作中去。我们集合在此崇拜，不是让自己卑躬屈膝，狂呼“和散那”，赞美哪位造出了一个桀骜不驯的宇宙的黑暗之神，或者哪位行奇迹做怪事、阴险的怪力乱神；而是来尽自己的义务，礼拜一位备受景仰的英国国教的造物主——一位尊贵的、含而不露的、绅士般的上帝，一位我们可以不失自尊、以礼相待地赞颂的上帝。

忧虑

我们在谈论人，其间提到了一个大家都熟悉的名字。于是各人都停下来互相望着；没过一会儿，靠着趣闻逸事和巧妙的润色，此君形象便重构完毕，似乎就在眼前，人高马大，红扑扑的，栩栩如生，还摆出几个典型的姿势来一个滑稽的自我造型。

真好玩！“可当然了，”我自忖，“这种事千万别落到我头上。”这玩意儿真不可思议，我意思是说，让自己心爱的形象，本

unthinkable, the notion, I mean, of my own dear image, called up like this without my knowledge, to turn my discreet way of life into a cake-walk.

Sanctuaries

She said 'How small the world is, after all!'

I thought of China, of a holy mountain in the West of China, full of legends and sacred groves and demon-haunted caves. It is always enveloped in mountain mists; through that white thick air the faint sound of bells reached me, the muffled footsteps of innumerable pilgrims, and the reiterated mantra, *Nam-Mo, O-mi-to-Fo*, which they murmured as they climbed its slopes. High up among its temples and monasteries marched processions of monks, with chants and services, and many prostrations, and lighted candles that glimmered through the fog. There in their solemn shrines stood the statues of the Arahats, and there, seated on his white elephant, loomed immense and dim, the image of Amitabha, the Lord of the Western Heavens.

She said, 'Life is so complicated!'

Climbing inaccessible dins of rock and ice, I shut myself within a Tibetan monastery beyond the Himalayan ramparts. I joined with choirs of monks, intoning their deep sonorous dirges and unintelligible prayers; I beat drums, I clashed cymbals, and blew at dawn from the Lamasery roofs conches, and loud

人不知情地就这么给唤出来，把我一生的谨慎变成了一场荒唐的嬉闹。

避难圣地

她说："世界，到底是小啊！"

我想起了中国，中国西部的一处神山，充满了传奇，布满了神人居住的树林和鬼蜮出没的洞穴。永远是山岚迷漫，透过那浓浓云雾，缥缈的钟声传到耳畔，还有无数朝圣者幽沉的脚步，以及他们一边登攀一边呢喃念着的"南无阿弥陀佛"。高高的庙堂寺院间穿行着僧侣的队列，吟诵经文做着佛事，有众多五体投地膜拜的善男信女，还有透过雾气闪闪烁烁的烛光。在他们庄严的神龛中立着一尊尊阿罗汉，而那骑着白象、巍峨而幽邃的，是西天主宰阿弥陀佛的神像。

她说："生活太复杂了！"

登上高不可攀的冰川巉岩，我幽居于喜马拉雅山屏障之上的一所西藏寺庙中。我与僧侣们一道诵经，吟唱他们那洪亮低沉的悲歌，念着听不明白的祷词；打鼓击钹，拂晓在喇嘛寺的屋顶吹着

discordant trumpets. And wandering through those vast and shadowy halls, as I tended the butter-lamps of the golden Buddhas, and watched the storms that swept across the barren mountains, I tasted an imaginary bliss, and then passed on to other scenes and incarnations along the endless road that leads me to Nirvana.

'But I do wish you would tell me what you really think?'

I fled to Africa, into the depths of the dark Ashanti forest. There, in its gloomiest recesses, where the soil is stained with the blood of the negroes He has eaten, dwells that monstrous Deity of human shape and red colour, the great Fetish God, Sasabonsum. I like Sasabonsurn: other Gods are sometimes moved to pity, to forgiveness, but to Him this weakness is unknown. He is utterly and absolutely implacable; no prayers, no human sacrifices can ever for one moment appease His cold, malignant rage.

Symptoms

'But there are certain people I simply cannot stand. A dreariness and sense of death come over me when I meet them—I really find it difficult to breathe when they are in the room, as if they had pumped all the air out of it. Wouldn't it be dreadful to produce that effect on people! But they never seem to be aware of it. I remember once meeting a famous Bore; I really must

螺号或响亮刺耳的长号。徜徉在那些空旷幽暗的殿堂里，照料着菩萨金像前的酥油灯，望着风暴扫过荒山，我尝到了一种想象中的福佑，接着继续前行，领略另外的景象和轮回转生，沿着这条无尽的道路通向极乐世界。

“可我真希望你能告诉我，你到底是怎么想的？”

我逃到非洲去，逃进黑暗的阿善蒂森林深处。在那里，在那最阴森的隐秘处，住着那个人形的红色魔神，那个伟大的物神沙沙波撒，那里的泥土都被让他吃掉的黑人的血染红了。我喜欢沙沙波撒：其他神祇有时会动恻隐之心，会手下留情，但他从没听说有这一弱点。他是完全的无情，绝对的无义；多少祷告、多少人命祭奠，都不能有一时一刻平息他那冷酷邪恶的暴怒。

征兆

“可就是有某些人，我简直一点也受不了。一见到他们我就觉得闷，觉得生不如死——那些人在房间里我真觉得透不过气来，好像他们把空气都抽光了似的。让人有这种感觉，难道还不恶心吗？但他们似乎从来就没意识到。记得有一次遇到一个出了

tell you about it, it shows the unbelievable obtuseness of such people.'

I told this and another story or two with great gusto, and talked on of my experiences and sensations, till suddenly I noticed, in the appearance of my charming neighbour, something—a slightly glazed look in her eyes, a just perceptible irregularity in her breathing—which turned that occasion for me into a kind of Nightmare.

Shadowed

I sometimes feel a little uneasy about that imagined self of mine—the Me of my daydreams—who leads a melodramatic life of his own, out of all relation with my real existence. So one day I shadowed him down the street. He loitered along for a while, and then stood at a shop-window and dressed himself out in a gaudy tie and yellow waistcoat. Then he bought a great sponge and two stuffed birds and took them to lodgings, where he led a shady existence. Next he moved to a big house in Mayfair, and gave grand dinner-parties, with splendid service and costly wines. His amorous adventures among the High-up Ones of this Earth I pass over. He soon sold his house and horses, gave up his motors, dismissed his retinue of servants, and went—saving two young ladies from being run over on the way—to live a life of heroic self-sacrifice among the poor.

名的闷蛋；我真得给你说说这事，看看这等人麻木不仁到了什么程度。”

我津津有味地讲了这个还有其他一两个故事，继续谈着自己的经历和感受，直到突然觉察到，我那位风韵迷人的邻座的表情——眼神微微有点呆滞，呼吸有点刚刚觉察得到的不规则——此情此景把那个场合变成了我的噩梦一场。

跟踪

我有时对自己想象出的那个自我觉得有点不安——那个白日梦中的“我”——他自己过着一种传奇情节剧般的生活，同我真正的存在一点关系也没有。因此有一天我就在街上跟踪他。他闲逛了一会儿，在一家店的橱窗前停下脚步，系上一条俗艳的领带，穿上一件黄色的马甲；接着，又买了一块大海绵、两个鸟标本带回住处，在那里他过着一种不为人知的生活。接着他搬到梅菲尔[28]的一所豪宅里，大宴宾客，有的是气派非凡的招待、昂贵的美酒。他在上流社会的猎艳偷欢我就略而不说了。不久他卖掉房子马匹，放弃他的几部汽车，辞退左右随从，出门——路上从车轮底下救了两名年轻女郎的性命——过一种自我牺牲的英雄式生活，与穷苦人为伍。

I was beginning to feel encouraged about him, when in passing a fishmonger's, he pointed at a great salmon and said, 'I caught that fish.'

The Incredible

'Yes, but they were afraid of you.'

'Afraid of *me*?'

'Yes, so one of them told me afterwards.'

I was fairly jiggered. If my personality can inspire fear or respect, the world must be a simpler place than I had thought it. Afraid of a twittering shadow, a make-believe like me? Are children more absurdly terrified by a candle in a hollow turnip? Was Bedlam at full moon ever scared by anything half so silly?

Terror

A pause fell on our conversation—one of those uncomfortable lapses when we sit with fixed smiles, searching our minds for some remark with which to fill up the unseasonable silence. It was only a moment—'But suppose,' I said to myself with horrible curiosity, 'suppose none of us had found a word to say?'

It is the dread of Something happening, Something

我渐渐开始觉得他有希望了，只见他路过一家鱼店，指着一条很大的鲑鱼说:“我逮的那鱼。”

不可思议

“是的，他们怕你。”

“怕我？！”

“没错，他们当中有人事后告诉我。”

我心里觉得很不是滋味。假如我的个性会引起他人害怕或尊敬，那世界就一定比我认为的要简单。怕我这样一个蹙然不安的影子，一个虚张声势的人？说小孩子叫空心萝卜头里的蜡烛吓着了，会比这更可笑吗？有哪个疯子在月圆之夜被只有这一半傻的什么东西给吓坏了？

恐怖

谈话突然断了——那种令人很不自在的静默，大家坐在那儿，脸上僵着笑容，在找话头来填充这尴尬的静默。只是片刻而已——“可是想想，”我带着可怕的好奇自语道，“要是我们谁也找不出一句话来说呢？”

正是因为害怕发生什么事，什么未知的、不堪的事，我们才

unknown and awful, that makes us do anything to keep the flicker of talk from dying out. So travellers at night in an unknown forest keep their fire ablaze, in fear of Wild Beasts lurking in the darkness ready to leap upon them.

Pathos

When winter twilight falls in my street with the rain, a sense of the horrible sadness of life descends upon me. I think of drunken old women who drown themselves because nobody loves them; I think of Napoleon at St. Helena, and of Byron, growing irritable and fat in the enervating climate of Italy.

Inconstancy

The rose that one wears and throws away, the friend one forgets, the music that passes; —out of the well-known transitoriness of mortal things I have made myself a maxim or precept to the effect that it is foolish to look for one face, or to listen long for one voice, in a world that is, after all, as I know, full of enchanting voices.

But all the same, I can never quite forget the enthusiasm with which, as a boy, I read the praises of Constancy, of True Love and the unchanged Northern Star.

想尽办法让话头忽闪着不致熄灭。同理，旅人夜里在陌生的森林中要保持他们的篝火燃烧不熄，生怕躲在暗地里的野兽朝他们扑过来。

伤感

当冬日的暮色随着雨点落到我这条街上时，一种可怕的人生悲情也降临在我心头。我想到喝醉酒的老女人，她们投水自尽是因为无人爱；我想到拿破仑沦落于圣赫勒拿岛[29]上，也想到拜伦，让意大利令人倦怠的气候变得焦躁肥胖。

世事无常

玫瑰戴过又扔掉、朋友相识又相忘、音乐过耳又飘走；——从凡世间那尽人皆知的无常之中，我为自己总结出一条座右铭或警诫，大意是，别愚蠢地找寻一张脸，或长久追听一个声音，毕竟这个世界，就我所知，充满了各种迷人的声音。

但尽管如此，我永远也无法真就忘却那份热忱。少年时代，我曾心怀这热忱阅读着那些赞美之词，赞美着地久天长、真挚之爱以及亘古不移的北极星。

The Poplar

There is a great tree in Sussex, whose cloud of thin foliage floats high in the summer air. The thrush sings in that umbrage, and blackbirds, who fill the late, decorative sunshine with a shimmer of golden sound. There the nightingale finds her green cloister; and on those branches sometimes, like a great fruit, hangs the lemon-coloured Moon. In the glare of August, when all the world is faint with heat, there is always a breeze in those cool recesses; always a noise, like the noise of water, among their lightly-hung leaves.

But the owner of this Tree lives in London, reading books.

On the Doorstep

I rang the bell as of old; as of old I gazed at the great shining Door and waited. But, alas! that flutter and beat of the wild heart, that delicious Doorstep Terror—it was gone; and with it dear, fantastic, panic-stricken Youth had rung the bell, flitted round the corner and vanished for ever.

白杨树

在苏塞克斯郡有一棵大树，细细的树冠云一般高高地飘浮在夏日空中。画眉在叶荫鸣唱，乌鸫在夕晖的晕染中撒开亮灿灿的金色歌喉。在这里，夜莺找到了她绿色的闺房；在那些枝头上，有时候，大果子似的，挂着柠檬色的月亮。在八月的亮光中，在世界热得昏昏沉沉时，总有一丝微风起于树下阴凉处；总有一阵悉索，如流水潺潺，在轻巧的绿叶间流淌。

但是这棵树的主人住在伦敦，在看书。

台阶前

同往日一样，我按响门铃；同往日一样，我盯着闪亮的大门等着。可是，哎哟哟！那颗狂跳不已的心，那份踏上门阶时甜滋滋的恐惧——不见了；一起的还有那珍贵的、美妙的、紧张兮兮的青春年华，也按了按门铃、闪过街角、永远消失了。

The Moon

I went in and shook hands with my hostess, but no one else took any special notice; no one screamed or left the room; the quiet murmur of talk went on. I suppose I seemed like the others; observed from outside no doubt I looked like them.

But inside, seen from within ...? Or was it a conceivable hypothesis that we were all really alike inside also, —that all these quietly-talking people had got the Moon too, in their heads?

Consolation

The other day, depressed on the Underground, I tried to cheer myself by thinking over the joys of our human lot. But there wasn't one of them for which I seemed to care a button—not Wine, nor Fame, nor Friendship, nor Eating, nor Making Love, nor the Consciousness of Virtue. Was it worth while then going way up in a lift into a world that had nothing less trite to offer?

Then I thought of reading—the nice and subtle happiness of reading. This was enough, this joy not dulled by Age, this polite and unpunished vice, this selfish, serene, life-long intoxication.

月亮

我进门，同女主人握了手，可屋内谁也没特别注意到我；没有人尖叫，没有人离开；低低的谈话声照旧。我料想自己似乎同别人一样，从外表看我无疑同他们没两样。

可是内心呢，从里面看呢……？或者有理由假定，我们内心也当真全都一样——这些在低声谈天的人，同样脑子里也有那月亮？

慰藉

那天，在地铁里心里觉得压抑，便试着想些做人在世的快活事来让自己高兴高兴。可那些事没有一件我似乎有一丁点儿兴趣——酒食、名声、友情、做爱、品德的意识，都不行。那还值得搭那么长的电梯上到一个没那么乏味的东西一样也拿不出来的世界吗？

接着，我想到了读书——阅读中那美妙又微妙的快乐。这就够了，这份愉悦，不因年岁而消减；这个恶习，不失礼又不受惩罚；这种陶醉，自私、安谧、受用终身。

The Lord Mayor

An arctic wind was blowing; it cut through me as I stood there. The boot-black was finishing his work and complaints.

'But I should be 'appy, sir, if only I could make four bob a day,' he said.

I looked down at him; it seemed absurd, the belief of this crippled, half-frozen creature. Happiness! the fabled treasure of some far-away heaven I thought it that afternoon; not to be bought with gold, not of this earth!

I said something to this effect. But four shillings a day was enough for the boot-black.

'Why,' he said, 'I should be as 'appy as the Lord Mayor!'

The Burden

I know too much; I have stuffed too many of the facts of History and Science into my intellectuals. My eyes have grown dim over books; believing in geological periods, cave-dwellers, Chinese Dynasties, and the fixed Stars has prematurely aged me.

Why am I to blame for all that is wrong in the world? I didn't invent Sin and Hate and Slaughter. Who made it my duty anyhow to administer the Universe, and keep the planets to their courses? My Atlantean shoulders are bent beneath the load of the Firmament; I grow weary of bearing the weight of the whole World.

市长大人

在北极刮来的风中，我站着觉得如刀刺骨。擦鞋匠一边完成他的活儿一边抱怨。

“但我会很幸福的，先生，只消一天里挣上四个先令。”他说。

我低头看他；似乎很可笑，一个瘸脚的、快冻僵了的人，有这个念想。幸福！那天下午我这么想着，它是神话虚构的某处遥远的天国中的宝藏，金钱买不到，这个地球上也没有！

我大约这么说了。但是一天四先令擦鞋匠便觉得够了。

“敢情是，”他说，“我会像市长大人那么幸福的！”

负担

我知道得太多了，我把太多历史和科学的事实塞进了头脑。我眼睛看书看花了；地质学分期、穴居人、中国的朝代，还有太空恒定的星体，信这些已然令我早衰。

为什么要把世上所有过错归罪于我？我并没有发明罪恶、仇恨、杀戮。总之是谁，要我来担责管理宇宙、保持行星沿轨道运行？我力大无比的双肩被苍穹压弯了；我又累又烦，还要驮着这整个世界。

Under an Umbrella

From under the roof of my umbrella I saw the washed pavement lapsing beneath my feet, the news-posters lying smeared with dirt at the crossings, the tracks of the buses in the liquid mud. On I went through this world of wetness. And through what long perspectives of the years shall I still hurry down wet streets—middle-aged, and then, perhaps, very old? And on what errands?

Asking myself this question I fade from your vision, Reader, into the distance, sloping my umbrella against the wind.

伞下

雨伞遮盖之下，我看到被雨水冲刷的人行道在脚下后退而去，新闻海报沾着污渍摊在十字路口的地面上，公车的轮胎印在泥泞中。我往前走着穿过这湿漉漉的世界。要穿过多么漫长的岁月画卷我依然还匆匆行走在雨中的街市呢？——中年，然后，也许是，很老的老年？行色匆匆所为何事？

问着自己这个问题，读者先生，我便从您眼中渐渐淡出，没入远方，斜撑着伞，顶着扑面而来的风。

MORE TRIVIA

巷陌续记

The Epithet

'Occult, night-wandering, enormous, honey-pale—or blanc, as Milton called her ——'

The morning paper lay there unopened; I knew I ought to look at the news, for the crash was awful, but I was too busy just then trying to find an adjective for the Moon—the magical, moony epithet, which could I only find or invent, what then would matter the quakes and sublunary conflicts of this negligible earth?

Reassurance

I look at my overcoat and my hat hanging in the hall with reassurance; for although I go out of doors with one individuality to-day, when yesterday I had quite another, yet my clothes keep my various selves buttoned up together, and enable all these otherwise irreconcilable aggregates of psychological phenomena to pass themselves off as one person.

The Great Adventure

I paused, before opening the front-door, for a moment of deep consideration.

修饰语

“神秘难测、夜游于天、硕大无朋、色淡如蜜——抑或白净光洁，如弥尔顿[30]这么说的她——”

晨报搁在那儿还没打开；我知道新闻是要看的，因为那起车祸很严重，可是我那时正忙着为月亮找一个形容词——这个神奇的、朦胧如月的修饰语，只要我能找得到或造得出，那么在这个微不足道的地球上，地壳的震颤和月下的纷争又算得了什么呢？

安心

看着挂在门厅里的大衣和帽子，我觉得挺安心的；因为虽然今天与我出门的是一个自己，昨天一起走的那个又颇不一样，但是这副衣着装束把我各式各样的自己扣在一起，使林林总总本来互不相容的这些心理现象得以凑得像一个人。

闯荡世界

打开大门前，我停下脚，默然沉思了一会儿。

Dim-lit, shadowy, full of menace and unimaginable chances, stretched all around my door the many-peopled streets. I could hear, ominous and muffled, the tides of multitudinous traffic, sounding along their ways. Was I equipped for the navigation of those waters, armed and ready to adventure out into that dangerous world again?

Gloves? Money? Cigarettes? Matches? Yes; and I had an umbrella for its tempests, and a latchkey for my safe return.

The Beatific Vision

Shoving and pushing, and pushed and shoved, a dishonoured bag of bones about London, or carted like a herring in a box through tunnels in the clay beneath it, as I bump my head in an omnibus, or hang, half-suffocated, from a greasy strap in the Underground, I dream, like other Idealists and Saints and Social Thinkers, of a better world than this, a world that might be, a City of Heaven brought down at last to earth.

One footman flings open the portals of my palace in that New Jerusalem for me; another unrolls a red path of velvet to the enormous motor which floats me through the city traffic—I leaning back like Edward VII, or like God, on hallowed cushions, smoking a big cigar.

灯光幽幽、暗影幢幢，充满凶险，也充满意想不到的机遇，从我门口向四面伸展出去的，是人来人往的一条条街道。听得见，森森然此起彼伏的，是车马沿路低沉的喧嚣。我是否已装备齐整，能在那些水域里航行？是否已披挂停当，能迈步出门，再次闯荡那危险的世界？

手套？钱？香烟？火柴？都有了；我还带有一把伞，用来抵御那不测风雨，以及一把钥匙，好让我归家有门。

荣福直观[31]

不体面的一副皮囊，在伦敦四处推推搡搡，被推被搡，或者像一条装箱的鲱鱼，在城底下黏土层里的隧道中运来运去，在巴士车上撞了脑袋，或者闷得半死不活地吊在地铁里一条油腻腻的皮带上，这时我便想入非非，像其他理想主义者、圣人、社会思想家那样，梦想着一个比眼前更好的世界，好得也许像天堂之城终于降临人间。

有一个男仆为我打开我在那个新耶路撒冷的宫门；另有一个铺开红色的天鹅绒地毯，一直接到那部巨大的汽车旁，那车载着我飘然穿过城中的车水马龙——我仰着身，状如爱德华七世[32]，或者上帝，靠在经祝圣的软垫上，抽着一根大雪茄。

Faces

Almost always the streets are full of dingy people; sometimes for weeks on end the poor face-hunter returns unblest from his expeditions, with no provision with which to replenish his daydream-larder.

Then one day the plenty is all too great; there are Princesses at the street-crossings, Queens in the taxi-cabs, Beings fair as the dayspring on the tops of buses; and the Gods themselves promenade up and down Piccadilly.

The Observer

Talk of ants! It's the precise habits, the incredible proceedings of human insects I like to note and study.

Walking to-day, a stranger dropped upon this planet, towards Victoria, a funny thing happened to me. I chanced to see a female of this species, a certain Mrs. Jones of my acquaintance, approaching from the opposite direction, and immediately I found myself performing the oddest set of movements. I straightened my back and simpered, I lifted my hat in the air; and then, seizing the cinquedigitated paw of this female, I moved it up and down several times, giving utterance to a set formula of articulated sounds.

These anthropological gestures and vocalizations, and my

人面

街上几乎总是充斥着邋遢的人们；有时一连几个礼拜，那个人面猎奇的可怜虫都要败兴而归，街头所见，无一可以补充其白日梦的给养储备。

然而有一天却多得叫人目不暇接；十字路口有公主王妃，的士车里坐着女王美后，巴士顶层有佳丽艳如曙色；各方神人自己，也都在皮卡迪利大街漫步逍遥。

观察者

说什么蚂蚁！是那些称为人类的昆虫，他们那精确无误的习性、那难以置信的行为方式，我才想注意研究呢。

我，一个掉到这行星上的外来者，今天正朝维多利亚车站走去时，遇到了一件有趣的事。我碰巧看到这一物种的一个雌性个体，某位我认识的琼斯太太，正从对面走来，我发觉自己马上就做出一套最奇怪的动作。挺直腰、脸皮笑着，帽子举在空中；接着，抓住这位雌性个体有五个开叉的爪子，上下摆动了几次，口中发出一套有既定公式的声音。

这些人类学的肢体和发声动作，以及我不随意志自动做出这

automatic performance of them, reminded me that it was from inside one of them I was observing those Bipeds.

Chaos

Punctual, commonplace, keeping all appointments, as I go my round in the obvious world, a bit of Chaos and old Night lingers on inside me; a dark bewilderment of mind, a nebulous sea of meditation; a looming of speculative universes out of nothing, and their collapse, as in a dream.

The Ghost

When people talk of Ghosts I don't mention the Apparition by which I am haunted, the Phantom that shadows me about the streets, the image or spectre, so familiar, so like myself, which lurks in the plate-glass of shop-windows, or leaps out of mirrors to waylay me.

The Suburbs

What are the beliefs about God in Grosvenor Gardens, the surmises of South Kensington concerning our fate beyond the

些动作的行为，使我记起自己是从他们当中一员的躯壳内，在观察那些两足动物的。

混沌

准时守约、平平淡淡，我在这一目了然的世界上度日如仪，而内里还流连着一点混沌、一抹古老的夜色；一种幽暗的内心迷惘，一片朦朦胧胧的玄想之海；忽而异想天开，忽而天塌地陷，恍惚如在梦中。

鬼魂

人们谈论鬼魂时我不提附在我身上的那个鬼，那个跟着我穿街过巷的幽灵，那个形象或幻象，是如此熟悉、如此像我本人，要么藏在商店橱窗的大玻璃中，要么突然从镜子里蹦出来给我个猝不及防。

市郊

伦敦市里[33]，格罗夫纳公园区的人是怎么信的上帝，南肯辛顿区的人对我们入土之后的命运又是怎么想的？凭什么认为皮姆

Grave? On what ground does life seem worth living in Pimlico; and how far in the Cromwell Road do they follow, or think they follow, the precepts of the Sermon on the Mount?

If I can but dimly discern the ideals of these familiar regions, how much more am I in the dark about the inner life of the great outer suburbs. In what works of local introspection can I study the daydreams of Hoxton, the curiosities and discouragements of Clapham or Ealing?

More than once I have paused before a suburban villa, telling myself that I had after all but to ring the bell, and go in and ask them. But alas, they would not tell me; they could not tell me, even if they would.

The Latchkey

I was astonished, I was almost horror-struck by the sight of the New Moon at the end of the street. In Blake-like wonder I stood and gazed at it on my doorstep. For what was I doing there? I, a wanderer, a pilgrim, a nomad of the desert, with no home save where the evening found me; —what was my business on that doorstep? At what commonplace had the Moon caught me with a latchkey in my hand?

利科区的生活似乎就值得过；在克伦威尔路上，他们对基督的山上宝训[34]跟得有多紧？或者他们自认为跟得有多紧？

假若我只能依稀看出这些熟悉地区居民的所思所求，那我对大片郊区的内心世界是有多么懵懂不察。有什么反思当地的作品可以让我来研究东区霍克顿居民的梦想？西南边克拉珀姆和西边伊林区平民觉得好奇或者扫兴的事物又有哪些？

不止一次我曾在一处郊区屋舍前驻足，跟自己说毕竟只要按响门铃，走进屋去问一下里面的人就是。可是，唉，他们不会告诉我的；即使想告诉我，也说不出来的。

门钥匙

我吃了一惊，几乎吓坏了——街尽头，竟然有一钩新月。怀着布莱克[35]般的惊诧，我站在我门前的台阶上凝神望着。我在那儿干吗呢？我，一个流浪汉、一名朝圣客、一个沙漠中的游牧人，没有家，天黑所到之处便是我栖身之所；——站在那台阶上到底有何贵干？什么样的寻常时刻啊，给月亮逮见了我手持一把门钥匙？

Good Practice

We met in an omnibus last evening. 'And where are you going now?' she asked, as she looked at me with amusement.

'I am going, if the awful truth must be told, to dine in Grosvenor Square.'

'Lord!' she colloquially replied, 'and what do you do that for?'

'I do it because I am invited. And besides,' I went on, 'let me remind you of what the Persian Mystics say of the Saints—that the Saints are sometimes rich, that God sometimes endows Those Holy Ones with an outward show of wealth to hide them from the profane.'

'Oh, does He?—Hides them in Grosvenor Square?'

'Very well then, I shall tell you my real reason for going to dine there. Do you remember what Diogenes replied when they wanted to know why he had begged money from a statue?'

'No; what did he say?'

'He said—but I must explain another time. I have to get off here. Good-night.'

I paused, however, at the door of the bus. 'He said,' I called back, 'I am practising Disappointment.'

Evasion

'And what do you think of the International Situation?'

训练有方

我们昨天傍晚在一部巴士上相遇。“你去哪儿?”她问道，望着我，饶有兴味的样子。

“我去嘛，如果不好听的真话非说不可的话，那就是去格罗夫纳广场吃饭。”

“天哪，”她大大咧咧地应道，“你这又为的啥?”

“因为有人请。而且，”我接着说，“让我提醒你波斯的神秘主义者是怎么说那些圣人的——他们有时很富有，上帝有时赐给那些圣洁之人富有的外表，把他们包藏起来躲开俗人。”

“哦，有这回事吗?——把他们藏在格罗夫纳广场?”

“好吧，好吧，我就把去那边吃饭的真实理由告诉你吧。你记得人们问第欧根尼[36]为什么向一尊塑像讨钱时，他是怎么回答的吗?”

“不知道，他是怎么说的?”

“他说——可是只能下次再告诉你了。我得在这儿下车。再见。”

我还是在车门处停了下来。“他说，”我回过头说道，“我在进行失望训练。”

闪烁其词

“对国际形势您有什么想法?”那位外国来的伯爵夫人问道，

asked that foreign Countess, with her foreign, fascinating smile.

Was she a Spy? I felt I must be careful.

'What do I think?' I evasively echoed; and then, carried away by the profound and melancholy interest of this question, 'Think?' I queried, 'do I ever really think? Is there anything inside my head but cotton-wool? How can I, with a mind full of grey monkeys with blue faces, call myself a Thinker? What am I anyhow?' I pursued the sad inquiry: 'A noodle, a pigwidgeon, a ninny-hammer—a bubble on the wave, Madame, a leaf in the wind!'

Dining Out

When I think of Etiquette and Funerals; when I consider the euphemisms and conventions and various costumes with which we invest the acts of our animal existence; when I bear in mind how elegantly we eat our victuals, and remember all the ablutions and preparations and salutations and exclamations and manipulations I performed when I dined out last evening, I reflect what creatures we are of ceremony; how elaborate, and polite a simian Species.

What's Wrong

From their corner of the half-empty drawing-room they

脸上带着异国的、迷人的微笑。

她是不是间谍？我觉得应该小心才是。

“我有什么想法？”我闪烁其词地跟着问；然后便陷入这个问题中深奥忧伤的意趣不能自拔。“想法？”我追问，“我可曾真的想过？我脑袋里充斥的除了棉絮一团外还有什么？我这个人，满脑子装着蓝脸灰猴，还怎能自认为是个有思想的人？我到底算什么？”这令人伤心的问题我一问到底：“一个笨蛋、傻瓜、糊涂虫——一个水面上漂的泡泡，夫人，一片风中的落叶！”

赴宴

当我想起礼节和葬礼；当我考虑到用来装点我们那与动物没两样的存在行为的那些委婉语和规矩，以及各式行头；当我心中记着我们进食时有多优雅，想起昨晚赴宴，我所做的那一番沐浴净身修饰、寒暄致意、应对交际，便心中思忖，万物之中，我们人是多么独擅礼仪，是一个多么不厌其烦、礼数周到的猿猴类物种啊。

问题所在

从他们坐的那个客厅角落，可以在一面大镜子中看到已经

could see in a great mirror the other dinner-guests linger and depart. But none of them were going on—what was the good?—to that evening party. They talked of satiety and disenchantment, of the wintry weather, of illness, of age and death.

'But what really frightens me most in life,' said one of them, 'what gives me a kind of vertigo or shiver, is—it sounds absurd, but it's simply the horror of space, *l'épouvante sidérale*—the dismay of Infinity, the black abysses in the Milky Way, the silence of those eternal spaces.'

'But Time,' said another of the group, 'surely Time is a worse nightmare. Think of it! the Past with never a beginning, the Future going on for ever and ever, and the little Present in which we live, twinkling for a second, between these black abysses.'

'What's wrong with me,' mused the third speaker, 'is that even the Present eludes me. I don't know what it really is; I can never catch the moment as it passes; I am always far ahead or far away behind, and always somewhere else. I am not really here now with you. And why should I go to the party? I shouldn't be there, either, if I went. My life is all reminiscence and anticipation—if you can call it life, if I am not rather a kind of ghost, haunting a past that has ceased to exist, or a future that is still more shadowy and unreal. It's ghastly in a way, this exile and isolation. But why speak of it, after all?'

They rose, and their figures too were reflected in the great mirror, as they passed out of the drawing-room, and dispersed, each on his or her way, into the winter night.

半空的厅里别的晚宴客人逗留了便走出去。但他们谁也不过去——有什么好去的？——出席那天晚上的宴会。他们谈论着满足感和幻灭感，谈论着冬天的天气，还有生老病死。

“但生活中真正叫我最害怕的，”他们中的一个说，“真正让我觉得有种头晕目眩、不寒而栗之感的是——听着荒唐，但说白了，就是空间恐惧感，*l'épouvante sidérale*——对星空的恐惧，面对无限，面对银河系黑幽幽的无底深渊、那层层太空永恒的沉默所产生的不安。”

“可还有时间呢，”另一个说，“时间肯定是个更可怕的噩梦。想想看吧！过去不见其始，未来不知其终，而我们身处的小小当下，须臾一忽闪，就夹在这两个幽黑的深渊之间。”

“我的问题是，”第三位若有所思地说，“连当下都把握不住。我不知道当下到底是什么；闪过的一刻从来都抓不住；要么远远在前，要么远远落后，总是准不到那个点。我现在也并不是真就同你们在一起。而我干吗要去那个宴会？就是去了，人也不在那边。我的生活全是回忆和期待——如果这能称作生活的话，如果我并非是什么鬼魂在一个不复存在的过去，或者比过去更虚更幻的未来纠缠不休的话。很有点恐怖，这种流放与隔绝。可是提它干吗呢，这种事？”

他们站起身，各人的身影照样也映在大镜子中，只见他们穿过客厅走出大门，四下散开，各走各的路，踏入冬日的夜色中。

Sir Eustace Carr

When I read the news about Sir Eustace Carr in the morning paper, I was startled, like everyone else who knew, if only by name, this young man, whose wealth and good looks, whose adventurous travels and whose brilliant and happy marriage, had made of him an almost romantic figure.

Every now and then one hears of some strange happening of this kind. But they are acts so anomalous, in such startling contradiction to all our usual ways and accepted notions of life and its value, that most of us are willing enough to accept the familiar explanation of insanity, or any other commonplace cause which may be alleged—financial trouble, or some passionate entanglement, and the fear of scandal and exposure. And then the Suicide is forgotten as soon as possible, and his memory shuffled out of the way as something unpleasant to think of. But I sometimes wonder about these cases, asking myself whether the dead man may not have carried to the grave with him the secret of some strange perplexity, some passion or craving or irresistible impulse, of which perhaps his intimates, and certainly the coroner's jury, can have had no inkling.

I had never met or spoken to Sir Eustace Carr—the worlds we lived in were very different—but I had read of his explorations in the East, and of the curious tombs he had discovered—somewhere, was it not? —in the Nile Valley. Then, too, it happened (and this was the main cause of my interest) that

尤斯迪斯·卡尔爵士

在晨报上看到有关尤斯迪斯·卡尔爵士的新闻，我不禁大吃一惊。知道他的人，哪怕只是听过他的名字，都会同我一样大吃一惊的。这位年轻人，他的家财、堂堂相貌、游历探险、美满婚姻，一时几成浪漫佳话。

时不时会听到诸如此类的怪事发生。但这类举动是如此有乖常理，同我们通常的生活方式和所接受的人生观价值观是如此格格不入，惊诧之余，我们大都也乐意将其归咎于精神错乱这一常见的原因，或者随便哪个可能是道听途说的老一套理由——钱财问题啦，感情纠纷啦，害怕丑闻曝光啦等等。接着呢，这起自杀事件人们忘得有多快便有多快，其人其事也就成了不愉快的回忆被抛诸脑后。可我有时却会寻思，在这类事件中，死者带进坟墓的是不是还有什么莫名的困惑与秘辛、一段激情与渴念、一份无可抗拒的冲动；这一切，他的至亲密友或许并不知情，而验尸陪审团更是不明就里。

我从未与尤斯迪斯·卡尔爵士交往或交谈过——我们所处的两个世界大不相同——但我读过有关他在东方的探险，有关他发现的那些神秘的陵墓——是不是？——在尼罗河谷的哪个地方。后来呢，又碰巧有个时候我不止一回看见过他（这是我对他

at one time I had seen him more than once, under circumstances that were rather unusual. And now I began to think of this incident. In a way it was nothing, and yet the impression haunted me that it was somehow connected with this final act, for which no explanation, beyond that of sudden mental derangement, had been offered. This explanation did not seem to me wholly adequate, although it had been accepted, I believe, both by his friends and the general public—and with the more apparent reason on account of a strain of eccentricity, amounting in some cases almost to insanity which could be traced, it was said, in his mother's family.

I found it not difficult to revive with a certain vividness the memory of those cold and rainy November weeks that I had happened to spend alone, some years ago, in Venice, and of the churches which I had so frequently haunted. Especially I remembered the great dreary church in the *campo* near my lodgings, into which I would often go on my way to my rooms in the twilight. It was the season when all the Venice churches are draped in black, and services for the dead are held in them at dawn and twilight; and when I entered this Baroque interior, with its twisted columns and volutes and high-piled, hideous tombs, adorned with skeletons and allegorical figures and angels blowing trumpets—all so agitated, and yet all so dead and empty and frigid—I would find the fantastic darkness filled with glimmering candles, and kneeling figures, and the discordant noise of chanting. There I would sit, while outside night fell

的事感兴趣的主要原因)，并且时间地点又非同寻常。现在我开始想起这件事。似乎算不了什么，可那一幕幕情景又挥之不去，不知怎么总觉得与他最后这举动有关联，而对他的自绝于世，除了精神方面突然失常之外，还提不出别的解释。这一解释，我觉得似乎并不能充分说明问题，虽然，我相信，业已为其朋友和公众所接受——而且基于其秉性中的某种怪僻更显得有道理，有一些情景几乎迹近精神错乱，源头据说呢，可以追溯到其母亲的家族。

我发现不难重新勾起那还有点栩栩如生的记忆，那个寒雨绵绵的十一月，一些年前了，我刚巧有几个星期一个人在威尼斯，想起了当时我常常流连的那些教堂。尤其是我住处附近广场上那座凄清的大教堂，我踏着暮色去我房间路过时，常常会拐进去。那个季节，威尼斯所有教堂都会披上黑色的帷幔，晨昏时分纪念死者的礼拜便在里面举行。我走进这巴洛克风格的内堂时，只见一排排弯弯扭扭的柱子和卷涡刻饰，阴森森的坟墓堆得很高，上面雕着骷髅、寓言人物，还有天使在吹喇叭——一切都如此喧腾不宁，然而又如此死气沉沉、空虚冰冷——我会发现眼前这怪诞的黑暗充斥着摇曳的烛光、跪拜的人影、缭乱的吟唱声。在那里我会坐着，一任外边夜色带雨降临威尼斯城；宫殿楼阁、碧绿的运

with the rain on Venice; the palaces and green canals faded into darkness, and the great bells, swinging against the low sky, sent the melancholy sound of their voices far over the lagoons.

It was here, in this church, that I used to see Sir Eustace Carr; would generally find him in the same corner when I entered, and would sometimes watch his face, until the ceremonious extinguishing of the candles, one by one, left us in shadowy night. It was a handsome and thoughtful face, and I remember more than once wondering what had brought him to Venice in that unseasonable month, and why he came so regularly to this monotonous service. It was as if some spell had drawn him; and now, with my curiosity newly wakened, I asked myself what had been that spell? I also must have been affected by it, for I had been there also in his uncommunicating company. Here, I felt, was perhaps the answer to my question, the secret of the enigma that puzzled me; and as I went over my memories of that time, and revived its sombre and almost sinister fascination, I seemed to see an answer looming before my imagination. But it was an answer, an hypothesis or supposition, so fantastic, that my common-sense could hardly accept it. For I now saw that the spell which had been on us both at that time in Venice had been nothing but the spell and tremendous incantation of the Thought of Death. The dreary city with its decaying palaces and great tomb-encumbered churches had really seemed, in those dark and desolate weeks, to be the home and metropolis of the King of Terrors; and the services at dawn and twilight,

河都隐入黑暗，教堂的大钟衬着低垂的夜空摇荡呜响，忧郁悲凉的钟声在一个个环礁湖上空传得很远很远。

就是在这里，在这座教堂里，我那时常常见到尤斯迪斯·卡尔爵士；进来时通常都会看到他待在同一个角落，有时也会端详一下他的脸，直到灭烛仪式，蜡烛一根根熄灭，将我们留在了暗夜幽影中。那是张英俊的、沉思的脸，记得不止一次我暗自寻思，到底是什么在这个时令不合的月份将他带来了威尼斯，为什么他这么定期不误地来做这千篇一律的礼拜。似乎有什么魔咒拖了他来；如今，我好奇心再发，自问那到底会是什么魔咒。我自己必定也受了这魔咒影响，因为我也来了，没有言语交流地陪着他。这里，我觉得，也许藏着我问题的答案，藏着我百思不得其解的谜底。我回想着当时的一幕幕，追忆着那幽暗得几乎是阴惨惨的迷幻之境，似乎看到有个答案隐约悬在我的想象之上。但这个答案，这个假设或推测，怪诞得连我凭常识都几乎接受不了。因为我现在明白，当时在威尼斯困住我们两人的魔咒不是别的，是死亡之思，是这一魔咒及其震魂慑魄的威力。那凄清的城市，城中颓圮的宫殿、墓茔累累的大教堂，在在都让人觉得，在那幽暗凄凉的几个星期中，似乎真成了死神的家园与都会；晨昏二度的礼拜，

with their prayers for the Dead, and funereal candles, had been the chanted ritual of his worship. Now suppose (such was the notion that held my imagination) suppose this spell, which I had felt but for a time and dimly, should become to someone a real obsession, casting its shadow more and more completely over a life otherwise prosperous and happy, might not this be the clue to a history like that of Sir Eustace Carr's—not only his interest in the buried East, his presence at that time in Venice, but also his unexplained and mysterious end?

Musing on this half-believed notion, I thought of the great personages and great nations we read of in ancient history, who have seemed to live with a kind of morbid pleasure in the shadow of this great Thought; who have surrounded themselves with mementoes of Death, and hideous symbols of its power, and who, like the Egyptians, have found their main interest, not in the present, but in imaginary explorations of the unknown future; not on the sunlit surface of this earth, but in the vaults and dwelling-places of the Dead beneath it.

Since this preoccupation, this curiosity, this nostalgia, has exercised so enormous a fascination in the past, I found it not impossible to imagine some modern favourite of fortune falling a victim to this malady of the soul; until at last, growing weary of other satisfactions, he might be drawn to open for himself the dark portal and join the inhabitants of that dim region. This, as I say, was the notion that haunted me, the link my imagination forged between Sir Eustace Carr's presence in that dark Venetian

那献给死者的祷词，那葬礼般的烛光，便是对这恐怖之君吟唱膜拜的仪式。那么设想一下（这就是牵动我想象的那个意念），设想这个魔咒，我不过是一时间隐隐有所感，却让一个人真的为之梦绕魂牵，把它的阴影越来越密实地罩在那个本来可以活得风光美满的生命之上。这个设想，有没有可能是洞悉类似尤斯迪斯·卡尔爵士这种身世生平的线索呢——不光是他为何会对葬于地下的东方感兴趣，会在那个时节现身威尼斯，还有他为何会那样无可解释地、神秘地殒殁？

心中转着自己这个半信半疑的念头，我想起了所读过的古代史上那些伟大的人物、那些伟大的民族，似乎都带着一种病态的快感活在死亡之思无远弗届的阴影里；让自己周遭包围着死亡的纪念物，以及它威力的各种面目可憎的象征物，就像埃及人那样，主要兴趣所在，不是当前，而是在想象中对不可知未来的探索；不是这个地球阳光照耀的表面，而是地下死人的窀穸家园。

既然前人能如此汲汲于此好，痴迷于这种好奇、这种思古幽情而欲罢不能，我觉得未尝不可想象一下今世也有哪个天生富贵命的人染上这一灵魂痼疾；终有一天，此人对其他乐趣变得兴味索然，难保就不会鬼使神差为自己打开那道黑暗的门洞，进去与冥界中人为伍。这就是，如我所说，在我心中挥之不去的念头，是我的想象力铸就的连接，将尤斯迪斯·卡尔爵士出现在那座幽

church, and his death some years later. But whether it is really a clue to that unexplained mystery, or whether it is nothing more than a somewhat sinister fancy, of course I cannot say.

At a Solemn Music

I sat there, hating the exuberance of her bust, and her high-coloured wig. And how could I listen to hushed music in the close proximity of those loud stockings?

Then our eyes met: in both of us the enchanted chord was touched; we both looked through the same window into Heaven. In that moment of musical, shared delight, my soul and the unembodied soul of that large lady joined hands and sang like the Morning Stars together.

The Communion of Souls

'So of course I bought it! How could I help buying it?' Then, lifting the conversation, as with Lady Hyslop one always lifts it, to a higher level, 'this notion of Free Will,' I went on, 'the notion, for instance, that I was free to buy or not to buy that rare edition, seems, when you think of it—at least to me it seems—a wretched notion really. I like to feel that I must follow the things I desire as—how shall I put it? —as the tide follows the Moon;

暗的威尼斯教堂和他一些年后的轻生联系起来。但这真是一个线索来了解那无可解释的秘辛，抑或只是有些不怀好意的自我作古？当然了，我还真不好说。

庄严的音乐会上

我端坐着，心中憎嫌着她那硕大丰腴的胸部、那高彩亮丽的假发。有颜色那么闹的一双长袜近在旁侧，我又怎能听得进轻婉的乐音？

接着我们目光相遇：两人着了魔的心弦被触动了，我们俩透过同一扇窗望向天国。就在那一刻的音乐中，那一点相通的欢乐里，我的灵魂和那位大个子女士不附形体的灵魂携起手来如晨星般同声歌唱。

灵魂交通

“啊，当然我买了！我怎么能不买呢？”接着，我便把话题拔高，就像每个人同海斯洛普夫人交谈都会拔高话题一样，拔到了一个更高的层面。“自由意志这个概念，”我继续说，“这个自由概念，比如说，我有自由买或不买那册珍本书，似乎是，你想想看——至少对于我似乎是——真的很糟糕。我喜欢觉得自己必须随心中欲求之物而行，如同——怎么说呢？——如同潮汐随月

that my actions are due to necessary causes; that the world inside me isn't a meaningless chaos, but a world of order, like the world outside, governed by beautiful laws, as the Stars are governed.'

'Ah, how I love the Stars!' murmured Lady Hyslop. 'What things they say to me! They are the pledges of lost recognitions; the promise of ineffable mitigations.'

'Mitigations?' I gasped, feeling a little giddy. But it didn't matter: always when we meet Lady Hyslop and I have the most sublime conversations.

Waxworks

'But one really never knows the Age one lives in. How interesting it would be,' I said to the lady next me, 'how I wish we could see ourselves as Posterity will see us!'

I have said it before; but on this occasion I was struck—almost thunder-struck—by my own remark. Like a rash exorcist, I was appalled by the spirit I had raised. For a queer second I did see us all in that inevitable mirror, but cadaverous, palsied, out-of-date, —a dusty set of old waxworks, simpering in the lumber-room of Time inanely.

'Better to be forgotten at once!' I exclaimed, with an emphasis that seemed somewhat to surprise the lady next me.

亮而动；觉得自己的行动自有必要之因由；觉得我内心的世界并非没有意义的一团混沌，而是有规有矩，如同外面的世界，为美好的定律所规管，管得如星星般错落有致。”

“啊，我多么喜欢星星啊！”海斯洛普夫人喃喃说道，“星星告诉我的有多好啊！它们是对失去了的认可的信约，是带着不可言喻的舒缓的许诺。”

“舒缓？”我一愣，觉得有点晕。但这无关宏旨：我们与海斯洛普夫人见面总是如此，而我则领略了最为崇高的交谈。

蜡像

“但一个人真的永远不了解自己所生活的时代。那会多有趣啊，”我对邻座的女士说，“我多么希望我们能够像后人看我们那样看看自己啊！”

这话我以前说过，但是这一次我竟然吃了一惊——几乎是如雷轰顶——被自己的话震住了。就像一个冒失的驱魔人，我被自己驱赶出来的精怪吓坏了。有那么诡异的一秒钟我真就看到我们个个都映在那面躲不开的镜子中，却像尸体一样僵直、古板——一套蒙着灰尘的旧蜡像，傻笑着立在时光的旧物仓里发呆。

“最好马上被人忘了！”我一声呼喊，语气之重似乎有点让邻座那位女士吃了一惊。

Adjectives

But why wasn't I born, alas, in an age of Adjectives; why can one no longer write of silver-shedding Tears and moon-tailed Peacocks, of eloquent Death, of the negro and star-enamelled Night?

Desperance

'Yes, as you say, life is so full of disappointment, disillusion! More and more I ask myself, as I grow older, what is the good of it all? We dress, we go out to dinner,' I went on, 'but surely we walk in a vain show, as the Bible puts it, and are crushed before the moth. How good this asparagus is! I often say asparagus is the most delicious vegetable of all. And yet, I don't know—when one thinks of fresh green peas. One can get tired of asparagus, as one can of strawberries—but I could eat tender peas for ever. Then peaches, and melons; —and there are certain pears, too, that taste like heaven. One of my favourite daydreams for the long evening of my life is to live alone, a formal, greedy, selfish old gentleman; in a square house, say, in Devonshire, with a square garden, whose walls are covered with apricots and figs and peaches: and there are precious pears, too, of my own planting, on espaliers along the paths. I shall walk out with a gold-headed cane in the autumn sunshine, and just at the ripe

形容词

可是我为什么没生在，唉，生在一个形容词的年代？为什么不得再写泻银如珠的泪水、屏开如月的孔雀，不得再写雄辩滔滔的死神、星如皓齿映黑脸的夜晚？

徒叹奈何

“没错，正如你说的，生活充满了失望，充满了幻灭！我越来越经常问自己，随着年岁增长，这一切到底为了什么。我们装束齐整，出去赴宴，”我接着讲，“但的确是，世人行动实系幻影[37]，就像《圣经》说的，被蠹虫所毁坏[38]。这芦笋多好啊！我常说，蔬菜中就芦笋最好吃。可是，我不知道——假如什么时候想起新鲜的绿豌豆呢。吃芦笋会腻，就像吃草莓会腻一样——但嫩豌豆我是百吃不厌。然后是桃子、蜜瓜；——还有某些梨子，也是这样，味道像人间仙果。我为自己漫长的人生暮年做的白日梦当中，最喜欢的一个就是一个人住，一个正儿八经、贪心自私的老绅士；住在一栋正方形的房子里，比如说在德文郡，有个正方形的园子，墙上披盖着杏子、无花果、桃子，还有珍贵的梨子，我亲手种的，长在园中小径旁的树墙上。我将步出门来，拄着一根金头手杖，在秋日

moment pick another pear. However, that isn't what I was going to say——'

Chairs

In the streets of London there are door-bells I ring (I see myself ringing them); in certain houses there are chairs covered with chintz or cretonne in which I sit and talk about life, explaining often after tea what I think of it.

A Grievance

They are all persons of elegant manners and spotless reputations; they seem to welcome my visits, and they listen to my anecdotes with unflinching attention. I have only one grievance against them; they will keep in their houses books full of stale epithets, which, when I only seem to smell their mawkish proximity, produce in me a slight feeling of nausea.

There are people, I believe, who are affected in this way by the presence of cats.

的阳光中，又摘下一个熟得刚刚好的梨子。不过，这不是我本来要说的——”

座椅

在伦敦街边，有我按响的门铃（我看到自己在按那些门铃）；在有些房子中，有套着印花布的座椅，我坐着谈论生活，常常是茶点过后在解释我的人生观点。

不满

他们这些人，个个仪态高雅，名声清白；他们似乎很欢迎我的次次到访，听我讲逸事趣闻时也心无旁骛地专注。我对他们只有一点不满：他们会在屋子里存着些净是陈词滥调的书籍；我只要闻到左近似乎有它们的酸腐味，便觉得有点反胃。

有些人，我相信，见到猫也有这种反应。

Misquotation

Some 'precious phrase by all the Muses trimmed,' he quoted.

I knew that the word was 'filed' —by all the Muses filed' —but I said nothing.

That I should permit a misquotation like this to pass made me doubt my own identity. Or, it occurred to me, perhaps my personality was changing; I was undergoing, perhaps, like an insect in the silence of its cocoon, some curious metamorphosis? I waited to see what I might be turning into—a Low Church Curate? a Major with a big moustache? or a Licensed Victualler, perhaps?

Victoria Street

We were talking of the state of the world as we walked towards Westminster—as we walked and were sad. The outlook, my companion said, was black beyond description.

Just then a gleam of sun gilded the Abbey Towers above the roofs of Victoria Street before us. 'But why,' I asked, as my eyes drank in this shining picture, 'why do we live for anything but Beauty? What is there that gives a meaning to the world but Beauty; —these splendours,' I said, 'that seem to fall upon us from the empyrean, from climes of bliss beyond the Constellations? '

引语出错

某一“佳言经所有缪斯之手修剪”[39]，他引了句诗。

我知道原话不是“修剪”而是“润色”——“经所有缪斯之手润色”——但我一声不吭。

引名言而出错如斯，自己竟会见怪不怪，我不禁怀疑自己的为人。或者，我突然觉得，也许是自己的个性在改变；我正在经历，说不定，像一只昆虫静静待在它的茧子中，经历着某种奇怪的蜕变？我等着，且看自己会变成什么——一个低教会派[40]的副牧师？一个蓄着大胡须的少校？或者一个领有酒牌的餐馆老板，也说不定？

维多利亚街

我们一边谈论着世局，一边往西敏寺走去——边走边黯然神伤。展望前景，我的伙伴说，一片暗淡，暗淡得无以言表。

就在这时，有一抹阳光将眼前高耸于维多利亚街屋顶上空的西敏寺塔楼镀成金黄。“可为什么，”我问道，眼睛陶醉于这幅熠熠生辉的画面，“为什么我们大小事操心，可就是不为美而活呢？还有什么赋予世界以意义呢，除了美；——这些壮丽与辉煌，”我说道，“翩然而至，仿佛来自苍穹的最高处，来自极乐的天境，远在众星座之外？”

Justification

Well, what if I did put it on a little at that luncheon party? Don't I owe it to my friends to assert now and then my claims to consideration; ought I always to allow myself to be juggernauted, trampled on and treated as dirt? And how about the Saints and Patriarchs of the Bible? Didn't Joseph tell of the dream in which his wheatsheaf was exalted; Deborah sing without blame how she arose a mother in Israel, and David boast of his triumph over the paw of the lion and the bear's paw? Nay, in His confabulations with His chosen people, does not the Creator of the Universe Himself make the most astounding efforts to impress upon those Hebrews His importance, His power, His glory?

Wasn't I made in His image?

The Hour-Glass

At the corner of Oakley Street I stopped for a moment's chat with my neighbour, Mrs. Wheble, who was waiting there for a bus.

'Do tell me,' she asked, 'what you have got in that odd looking parcel?'

'It's an hour-glass,' I said, taking it out of its paper wrapping. 'I've always wanted an hour-glass to measure time by.

理据

嗯，就算我在那午餐会上装点腔作点势了，又怎么样？难道我不是为了朋友才不时要张扬一下让人另眼相看吗？难不成我应该总是给人欺凌、践踏，视如尘土吗？《圣经》中的那些圣人、那些先祖元老又怎样呢？难道约瑟没有说他做的梦吗，梦里他在田里捆的禾稼立着，由他哥哥们捆的禾稼围着下拜[41]？底波拉不是理直气壮地作歌，唱她如何兴起成为以色列之母[42]的吗？大卫不也夸口自己战胜了狮和熊的爪牙吗[43]？可不是，就连宇宙的造物主本身，在同他所拣选的人交谈时，不也令人惊讶不已地尽力要那些希伯来人铭记自己的地位、权柄、荣耀吗？

我不就是照着他的形象造的吗？

沙漏

在奥克利街角我停下来和邻居卫波太太聊会儿天，她刚好在那里等巴士。

“告诉我吧，”她问道，“你那怪怪的包裹中装的什么？”

“是个沙漏，”我答道，说着就把东西从纸包里拿出来，“我一直想要个沙漏来计时间。时间啊，还真是太神秘了，你想想！看，

What a mystery Time really is, when you think of it! See, the sands are running out now while we are talking. I've got here in my hand the most potent, the most enigmatic, the most fleeting of all essences—Time, the sad cure for all our sorrows; —but I say! There's your bus just starting. You'll miss it if you don't look out!'

Action

I am no mere thinker, no mere creature of dreams and imagination. I pay bills, post letters; I buy new bootlaces and put them in my boots. And when I set out to get my hair cut, it is with the iron face of those men of empire and unconquerable will, those Caesars and Napoleons, whose footsteps shake the earth.

Waiting

We met at Waterloo; as we were paying the same visit, we travelled in the train together; but when we got out at that country station, she found that her boxes had not arrived. They might have gone on to the next station; I waited with her while enquiries were telephoned down the line. It was a mild spring evening: side by side we sat in silence on a wooden bench facing

我们这边在说话，那边沙就在流出来。我这会儿手中握住了天地间最强大、最玄乎、最不可捉摸的要素——时间，这治愈万千悲伤的可悲的良药；——但是，快看！你等的巴士要开了。一不小心你就要错过了！”

行动

我绝非一个只会思想、只会做梦想象的家伙。我付账、寄信；我买新鞋带，还往鞋子上穿呢。出去理发时，脸上的表情坚硬如铁，一如君临帝国、百折不挠的一众人等，如那些恺撒们、拿破仑们，脚步落处大地发抖。

等待

我们俩是在滑铁卢[44]遇见的，因为去的地方相同，便一起搭火车前往。可是等我们在那个乡村火车站下了车，她发现她的行李没到。说不定送去了下一站；我便陪着她，等他们沿线打电话问过去。那是个和煦的春日傍晚，我们并排坐在一条木长椅上默

the platform; the bustle caused by the passing train ebbed away; the dusk deepened, and one by one the stars twinkled out in the serene sky.

'How peaceful it is!' I said. 'Is there not a certain charm,' I went on after another pause, 'in waiting like this in silence under the stars? It's after all a little adventure, is it not? a moment with a certain mood and colour and atmosphere of its own.'

'I often think,' I once more mused aloud, 'I often think that it is in moments like this of waiting and hushed suspense that one tastes most fully the savour of life, the uncertainty, and yet the sweetness of our frail mortal condition, so capable of fear and hope, so dependent on a million accidents.'

'Luggage!' I said, after another silence, 'is it not after all absurd that minds that voyage through strange seas should carry about with them brushes and drapery in leather boxes? Suppose all this paltry junk,' I said, giving my suitcase a poke with my umbrella, 'Suppose all this junk should disappear, what after all would it matter?'

At last she spoke. 'But it's my luggage,' she said, 'which is lost.'

Ions

'Self-determination,' one of them insisted. 'Arbitration!' cried another.

不作声，面对着月台；火车过站带来的忙乱消退了；暮色渐浓，星星一颗颗闪现在宁谧的天幕上。

“多么宁静啊！”我说道，“这不是别有一番风味吗？”我顿了顿继续说：“就这么等着，默不作声，在一片星空之下？怎么说这都是小小的一次历险，是不是？片刻之间，自有某种心绪、某种色调、某种氛围。”

“我常常想，”我再次陷入沉思，自言自语道，“我常常想，就是在这样的片刻中，在这样的等待和屏息悬念中，一个人最能完整地领略生活的真味，生老病死的脆弱中那无常然而甜美的况味，动辄担惊受怕，动辄希望满怀，一切又如此仰赖祸福之间的万千偶然。”

“行李！”我沉默了一会儿又说开了，“归根结底这不是很荒唐吗，有心之人漂洋过海旅行还要拎着皮箱装着些刷子衣服什么的？要是这些劳什子，”我说着用雨伞捅了捅我的手提箱，“要是这些劳什子全不见了，那又会怎样？”

她终于开口了。“可这是我的行李，”她说，“给弄丢了啊。”

制

“自决制。”他们当中有人坚持说。“仲裁制！”另一个嚷道。

'Co-operation?' suggested the mildest of the party.

'Confiscation!' answered an uncompromising female.

I, too, became slightly intoxicated by the sound of these vocables. And were they not the cure for all our ills?

'Inebriation!' I chimed in, 'Inundation, Afforestation, Flagellation, Transubstantiation, Co-education!'

The Wrong Word

We were talking of the Universe at tea, and one of our company declared that he at least was entirely without illusions. He had long since faced the fact that Nature had no sympathy with our hopes and fears, and was completely indifferent to our fate. The Universe, he said, was a great meaningless machine; Man, with his reason and moral judgements, was the product of blind forces, which, though they would so soon destroy him, he must yet despise. To endure this tragedy of our fate with passionless despair, never to wince or bow the head, to confront the hostile powers with high disdain, to fix with eyes of scorn the Gorgon face of Destiny, to stand on the brink of the abyss, clenching his fist at the death-pale stars—this, he said, was his attitude, and it produced, as you can imagine, a powerful impression on the company. As for me, I was carried away completely.

'By Jove, that is a stunt!' I cried.

“合作制？”这群人里最温和的一个建议道。

“充公制！”一位女性不肯妥协。

我，听着这些“制”“制”声，不觉也有一点酩酊。这些不就是医治我们各种弊病的良药吗？

“放任制！”我插进话来，“漫灌制、绿化制、鞭刑制、组织代换制、男女同校制！”

错词

茶点时我们谈起了宇宙，同桌的一位宣称他至少是完全不存幻想。他很久以来便面对这个事实，亦即大自然对我们的希望与恐惧不怀同情，对我们的命运完全无动于衷。宇宙嘛，他说，是部没有意义的大机器；人嘛，带着理性和道德判断，是各种盲目之力的产物，虽然这些力很快就会将人摧毁，人还是得藐视它们。忍受我们命运的这一悲剧，淡漠而绝望，永不畏缩，永不低头，以高慢的鄙夷直面种种敌对的力量，以不屑的眼光逼视命运的狰狞，立于深渊边缘，攥拳对着满天死灰般的星星——这，他说，就是他的态度。这番话，你可以想见，可谓语惊四座。至于我呢，则听得飘飘然不能自已。

“天哪，那可是一项特技啊！”我嚷道。

Becalmed

Half-way along the street I stopped; I had forgotten the errand which had brought me out. What was it I wanted? There was nothing on earth I wanted; I stood there, motionless, without desire, like a ship at sea, deserted of all winds. It seemed as if I might stand there for ever.

Then, as with the shadow of a cloud, or ripple of the returning breeze, the wind of impulse darkened across the waters and filled my sails again. Life was again momentous, full of meaning; and radiant to my imagination the stamps I had hurried out to buy.

A Slander

'But I'm told you don't believe in love ——'

'Now who on earth could have told you that?' I cried indignantly. 'Of course I believe in it; —there is no one more enthusiastic about Love than I am. I believe in it at all times and seasons, but especially in the Spring. Why, just think of it! True-love amid the apple-blossoms, lovers who outwake the nightingales of April, the touch of hands and lips, and the clinging of flower-soft limbs together; and all this with, for a background, the gay, musical, perfumed landscape of the Spring. Why, nothing could be more genial, Miss Tomkins, more

风住船止

在街上走了一半我停下脚步，忘了是什么事让我出的门。要买什么吗？我什么也不缺啊。我站在那里，一动不动，无欲无求，就像海面上一艘船，没了风动不了。看样子我似乎要永远这么站下去了。

然后，宛如云过影来，风起波兴，一阵冲动如风吹过扫暗水面，重又鼓起了我的船帆。生活重新变得重要，充满意义；照亮我想象力的光彩是我急匆匆赶出门要买的邮票。

诽谤

“可是听人说你不相信爱——”

“到底是谁会这么说我？”我气冲冲地大声问，“我当然信了；——谁都不像我对爱这么热诚。我从早到晚地信，一年四季地信，尤其是在春季。怎么样，只消想想！苹果花丛中的真爱、连四月的夜莺也自叹不如的爱侣的不眠、手与唇的相触相碰、花般温软的相拥相偎；这一切，作为背景衬托的，是欢欣、悦耳、花香一片的春色。怎么样，汤金斯小姐，还有什么能比这更可心可意、更

appropriate and pretty!

'Haven't I said so again and again, haven't I published it more than once in the weekly papers?'

Synthesis

'It's awful,' I said, 'I think it simply wicked, the way you tear your friends to pieces.'

'But you do it yourself, you know you do! You analyse and analyse people, and then you make them up again into creatures larger than life ——'

'That's exactly it,' I answered gravely. 'If I take people to pieces, I do it in order to put them together again better than they were before; I make them more real, so to speak, more significant, more essentially themselves. But to cut them up, as you do, and leave the fragments anyhow on the floor—I can't tell you how cruel and heartless and wrong I think it!'

Shrinkage

Sometimes my soul floats out beyond the constellations; then all the vast life of the Universe is mine. Then again it evaporates, it shrinks, it dwindles; and of that flood which overbrimmed the bowl of the great Cosmos there is hardly enough

相得益彰、更俏丽妩媚呢！

“这些话，我不是说了一遍又一遍，我不是在周报上不止一次发表过了吗？”

整合

“太可怕了，”我说，“我觉得这简直是邪恶，看你这么把你的朋友们撕成碎片。”

“但你自己也这样，你知道你也这么干！你把人分析来分析去，再把他们拼合成夸张不实的东西——”

“一点不错，”我郑重答道，“如果我把人拆成一块块，那是为了把他们重新整合，成为比原来更好的人；我让他们显得更真实，这么说吧，更有意义，更是他们的本真之人。但是把他们大卸八块，就像你干的那样，一块块就这么随便丢在地板上——我不知道该怎么跟你说，这在我看来是多么残忍，多么狠心，多么离谱！”

萎缩

有时候，我的灵魂飘飘悠悠飞到了星辰之外；这一刻宇宙汗漫的生命便全归我了。接着，它又化为云烟，萎缩了，衰减了；而

now left to fill a teaspoon.

Comfort

People often said that there was nothing sadder, she mourned, than the remembrance of past happiness; but to her it seemed that not the way we remembered, but the way we forgot, was the real tragedy of life. Everything faded from us; our joys and sorrows vanished alike in the irrevocable flux; we could not stay their fleeting. Did I not feel, she moaned, the sadness of this forgetting, this outliving all the things we care for; this constant dying, so to speak, in the midst of life?

I felt its sadness very much; I felt quite lugubrious about it. 'And yet,' I said (for I did really want to think of something that might console this lamentable lady) 'and yet can't we find, in this fading of recollection, some recompense, after all? Think, for instance —.' But what, alas, could I suggest?

'Think,' I began once more after a pause of deep consideration, 'think of forgetting, and reading, and re-forgetting and re-reading Jane Austen's novels!'

Ebury Street

'Do you mean to cut me? How odd you look! What are you

那漫溢于苍穹之巨鼎的滔滔洪波，此刻所余已盛不满一茶羹了。

安慰

人们常说再伤心，她哀哀说道，也伤心不过追忆往日的幸福；但是对她而言，似乎不是我们如何记，而是我们如何忘，才是生活真正的悲剧所在。一切都从我们心中黯然退去；欢乐和悲伤，都一样化为乌有，无可奈何地流逝；逃遁匆匆，拦也拦不住。难道我感受不到吗，她悲叹，这忘却留下的悲哀，悲的是人尚在而珍爱之物皆不存，悲的是，可以说，一生中这恒常不绝的亡故？

这份悲哀我深有感受，有锥心刺骨的感受。"然而，"我说道(因为我真希望能想些什么，说来或者可以安慰这位可怜兮兮的女士)，"然而不管怎样，我们难道不能在这记忆的消退中找着某些补偿吗？想想吧，比如说——"但是，比如说什么呢，唉，我有什么可说的呢？

"想想吧，"我沉思了一会儿又开始说，"想想吧，忘了就看，再忘再看简·奥斯丁[45]写的小说！"

伊伯利街[46]

"你是不是想装着没看见我？瞧你那模样真怪！你来伊伯利

doing in Ebury Street?' she asked.

I felt a large, healthy blush suffuse my features, 'There's a lady who lives here—no, I don't mean what you think—a lady,' I said desperately, 'a Mrs. Whigham, who hates the way I write, and threw my last book out of her window. I walk by her house now and then to practise humility, and learn—as we all should learn—to endure the world's contempt.'

This Mrs. Whigham was, however, an invented being; I had really come to Ebury Street for another look, in the window of a shop there, at an old Venetian mirror, in whose depths of dusky glass I had seen a dim, romantic, well-dressed figure, as I went by one day.

The Welsh Harp

What charming corners one can find in the immense dinginess of London, and what curious encounters become a part of the London-lovers experience! The other day, when I walked beyond the Edgware Road, and stopped for tea at the Welsh Harp, on the banks of the Brent Reservoir, I found, beyond the modern frontage of this inn, a garden adorned with sham ruins and statues, and full of autumn flowers and the shimmer of clear water. Sitting there and drinking my tea—alone, as I thought at first, in the twilight—I became aware that the garden had another occupant; that at another table, not far from me, a vague

街有什么事？”她问道。

我觉得一大片健康的红晕涌上脸来。“有一位女士住在这里——不，不是你想的那样——一位女士，”我气急败坏地说，“一位名叫卫格翰太太的，她讨厌我的写作方式，将我最新出的书丢出了窗外。我不时要从她屋前走过，来修炼我的谦卑之心，来学习——就像我们大家都得学习——怎么忍受世人的鄙夷。”

然而，这位卫格翰太太是我编出来的；我来伊伯利街其实是想再看看，那里一家铺子橱窗里摆有一面威尼斯款旧镜子，映在那幽暗的镜面纵深处，我有一天路过时，见到了一个模模糊糊、气质浪漫、衣着光鲜的人影。

威尔士竖琴酒馆

在伦敦那一大片沉沉的阴暗中，原来找得到那么别有洞天的角落啊，而令人惊艳的邂逅又成了喜欢伦敦的人怎样的一份经历啊！前两天，我信步走过了艾奇韦尔路那头，在布伦特水库边的威尔士竖琴酒馆歇脚饮茶。我发现，在这小酒馆现代装修的门面背后，有一个花园，装点着仿制的废墟和雕像，开满了秋天的花卉，荡漾着清澈的秋水。坐在那里喝着茶——一个人，我刚开始还以为，一片暮色——接着便意识到园中还有一个人；在另一张桌边，离我不远处，隐隐约约坐着一个女的，戴着一顶破旧的圆

woman in a shabby bonnet was sitting, with her reticule lying by her, also drinking tea and gazing at the after-glow of the sunset. An elderly spinster I thought her, a dressmaker perhaps, or a retired governess, one of those maiden ladies who live alone in quiet lodgings, and are fond of romantic fiction and solitary excursions.

More than once, as we sat there, we two alone in the growing dusk, our glances met, and a curious relation of sympathy and understanding established itself between us; we seemed to carry on a dialogue full of tacit avowals. 'Yes,' we seemed to say, as our eyes met over our suspended tea-cups, 'yes, Beauty, Romance, the Blue Bird that sings of Happiness—these are the things we care for; —the only things that, in spite of everything, we still care for. But where can we find them in the dingy London streets?'

'And yet,' our eyes seemed to ask each other, 'isn't this garden, in its shabby, pretentious way, romantic; isn't it like something in a poem of Verlaine's; hasn't it now, in the dim light, a curious beauty? And this mood of meditation after our excellent tea, what name, if we are honest, can we call it by, if we don't call it Happiness?'

Misapprehension

People often seem to take me for some one else; they talk

帽，手提袋放在身边，也在喝茶，凝神看着落日的余晖。我看这是个有些年纪的老处女，一个裁缝也说不定，或者退了休的家庭教师，那些没有嫁人的女士中的一位，她们安安静静地独居，都爱看言情小说，喜欢单人外出。

不止一次，当我们坐在那里，暮色渐浓中独自坐着的两个人，目光相遇，有一种奇怪的同情与理解在两人间建立；我们似乎心照不宣地在进行着一场对话。“是的，”我们似乎在说，目光从举在面前的茶杯上对望相遇，“是的，美、浪漫、歌唱幸福的青鸟——这些是我们念兹在兹的东西；——万物虽繁，但只有这些，才是我们心中所念。但是这些我们在伦敦街道的幽暗中上哪儿找去呢？”

“然而，”我们的目光似乎在互相询问，“这花园，看它那破旧、矜夸的模样，不是很浪漫吗？不是挺像魏尔伦[47]诗中所描写的那样吗？此时此刻在这片朦胧中，它不是有一种奇特的美吗？而好茶过后的这种玄思冥想的心境，真心说来，该叫它什么呢，如果我们不称之为幸福？”

误解

人们似乎常常把我当成另外一个人，跟我说话时好像我是一

to me as if I were a person of earnest views and unalterable convictions. 'What is your opinion of Democracy?' they ask. 'Are you in favour of the Channel Tunnel?' 'Do you believe in existence after Death?'

I assume a thoughtful attitude, and by means of grave looks and evasive answers, I conceal—or at least I hope I conceal—my discreditable secret.

The Lift

What on earth had I come up for? I stood out of breath in my bedroom; I had completely forgotten the errand which had carried me upstairs, leaping two steps at a time.

Gloves! Of course it was my gloves which I had left there. But what did gloves matter, I asked myself, in a world, as Dr. Johnson describes it, bursting with Sin and Misery?

O stars and garters! how bored I am by this trite, moralizing way of regarding natural phenomena—this crying of vanity on the beautiful manifestations of mechanical forces. This desire of mine to appear out of doors in appropriate apparel, if it can thus overcome the law of gravitation; if it can lift twelve stone of matter thirty or forty feet above the earth's surface; if it can do this every day, and several times a day, is it not quite as remarkable and convenient in the house as a hydraulic lift?

个实话实说、信念坚定的人。“你对民主有什么看法?”他们问,“你赞成建海底隧道吗?”“你相信人死后还存在吗?”

我摆出若有所思的模样,加以一副凝重的神态和含糊其词的回答,隐瞒了——或者至少我希望是隐瞒了——我那说出去会败坏名声的秘密。

升降机

我上来到底是要干什么?我上气不接下气站在卧室中,忘得一干二净是什么事让自己上得楼来,还一步两级地跑呢。

手套!当然是手套,我忘在那里了。但手套真就那么重要吗,我问自己,在这么一个世界,如约翰逊博士[48]所描绘的,一个罪孽与哀苦横流的世界上?

啊,老天爷啊!我真是腻透了这种陈腐的、道德化地看待自然现象的德行——看到机械力美妙的体现就如此大叫虚荣。我的这个出门应该衣着得体的欲望,假如能因此克服引力定律,假如能把一百六十八磅的物体举到地球表面三四十英尺高,假如它能天天这么举、一天举几次,那房子内有了它不就同有一部液压升降机一样了得,一样方便吗?

Sloane Street

When I walk out, middle-aged, but still sprightly, and still, if the truth must be told, with an idiot dream in my heart of some romantic encounter, I look at the passers-by, say in Sloane Street, and then I begin to imagine moonfaces more alluring than any I see in that thoroughfare. But then again vaster thoughts visit me, remote metaphysical musings; those faces like moons I imagined begin to wane as moons wane, the passers-by vanish; and immortal Reason, disdaining the daymoth she dwells with, turns away to her crystalline sphere of contemplation. I am lost out of Time, I walk on to Sloane Square in a world of white silence.

Regent's Park

I wondered, as I passed Regent's Park on my way to Hampstead, what kind of people live in those great stuccoed terraces and crescents, with their solemn facades and friezes and pediments and statues. People larger than life I picture the inhabitants of those august, unfashionable houses, people with a dignity of port, an amplitude of back, an emphasis of vocabulary and conviction unknown in other regions; Dowagers and Dignitaries who have retired from a world no longer worthy of them, ex-Governors of Dominions, unavailing Viceroys,

斯隆街[49]

我走出门来，已是中年但仍然精力旺盛，仍然，如果实话非说不可，心中还怀着个痴痴傻傻的梦，希冀有什么浪漫的邂逅。我看着眼前走过的路人，比如说在斯隆街吧，就开始想象一些月亮般的脸庞，比我在这闹市大街上所见的都要迷人。但接着又有一些更不着边际的形而上思绪造访我心；那些想象出来的月亮般的脸蛋便开始由盈转亏如同月亮一样，眼前的路人也消失了；不朽的理性不屑再与同住的白日飞蛾为伍，转身投入她水晶般透明的沉思之境。我迷失在时间之外，继续往斯隆广场走去，身边的世界是白茫茫的一片沉默。

摄政公园

去汉普斯特德的路上经过摄政公园时，我心中思忖，是什么人住在那些拉毛外墙的临街大宅和新月形排屋中，门面如此庄严，装点着雕画的门梁、三角墙和一座座雕像。是些不近人间烟火之人，我心中勾画着，住在那些气派而不时髦的豪宅里，威仪凛然，背影雄阔，讲究的词汇和信念其他地区的民众闻所未闻；有从不再配得上他们的世界退隐的达官与贵妇，有自治领地的

superannuated Bishops and valetudinarian Generals, who wear top-hats and drive around the Park in old-fashioned barouches; — a society, I imagine it, not frivolous, not flippant, entirely devoid of double meanings; a society in which the memory of Queen Victoria is still revered, and regrets are still felt, perhaps, for the death of the Prince Consort.

Or, as I have sometimes fancied, are those commodious mansions the homes of the Victorian Statesmen and Royal Ladies and distinguished-looking Murderers who, in the nearby wax-work Exhibition, gaze on the shallow, modern generation which chatters and pushes all day before the glassy disapprobation of their eyes?

The Aviary

Peacock Vanities, great, crested Cockatoos of Glory, gay Infatuations and painted Daydreams; —what a pity it is all the Blue Birds of impossible Paradises have such beaks and sharp claws, that one really has to keep them shut up in their not too-cleanly cages!

St. John's Wood

As I walked on, the air soon lightened; the Throne, the Altar and the Top-Hat cast fainter shadows, the figures of John

前长官，有无甚建树的总督，有退休的老主教和潜心颐养病体的将军——头戴大礼帽，坐着老式的双马四轮大马车在公园里兜风；——一个社会圈子，就我想象，不轻狂、不轻佻、绝不含糊其词，追忆起维多利亚女王仍然尊敬有加，对王夫阿尔伯特的死，说不定呢，仍然心有戚戚。

或者，像我有时异想天开揣度的，那些大楼广厦会不会是维多利亚时代的经国才俊、皇族的仕女贵妇，以及道貌岸然的杀人凶手的宅邸，这些人摆在附近的蜡像展馆里，盯着肤浅的现代人如何在他们呆滞无神、挑剔非难的目光下说长道短，推推搡搡？

鸟舍

孔雀的虚荣、大鹦鹉华冠巍巍的光彩、美滋滋的痴迷和五颜六色的白日梦；——多可惜啊，所有从那些可望不可即的天堂来的青鸟都这般尖喙利爪，弄得人真只好把它们关进它们那并不太干净的笼子里！

圣约翰树林[50]

我信步走着，空气不久就变得轻快了；王座啊，圣坛啊，高顶礼帽啊，投下的影子渐渐变淡，约翰·布赖特[51]和威廉·格莱斯

Bright and Gladstone and Queen Victoria faded from my mind. I had entered the precincts of St. John's Wood; and as I went past its villas of coquettish aspect, with gay Swiss gables, with frivolously Gothic or Italian or almost Oriental faces, their lighter outlook on existence, the air they have of not taking life too earnestly, began to exert an influence.

St. John's Wood is the home in fiction of adventuresses and profligacy and outrageous supper-parties; often have I read about those foreign Countesses of unknown history and unbelievable fascination, who decoy handsome young officials of the Foreign Office to these villas; —and rob them, in dim-lit, scented bedrooms, of important documents. But I at least have never too severely blamed these young diplomatists. Silent is the street as the mysterious brougham pauses, lovely the eyes that flash, and graceful the white-gloved hand that beckons from the carriage-window; and how can they resist (for they are only human) the lure of so adventurous, so enchanting an invitation?

The Garden Suburb

I had often heard of the Hampstead Garden Suburb, and the attempt of its inhabitants to create an atmosphere of the Higher Culture, to recreate, as it were, the Golden Age in that region. But I must now confess that it was in a spirit of profane curiosity that I walked up towards its courts and closes. And

顿[52]还有女王维多利亚的身影，也从我心头隐去。我走进了圣约翰树林地界；路过它那些风姿妩媚的别墅，看到那些花哨的瑞士山墙、轻佻地摆着的或者哥特式或者意大利式或者几乎是东方式的门面，它们那种较为轻俏的人生态度、那种逢场作戏的逍遥，开始产生影响了。

圣约翰树林区是小说中女冒险家的居所，是花天酒地、纸醉金迷的浪荡之乡；我常常读到那些异国伯爵夫人，身世不明，魅力无敌，把外交部漂亮的年轻官员勾引到这些别墅中来；——在灯光迷离、熏了香的内室攫走他们的重要文件。但至少我从不会太过苛责这些年轻的外交官。静悄悄的是这条街路，有神秘的马车逗留，楚楚可爱的是那忽闪着的眼睛，风情万种透过车窗招摇着的是那只戴着白手套的手；他们怎么抵挡得住（怎么说不过是人哪）这芳泽探险、勾魂摄魄的诱惑，如此令人心旌摇荡的邀请呢？

花园郊区

我常常听到汉普斯特德花园郊区这地方，听到那里的居民有意要创造一种高端文化的氛围，宛如要在该地区重建黄金时代[53]。但我现在必须坦白，自己当时是怀着一种粗鄙不敬的好奇心走上去看那地区的庭院和街巷的。当看到贴着的公告有育儿术、手工

when I saw the notices of the Societies for Mothercraft and Handicraft and Child Study, the lectures on Reincarnation, the Holy Grail, and the Teaching of the Holy Zoroaster, I am afraid I laughed. But how thin this laughter sounded amid the quiet amenity, the beautiful distinction of this Utopia! It was an afternoon of daydreams; the autumnal light under the low clouds was propitious to inner recollection; and as I walked the streets of this transcendental city, soothed by the sense of order and beautiful architecture all around me, I began to feel that I too was an Idealist, that here was my spiritual home, and that it would be a seemly thing to give up the cinemas and come and make my abode on this hill-top. Pictures floated before my eyes of tranquil days, days of gardening and handicrafts and lectures, evenings spent in perusing the world's masterpieces.

Although I still frequent the cinemas, and spend too much time gazing in at the windows of expensive shops, and the reverie of that afternoon has come to no fruition, yet I feel myself a better person for it: I feel that it marks me off from the merely cynical and worldly. For I at least have had a Pisgah sight of the Promised City; I have made its ideal my own, if but for an afternoon, and only in a daydream.

Sunday Calls

'Well, I must say!' Reason exclaimed, when we found

艺术、儿童学习等社团的，有关于轮回转世、关于圣杯、关于圣人琐罗亚斯德[54]教诲的讲座的，我怕我当时是哑然一声笑。但这一声笑，在眼前一片幽静中，在这美好独特的乌托邦氛围里，显得多么单薄啊！那是个做白日梦的下午；低垂的云彩下一派秋色，正是诱发内心遐思的大好时光；我沿着这超然世外的街市走着，那种井井有条的感觉，那些举目皆是的漂亮建筑，让我心神舒泰，开始觉得自己也是个理想主义者，此地是我的精神家园，觉得要是放弃那些电影院，把家安在这山顶上，会是很惬意的一件事。眼前浮现一幅幅岁月静好的画面：白天养花修草、做做手工、听听讲座，晚上开卷细读世界名作。

虽然我还是常常光顾电影院，花太多时间在高档商店的橱窗前端详，而且那天下午的一场遐思也不了了之，但我觉得自己因此变好了：觉得那个下午令我从无非是玩世不恭的俗人中脱颖而出。因为我至少像摩西上了毗斯迦山[55]那样见过上帝的应许之城；我把那个花园郊区的理想变成了自己的理想，尽管不过是一个下午的光景，不过是一场白日梦中的遐想。

星期天的叩问

“这下，我非说不可！”我们发觉自己又在街上时，理性大叫。

ourselves in the street again.

'What's the matter now?' I asked uneasily.

'Why are you always trying to be some one else? Why not be what you really are?'

'But what am I really? Again I ask you!'

'I do hate to see you playing the ass; and think how they laugh at you!'

The glossy and respected image of myself I had left in the house behind us began to tarnish.

'And what next?' my querulous companion went on. 'What will you be in South Kensington, I wonder? a sad, subtle, solitary Satan, disillusioned and distinguished; or a bluff, breezy sailor, fond of his bottle and boon companions?'

An Anomaly

When people embellish their conversation with a glitter of titles, and drag into it self-aggrandizing anecdotes, though I laugh at this peacock vein in them, I do not harshly condemn it. Nay, since I too am human, since I too belong to the great household, would it be surprising if—say once or twice in my life—I also should have yielded to this tickling relish of the tongue?

No; —but what is surprising is the way that I alone always escape detection, always throw dust in other people's eyes.

“这次又怎么啦？”我不安地问道。

“你干吗老要把自己当成别的人？干吗不做回真正的自己？”

“但什么是我真正的自己？我再问你！”

“我真讨厌看你装癫卖傻，想想他们怎么笑话的你！”

我留在身后屋中那受人尊敬的亮丽形象开始失色。

“接着呢？”我那满腹牢骚的伙伴继续说，“等你在南肯辛顿时又会是个什么人呢，我问你？一个哀伤又暧昧的独行魔鬼，心灰意冷又心气不凡；还是一个满腔热忱、满面春风的水手，好的是老酒老友相伴？”

另类

看到人们用些闪亮的头衔来点缀谈资，用些奇闻逸事来自我吹嘘，虽然这种孔雀开屏式的做派令我发笑，我却不会严词苛责。不会的，因为我也是人，也属于人类这一大门大户，万一——万一我这辈子有那么一两次——抵不住痒也坠入了这口舌之乐，也值得大惊小怪吗？

大可不必；——但怪就怪在怎么就我一个人总是做得神不知鬼不觉，总是能瞒天过海。

The Listener

The topic was one of my favourite topics, but I didn't at all feel on this occasion that it was I who was speaking. No, it was the Truth shining through me; the light of the Revelation which I had been chosen to proclaim and blazon to the world. No wonder they were all impressed by my tones and gestures; no wonder even the fastidious lady whom it was most difficult to please kept watching me with an almost ecstatic attention.

As a cloud may obscure the sun in his glory, so from the morass of memory arose a tiny mist of words to darken my mind for a moment. I brushed them aside; they had no meaning. Sunning myself in the mirror of those eyes, never, for a moment, could I credit that devil-suggested explanation of their gaze.

Oh, no! that phrase I had heard, I had heard, the phrase, 'She mimics you to perfection,' was nothing but a scrap of unintelligible jabber.

Caviare

'Aren't you ashamed of yourself?' asked my hostess, when she found me alone in the supper-room, after all the other guests had gone.

'Ashamed? Why should I be ashamed?' I asked, as I went on eating. 'I am simply following the precept of Aristippus of

听者

话题是我最喜欢讲的一个，但我一点都不觉得这一次在讲话的是我。不，是真理透过我在闪光；是启示之光，选了我来彰显，来向世界宣扬。怪不得我的抑扬顿挫、举手投足令他们个个为之心动；怪不得即便是爱挑剔、最难讨好的那位女士也目不转睛地看着我，一脸如痴如醉的神情。

正如一片云可以遮住太阳的光辉，从记忆的泥沼中升起了一小团词语的迷雾，一时间蒙蔽了我的心。我把那些词语拨开；它们毫无意义。那些镜子般的眼睛令我如沐春光，我绝不会、一刻也不会，去相信那魔鬼建议的对那一片目光所做的解释。

啊，不！那句话，我听到的，我听到的，那句话，“她把你模仿得惟妙惟肖”，只不过是令人不知所云的嚼舌罢了。

鱼子酱

“你没觉得不好意思吗？”我的女主人问道，她看到我一个人还坐在晚餐室，而其他客人全都走了。

“不好意思？我干吗要不好意思？”我反问她，一边径自吃着，“我只不过是在遵循昔勒尼的亚里斯提卜[56]的教诲，他坚持要

Cyrene, who maintains that we should live wholly in the present moment, which alone exists, and in which alone the absolute Good of life is before us. It is only by regarding each Moment as an eternity, with no before or after, and by calmly and resolutely culling, without fear, or passion, or prejudice, the Good it offers—it is only thus, he says, that Wisdom is made manifest; only thus,' I explained, as I took another caviare-sandwich, 'that mortals may participate in the felicity of the Gods—the bright Gods, who feed on happiness for ever.'

Above the Clouds

'I do so hate gossip,' she murmured.

'How I hate it too!' I heard myself exclaim.

'There is so much that is good and noble in human nature; why not talk of that?'

'Why not indeed?' I sighed.

'I always feel that it is one's own fault if one dislikes people, or finds them boring.'

'How I agree with you!' I cried, as Virtue crept like a guilty thing into my heart.

'But people are nowadays so cynical—they sneer at everything that makes life worth living—Love, Faith, Friendship—'

'And yet those very names are so lovely that even when used

我们完完全全活在当下，只有当下一刻才存在，只在这一刻生活的绝对之好才摆在我们面前。只有将每一刻都视为永恒，无前无后，只有冷静地、坚决地采撷其所提供的好处，心中无畏惧、无激情也无偏见——唯有如此，他说了，方得见智慧；唯有如此，”我解释道，顺手又拿起一块鱼子酱三明治，“凡人方得以分享诸神之福——那些聪明的神祇，他们以幸福为食，永永远远。”

高上云端

“我最讨厌说人闲话了。”她嘟哝着。

“这我也讨厌透了！”我脱口感叹。

“人性中有这么多善良高尚的东西，为什么不拿出来说呢？”

“的确是，为什么不呢？”我叹了一口气。

“我向来觉得，要是谁看别人不顺眼，觉得他们没意思，那错在自己。”

“我太同意了！”我嚷道，这时美德像负罪似的悄悄爬上心头。

“可是当今世人都变得这么愤世嫉俗——能让生活值得一过的东西他们通通嗤之以鼻——爱情啊，信仰啊，友谊啊——”

“而这些东西光叫名字都这么可爱，即使拿来嘲弄讥笑，也闪

in mockery they shine like stars.' (I should have died then; never again shall I be so fit for Heaven.)

'How beautifully you put it! I have so enjoyed our talk.' I had enjoyed it too, and felt all the better for it; only a little giddy and out of breath, as if I had been up in a balloon.

The Bubble

Walking home at night, troubled by the world's affairs, and with its weight of Wrong crushing down my poor shoulders, I sometimes allow my Thoughts an interlude of solace. From the jar in which I keep my Vanity bottled, I remove the cork; out rushes that friendly Jinn and swells up and fills the sky. I walk on lightly through another world, a world in which I cut a very different figure.

I shall not describe that exquisite, evanescent universe; I soon snuff it out, or it melts of itself in thin air.

Paradise Regained

The fields and old farm, the little river, the village church among its elms, the formal gates of the park with the roofs of the great house beyond, all made, in the evening air, a dream-like picture. I was strangely happy; and how familiar was every

亮如星星。”（我当时就该死了的好，此后我绝不会再像那一刻那么适合进天堂了。）

“说得多好啊！同你谈话真愉快。”我也很愉快呢，而且感觉更加好了；只是有点晕，有点透不过气，好像坐气球升空了。

泡沫

晚上走回家，心中为世事所困扰，其不公不义重重压在我可怜的双肩上，我有时就让自己的思绪来一段自我抚慰的幕间曲。我把封着自己虚荣心的那个罐子的软木塞拔开，冲出来那个友善的精灵，膨胀起来充满了天空。我脚步轻盈地走过另一个世界，在那个世界我的形象大不相同。

我就不细说那个瞬间即逝的美妙天地了；我很快便将它掐灭，或者它自己化成空气飘散了。

乐园复得

连片的田畴、古朴的农庄、小河流水、榆树掩映的乡村教堂、公园的大门和后边巨宅的层层屋顶，这一切，在黄昏暮色中勾画出一幅梦幻般的图景。我感到莫名欣悦；眼前所见，一点一滴多

detail of the scene before me! There was the trout-stream I had fished in, there were the meadows I had galloped over; —through how many countless, quiet English years had I not lived in this landscape, and loved and hunted, courting innumerable vicars' daughters from cover to cover of all the countless, mild, old-fashioned novels of English country life which I have dreamed away my own life in reading?

Moments

'Awful moments? Why, yes, of course,' I said, 'life is full of them—let me think——'

'To find other people's unposted letters in an old pocket; to be seen looking at oneself in a street-mirror, or over-heard talking of the Ideal to a Duchess; to refuse Nuns who come to the door to ask for subscriptions, or to be lent by a beautiful new acquaintance a book she has written full of mystical slip-slop, and dreadful musings in an old-world garden——'

Interruption

'Life,' said a gaunt widow, with a reputation for being clever— 'life is a perpetual toothache.'

In this vein the conversation went on: the familiar

么熟悉啊！有我曾经垂钓过鳟鱼的溪流，有我曾经策马奔腾过的草地；——说不清有多少个恬静的英伦岁月我不就是住在这田园风光中，在这儿恋爱狩猎，在多不胜数的一本本温煦老派的英国乡村小说中把数不清的牧师女儿从封面追到封底，读着读着，梦掉了自己的人生吗？

瞬间

“可怕的瞬间？哦，是的，当然了，”我说，“生活充满了这种可怕的瞬间——让我想想——”

“在一个旧衣口袋里发现了别人没寄出的信件；让人看到自己在照着街边的一面镜子，或者让人无意间听到在跟一位公爵夫人谈理想；拒绝登门求捐的修女；或者收下一位漂亮的新交硬借的一本她写的书，书中满纸不知所云的无聊话，以及在一个旧世花园中百无聊赖的冥想——”

打岔

“生活，”一位瘦骨嶙峋的寡妇说，她以聪明著称——“生活是无休止的牙痛。”

顺着这个调调谈话继续着：讨论了熟悉的话题如劳工问题、

topics were discussed of labour-troubles, epidemics, cancer, tuberculosis, and taxation.

Near me there sat a little old lady who was placidly drinking her tea, and taking no part in the melancholy chorus. 'Well, I must say,' she remarked, turning to me, and speaking in an undertone, 'I must say I enjoy life.'

'So do I,' I whispered.

'When I enjoy things,' she went on, 'I know it. Eating, for instance, the sunshine, my hot-water bottle at night. Other people are always thinking of unpleasant things.'

'It makes a difference,' she added, as she got up to go with the others.

'All the difference in the world!' I answered.

Alchemy

It's too bad that I had no chance for a longer colloquy with this old lady. I felt that we were congenial spirits, and had a lot to tell each other.

For she and I are not among those who fill the mind with garbage; we make a better use of that divine and adorable endowment. We invite Thought to share, and by sharing to enhance, the pleasures of the delicate senses; we distil, as it were, an elixir from our goldenest moments, keeping out of the shining crucible of consciousness everything that tastes sour.

流行病、癌症、肺结核，以及税收。

我旁边不远处坐着一位小个子老太太，心平气和地喝着茶，不参与这场忧郁大合唱。“嗯，我得说，”她开口道，转身向我，声音低低的，“我得说我很享受生活。”

“我也是。”我悄悄说道。

“享受什么时，”她继续说，“我心里清楚。饮食，比如说，还有阳光、我夜里焐的热水袋。其他人老是想些不愉快的事情。”

“差别就在这里。”她加了一句，说着起身要同那些人离去。

“世间差别全在这里！”我答道。

炼金之术

太可惜了，没机会同这位老太太晤谈得久一些。我觉得我们俩灵犀相通，有很多话可以彼此交流。

因为她和我都不是那种人，心中塞满了垃圾；我们把这可敬可爱的天赋灵性用得更好。我们邀请思想来分享，通过分享来加强微妙的感官带来的愉悦；我们犹如从最辉煌的黄金时刻提炼出一种不老的妙药，不让意识这一锃亮的坩埚沾一点酸溜溜的东西。

I do wish that we could have discussed at greater length, like two Alchemists, the theory and practice of our art.

The Ear-Trumpet

They were talking of people I did not know. 'How do they spend their time there?' someone asked.

Then I, who had been sitting too long silent, lifted up my voice. 'Ah, that's a mysterious question, when you think of it, how people spend their time. We only see them after all in glimpses; but what, I often wonder, do they do in their hushed and shrouded hours—in all the mysterious interstices of their lives?'

'In the what?'

'In the times, I mean, when no one sees them. In the intervals.'

'But that isn't the word you used?'

'It's the same thing—the interstices—'

Of course there was a deaf lady present. 'What did you say?' she inquired, holding out her ear-trumpet for my answer.

Guilt

What should I think of? I asked myself as I opened my

我真希望我们能更加周详地谈谈，就像两位炼金师那样，讨论一下我们这门艺术的理论与实践。

号角状助听筒

他们在谈些我不认识的人。“他们在那里是怎么打发时间的呢？”有人问。

我在一旁干坐太久，便扬声说道：“啊，这个问题可玄乎了，你想想看，人们是怎么打发时间的。毕竟我们看人，每次无非是一瞥而过的见识；但我常常思忖，他们不声不响、行踪隐秘的时候，在干什么呢——我是说在他们生活中所有那些神秘的暇隙中？”

“在什么？”

“在那些时分，我的意思是，当没有人看到他们时。在这样的空当儿。”

“但这可不是你刚才用的那个词啊？”

“是一回事——暇隙——”

没错，在场有一位女士耳背。“你刚才说什么来着？”她探问，手持她的助听筒伸过来等我的回答。

愧疚

我该想些什么呢？我一边问自己，一边撑开雨伞。我该让自

umbrella. How should I occupy my imagination that harsh, dusky, sloshy, winter afternoon, as I walked to Bedford Square? Should I think of Arabia or of exotic birds; of Albatrosses, or of those great Condors who sleep on their outspread wings in the high blue air above the Andes?

But a sense of guilt oppressed me. What had I done, or left undone? And the shadowy figures that seemed to menace and pursue me? Yes, I had wronged them; it was again those Polish Poets, it was Mickiewicz, Slowacki, Szymonowicz, Krasicki, Kochanowski; —and I had never read one word of all their works!

Cadogan Gardens

Out of the fog a dim figure accosted me. 'I beg your pardon, Sir, but could you tell me how to get to Cadogan Gardens?'

'Cadogan Gardens? I am afraid I am lost myself. Perhaps, Sir,' I added (we two seemed oddly intimate in that white world of mystery together), 'perhaps, Sir, you can tell me where I can find the Gardens I am looking for?' I breathed their name.

'Hesperian Gardens?' the voice repeated. 'I don't think I have ever heard of Hesperian Gardens.'

'Oh, surely!' I cried, 'the Gardens of the Sunset and the singing Maidens!'

己的想象力忙些什么呢，在这个阴冷、昏暗、泥泞的冬日下午，人走在去贝德福德广场[57]的路上？我是不是该去想阿拉伯，或者什么异域珍禽；想信天翁，还是那些身形硕大的南美神鹰，在安第斯山上空高高的蓝天中安睡在自己舒展的双翼上？

但是有一阵愧疚感压在心头。有什么我做了，或者该做而未做？影影绰绰的还有那些人似乎逼过来追着我？对了，我亏欠了他们；还是那些波兰诗人，密茨凯维奇、斯沃瓦茨基、斯基莫诺维兹、克拉西茨基、科哈诺夫斯基[58]；——这些人的作品我一个字都没读过！

卡多根花园[59]

从雾中出来个模糊的人影跟我搭讪。“对不起，先生，可否告诉我如何去卡多根花园？”

“卡多根花园？我怕我自己也迷路了。也许，先生，”我补充道（在这个神秘的白色世界中我们两人走在一起似乎很奇怪地亲近起来），“也许，先生，你知道我在找的花园在哪里？”我轻声说出花园的名字。

“金苹果圣园[60]？”那声音重复了一下，“我想我从来没听说过金苹果圣园。”

“啊，当然有！”我高声说，“日落与欢歌少女之园！”

The Rescue

As I sat there, hopeless, with my coat and hat on in my bedroom, I felt I had no hold on life, no longer the slightest interest in it. To gain all that the world can give I would not have raised a listless finger; and it was entirely without intention that I took a cigarette, and felt for matches in my pocket. It was the act of an automaton, of a corpse that twitches a little after life has left it.

But when I found that I hadn't any matches, that—hang it! —there wasn't a box of matches anywhere, then, with this vexation, life came flooding back—the warm, familiar sense of my own existence, with all its exasperation, its irrevocable charm.

The Epitaph

'But perhaps he is a friend of yours?' said my lips: 'Is it safe?' my eyes asked. 'Dare I tell you how awful I think him?'

It was safe; only silence fell upon them, those Sad Ones, who at my decease should murmur, 'He never said an unkind word of anyone.'

'Alas, Farewell!' breathed, as it faded, that boyish day-dream of my Funeral.

解救

我坐在那里，万念俱灰，身穿外衣头戴帽子坐在卧室中，感觉对生活毫无把握，不再有一点点兴趣。就是世界把能给的都给我，我也无精打采懒得动一根手指去要；完全是毫无目的地，我掏出一根香烟，在口袋里摸火柴。无心自动，就像一具尸体在生命离去之后的几下抽搐。

但是等我发现没有火柴，发现——岂有此理！——哪儿都找不到一盒火柴，不禁怒从心头起，生命潮水般涌了回来——那种温暖的、熟悉的自我存在感，带着它所有的懊恼，还有它挡不住的魅力。

墓志铭

“但他也许是你的朋友？”我的嘴唇说。“妥当吗？”我的眼睛问，“我敢跟你说我觉得他有多坏吗？”

很妥当；只有沉默盖下来，笼罩住那些伤心人，他们在我去世时应该会喃喃说一声：“他从来没讲过谁一句坏话。”

“唉呀，永别了！”呼出了这一句话，随它飘散的，是关于我自己葬礼的这场孩子气的白日梦。

The Popes of Rome

I love to lie in bed and read the lives of the Popes of Rome. I think I could read for ever the biographies of those Pontiffs. For while I am absorbed in the goings-on of one Innocent or Pius, the Pope before him fades away; the earlier Vicars of Christ have all vanished from my failing memory; I am ready to read anew, with ever-renewed astonishment, the outrageous doings of those holy and obstinate old men.

Charm

'Speaking of Charm,' I said, 'there is one quality which I find very attractive, though most people don't notice it, and rather dislike it if they do. That quality is Observation. You read of it in eighteenth-century books— "a Man of much Observation," they say. So few people,' I went on, 'really notice anything—they live in theories and thin dreams, and look at you with unseeing eyes. They take no real interest in the real world; but the Observers I speak of find it a source of inexhaustible fascination. Nothing escapes them; they can tell at once what the people they meet are like, where they belong, their profession, the kind of houses they live in. The slightest thing is enough for them to judge by—a tone of voice, a gesture, the way they put their hats on.'

罗马教皇

我喜欢躺在床上阅读一个个罗马教皇的生平，觉得这些教皇们的传记我可以永远读下去。因为我一沉浸在哪位号称“庇护”或者圣洁“意诺增爵”几世的行状时，他之前的那个教皇便就淡去；更早的基督之代表则全都从我逐渐衰退的记忆中消失了。我愿意重新开始，带着常读常新的惊奇，阅读这些神圣又固执的老头荒唐无道的作为。

魅力

“谈到魅力，”我说，“有一种品质我发现非常吸引人，虽然大多数人没注意到，注意到了也很不喜欢。那种品质就是观察力。你在十八世纪的书上可以读到——‘一个颇具观察力的人。’他们说。太少人，”我接着说，“真正注意到什么——他们活在理论中，活在虚梦中，看着你又视而不见。他们对真实的世界没有真正的兴趣；但我说的那种具观察力的人却发现这世界是一个取之不尽的魅力之源。什么都逃不过他们的眼睛；一看就说得出见到的是什么样的人，何方神圣，干的哪一行，住的哪一种房子。一点蛛丝马迹便足以让他们做出判断——一个声调、一个手势，或者戴帽子的动作。”

'I always judge people,' one of the company remarked, 'by their shoes. It's people's feet I look at first. And shoe-laces now—what an awful lot shoe-laces can tell you!'

As I slipped my feet back under my chair, I subjected to a rapid reconsideration my notion of Charm.

The Concerto

'What a beautiful movement!' she murmured, as the music paused.

'Lovely!' I roused myself to echo, though I hadn't heard a note.

Immediately I found myself again in the dock; and again the trial began, that ever-recurring criminal Action in which I am both Judge and culprit, all the jury, and the advocate on either side.

I now pleaded my other respectable attainments and general good character; and then dropped back into my dream, letting the violins wail unheard through the other movements, and the Grand Piano tinkle.

Somewhere

Somewhere, far below the horizon, there is a City; some

"我判断人总是，"同伴中有一个说，"看穿的鞋子。我最先看的是脚。现在是看鞋带——小小鞋带大有文章！"

我一边暗暗把脚缩回到椅子底下，一边不得不飞快地重新考虑起自己的魅力观。

协奏曲

"多美的乐章啊！"音乐暂停时她喃喃说道。

"很好听！"我打起精神附和道，尽管我一个音符都没听进去。

旋即我发现自己又进了被告席；庭审又开始了，在那场反复不断的刑事诉讼中我既是法官又是犯人，还是全体陪审团，以及双方的辩护律师。

我一会儿以自己在其他方面足以称道的成就和整体的优良品格申辩；一会儿又坠回我的遐思神游，听而不闻，任凭接下来的乐章中一众小提琴如何号叫，大钢琴如何叮咚作响。

有一个地方

有一个地方，远远地在地平线之下，那里有一座城市；有一天

day I shall sail to find its harbour; by what star I shall steer, or where that seaport lies, I do not know; but somehow or other through calms and storms and the sea-noises I shall voyage, until at last some mountain peak shall rise, telling me I am near my destination; or I shall see, at dusk, a lighthouse, twinkling at its port.

The Miracle

After lighting the spirit-lamp in preparation for tea she turned with her earnest eyes and gave me all her attention:

'But we have never had a real talk about serious things.' she said.

As she said it, I saw my danger; I was alone with that enthusiast, and she was going to talk to me about my Soul.

'Now help me, O ye Guardian Powers!' Thus did I invoke those more than mortal combatants who succour heroic minds in their worst extremities, aiding the pure Knight to defend his honour and life, and struggling Damsels to preserve that which is dearer to them than life itself.

Not too long was I forced to emulate those ladies; for, at the very crisis of my peril, the spirit-lamp flared up and almost exploded; the kettle was upset, and I found myself soon after in the safe street, with soul as inviolate as the mountain snow.

我将扬帆去寻找它的港湾；靠哪颗星星导航，哪里又是那海港所在，我不知道；但无论如何，或风平浪静或狂风暴雨，穿越浪涛的喧哗我将远航，直到有某座山峰终将升起，告诉我快到目的地了；或者我将看到，暮色中，一座灯塔，在它的港口闪闪发亮。

奇迹

点上酒精灯准备沏茶后，她转过头来，目光诚挚、全神贯注地看着我：

“可我们还从来没真正谈过严肃的事情呢。”她说。

听着这句话，我知道有危险了；我孤身面对这位热心人，她这就要跟我讨论我的灵魂问题。

“救救我吧，啊，各方神灵！”如此这般我呼召那些超越凡人的神兵，他们救英雄于大危大难中，助纯洁的骑士捍卫名誉和生命，帮落难少女保全那比生命还宝贵的东西。

过不了多久我就不用被迫仿效那些女士了；因为，就在我走投无路之时，酒精灯腾起烈焰差点爆炸；水壶翻了，而我一会儿就发现自己安然来到街上，灵魂如远山白雪一样未受侵犯。

The Platitude

'It's after all the little things in life that really matter!'

I was as much chagrined as they were flabbergasted by this involuntary outbreak; but I have become an expert in that Taoist art of disintegration which Yen Hui described to Confucius as 'the art of sitting and forgetting.' I have learnt to lay aside my personality in awkward moments, to dissolve this self of mine into the All Pervading; to fall back, in fact, into the universal flux, and sit, as I now sat there, a blameless lump of matter, rolled on according to the heavens' rolling, with rocks and trees.

The Fetish

Enshrined in a box of white paste-board I keep upstairs a black ceremonial object: it's my last link with Christendom and grave Custom: only on sacred occasions does it make its appearance, only at some great tribal dance of my race. To pageants of Woe I march with it, or of the hugest Felicity: at great Hallelujahs of Wedlock, or at last Valedictions, I hold it bare-headed as I bow before altars and tombs.

陈词滥调

“毕竟,生活中的小事情才重要呢!”

脱口而出的这句话,他们听了有多惊愕,我便有多懊恼;但我已经精通道家那种置身事外的分离术,就是颜回跟孔夫子说的“坐忘”之术。我学会了尴尬时将自己的人格搁置一旁,将这个自我分解化入统摄万物的天地;事实上,是回归宇宙之流动,安坐,如同我现在安坐于此,一尊无责无错的物质,随苍天的运转而流转,与山石树木相伴。

神物

我供在一个白色的纸板盒中放在楼上的,是一件黑色的礼器:那是我同基督教世界和盛典大礼的最后一线联系:只有在一些神圣的场合,只有在我这个族类某种盛大的部落舞会中,它才会现身。向着大悲,或者大喜的露天盛会我与它共同前行:在喜结良缘的哈利路亚赞美声中,在与逝者告别的悼念声中,我把它拿在手里,头部裸露朝着圣坛和坟墓鞠躬。

Things to Say

'How did you get on with Mrs. Hearse? You didn't seem to have much to say!'

'Have you ever noticed,' I asked, 'how, when you are trying to talk to people, all sorts of inappropriate things to say float by with appealing faces?'

'With me,' I went on, 'these ghosts of the unspoken are sometimes platitudes; sometimes dreadful facts; or I am deafened, as I was just now, by wicked stories, which clamour like wild beasts behind the grating of my teeth.'

The Echo

Now and then, from the other end of the table, words and phrases reached us as we talked.

'What do they mean by Complexes?' she asked.

'Oh, it's only one of the catchwords of the day,' I answered. 'Everything's a Complex just now.'

'The talk of most people,' I went on, 'is simply—how shall I put it? —simply the ticking of clocks; it marks the hour, but it has no other interest. But I like to think for myself, to be something more than a mere mouthpiece—a mere sounding-board and echo of contemporary chatter.'

'Just listen!' I said, as again their voices reached our ears.

欲言……

“你跟荷尔斯太太相处得怎样？你们好像没什么话好说！”

“你可曾注意到，”我问，“想要跟人说什么时，各种各样难以启齿的情事会怎样以一副副媚人的面孔从眼前飘过？”

“就我而言，”我接着说，“这些没有说出口的幽灵有时是些陈词滥调，有时是吓人的实情；或者，就像刚才，丑闻坏事震得我耳聋，只觉得它们像野兽一般在我牙齿的两排栅栏后嘶吼着。”

回音

不时地，在我们聊天时，从桌那头会传过来只言片语。

“他们说的‘情结’是什么意思？”她问。

“哦，只是当今一个时髦词罢了，”我回答，“如今什么都是‘情结’。”

“大多数人的话，”我继续说，“只不过——该怎么说呢？——只不过是时钟的嘀嗒声而已；除了报时辰，没别的意味。但我喜欢自己去思考，不能只当他人喉舌——当一块增音板，成为时下清谈的回音。”

“你听！”我说，桌那头的声音又传到我们耳朵里。

'It's simply one of the catchwords of the day,' someone was shouting, 'the merest echo of contemporary chatter!'

Routine

I live by the clock; all my activities, my exits and entrances, my times for smoking cigarettes and reading murder-stories, are synchronized and set in harmony with the earth's motion and the sun's. Much more than happiness I love my habits, the timely routine and oscillation of the hours which carry me on through months and seasons. Thus my life spins silent on its axle; but at the least dislocation or jar—if the Post is late, or the Morning Paper doesn't turn up—I am giddy, I am undone; the ground rocks beneath my feet.

The Scavenger

'The parlour-maid and cook both gave notice——'

'My stomach is not at all what it should be——'

'Of course the telephone was out of order——'

'The coal they sent was all stones and coal-dust——'

'All the electric wiring has had to be renewed——'

'I find it impossible to digest potatoes——'

'My aunt has had to have eighteen of her teeth

“只不过是当今一个时髦词罢了，”有个谁在大声说，“充其量不过是时下清谈的一声回音罢了！”

起居成规

我按照钟点生活；一切活动，上落进出、抽烟喝茶、看凶杀小说，全都搭配有序，与地球和太阳的运转协调同步。我爱我的习惯远胜过爱喜乐，那有条不紊的成规，那一小时一小时的往返交替，带着我过了一月又一月，一季又一季。就这样，我的生活静静地绕着它的轴心自传；但只要有一点点脱节或者颠簸——要是邮件来迟了，或者早报没送到——我便昏昏然，失魂落魄的；地面都在脚下晃动起来。

收垃圾的

“客厅女仆和厨子都提出辞呈了——”

“我的胃真是不行了——”

“可不是，电话坏了——”

“送来的煤全是石块和煤屑——”

“电线全部都得换新的——”

“我发觉消化不了马铃薯——”

“我姑妈得把十八颗牙齿拔掉——”

extracted——'

Am I nothing but a dust-bin or kitchen sink for other people's troubles?

Have I no agonies, no indigestions of my own?

The Hot-Bed

It was too much; the news in the paper was appalling; Central Europe and the Continent of Asia in a state of chaos; no comfort anywhere; tempests in the Channel, earthquakes, famines, strikes, insurrections. The burden of the mystery, the weight of all this incorrigible world—this theatre of man's baseness—was really more than I could cope with.

'To prepare a hot-bed for early vegetables, equal quantities are taken of horse-manure and fallen leaves; a large heap is built in alternate layers,' I read with passionate interest, 'of these materials; it is left for several days, and then turned over. The site of the hot-bed must be sheltered from cold winds, but open to the sunshine. Early and dwarf varieties of potatoes should be chosen; asparagus plants may be dug up from the open garden——'

Aphasia

'But you haven't spoken a word—you ought to tell us what

难道我什么都不是，只是个垃圾桶、洗碗槽，用来给人装烦恼的吗？

难道我自己就没有糟心事，不会消化不良吗？

温床

受不了了；报纸上的新闻不忍卒读；中欧和亚洲大陆乱成一团；世上无一安生之处；英吉利海峡的风暴，还有那些地震、饥荒、罢工、暴乱。天意莫测的重负，还有人世——在在上演着人性卑劣的这个世界——那无可救药的沉疴，真的让我应付不了。

“为蔬菜幼苗准备温床，取等量马粪与枯叶；两样材料分层交替摞成一大堆；”我读得津津有味，“放置若干天之后再将其翻转。温床位置必须避风向阳。务必选用矮种马铃薯幼苗；芦笋苗株可以从露天园地挖来——”

失语症

“但你一句话都没说——你总得告诉我们你的想法啊。”

you think.'

'The truth is,' I whispered in her unaverted ear, 'the truth is, I talk too much. Think of all the years I have been wagging my tongue; think how I shall go on wagging it, till it is smothered in dust! '

'And the worst of it is,' I went on hoarsely whispering, 'the horror is that no one understands me; I can never make clear to anyone my view of things. I may talk till I am black in the face, and no one will ever know—I shall go down to the grave—and no one will know what I mean.'

Mrs. Backe

Mrs. Backe would be down in a few minutes, so I waited in the drawing-room of this new acquaintance who had so kindly invited me, to tea.

It is indiscreet, but I cannot help it; if I am left alone in a room, I cannot help peering about at the ornaments and books. The habitations people make for their souls interest me like sea-shells, or the nests of birds.

'A lover of Switzerland,' I inferred, 'has travelled in the East—the complete works of Canon Farrar; —that big bust with whiskers is Mendelssohn, no doubt. Good heavens! a stuffed cat! And that Moorish plaque is rather awful. Still, many of the nicest people have no taste——'

“实情是，”我对着她没避开的一边耳朵低声说，“实情是，我说得太多。想想这些年来我都在磨嘴皮子；想想我还要磨下去，磨到被土尘堵上！”

“最糟糕的是，”我声音沙哑地继续低声说道，“可怕的是没有人理解我；我根本无法和谁说得清我对事物的看法。我可以说到脸色发黑，也绝不会有人听明白的——我将要进坟墓的——也没有人会明白我说的啥。”

巴克太太

巴克太太等几分钟后会下来，我便在这位新交朋友家的客厅里等着，她一番美意邀请我来共进茶点。

这么做很失礼，但我还是忍不住；如果留我独自在一个房间里，我便会忍不住窥视房里的装饰品和藏书。人们为自己的灵魂营造的居所让我感兴趣，一如海边的贝壳和树上的鸟窝。

“喜欢瑞士，”我推想，“在东方旅行过——法拉尔牧师[61]著作全集；——那尊络腮胡子的大半身像是门德尔松[62]无疑。天哪！一个填制的猫标本！那块摩尔人[63]牌匾很是讨人嫌。算了吧，很多大好人没有好品位——”

Then I saw the clock—the pink china clock with the face of a monkey. Softly I stole from the room and downstairs, and closed the front-door for ever behind me.

Magic

'Do you think there are Ghosts?' she foamed, her eyes ablaze, 'do you believe in Magic?'

'Are you interested in etymology?' I asked. 'To my mind there is nothing more fascinating than the derivations of words; — I could spend my life just looking them up in the dictionary. That's the way to learn the wonder of real life and history. Think of *Magic*, for instance, it comes, as no doubt you know, from the Magi, or ancient priests of Persia.'

'Don't you love our deposit of Persian words in English? To me they glitter like jewels in our northern speech. *Magic* and *Paradise*, for instance; and the names of flowers and gems and rich fruits and tissues—*Tulip* and *Lilac* and *Jasmin* and *Peach* and *Lapis Lazuli*,' I chanted, 'and *Azure* and *Taffeta* and *Scarlet*.'

Fame

Somewhat furtively I bowed in Knightsbridge to the new Moon; the little ceremony was no doubt a survival of prehistoric

然后我看到了那个座钟——那个粉红色的瓷钟，钟面是个猴子脸。悄悄地，我从房间里溜出来下了楼梯，转身把前门在我身后永远地关上了。

魔法

“你说有鬼吗？”她说得唾沫四溅，两眼发光，“你相信魔法吗？”

“你对语源学感兴趣吗？”我问，“对我来说没有什么比追寻词语衍生更令人着迷了；——我可以一辈子就这么在词典里查下去。这是了解真实生活和历史之奇妙的不二法门。想想那称为‘魔法’的Magic，比如说，就来自，你无疑是知道的，来自Magi，说的是东方三博士，或者古波斯的祭司。”

“你难道不喜欢我们英语中积存的波斯语词吗？在我看来这就像闪亮的宝石映嵌在我们这北方的语言中。比如，说‘魔法’的Magic和‘天堂’的Paradise；还有花、珠宝、五花八门的水果和织品的名称——‘郁金香’的Tulip和‘紫丁香’的Lilac，还有‘茉莉’的Jasmin、‘桃子’的Peach、‘青金石’的Lapis Lazuli，”我吟哦着，“还有‘天蓝’的Azure、‘塔夫绸’的Taffeta、‘深红色’的Scarlet。”

名声

有些偷偷摸摸地，我在骑士桥[64]向新月鞠了一躬；这小小仪

feelings, but the Wish that I breathed was an inheritance from a later epoch. It was an echo of Greece and Rome, the ideal ambition of their poets and heroes; the thought of it seemed to float through the air in starlight and music; I saw in a bright constellation those stately Immortals, their names rang in my ears.

'May I, too, —' I whispered incredulous, as I lifted my hat to the Moon.

News-Items

In spite of the delicacy of my moral feelings, and my unrelaxed solicitude for the maintenance of the right principles of conduct, I find I can read without tears of the retired Colonels who forge cheques, and the ladies of unexceptionable position who are caught pilfering furs in shops. Somehow the sudden lapses of respected people, odd indecorums, backbitings, bigamies, embezzlements, and attempted chastities—the surprising leaps they make now and then out of propriety into the police-courts—somehow news-items of this kind do not altogether—how shall I put it? —well, they don't absolutely blacken the sunshine for me.

And Clergymen? If a Clergyman slips up, do not, I pray you, gentle Reader, grieve, on my account, too much——

式无疑是残存的一点史前情感，但是我悄声许下的愿望却是其后一个时代的余绪。那是古希腊和古罗马的一个回声，是当时诗人和英雄们理想的志向；那份情怀似乎透过空气飘在星光与音乐中；我在一个明亮的星座里看到那些庄严的不朽之身，他们的名字回响在我的耳畔。

“但愿我，也能，——”我一边轻声说，将信将疑地，一边扬起帽子对着月亮欠了欠身。

新闻

尽管我道德情操敏锐周全，毫不松懈地秉持待人处事该有的原则，我发现自己能眼不带泪地读着退役上校伪造支票、极为体面的淑女在店里偷皮草被抓这样的新闻。不知何故，可敬之人突然有失检点、怪诞无品、两面三刀、重婚出轨、盗用公款、强暴未遂——时不时那些出乎意料的失足令他们跌破法纪掉进法庭——不知何故这种新闻并不会完全——我该怎么说呢？——嗯，并不会绝对遮住我的阳光。

牧师们呢？如果有哪位牧师误入歧途，不要，我求求你们，读者诸君，不要伤心，看在我的分上，不要伤心太过——

Whiskers

There was once a young man who thought he saw Life as it really is; who prided himself on looking at it grimly in the face without illusions. And he went on looking at it grimly, as he thought, for a good many years. This was his notion of himself; but one day, meeting some very young people, he saw, reflected as it were in their eyes, a bland old gentleman with a white waistcoat and Victorian whiskers, a lover of souls and sunsets, and noble solutions for all problems——

That was what he saw in the eyes of those atrocious young men.

The Spelling Lesson

The incident which had caused the laughter of those youngsters was not a thing to joke about. I expressed my conviction briefly; but the time-honoured word I made use of seemed unfamiliar to them; —they looked at each other and began whispering together. Then one of them asked in a hushed voice, 'It's *what*, did you say?'

I repeated my monosyllable loudly.

Again they whispered together, and again their spokesman came forward.

'Do you mind telling us how you spell it?'

络腮胡须

曾经有个年轻人，觉得自己看透生活，很自豪能凛然直面人生而不存幻想。他继续凛然地，就他以为，逼视了人生好多年。那是他的自我认定；但是有一天，遇见一些年纪非常轻的人，他看到，可以说映在这些年轻人眼中的，是一个干巴巴的老绅士，身穿白色马甲，蓄着维多利亚时代的连鬓胡须，钟爱灵魂与夕阳，以及高而雅之地解决一切问题——

这就是他在那些顽劣的小青年眼中所看到的。

单词拼写课

这事让那班小年轻发笑，但这可是不能闹着玩儿的一件事。我简短地说了我的评判；但我用的那个沿用经久的单词他们似乎并不熟悉；——只见他们面面相觑，交头接耳起来。接着有一人压低声音问道："是什么，您说的？"

我把这个单音节词大声重复了一遍。

他们又窃窃私语开来，那个代言人又走上前。

"您可以告诉我们这个词怎么拼写吗？"

'I spell it, I spell it with a W!' I shouted. 'W-W-R-O-N-G—WRONG!'

At the Club

'It's the result of Board School Education——'

'It's the popular Press——'

'It's the selfishness of the Working Classes——'

'It's the Cinema——'

'It's the Jews——'

'Paid Agitators!——'

'The decay of Faith——'

'The disintegration of Family Life——'

'I put it down,' I said, 'to Sun-spots. If you want to know,' I went inexorably on, 'if you ask me the cause of all this modern Unrest——'

Delay

I was late for breakfast this morning, for I had been delayed in my heavenly hot bath by the thought of all the other Earnest Thinkers, who, at that very moment—I had good reason to believe it—were soaking the time away in hot baths all over London.

“我拼出来，我用个W拼出来！”我大喊，“W-W-R-O-N-G——WRONG，一个字：‘错’！”

俱乐部里

“这是寄宿学校教育的结果——”

“是通俗出版物——”

“是劳工阶级的自私——”

“是电影——”

“是犹太人——”

“用钱雇的煽动者！——”

“信仰的堕落——”

“家庭生活的解体——”

“我将之归咎于，”我说，“太阳黑子。如果你们想知道，”我不由分说地讲下去，“假如你们问我现代所有这些动乱的原因何在——”

耽搁

今天早餐吃迟了，耽搁的原因是我在舒服无比的热水中泡澡，想起了所有其他那些认真的思想家，此时此刻，伦敦上下——我完全有理由相信——都在澡盆中把时间泡掉。

Smiles

When people smile to themselves in the street, when I see the face of an ugly man or uninteresting woman light up (faces, it would seem, not exactly made for happy smiling), I wonder from what visions within those smiles are reflected; from what footlights, what gay and incredible scenes, do they gleam of vain glory?

The Pear

'But every one in Bloomsbury is enthusiastic about the book!' I protested.

'Well, what if they are?' was the answer.

I too am a Superior Person, but the predicament was awkward. To figure as the dupe of a vulgar admiration, to be caught crying stale fish at a choice luncheon party!

'Oh, of course!' I hit back, 'I know it's considered the thing just now to despise the taste of the age one lives in. No one, even in Balham, will admit that they have read the books of the day. But my attitude has always been' (what had it been? I had to think in a hurry) 'I have always felt that it was more interesting, after all, to belong to one's own epoch: to share its dated and unique vision, that flying glimpse of the great panorama which no subsequent generation can ever recapture. To be Elizabethan

微笑

当人们在街上自顾自地微笑，当我看到一个丑陋的男人或者一个乏味的女人脸上粲然一笑（那些脸，似乎并非生来就是为了开心欢笑），我就纳闷，是什么内心景象在那些笑容中反映出来；打的是什么脚灯，是从什么欢悦又难以置信的场景，它们闪烁出虚华的荣光？

梨子

“但是在布卢姆茨伯里[65]，每个人对这本书都喜爱有加呢！”我不服。

“嗯，喜爱又怎样？”对方答道。

我也不是等闲之辈，但眼前的窘境还是令人尴尬。不小心就成了个品味低俗的傻乎乎的崇拜者，就像在精致的午餐会上高喊臭鱼一样丢人现眼！

“哦，当然了！”我还击过去，“我知道眼下时髦的是鄙视自己所生活的这个时代的品味。没有人，即使在巴勒姆[66]，会承认读过当今出的书。但是我的态度向来是”（什么态度？我得赶紧想想）“我从来都觉得更有意思的，毕竟是，归属于自己的时代：分享它打上时间印记的独一无二的愿景、它恢宏的全景那飞闪而过的一瞥，这一切将来没有哪一代能再度领略。在伊丽莎白时代就得是

in the age of Elizabeth; romantic at the height of the Romantic Movement——'

But it was no good: I saw it was no good, so I took a large pear and ate it in silence.

I know a good deal about pears, and am particularly fond of them. This one was a *Doyenné du Comice*, the most delicious of all.

The Dawn

My imagination has its dancing-places, like the Dawn in Homer; there are terraces, with balustrades and marble fountains on them, where Ideal Beings smile as I draw near; there are ilex-groves and beech trees under which I hold forth for ever; gardens fairer than most earthly gardens where groups of ladies never grow weary of listening to my voice.

Insomnia

Sometimes, when I am cross and cannot sleep, I engage in angry contests with the Opinions I object to. Into the room they flop, those bat-like monsters of Wrong-Belief and Darkness; and though they glare at me with the daylight faces of bullying talkers, and their voices are the voices that shout me down in argument, yet, in these nocturnal controversies, it is always my

伊丽莎白的范儿；在浪漫主义的高潮就得浪漫——”

但是没有用：我看出没有用，于是拿起一个大梨子，不说话径自吃起来。

我对梨子知道得很多，也特别喜欢吃梨。这一个是*Doyenné du Comice*，世纪梨，最好吃的那种。

黎明

我的想象力有它的欢舞之地，就像荷马诗中的黎明；那里有庭院露台，上有栏杆扶手、玉石喷泉。在那里，理想之人微笑着看我走近前来；那里有榉木林和冬青树丛，我站在树下滔滔不绝高论不止；那里的花园之美，少有尘世园林可比，园中有成群结队的淑女，我的声音她们百听不厌。

失眠

有的时候，我生气睡不着，便会跟我所反对的那些意见狠狠较量一番。扑腾着闯进房来的，是那些蝙蝠怪般的歪理和暗黑的邪念；虽然它们盯着我，顶着白天里说话人那一副副欺人太甚的面孔，声音也是争论中把我压倒的那些大嗓门，但是，在这些夜间

assertions which admit no answer.

I do not spare them; it is now their turn to be lashed to fury; made to eat their words.

Reading Philosophy

'The abstractedness of the relation brings to consciousness no less strongly the foreignness of the Idea to natural phenomena. In its widest formulation—'; mechanically I turned the page, but what on earth was it all about? Some Fancy must have been fluttering between my spectacles and book.

I turned and caught that pretty Daydream. To be a Wit—yes, while my eyes were reading Hegel, I had stolen out myself to amaze the world with my epigrams. Each conversation at its most breathless moment I had crowned with words of double meaning which had echoed all through Chelsea. Feared all my life-time for my repartees, when my ashes had been swept at last into an urn of moderate dimensions, I had still lived on the lips of men; still my plays on words had been laughed at, my sayings handed down in memoirs to ensuing ages.

Moral Triumph

When I see motors gliding up at night to great houses in

的争辩中，总是我的话斩钉截铁、强嘴不得。

我不依不饶；现在轮到它们被大举挞伐气得直跳脚，词穷之下唯有认错。

读哲学

"关系的提取性同样强烈地带给意识的是理念对于自然现象的外来性。在其最宽泛的构式中——"机械地，我翻过这一页，但这到底说的什么？刚才必定有什么幻想在我的眼镜和书页之间晃动。

我转身逮住了那个可爱的白日梦。做个智者——没错，眼睛一边在读着黑格尔，我人却一边偷溜了出来用我的警句让世人叫绝。每逢交谈到了最令人翘首屏息的一刻，我便用了一语双关的言辞为其加冕，让整个切尔西[67]一时间回声朗朗。这一辈子人们都怕我的话中机锋，等骨灰终于被扫进一个尺寸中等的陶罐时，我仍然活在人们的唇舌间；我的文字游戏仍然供人哂笑，我的格言也在回忆录中传于后世。

道德胜利

看到汽车在晚间翩翩然驶往那些时髦广场上的豪宅时，我便

the fashionable squares, I journey in them: I ascend the stairways of those palaces; and, ushered with éclat into drawing-rooms of splendour, I sun myself in the painted smiles of Mayfair Jezebels, and in that world of rouge and diamonds, I glitter like a star. There I quaff the elixir and sweet essence of mundane triumph, eating truffles to the sound of trumpets, and feasting at sunrise on lobster-salad and champagne.

But it's all dust, it's all emptiness and ashes. Ah! far away from there I retire into the desert or the cloister to contend with Demons; to overcome in holy combats unspeakable Temptations, and purify, by prodigious purges, my heart of base desire.

The Springs of Action

What am I? What is Man?

I had looked into a number of books for an answer to this problem, before I came on Jeremy Bentham's simple and satisfactory solution: Man is a mechanism, moved by just so many springs of Action. These springs he enumerates in elaborate tables; and glancing over them this morning before getting up, I began with *Charity*, *All-embracing Benevolence*, *Love of Knowledge*, *Laudable Ambition*, *Godly Zeal*. Then I waited, but there was no buzz of any wheel beginning to move in my inner mechanism. I looked again: I saw *Arrogance*, *Ostentation*, *Vainglory*, *Abomination*, *Rage*, *Fury*, *Revenge*; and I

是车里人去走一回：我登上那些宫殿的楼梯；在一片赞叹声中让人引进金碧辉煌的客厅，日光浴般沉浸在梅菲尔名媛贵妇的脂粉笑面中，在那个粉黛与宝石的世界中，我璀璨如一颗星。在那里，我畅饮俗世荣华酿就的仙液琼浆，啖着松露听管乐，日出时分就着香槟饱餐龙虾沙拉。

但这一切无非是尘泥，无非是虚空与浮灰。啊！远远地我从那里退回，退入沙漠或灵修之地去同魔鬼争战；在神圣的战斗中征服难以启齿的诱惑，洁净自己，酣畅淋漓地荡涤内心下作的欲念。

行动发条种种

我是什么？人是什么？

我查了许多书想找答案，最终在杰里米·边沁[68]那里找到了既简单又令人满意的答案：人是一种机械结构，无非由这么多的行动发条驱动。这些发条他精细地列表枚举。今早起床前我浏览了一下，开始是“慈善”“无所不包的仁爱”“对知识的喜爱”“值得赞赏的雄心”“虔诚的热心”。然后我等着，可是并没有什么轮子在我内里的机械结构中转动的声音。我又瞧了一眼，看到“骄傲”“炫耀”“虚荣”“憎恨”“愤怒”“狂暴”“复仇”；怀着火

was about to leap out of bed in a paroxysm of dreadful passions, when fortunately my eye fell on another set of motives: *Love of Ease, Indolence, Procrastination, Sloth.*

In the Cage

'What I say is, what I say!' I vociferate, as—a Parrot in the great cage of the World—I hop screeching, 'What I say is!' from perch to perch.

Voices

'You smoke too much!' whispers the still small voice of Conscience .

'You are a failure, nobody likes you,' Self-contempt keeps muttering.

'What's the good of it all?' sighs Disillusion, arid as a breath from the Sahara.

I can't tell you how these Voices bore me; but I can listen all day with grave attention to that suave bosom-Jesuit who keeps on unweariedly proving that all my acts and appetites and inclinations are in the most amazing harmony with the dictates of the Moral Law.

爆的激情，我这就要一跃跳下床时，幸好眼光落到另外一套动机上：“喜爱安逸”“慵懒”“拖延”“懈怠”。

笼中

“我说的就是，我所说的！”我大叫，就像——一只鹦鹉困在了世界这个大鸟笼内——我一边叫着“我说的就是！”，一边在一根根栖木上跳来跳去。

声音

“你烟抽得太多了！”良知低语道，声音还是小小的。

“你这窝囊废，人见人厌。”自轻自贱在不断嘟哝着。

“这都有什么用呢？”幻灭叹息道，干巴巴地像一丝撒哈拉吹来的风。

我无法告诉你这些声音有多烦人；但是我可以认真严肃听一整天那位和颜悦色的耶稣会朋友的知心话，听他不厌其烦地证明我的行为、欲念、嗜好无不与道德律的制约非常惊人地合拍。

Complacency

Dove-grey and harmless as a dove, full of piety and innocence and pure thoughts, my Soul brooded unaffectedly within me; —I was only half listening to that shrill conversation. And I began to wonder, as more than once in moments like this I have wondered, whether I might not be something more, after all, than a mere echo or compilation—could not claim, in fact, to possess a personality of my own.

Might it not be worth while, I now asked myself, to follow up this pleasing conjecture; to retire like Descartes from the world, and spend the rest of life, as he spent it, trying to prove my own existence?

The Rationalist

Occultisms, incantations, glimpses of the Beyond, intimations from another world—all kinds of supernaturalisms are most distasteful to me; I cling to the known world of explicable phenomena; and I was much put out to find this morning a cabalistic inscription written in letters of large menace on my bath-room floor. TAM HTAB—what could be the meaning of these awful words, and how on earth had they got there? Like Belshazzar, my thoughts were troubled by this writing, and my knees smote one against the other; till majestic Reason, deigning

自得

灰色如鸽，温良如鸽，满怀虔诚、纯真、无邪的念头，我的灵魂正声色不动地在我的内心孵化；——我只是入耳不入心地听着那场尖声交谈罢了。我也开始纳闷，不止一次碰到这种情形我都纳闷过：我可不可以，到头来，不只是个应声虫或者由人编排的东西——难道不能声称，事实上，我拥有一个自己的人格？

难道不值得吗，我在问自己，追随这个愉快的推想；就像笛卡儿[69]那般退隐避世，试将余生，如他那样，用来证明我自己的存在？

理性主义者

神秘主义、魔法咒语、窥探未知、来自另一世界的暗示——凡此种种超自然主义我都深恶痛绝；我紧拽着的是由可解释的现象组成的已知世界；可今天早上让我心烦意乱的是发现有一组犹太神秘哲学那样的文字，凶神恶煞般赫然写在我浴室的地板上。TAM HTAB——这些吓人的字母会是什么意思呢？究竟是怎么跑到那里去的？就像伯沙撒[70]，我让这一行字母弄得心神不宁，双腿打战；直到庄严的理性从她对永恒因果的思考中屈尊旁顾，

to look downward from her contemplation of eternal causes, spelt backwards for me, with a pitying smile, the homely inscription on the BATH MAT, which was lying there, wrong side up.

Phrases

Is there, after all, any solace like the solace and consolation of Language? When I am disconcerted by the unpleasing aspects of existence, when to me, as to Hamlet, this earth seems a sterile promontory, it is not in Metaphysics nor in Religion that I seek for reassurance, but in fine phrases. The thought of gazing on life's Evening Star makes of ugly old age a pleasing prospect; if I call Death mighty and unpersuaded, it has no terrors for me; I am perfectly content to be cut down as a flower, to flee as a shadow, to be swallowed like a snowflake on the sea. These similes soothe and effectually console me. I am sad only at the thought that Words must perish like all things mortal; that the most perfect Metaphors must be forgotten when the human race is dust.

'But the iniquity of Oblivion blindly scattereth her poppy.'

Athanasius

Since I have reason to believe that the age I live in is not

替我倒过来拼了一下，怜悯地微笑着，读出这个家常词语：BATH MAT，“浴垫”，摆在那里，放反了而已。

语词

毕竟，还有什么慰藉，堪比语言的安抚与慰藉？当我因生存的不顺意而心乱，当看在我眼里，就像看在哈姆雷特眼里那样，这个地球似乎是一个寸草不长的海角，这时，既不是在形而上学也不是在宗教那里我寻求安慰，而是在美妙的语词中。眺望生命的晚星，这么一想难看不堪的老境便成了一道愉快的风景；要是我说死神强大顽梗，它可一点也吓不着我；我毫无遗憾，哪天像一朵花般被剪下来，像一道影子般逃去如飞，像一片雪花般被大海吞没。这些比喻安抚着我，确实让我宽心释怀。让我伤心的只是想到语词必定会消亡，与凡间万物无异；想到最完美的比喻，也必定会被忘记，随着人类化作尘土。

“但遗忘不公不义，盲目地把她的罂粟花挥撒。”[71]

圣亚他那修信经[72]

既然我有理由相信自己所处的并非一个黄金时代，也很不指

an Age of Gold, and am quite disenchanted of all hope that the earth will turn to Paradise at present, I have abandoned the supervision of public occurrences, and given over the helm and pilotage of the Ship of State to other hands. Concerned no longer with the fate of the Empire and the Universe, and quite undistracted by the supposed onrush of all things to darkness and the dogs, I sit at home and ruminate on the qualities of certain little books like this one—little elixirs of perfection, full of subtlety and sadness—which I can read and read again.

Although my taste in letters is by now, I must believe, almost absolutely flawless, yet conceivably, in some minute particulars, I may polish and improve it; that thus—zealous, like all the elect to narrow the privilege of Salvation—I may promulgate, and if necessary maintain alone against the world an Athanasian creed of literary judgements, which whosoever shall not keep pure and undefiled, without doubt he shall perish everlastingly.

Ask me no more

Where are the snows of yesteryear? Ask me no more the fate of Roses, or of Nightingales, or where the old Moons go, or what becomes of last year's Oxford poets.

望人间现在能变天堂，便也就放弃了对公共事务的监督，将国家之巨轮的掌舵和领航交于他人。不再关心帝国和宇宙的命运，也很没心思搭理人说的滔滔万物如何争相堕落坠入黑暗，我坐在家中反复咀嚼细品某些小书的风味特质，就像这一本——一份份至美的小小灵药，饱含婉妙与哀伤——我可以一读而再读。

尽管我的文字品味到现在，我必须相信，几乎是无可挑剔，然而可以想见，在某些细微奇特处，我仍可推敲改善；于是乎——热心得像所有上帝选民缩聚得救的特权那样——我可以传播，必要的话还可以以一身抗万众地秉持一套文学评判的亚他那修信经，无论谁要是对其教义不诚不敬，必将万劫不复无疑。

别再问我

去年的雪在哪里？别再问我什么玫瑰花的命运、夜莺的命运了，或者旧时明月都去了哪里，或者去岁牛津的诗人们都怎样了。

Joy

Sometimes at breakfast, sometimes in a train or empty bus, or on the moving stairs at Charing Cross, I am happy; the earth turns to gold, and life becomes a magical adventure. Only yesterday, travelling alone to Sussex, I became lightheaded with this sudden joy. The train seemed to rush to its adorable destination through a world new-born in splendour, bathed in a beautiful element, fresh and clear as on the morning of Creation. Even the coloured photographs of South Coast watering-places in the railway carriage shone with the light of Paradise upon them. Brighton faced me; next to it divine Southsea beckoned; and oh, the esplanade at Ryde! Then I saw the beach at Sidmouth, the Tilly Whim caves near Swanage; —was it in those unhaunted caves, or amid the tumult of life which hums about the Worthing bandstand, that I should find Bliss in its quintessence?

Or on the pier at St. Peter Port perhaps, in the Channel Islands, amid that crowd who watch in eternal ecstasy the ever-arriving, never-disembarking Weymouth steamer?

In Arcady

When I retire from London to my rural solitudes, and taste once more, as always, those pure delights of Nature which the Poets celebrate—walks in the unambitious meadows, and

欣喜

有时在用早餐时，有时在火车或无人的巴士上，或者在查令十字[73]车站的自动扶梯上，我很快乐；大地变成金色，生活成了一场神奇的冒险。就在昨天，我一个人乘车去萨塞克斯，这突然的欣喜让我觉得眩晕。火车向它可爱的目的地疾驶，似乎在穿越一个辉煌的新天新地，沐浴着一种美丽的元素，清新明澈如创世之日的早晨。就连车厢中挂着的南边海岸温泉盛景那些着色的照片，都闪亮着天堂之光。布莱顿迎面而来；紧接这滨海城镇的是仙境般的南海在召唤；啊，怀特岛上莱德镇边那一片空阔的游憩场！接着我看到了锡德茅斯镇的海滩、斯沃尼奇附近的梯利·怀姆采石洞[74]；——该是在这些人迹罕至的洞穴中，还是在沃辛城音乐台边嗡嗡嗡的喧哗中，我会寻得天赐之福的极致？

或者在圣彼得港码头上也说不定，在海峡群岛那里，在那人群中，看他们怀着永恒的狂喜眺望那永在到埠、从不下客的韦茅斯汽轮？

人在世外[75]

每一次，从伦敦退隐到乡野的寂寥中，我总是会再度品尝到大自然那些纯粹的喜悦，那为诗人所讴歌礼赞的喜悦——漫步于淡泊无求的青草地上，无比满足地混迹于菜蔬花草间——但心境

the ever-satisfying companionship of vegetables and flowers—I am nevertheless haunted now and then (but tell it not to Shelley's Skylark, nor whisper to Wordsworth's Daffodils, the disconcerting secret) —I am incongruously beset by longings of which the Lake Poets never sang. Echoes and images of the abandoned City discompose my arcadizings; I hear, in the babbling of brooks, the delicious sound of London gossip, and newsboys' voices in the cries of birds. Sometimes the gold-splashed distance of a country lane seems to gleam at sunset with the posters of the evening papers; I dream at dawn of dinner-invitations, when like a telephone-call, I hear the Greenfinch trill his electric bell.

Worries

In the woods about my garden and familiar precincts lurk the fears of life; all threaten me, some I may escape, of others I am the destined and devoted victim. Sooner or later—and yet in any case how soon! —I shall fall, as I have seen others fall, touched by an unseen hand.

But I do not think of these Terrors often, though I seem to hear them sometimes moving in the thickets. It is the little transitory worries that bite and annoy me, querulous insects, born of the moment, and perishing with the day.

还是不时受到滋扰（可别把这告诉雪莱的夜莺，或者偷偷说给华兹华斯[76]的水仙花们听哟，这挺让人难为情的秘密）——我还是很煞风景地让湖畔诗人们从未歌唱过的一些渴念弄得心绪不宁。已抛诸脑后的那座城市的串串回响和影像搅散我世外田园的清净；我听到，在溪流的潺潺声中，响着伦敦悦耳的飞短流长，在鸟鸣中又有报童的声声呼叫。有时候，在一条乡村小巷金光泼洒的远处，落日中似乎闪出一张张晚报的招贴；黎明时我梦见赴宴的邀请，像来电话似的，听到金翅雀按响他的电铃。

忧烦

在我花园四周的林子和熟悉的周边地区潜藏着生活中令人心惊的东西；无不在威胁着我，有些躲得了，有些我是命该投身供其戕害。或迟或早——但无论如何早得很！——我会跌跤，就像我见到别人跌的那样，被一只看不见的手碰了就倒下。

但是我并没有常常去想这些吓人的东西，虽然我似乎听到它们有时在树丛中挪动。反而是小小的、转瞬即逝的忧烦在叮咬、滋扰着我，这些满腹牢骚的蚊虫，生于当时，死于当日。

Property

I should be very sorry to think that there was anything fishy or fraudulent about the time-honoured institution of Private Property. It is endorsed by Society, defended by the Church, maintained by the Law, and the slightest tamperings with it are severely punished by elderly Judges in large horsehair wigs. Oh, certainly it must be all right; I have a feeling that it is all right; and one of these days I shall get some one to explain why the world keeps on putting adequate sums of its currency into my pocket.

But of course it's all right—

Mrs. Braye

'Mrs. Braye is so sorry she couldn't come. She longs to see your garden; but she is shut up with an awful cold.'

'Thank God!' I exclaimed.

'But I thought you liked Mrs. Braye?'

'Indeed I do—I do like her immensely! Who could help liking her? her generous nature, her gift for appreciation, her wholehearted, fervid enthusiasm?'

'It's only that I am afraid—I am awfully afraid, to tell you the truth—of her adjectives.'

财产

我会很过意不去的，要是认为那历史悠久的私有财产体制有什么蹊跷的话。这个体制，为社会认可，得教会捍卫，由法律维持，要是给谁损害哪怕一丁点儿，头戴大大的马鬃假发的老法官都会严加惩罚。这个体制啊，当然不会有问题的；我有个感觉它没有问题的；这几天我应该找个人来解释一下，为什么这个世界把它的货币一笔笔够我花的不断放进我的口袋。

但当然了这没问题——

布雷耶太太

"布雷耶太太说她非常抱歉不能来。她一直很想看看你的花园，但是得了严重的感冒不能出门。"

"感谢上帝！"我大声说。

"但我还以为你喜欢布雷耶太太呢？"

"我的确喜欢她——喜欢得不得了！谁能不喜欢她呢？慷慨大方、慧眼独具、全心待人、热情有加的一个人？"

"只是我怕——我太怕了，跟你说真的——怕她的形容词。"

The Danger of Going to Church

As I came away from the Evening Service, walking home from that Sabbath adventure, some neighbours of mine met and passed me in their motor, laughing. Were they laughing at me? I wondered uneasily; and as I sauntered across the fields I vaguely cursed those misbelievers. Yes, yes, their eyes should be darkened, and their mocking lips put to silence. They should be smitten with the botch of Egypt, and a sore botch in the legs that cannot be healed. All the teeth should be broken in the mouths of those bloody men and daughters of backsliding; their faces should become as flames, and their heads be made utterly bald. Their little ones should be dashed to pieces before their eyes, and brimstone scattered upon their habitations. They should be led away with their buttocks uncovered; they should stagger to and fro as a drunken man staggereth in his vomit.

But as for the Godly Man who kept his Sabbaths, his should be the blessings of those who walk in the right way. 'These blessings' —the words came back to me from the Evening Lesson— 'these blessings shall come upon thee, and overtake thee.' And suddenly, in the mild summer air, it seemed as if, like a swarm of bees inadvertently wakened, the blessings of the Old Testament were actually rushing after me. From the hot, remote, passionate past of Hebrew history, out of the Oriental climate and unctuous lives of that infuriate people, gross good things were coming to overwhelm me with benedictions for which I

上教堂的危险

我做完晚礼拜，由那场安息日会的历险出来，走路回家，我的几个邻居坐在他们的汽车里遇见我，从我身边开过去，哈哈笑着。他们这是在笑我吗？我不高兴地嘀咕着，漫步穿过田野时隐隐约约诅咒着那些异教徒。是的，是的，他们的双眼要被黑暗蒙蔽，他们讪笑的嘴唇要被封住。他们应该浑身长满埃及脓疮，腿上一个脓疮痛得很又好不了。那些堕落的狗男女，满嘴牙齿要全部打断，脸要变成火焰，头发要掉得一根不剩。他们的小孩要当着他们的面被撕成碎片，硫黄石要撒遍他们的住所。他们要光着屁股被带走；他们要来回跌跌撞撞像醉鬼在自己呕吐的污秽中打转。

但是谨守安息日的信神之人呢，他的福分应该是行正道之人的福分。“这些福分”——这话从晚课上传回我耳边——“这些福分将临到你们身上，赶过你们。”突然间，在夏日温煦的空气中，仿佛有一群蜜蜂被无意间弄醒了似的，《旧约》中所说的福分似乎真的就一阵阵从后面向我赶来。从希伯来历史上那炎热的、遥远的、激情充盈的过去，从那一方东土风情，从那脾气暴躁的民族油腻的生活中，大大的好事正向我涌来，带着我并不希图的祝祷要

had not bargained. Great oxen and camels and concubines were panting close behind me, he-goats and she-goats and rams of the breed of Bashan. My barns should burst their doors with plenty, and all my paths drop fatness. My face should be smeared with the oil of rejoicing; all my household and the beasts of my household should beget and bear increase; and as for the fruit of my own loins, it should be for multitude as the sands of the sea, and as the stars of heaven. My little ones should be as olive plants about my table; sons and daughters, and their sons and daughters to the third and fourth generation, should rise up and call me blessed. My feet should be dipped in butter; I should sit under my fig-tree with my heel on the neck of my enemy, and my eyes stand out with fatness; I should flourish as the Cedar of Lebanon that bringeth forth fruit in old age.

Things to Write

What things there are to write, if one could only write them! My mind is full of gleaming thoughts; gay moods and mysterious, moth-like meditations hover in my imagination, fanning their painted wings. They would make my fortune if I could catch them; but always the rarest, those freaked with azure and the deepest crimson, flutter away beyond my reach.

The ever-baffled chase of these filmy nothings often seems, for one of sober years in a sad world, a trifling occupation. But

将我淹没。又壮又大的牛和骆驼、大妾小妾，气喘吁吁地紧跟在我后面，还有公山羊和母山羊、巴珊的良种公羊。我的谷仓会满得仓门爆开，我的道路条条富得滴油。我的脸庞会抹满喜悦的油膏；我全家人畜兴旺；至于己之所出的子嗣，会多如海边沙粒、天上繁星。我的孩子会像橄榄树般围在我桌旁；子子女女、他们的子子女女，到三代四代，会起身说我是蒙福之人。我的双脚会浸在牛油中；我会坐在我的无花果树下，一只脚架着敌人的脖子，两眼肥得突了出来；我会像黎巴嫩雪松那样繁茂，那样老树结籽。

可写的东西

有多少东西可写啊，只要你写得了！我满脑海是闪亮的念头；欢快的心情和神秘的、飞蛾似的玄思盘旋在我的想象中，呼扇着彩画般的双翼。它们会让我发财的，要是我抓得住的话；但总是那些最为稀罕、蔚蓝色和红得发紫的怪诞念头，扑扇着飞走了，逮也逮不着。

枉费心机追逐这些稀薄透明的虚幻之想，对一个悲惨世界中已活到心清之年的人来说，似乎常常是不足一提的营生。但我不

have I not read of the great Kings of Persia who used to ride out to hawk for butterflies, nor deemed this pastime beneath their royal dignity?

The Vicar of Lynch

When I heard through country gossip of the strange happening at Lynch which had caused so great a scandal, and had led to the disappearance of the deaf old Vicar of that remote village, I collected all the reports I could about it, for I felt that at the centre of this uncomprehending talk and wild anecdote, there was something with more meaning than a mere sudden outbreak of blasphemy and madness.

It appeared that the old Vicar, after some years spent in the quiet discharge of his parochial duties, had been noticed to become more and more odd in his appearance and behaviour; and it was also said that he had gradually introduced certain alterations into the Church services. These had been vaguely supposed at the time to be of a High Church character, but afterward they were put down to a growing mental derangement, which had finally culminated at that notorious Harvest Festival, when his career as a clergyman of the Church of England had ended. On this painful occasion the old man had come into church outlandishly dressed, and had gone through a service with chanted gibberish and unaccustomed gestures, and prayers

是读过那些伟大的波斯王常常会骑马出去捉蝴蝶，并不觉得这么玩配不上他们的王室之尊吗？

临齐的牧师

从乡下的传言中我得知临齐那地方出了怪事，已经传成一件大丑闻，弄得那个偏僻小村里耳聋的老牧师都失踪了，我便尽量把所有相关的传闻集拢，因为我觉得这桩荒诞不经的怪事和人云亦云的说辞当中另有文章，其意义不只是一时突然亵渎神明和头脑发疯那么简单。

事情好像是这样：那位老牧师安安静静做他的教区工作有些年头之后，人们注意到他外表和行为越变越古怪；还有人说他慢慢在教堂礼拜中引进某些变动。当时大家隐约认为这些是高派教会[77]的特点，后来则归因于日趋严重的神志错乱，日积月累终于在那个丢人现眼的丰收节庆典上总暴发，自己在英格兰教会的神职也因此了结。在这个令人难堪的庆典上，老头一身奇装异服走进教堂，做礼拜时胡言乱语地哼唱着，怪里怪气地比画着，说的

which were unfamiliar to his congregation. There was also talk of a woman's figure on the altar, which the Vicar had unveiled at a solemn moment in this performance; and I also heard echo of other gossip—gossip that was, however, authoritatively contradicted and suppressed as much as possible—about the use of certain other symbols of a most unsuitable kind. Then a few days after the old man had disappeared—some of the neighbours believed that he was dead; some, that he was now shut up in an asylum for the Insane.

Such was the fantastic and almost incredible talk I listened to, but in which, as I say, I found much more meaning than my neighbours. For one thing, although they knew that the Vicar had come from Oxford to this remote College living, they knew nothing of his work and scholarly reputation in that University, and none of them had probably ever heard of—much less read—an important book which he had written, and which was the standard work on his special subject. To them he was simply a deaf, eccentric, and solitary clergyman; and I think I was the only person in the neighbourhood who had conversed with him on the subject concerning which he was the greatest living authority in England.

For I had seen the old man once—curiously enough at the time of a Harvest Festival, though it was some years before the one which had led to his disappearance. Bicycling one day over the hills, I had ridden down into a valley of cornfields, and then, passing along an unfenced road that ran across a wide expanse of

祷告词会众都不熟悉。传说圣坛上还摆了个女人像，那牧师在庆典的一个庄严时刻为那尊人像揭幕；我还听到传来传去有其他闲言——权威方面则对此尽量辩驳压制——说是用了别的一些非常不合适的标志。在老头不见了几天之后——有些邻居相信他已经死了，有些又说他现在被关进了疯人院。

这些就是我听人说的简直匪夷所思的荒唐事，但就像我说的，个中意义我看到的比邻居们要多得多。比如说吧，他们虽然知道牧师来自牛津，在此地过这乡僻的教士生涯，可是对他在那所大学从事的工作和学术声望一无所知，大概谁也没听说过——更别说读过——他写的一本重要著作，那可是他专业领域里的标杆之作。在他们看来，他无非是个又聋又怪的孤身老教士罢了；我觉得这一带只有我跟他谈过那个他贵为英格兰当世最高权威的课题。

因为我见过老人一面——巧的是就在有一年的丰收节，虽然比这次令他失踪的丰收节要早一些年。有一天我骑着车翻过山头，下到一个有麦地的山谷，再沿着一条没有篱笆隔着的路往前骑，穿过一大片麦茬，下车开了三四道栅门之后，突然看到前面是

stubble, I came, after getting off to open three or four gates, upon a group of thatched cottages, with a little, unrestored Norman church standing among great elms. I left my bicycle and walked through the churchyard, and as I went into the church, through its deeply-recessed Norman doorway, a surprisingly pretty sight met my eyes. The dim, cool, little interior was set out and richly adorned with an abundance of fruit and vegetables, yellow gourds, apples and plums and golden wheat-sheaves, great loaves of bread, and garlands of September flowers. A shabby-looking old clergyman was standing on the top of a step-ladder, finishing the decorations, when I entered. As soon as he saw me he came down, and I spoke to him, praising the decorations, and raising my voice a little, for I noticed that he was deaf. We spoke of the Harvest Festival; and as I soon perceived that I was talking with a man of books and University education, I ventured to hint at what had vividly impressed me in that old, gaudily-decorated church—its pagan character, as if it were a rude archaic temple in some corner of the antique world, which had been adorned, two thousand years ago, by pious country folk for some local festival. The old clergyman was not in the least shocked by my remark; it seemed indeed rather to please him; there was, he agreed, something of a pagan character in the modern Harvest Festival—it was no doubt a bit of the old primitive Vegetation Ritual, the old Religion of the soil; a Festival which, like so many others, had not been destroyed by Christianity, but absorbed into it, and given a new meaning. 'Indeed,' he added, talking on

几座茅草屋，有一座未经修复的诺曼底式小教堂，掩映在高大的榆树间。我把车停在外面，穿过教堂墓园，从那深深嵌入墙内的诺曼底式大门走进教堂，映入眼帘的是一幅漂亮得令人吃惊的景象。小小的教堂内清幽凉爽，陈列着各色水果菜蔬，装点得琳琅满目，黄熟的葫芦瓜、苹果、李子、金色的麦束、大块大块的面包，还有九月的鲜花扎成的一个个花环。我进去时，有一位模样寒酸的老教士正站在一座折叠梯顶上把各样摆设弄停当。他一看到我便下了梯子，我跟他说话，夸教堂的装饰漂亮，声音也提高了一点，因为我注意到他耳背。我们谈到丰收节；言谈间我很快看出对方是位饱学之士，受过大学教育，于是斗胆暗示说那间装饰俗艳的旧教堂给我留下的生动印象是——它的异教色彩，宛如古代世界某个角落里一间粗陋的古神庙，虔诚的乡下人，两千年前，装点了来庆祝当地某个节日。老教士听了我这一番话，一点也不诧异，反而真还显得很高兴；现代的丰收节庆，他同意，是有一些异教色彩——毫无疑问有点古老的原始植物祭祀遗风、古老的拜土宗教余韵；就像别的那么多节日一样，这也是一个没有被基督教毁掉的节日，而是让基督教吸收了并赋予新的意义。“的确，”他

as if the subject interested him, and expressing himself with a certain donnish carefulness of speech that I found pleasant to listen to, 'the Harvest Festival is undoubtedly a survival of the prehistoric worship of that Corn Goddess who, in classical times, was called Demeter and Ioulo and Ceres, but whose cult as an Earth-Mother and Corn-Spirit is of much greater antiquity. For there is no doubt that this Vegetation Spirit has been worshipped from the earliest times by agricultural peoples; the wheat fields and ripe harvest being naturally suggestive of the presence amid the corn of a kindly Being, who, in return for due rites and offerings, will vouchsafe nourishing rains and golden harvests.' He mentioned the references in Virgil, and the description in Theocritus of a Sicilian Harvest Festival—these were no doubt familiar to me; but if I was interested in the subject, I should find, he said, much more information collected in a book which he had written, but of which I had probably never heard, about the Vegetation Deities in Greek Religion. As it happened I knew the book, and felt now much interested in my chance in meeting with the distinguished scholar; and after expressing this as best I could, I rode off, promising to visit him again. This promise I was never able to fulfil; but when afterward, on my return to the neighbourhood, I heard of that unhappy scandal, my memory of this meeting and our talk enabled me to form a theory as to what had really happened.

It seemed plain to me that the change had been too violent for this elderly student, taken from his books and college rooms

补充道，好像很有兴致似的接着说，语气还带上一种大学讲课字斟句酌的认真，我听了觉得很舒服，“丰收节无疑是史前谷神崇拜遗留下来的，在古代，谷物女神称为狄米特、艾欧罗，还有希若司，但是将谷神作为大地之母和谷物精灵来崇拜，则更为古老。因为毫无疑问，这位植物精灵在最早的时候就为农业部族所崇拜；麦田和庄稼成熟的收成很自然地提示在谷物间有一位仁慈的灵物，只要礼仪行足、祭献不误，便会以好雨润泽大地，以金秋的丰收回报众生。”他提及维吉尔[78]诗中的典故，以及忒奥克里托斯[79]笔下西西里岛上的丰收节庆——这些我当然熟悉；但如果对这个课题感兴趣的话，他说，那我应该会发现比这多得多的材料搜集在他写的一本书中，只是那本书我很可能从未听说过，写的是希腊宗教里的各种植物神祇。碰巧那本书我知道，听他说了之后觉得邂逅这位杰出的学者真很有意思。我把这个意思尽量得体地表达了之后，便骑车离去，答应以后再来拜访。答应了，我却一直未能履约；但是后来，刚回到那地方，就听说了那桩令人不快的丑闻，回想这次偶遇交谈，我对到底发生了什么便有了自己的看法。

依我看事情似乎很明显，对这位老先生来说，变化太剧烈了：从书本和学院校舍给支到这个偏僻的山谷，形单影只结庐于大自

and set down in the solitude of this remote valley, amid the richness, and living sap of Nature. The gay spectacle, right under his old eyes, of growing shoots and budding foliage, of blossoming and flowering, and the ripening of fruits and crops, the pairing of birds and the mating of cattle, had little by little (such was my theory) unhinged his brains. More and more his thoughts had come to dwell, not on the doctrines of the Church in which he had long ago taken orders, but on the pagan rites which had formed his study, and which had been the expression of ways not unlike the agricultural life amid which he now found himself living. So as his derangement grew upon him in his isolation, he had gradually transformed, with a maniac's cunning, the Christian services, and led his little congregation, all unknown to themselves, back toward their ancestral worship of the Corn-Goddess. At last he had thrown away all disguise, and had appeared as a hierophant of Demeter, dressed in a fawn skin, with a crown of poplar leaves, and pedantically carrying the mystic basket and the winnowing fan appropriate to these mysteries. The wheaten posset he offered the shocked communicants belonged to these also, and the figure of a woman on the altar was of course the holy Wheatsheaf, whose unveiling was the culminating point in that famous ritual.

It is much to be regretted that I could not recover full and more exact details of that celebration, in which this great scholar had probably embodied his mature knowledge concerning a subject which has puzzled generations of students. But what

然的丰沛与勃勃生机间。这一派欣欣向荣的景象就展现在他老眼之前，新枝萌发、绿树吐芽、鲜花怒放、春华秋实、燕雀比翼、牲口配种，所有这些都一点一点地（我的看法）让他的头脑失了方寸。他越来越念兹在兹的不是他早年受命服膺的教会信条，而是形成他研究领域的异教礼俗，其所表达的生活方式也与他发现自己眼下身处的农耕生活不无相似之处。于是乎，随着在与世隔绝中变得越来越糊涂，他怀着一种癫狂之人的狡黠，渐渐改变了基督教的礼拜仪式，带领他的小小会众，不明就里的这些人，向着他们祖先的谷物女神崇拜回归。最终他丢开所有伪装，以狄米特显灵的形象出现，身裹幼鹿皮，头戴白杨树叶编成的冠冕，还学究气地依足祭神规矩挎着神秘的篮子摇着扬谷的扇子。领圣餐时他给大吃一惊的会众喝的麦酒也属于这规矩的一部分，而祭坛上的那尊女像当然是麦束的圣洁之身，揭像一幕则把那场远近闻名的祭礼推向高潮。

很令人遗憾的是我无法更精确地复原那次庆典的所有细节，当时这位大学者很可能在一个世代学人为之困惑的学科领域，将自己厚积而发的知识以肉身演示于人前。可是，能期望那些人有

powers of careful observation could one expect from a group of labourers and small farmers? Some of the things that reached my ears I refused to believe—the mention of pig's blood, for instance, and especially the talk of certain grosser symbols, which the choir boys, it was whispered, had carried in their hands about the church in ceremonious procession. Village people have strange imaginations; and to this event, growing more and more monstrous as they talked it over, they must themselves have added this grotesque detail. However, I have written to consult an Oxford authority on this interesting point, and he has been kind enough to explain at length that although at the *Haloa*, or winter festival of the Corn-Goddess, and also at the *Chloeia*, or festival in early spring, some symbolization of the reproductive powers of Nature would be proper and appropriate, such ritualism would have been quite out of place at the *Thalysia*, or autumn festival of thanksgiving. I feel certain that a solecism of this kind—the introduction into a particular rite of features not sanctioned by the texts—would have seemed a shocking thing to one who had always been so accurate a scholar.

In a Fix

To go, or not to go? Did I want or not want to bicycle over to the Hanbury-Belchers at Pokemore? Wouldn't it be pleasanter to stay at home?

多少眼光和细致的观察力呢，一众劳工和小农场主？有些事传到我耳朵但我拒绝相信——比如说猪血，特别还提到某些更不堪入目的标志，并窃窃私语，说仪式中唱诗班的男孩手持这些标志在教堂内四处游行。乡野之人有着很奇特的想象力；就此事而言，人们越是谈论，其想象力就变得越发荒诞狰狞，这个诡怪离奇的细节一定是他们自己添加的。这个饶有趣味的问题，我可是写信请教了牛津的一位权威，他很客气，详细解释给我听了，说是在哈罗阿节，或者说谷物女神的冬节庆典上，还有在科罗伊亚节，即早春节的庆典上，出现某种对大自然繁育能力的象征标志是合乎体统没问题的，但这种仪式要是用在萨里希亚节，或者说秋季的感恩节庆，就很不合适了。我确信，这种忤逆——在一个特别的祭典上引入不为经书认可的环节——对一个向来如此精确严谨的学者来说，似乎会是骇人听闻的一件事。

两难

去，还是不去？我是想，还是不想，骑车去波克摩的汉波利-贝尔彻家？在家里待着不是更快活吗？

I liked the Hanbury-Belchers—

Or did I really like them?

Still, it might be pleasant?

But how beforehand can one ever tell? Experience? I was still, I felt, as ignorant of life as a newborn infant; experience has taught me nothing; what I needed was some definite, a priori principle, some clear conception of the meaning of existence, in the light of which problems of this kind would solve themselves at once.

I leant my bicycle against the gate, and sat down to think the matter out. Calling to mind the moral debates of the old philosophers, I meditated on that *Summum Bonum*, or Sovereign Felicity of which they argued; but from their disputes and cogitations what came back most vividly—what seemed to fall upon me almost in a hush of terror—was that paralysis or dread balance of desire which they wrote of; the predicament, in fact, of that philosophic quadruped, who, because he found in each of them precisely the same attraction, stood between two bundles of hay, unable to move, until he perished of hunger.

The Garden Party

'Yes, I suppose it is rather a dull Garden Party,' I agreed, though my local pride was a little hurt by the disdain of that visiting young woman for our rural society. 'Still we have some

我喜欢汉波利-贝尔彻一家——

我是真的喜欢他们吗？

怎么说，去也许很愉快呢？

但事前真还怎么说得准呢？凭经验？可我仍然，我觉得，对生活一无所知像个初生小儿；经验没教给我一点东西；我需要的是一个明确的、先验的原则，对生存之意义的某种清晰的概念，根据这个概念，诸如此类的问题自己会迎刃而解。

我把车靠在门边，坐下来要琢磨出个究竟。回想起古代哲学家的道德辩论，细思他们争论的那个*Summum Bonum*，或者说至善；但看他们争来争去，思来想去，从中最活灵活现回想起的——似乎是在一阵无声的恐怖中砸在我身上的——是他们所写的欲望瘫痪或欲望的可怕平衡；两难困境，事实上，就是那头有哲学心的四足动物面临的窘况：发现两捆干草具有同样的吸引力，于是乎站在二者之间，动弹不得，结果活活饿死。[80]

游园会

“没错，我看这游园会是没什么意思，”我附和道，虽然我这当地人的自尊心因为那位年轻女宾看不起我们的乡村社会而有点受伤，“我们一些邻居还是很有趣的，等你认识他们了就知道。

interesting neighbours, when you get to know them. Now that fat lady over there in purple—do you see her? Mrs. Turnbull—she believes in Eternal Torment. And that old gentleman with whiskers and white spats, Colonel Bosco, is convinced that England is tottering on the very brink of the Abyss. He expects to hear at any moment the final crash of Empire, Church, and Throne; and it gives him, he says, a kind of giddy feeling. And the pie-faced lady he is talking to, Miss Stuart-Frisby, was, she tells us, Mary Queen of Scots in a previous existence. And our Curate—we're proud of our Curate, he's a great cricketer, and a kind of saint as well. They say he goes out in Winter at three o'clock in the morning, and stands up to his neck in a pond, to cool and overcome his appetites.'

Weltschmerz

'How depressed you look! What on earth's the matter?'

'Central Europe,' I said, 'and the chaos in China is something awful. There's a threatened shortage, too, of beer in Copenhagen.'

'But why should that worry you?'

'It doesn't. It's what I said to Mrs. Rumbal—I do say such idiotic things! She asked me to come to see them. "I shall be delighted," I said, "as delighted—" '

'But it's your fault for making me read that book of Siamese translations!' —

喏，那边那位胖胖的女士，穿紫色衣服的——你看到了吗？特恩布尔太太——她信奉永世磨难。还有那位老先生，蓄连鬓胡、鞋上套着白鞋罩的那位，波斯科上校，他相信英格兰正在地狱的深渊边上摇摇欲坠。他随时都等着听帝国、教会和皇室垮台的最后一声轰隆；这让他，他说，有种眩晕的感觉。正在跟他说话的那位馅饼脸女士，斯图亚特-弗里斯比小姐，她跟我们说，自己前世是苏格兰玛丽女王。我们的助理牧师呢——我们都为我们的助理牧师感到自豪，他是个板球高手，也算是个圣人来着。他们说他冬天凌晨三点出去，站在一个水塘中，水浸到脖子，以此来冷却克服自己的欲念。”

悲观

“看你那副沮丧的样子！到底是怎么回事？”

“中欧，”我说，“还有中国的乱象也挺揪心的。哥本哈根眼看也要啤酒短缺了。”

“但你为什么要担这些心呢？”

“不是这些。担心的是我对伦波尔太太说的话——我还真说了这些蠢话！她请我过来看他们。‘我将会很高兴，’我说，‘高兴得像——’”

“但那是你的错，不该让我读那本暹罗语翻译的书！”——

' "As delighted," I said, "Mrs. Rumbal, as a royal flamingo, when he alights upon a cluster of lotuses."'

Life-Enhancement

I was simply telling them at tea the details of my journey—how late the train had been in starting, how crowded the railway carriage, how I had mislaid my umbrella, and nearly lost my Gladstone bag.

But how I enjoyed making them listen, what a sense of enhanced existence I found it gave me (and to think that I have pitied bores!) to force my doings, my interests, my bag and umbrella, down their throats!

The Pyramid

'To read Gibbon,' I said, as we paced that terrace in the sunshine, 'to peruse his metallic, melancholy pages, and then forget them; to re-read and re-forget the *Decline* and *Fall*; to fill the mind with that great, sad, splendid, meaningless panorama of History, and then to watch those Kings and Conquerors, those Heresiarchs and monks and Patriarchs and Councils, all fade away from our memory, as they have faded from the glass of Time—'

As she turned to me with a glance full of enthusiasm, 'What

"'高兴得像,'我说,'伦波尔太太,像一只气派的火烈鸟君临荷花丛。'"

生命强化

我不过是在喝茶时告诉他们我旅行的细节罢了——火车发车晚点了多少,车厢有多拥挤,我怎么忘了雨伞放哪儿,还差点弄丢了我的格莱斯顿旅行包。

但我是多么喜欢让他们听我说啊!我发现这给了我怎样一种强化的存在感啊(想想我还可怜过闷蛋们!)——将我所做的、我所感兴趣的、我的旅行包和雨伞,一股脑儿强灌给他们!

金字塔

"读吉本,"我说,两人一边在露台上的阳光中踱着步,"细细读他那铿锵、忧伤的文字,然后忘掉;再读再忘那罗马帝国的衰与亡;让内心充满那宏大的、悲伤的、辉煌的、没有意义的历史画卷,然后看着那些国王和征服者、那些异教首领和僧侣和长老还有议事会的衮衮诸公,一个个淡出我们的记忆,一如他们从时间的沙漏中流逝——"

她转脸看了我一眼,目光洋溢着热情。"能有什么这么令人

is so enchanting,' I reflected, 'as the dawn of an acquaintance with a clever woman with whom one can share one's thoughts?'

It was her remark about History, how she believed that the builders of the Great Pyramid had foreseen and foretold many events of Modern History, which made a gigantic shadow, an Egyptian darkness, loom between us on that terrace.

Eclipse

A mild radiance and the scent of flowers filled the drawing-room, whose windows stood open to the summer night. I thought our talk delightful; the topic was one of my favourite topics; I had much that was illuminating to say about it, and I was a little put out when we were called to the window to look at the planet Jupiter, which was shining in the sky just then, we were told, with great brilliance.

In turns through a telescope we gazed at the Planet. I thought the spectacle over-rated. However I said nothing. Not for the world, not for any number of worlds would I have wished them to guess why I was displeased with that star.

Reflections

When I walk to the side of the thought-suggesting sea,

陶醉，”我心想，“比得上初识一位聪慧的女子，得以分享你的想法？”

是她关于历史的评说，说她如何相信大金字塔的建设者们已经预见并预告了现代历史中的许多事件，令一道巨大的阴影、一道古埃及的暗影，在那露台上幽幽地悬在我们两人之间。

黯然

温煦的亮光和着花香弥漫在客厅中，客厅窗户开处，对着一片夏天的夜色。我觉得我们谈得很愉快；话题是我最喜欢的一个；对此我有许多振聋发聩的话要说，突然被打断了，顿觉有些懊恼，因为有人叫大家到窗口看木星，说什么夜空中那颗星刚好亮着，正大放光芒呢。

大家轮流用一部望远镜观看那颗行星。我觉得并没有说的那么好看。但我一声不吭。就是用世界来换，不管用多少个世界来换，我也不想让他们去猜我为什么对那颗星耿耿于怀。

反思

走到令人浮想联翩的海边，坐在沙滩上对着不远处的潮涨潮

when I sit on the sand not far from the margin of the incoming or retreating tide, I often gaze on that waste of undulating water until it assumes in my eyes a moral meaning—seems to lie there on the page of Nature's book as an immense and shining metaphor, re-presenting the instability and transience of all things in the stream of Time. And the waves, as they hasten towards the pebbled shore, remind me, as they have reminded others, of our own moments hastening to their end.

But as they keep on reiterating this monotonous lesson, and my thoughts ebb and flow to their melancholy music, they seem to efface and wash away their own monitions: my sense of the transience of things proves itself but a transient reflection; and reclining there in the shade of my white cotton sun-umbrella, I float agreeably off into an oblivion of Time, the Sea, and Mortality.

The Ideal

Bright shone the morning, and as I waited (they had promised to call for me in their motor) I made for myself an enchanting picture of the day before me, our drive to that forest beyond the dove-blue hills, the ideal beings I should meet there, feasting with them in the shade of immemorial trees.

And when, in the rainy twilight, I was deposited, soaked, and half-dead with fatigue, out of that open motor, was there

落，我常常会凝视这空自起伏的一片荒凉，直到它在我眼中呈现出一种道德意义——似乎是躺在自然之书页面上的一个磅礴闪亮的隐喻，再现万物在时间之流中的飘忽与浮沉。那一排排浪花，匆匆涌向沙滩上的卵石，提醒着我，就像以前提醒过其他人那样，我们自己人生的时时刻刻也在涌向它们的终结。

但随着浪花喋喋不休地重复着这单调的说教，随着我的思绪伴着它们忧郁的音乐起伏跌宕，它们似乎在抹去、在冲刷掉自己的训诫：我那万物飘忽之感最终证明自己不过是个飘忽而过的念头；斜倚在我白色的棉布太阳伞的伞阴之下，我飘飘然忘却了时间、大海，以及生死。

理想

晨光明媚，我一边等着（他们答应开车来接我）一边给自己眼前这一天勾画出一幅醉人的图景：我们驱车来到鸽蓝色的小山那边的森林，遇见一些理想之人，一起在古树的浓荫下宴饮作乐。

雨中的暮色里，我从那部无盖汽车上给卸了下来，浑身湿透，累得半死，这时候，难道内心就空落落地只剩寒气与幻灭？即使

nothing inside me but chill and disillusion? If I had dreamed a dream incompatible with the climate and social conditions of these Islands, had I not, out of that very dream and disenchantment, created, like the Platonic Lover, a Platonic and imperishable vision—the ideal Picnic, the Picnic as it might be—the wonderful windless weather, the Watteauish landscape, where a group of mortals talk and feast as they talked and feasted in the Golden Age?

Bogeys

I remember how charmed I was with these new acquaintances, to whose house I had been taken that afternoon to call. I remember the gardens through which we sauntered, with peaches ripening on the sunny walls; I remember the mellow light on the old portraits in the drawing-room, the friendly atmosphere and tranquil voices; and how, as the quiet stream of talk flowed on, one subject after another was pleasantly mirrored on its surface; —till, at a chance remark, there was a sudden change and darkening, an angry swirl, as if a monster were raising its head above the waters.

What was it about, the disputation into which we plunged, in spite of our desperate efforts to clutch at other subjects? Was it Tariff Reform or Table-rapping—Bacon and Shakespeare, Disestablishment, perhaps—or Anti-Vivisection? What did any

我做了一个梦，即使这梦与这些岛屿的气候和社会环境不合，难道我就没有从这个梦境、从这场梦醒当中，就像柏拉图式恋人般，创造出一个柏拉图式的不朽意境——理想的野餐，夫复何求的野餐——微风不兴的美妙天气，如华托[81]笔下的田园风光，一群凡人在边谈边吃，一如他们在黄金时代那般高谈阔论，宴饮作乐？

妖怪

还记得这些新结识的人是多么让我着迷，那天下午也带我去拜访了他们家。我记得我们漫步穿过的花园，阳光朗照的墙上桃子正要成熟；我记得客厅中古肖像画上醇和的光泽、友善的氛围和安宁柔和的话音；随着谈话如静水无波而流，一个接一个话题又是如何愉快地倒映其上；——直到有人随口说了句什么，气氛急转直下，天昏地暗中怒涛涌起，有如一个妖怪正从水中探出脑袋。

说的什么呢，看我们一头扎进去争成那样，大家拼命想扭转话题也扭不转？是说关税改革还是击桌通灵[82]——是培根和莎士比亚、政教分离吧，说不定——或者是反对动物活体解剖？这些

of us know or really care about it? What force, what fury drove us into saying the stupid, intolerant, denunciatory things we said; that made us feel we would rather die than not say them? How could a group of humane, polite, and intelligent people be so suddenly transformed into barking animals?

Why do we let these Abstractions and implacable Dogmatisms take possession of us, glare at each other through our eyes, and fight their futile, frenzied conflicts in our persons? Life without the rancours and ever-recurring battles of these Bogeys might be so simple, friendly, affectionate, and pleasant!

Weltanschauung

When, now and then, on a calm night I look up at the Stars, I reflect on the wonders of Creation, the unimportance of this Planet, and the possible existence of other worlds like ours. Sometimes it is the self-poised and passionless shining of those serene orbs which I think of; sometimes Kant's phrase comes into my mind about the majesty of the Starry Heavens and the Moral Law; or I remember Xenophanes gazing up at the broad firmament, and crying, 'The All is One!' and thus, in that sublime assertion, enunciating for the first time the great doctrine of the Unity of Being.

But these Thoughts are not my thoughts; they eddy through my mind like scraps of old paper, or withered leaves in the wind.

东西我们又有谁知道了什么，有谁真的关心？是什么力量、什么怒火驱使我们讲了那些愚蠢的、褊狭的、相互斥责的话，讲了那些不说宁可去死的话？一班仁心仁德、文质彬彬的聪明人，怎么会骤然变成一群汪汪狂吠的动物？

为什么我们让这些抽象的观念和执拗僵化的教条迷了心窍？让它们透过我们的眼睛怒目相向，以我们之身剑拔弩张地大打口水仗？生活要是没了这些妖怪搅起的敌意、翻来覆去挑起的争端，会多么简单，多么温馨，多么愉快啊！

世界观

不时地，我会在安静的夜晚抬头看星星，细思造物的神妙，这颗行星的卑微，以及天外可能存在的与我们类似的世界。有时候，是那些自悬于天、冷峻无情、安静坦然地发着光的星球惹我心思；有时候，康德[83]的话跑进了我的头脑，说的是星空与道德律的威严；或者我会记起克塞诺芬尼[84]，他凝望广袤的苍穹，呼喊着："万有为一！"于是乎，以这个崇高的断言第一次明确提出了存在同归于一这一伟大的学说。

但是这些思想并非我的思想；它们在我心中兜转而过，像片片旧纸，像枯叶随风。我真正感觉到的是一种原始得多的心境的

What I really feel is the survival of a much more primitive mood—a view of the world which dates indeed from before the invention of language. It has never been put into literature; no poet has sung of it, no historian of human thought has so much as alluded to it; astronomers in their glazed observatories, with their eyes glued to the ends of telescopes, seem to have had no notion of it.

But sometimes, far off at night, I have heard a dog howling at the Moon.

The Alien

The older I grow, the more of an alien I find myself in the world; I cannot get used to it, cannot believe that it is real. I think I must have been made to live on some other Star. Or perhaps I am subject to hallucinations and hear voices; perhaps what I seem to see is delusion and doesn't happen; perhaps people don't really say the things I think I hear them saying.

Ah, some one ought to have told me when I was young, I should certainly have been told of the songs that are sung in drawing-rooms; they ought to have warned me about the fat women who suddenly get up and bellow out incredible recitations.

余绪——一种世界观，其发端的确可追溯至语言发明之前。这种世界观，从未载于文学；从未有诗人歌咏过，从未有人类思想史家哪怕是隐约提到过；天文学家在他们罩着玻璃的观测台上，眼睛贴着望远镜，对此似乎也全无概念。

但是有些时候，夜晚时分远远地，我听到了一只狗在对着月亮吠叫。

异类

我年纪越大，越觉得自己在世界上是异类一个；我无法适应它，无法相信它是真的。我想我生来必定是要活在别的哪个星球上的。或者，我也许有幻觉，有幻听；也许我眼睛似乎看到的本是错觉，并没有发生；也许人们并没有真的说过我觉得自己听到他们在说的那些话。

啊，我年轻时有人就应该告诉我，肯定有人应该告诉过我客厅里唱的那些歌；他们就应该警告我有那些胖女人，她们会突然站起身来吼出不可思议的朗诵词。

Achievement

'Yes, as you say, one certainly ought to try to make something of one's life. It's an experience after all, full of exasperation of course, but full of interest. And making love, and the warmth of the sun are pleasant, and money, and the taste of food. And how pleasant it is, too, to shine in conversation!'

'What I think would be perfectly charming,' I confided to our Vicar's wife, 'what above all things I should like, would be to make out of my life—how shall I put it? —something delicate and durable, something privileged to win the approbation of the high authorities of the Universe. To live on, in fact, after my funeral in a perfect phrase.'

成就

“没错，如您所说，人生应当努力有所作为。这毕竟是一份经历，充满恼怒激愤当然了，但也饶有兴味。做爱、温煦的阳光，都令人愉快，还有金钱，以及食物的滋味。而这，也多么愉快啊，能在交谈中一展口才！”

“我觉得最令人神往的，”我向我们的牧师太太吐露心迹，“比我会喜欢的一切都要好的，是以我一生来成就——我该怎么说呢？——成就某种精妙且经久不衰的东西，一种有幸赢得宇宙最高权威们赞许的东西。实际上就是，能在我葬礼之后，还活在一句完美的话语中。”

AFTERTHOUGHTS

'Little fish are sweet'

追记

“小鱼甜美”

Ⅰ. Life and Human Nature

We are the children of our age, but children who can never know their mother.

It is just as well to be a little giddy-pated, if you are to feel at home on this turning earth.

The future looms a dark fog before us, but through it we see the eyes of Posterity, gazing at us coldly.

How furious it makes people to tell them of the things which belong to their peace!

All mirrors are magical mirrors; never can we see our faces in them.

Our lives within may be mysteries and marvels; but our names and noses are familiar to the world.

There are two things to aim at in life: first, to get what you want; and, after that, to enjoy it. Only the wisest of mankind achieve the second.

Happiness is a wine of the rarest vintage, and seems insipid to a vulgar taste.

That amusing stories are told about us does not amuse the Soul.

一、人生与人性

我们是我们时代的孩儿，但却是永远不认识自己母亲的孩儿。

有点晕头转向有何不可，假如你要自在地待在这个转动的地球上。

未来把一重暗黑的雾悬在我们面前，但是透过这雾我们看见后人的眼睛凝视着我们，冷冷地。

告诉人们属于他们安宁的事情，这让他们多么怒火中烧啊！

一切镜子都是魔镜，我们永远看不见自己的面孔照在里面。

我们内心的生活可以神秘又神奇，但我们的名字和鼻子世人都熟悉。

人生目的有二：其一，得己所要；其后，享受所得。唯智慧最高之人可达其二。

幸福乃一至珍佳酿，若品味低俗尝之则似乎索然。

拿我们当笑话说，这可让灵魂笑不起来。

How awful to reflect that what people say of us is true!

Our names are labels, plainly printed on the bottled essence of our past behaviour.

As oysters secrete scale by scale the shells which over-crust their pearly seclusion, so our souls exude act by act the rough personage which hides softly away from the world an irrelevant dream of existence.

My festival is a festival of imagination on the way to the palace.

How exquisitely ironic is the entertainment we can derive from our disillusions!

For souls in growth, great quarrels are great emancipations.

The actual is egregious and disconcerting, and never more so than when the Ideal becomes real, and Heaven touches earth for a moment.

How many of our daydreams would darken into nightmares, were there a danger of their coming true!

What happens in life is mere litter; but from this wastepaper of perishable events Thought can unpack imperishable meanings.

Amid the vast unimportance of all things, how beyond all calculation important we find it each morning to have at hand,

太可怕了，想想人家这么说我们，还说对了！

我们的名字是标签，明明白白印在瓶装了的我们过往行为的精髓上。

如同牡蛎一层一层地分泌出外壳来包裹它们含珠的幽居之身，我们的灵魂也一言一行地渗出有头有脸的粗糙形象，悄悄地瞒着世界包藏起一个与之不相干的存在之梦。

我的节日，便是行在去宫中路上的一个想象力的节日。

多么妙不可言的反讽啊，那从自己的幻灭中得出的娱乐！

对于成长中的灵魂，大吵架是大解放。

所谓真实，其坏无以复加，也令人不安；而最坏者莫过于理想成真，天堂有一刻碰到了地面。

我们的白日美梦有多少会黯然变成噩梦啊，要是这些梦有实现的危险！

生活中所发生的无非是垃圾而已；但大小事湮灭化成的这团废纸，思想却能从中拆解出不灭的意义。

万事悠悠无一重要，唯有一样重要非常：每天早晨坐着面对

as we sit facing Time and Eternity, an adequate supply of thin paper!

Solvency is entirely a matter of temperament and not of income.

All-glorious within us are our gay pretensions; but when they fly from our lips, how are their wings bereft of their glory!

That we should practise what we preach is generally admitted; but anyone who preaches what he and his hearers practise must incur the gravest moral disapprobation.

It is only those who can declare without guile that they are doing the very opposite of what they are really doing—meat-eating vegetarians for instance, and snob-hating snobs—who keep stainless their serene ideals, and walk the earth in white, like angels.

Self-respecting people do not care to peep at their reflections in unexpected mirrors, or to see themselves as others see them.

Are we all alike, all pleased alike and troubled by that wanton eye so reprobated by the Founder of our Faith?

Only those who get into scrapes with their eyes open can find the safe way out.

The lusts of the Body scandalize the Soul; but it has to come to heel.

时间和永恒时，我们手边必须见到有薄薄的报纸足份送来！

偿付能力完全是气质秉性的问题，与收入无关。

在心里头风光无限的是我们华丽的矫饰；但要是从口中飞出，翅膀便顿失光彩！

应该践行自己所宣扬的，这一点大家都认；但如果谁宣扬的是自己和他的听众所践行的，则必定会招致最严正的道德责难。

只有能不虚与委蛇地宣告自己正在做的与自己真正在做的事截然相反的那些人——吃肉的素食者比如说，还有讨厌势利鬼的势利鬼——才把他们清净的理想保持得一尘不染，穿着白衣行走于世，宛如天使在人间。

自尊之人不屑于瞟一眼不期而遇的镜子中的自己，或者像别人那样看待自己。

我们是不是都一样，都一样喜滋滋但又心烦意乱，就因为那个不老实的眼神，那个为我们信仰的缔造者所深恶痛绝的眼神？

只有那些睁着双眼走入困境的人才找得到安全的脱身之路。

肉体的贪欲让灵魂震惊，但它唯有屈就。

Money and sex are forces too unruly for our reason; they can only be controlled by taboos with which we tamper at our peril.

If you eradicate a fault, you leave room for a worse one to take root and flourish.

There are few sorrows, however poignant, in which a good income is of no avail.

What is more mortifying than to feel that you have missed the plum for want of courage to shake the tree?

Great felicities are often great misfortunes.

Little superstitions are the spiders of the mind; we must keep brushing them away, or they will choke it with their webs.

We need bogeys and awful apprehensions to keep us from being dull.

'On the hill at Bomma, at the mouth of the Congo River,' Frazer tells us, in a sentence which seems to solve all the problems, 'dwells Namvulu Vulu, king of the rain and storm.'

Sound is more than sense.

That we are all lost in a world of vain illusion; and that somewhere, somehow, we must all seek Salvation and a more Abiding City—this is what old-fashioned parsons keep droning from their pulpits. The worst of it is, what they say is true.

钱和性这两种力对我们的理性来说太桀骜不驯了，只能套之以禁忌来控制；若在禁忌上动手脚，则风险自负。

拔除一个缺点，便留下地方让一个更坏的缺点生根壮大。

很少有什么悲伤，无论多么痛彻心扉，会让一份好的收入派不上用场。

有什么比这更令人愧悔无地的呢：觉得自己没吃到梅子，是因为缺了摇树的勇气？

大福常常是大难。

小迷信是心中的蜘蛛；我们必须不断拂拭驱赶，不然心就给它们的网噎住了。

我们需要妖怪，需要吓人的一惊一乍，让我们不至于木然无趣。

“在波马的山上，在刚果河的河口，”弗雷泽告诉我们，他这一句话似乎要解决一切问题，“住着纳姆乌鲁·乌鲁，暴风雨之王。”[85]

声音不止意义。

我们都迷失在一个虚幻的世界里；在某个地方，以某种方式，我们都必须寻求救赎，寻找一个更为永恒的城市——这些就是老派的牧师们在布道坛上嗡嗡嗡说个不停的话。最糟糕的是，他们所说可是真的。

'Seven great poplars, and amid those poplars, a golden well.'

It is through the cracks in our brains that ecstasy creeps in.

An echo of music, a face in the street, glimpses of the moon or wanton thoughts; —only in the iridescence of things the vagabond soul is happy.

An act of folly ceases to be foolish, when you know it for the folly that it is.

Look at the Moon! You may not know it, but there is something wrong about the Moon. She will not keep her appointments, nor conform to the programme laid down for her by the lunar theorists. At the end of the nineteenth century she arrived ten seconds late: was fourteen seconds ahead of time a hundred years before.

There are tens of thousands, we are told, who are capable of achieving success in the ordinary walks of life; hundreds there are who can rule their fellow-men and wield empires, to one who can even understand the problem presented by the retardations and accelerations of this incalculable orb. But even these aristocrats of the intellect, ranking, we are told, above all other aristocracies in the scale of being, and including Ernest W. Brown and G. W. Hill among their most illustrious members, have never been able to calculate the motion of the Moon: still she laughs at their attempts to account for her behavior.

“七棵高高的白杨树，在这些杨树间，一口金井。”

是从我们大脑的缝隙间销魂之乐偷偷爬了进来。

音乐的一声回响，街上的一张面孔，忽明忽暗的月影，或者心猿意马的思绪；——只有在万物的七彩中，游荡的灵魂才觉得高兴。

一件蠢事不再蠢，一旦你明知它蠢还去做。

看看月亮吧！你可能不知道，但月亮是出了状况。她不会准时赴约，也不遵守月相理论家们为她定下的规程。在十九世纪结束时她迟到了十秒钟：一百年前是早到十四秒。

据说，有千千万万人能够在普通的各行各业中取得成功；有数以百计的人能统治他们的同胞，能操控帝国，相比之下有一人甚至能理解这个捉摸不定的星球那快快慢慢的行踪带来的问题。但据说，这些智力超群、地位崇高的人中俊杰中的俊杰，包括其最亮眼的成员中的欧内斯特·威廉·布朗[86]和乔治·威廉·希尔[87]，也从未能算出月亮的运行规律：她仍然在嘲笑这些人想把她的行为弄明白的企图呢。

Ⅱ. Age and Death

It seemed so simple when one was young, and new ideas were mentioned, not to grow red in the face and gobble!

But we are forced like the insects, and cannot help it, to undergo all the metamorphoses preordained for our species.

We grow with years more fragile in body, but morally stouter, and can throw off the chill of a bad conscience almost at once.

An evil name, which is a drawback at first, sheds a kind of lustre on old age.

There are people who are beautiful in dilapidation, like houses that were hideous when new.

What is more enchanting than the voices of young people, when you can't hear what they say?

Don't laugh at a youth for his affectations; he is only trying on one face after another to find his own.

Youth is at war with Time; but why should a youth of high fancy quarrel with that Abstraction which can ripen his talent, and mellow his portrait with the varnish of years?

If we shake hands with icy fingers, it is because we have burnt them so horribly before.

二、年岁与死亡

年轻时这似乎简单得不得了——听人谈起新想法时不会面红耳赤嗷嗷叫！

但我们万般无奈，唯有像昆虫一样，被迫经历我们这个物种命定的所有蜕变。

我们随着年岁增长身体越发衰弱，但道德却越发硬朗，几乎能将亏心带来的寒意一把甩掉。

恶名，起初是瑕疵，却给晚年投下一种辉光。

有人衰败中显出美，一如有些房子崭新时窳劣不堪。

有什么能比年轻人的声音更迷人呢，要是你听不见他们说的是什么？

别笑年轻人造作，他只不过是在一张一张脸地试着要找出自己的那一张。

青春和时光交战；可是一个才思发越的年轻人为什么要同那“抽象”争拗呢？抽象让他的才气变得老成，让他的肖像因岁月的漆光而变得淳厚。

如果我们握手碰到的是冰冷的手指，那是因为我们以前把它们烧得够狠了。

Just when they sit down to enjoy in peace their evening meal of existence, the tables of most people are pounced upon as by harpies, and pillaged by their children.

Parents used to care more for their money than their family; now they pay for their children's friendship through the nose.

The fiery thought of a social slip which makes us feel hot all over, may mellow into a glow to warm our ageing bones.

I cannot forgive my friends for dying; I do not find these vanishing acts of theirs at all amusing.

We all do ugly things, and our last great act is the ugliest of all.

Why are happy people not afraid of Death, while the insatiable and the unhappy so abhor that grim feature?

Ⅲ. Other People

There are men and women born into the world to do its work and win its prizes; others, simply to look on and see what happens. These two kinds of people are apt to feel ashamed when they meet each other.

It's an odd thing about this universe that though we all

大多数人，就在他们刚坐下来要安安静静享受生活的晚餐时，饭桌便有如被鹰身女妖扑上来霸住似的，任由他们的孩子洗劫。

父母惯于守财先于顾家，过后则为买得儿女的情谊大破其财。

想起一次社交失误而心里窝着的那把令人浑身发热的火，可以焐成一片醇和的亮光来给我们渐渐老去的身子骨取暖。

我无法饶恕朋友过世，我觉得他们的这些遁身把戏一点也不好玩。

我们都做过丑事，而最后的那幕大戏最丑不过了。

为什么快乐的人不怕死神，而无法满足和不快乐的那些人又对这一副狰狞面孔如此深恶痛绝？

三、他人

男男女女，有些生来世上是要干它的活赢它的奖；其他的呢，无非旁观世事而已。这两种人相遇，往往会感到难堪。

这天地间有件事很怪，就是大家虽然相互不以为然，但我们

disagree with each other, we are all of us always in the right.

If with an excess of interest you peer into the lives of others, what you will probably find is that you have to pay their debts.

Those who set out to serve both God and Mammon soon discover that there is no God.

How much of our disparagement is the talk of foxes who have lost their tails!

There are people of whose lives I know such horrid details, that I feel ashamed of myself when I meet them in drawing-rooms, making a good impression.

When we say we are certain so-and-so could not have done it, what we mean is that we think he very likely did.

If we disregard what the world says of someone, we live to repent it.

The world is not unkind, and reprobates are worse than their reputations.

If you set out to fight the battles of discredited people, don't be too much surprised when they snipe you from the rear.

Most people sell their souls, and live with a good conscience on the proceeds.

又总是个个都对。

假如过分的兴趣让你窥视了他人的生活，那么你很可能发现的是自己得为他们还债。

那些存心服侍上帝金钱两不误的人很快就会发现没有上帝。

我们口中所出的非议，有多少是丢了尾巴的狐狸说的话啊！

有些人，我知道他们生活中如此不堪的丑事，结果都替自己觉得羞愧：与他们在聚会客厅里相遇还给人留下个好印象。

我们说我们肯定某件事不会是某某人干的时候，我们的意思是我们认为非常可能是他干的。

如果我们不理世人对某人的评说，那迟早会后悔的。

世界并非不仁，而恶人比他们的恶名更恶。

假若你成心要为失信之人征战，那等背后挨他们枪子儿时就别太觉得意外了。

大多数人卖自己的灵魂，问心无愧地靠所得过活。

To sell one's soul and not be paid for it, and do the Devil's work without his wages, is perhaps in Heaven's eyes a less flagitious bargain.

It is almost always worth while to be cheated; peoples' little frauds have an interest which more than repays what they cost us.

When people come and talk to you of their aspirations, before they leave you had better count your spoons.

All Reformers, however strict their social conscience, live in houses just as big as they can pay for.

When they come downstairs from their Ivory Towers, Idealists are apt to walk straight into the gutter.

The tone of people with low aims is always a high one: the talk of those who live purely for the Good is appalling.

People before the public live an imagined life in the thought of others, and flourish or feel faint as they grow bright or dwindle in that mirror.

A virtuous king is a king who has shirked his proper function—to embody for his subjects an ideal of illustrious misbehaviour beyond their reach.

Some human roles are so fixed that it is too great a strain to act them in any but the accepted manner. Fathers should

卖自己的灵魂而没收到钱，干魔鬼的活而没有魔鬼的工钱，也许在上天眼里是一桩不那么穷凶极恶的买卖。

上当受骗几乎总是值得的；人们的小诡计有利息，偿还我们为他们付出的代价足足有余。

有人来跟你谈他们的宏图大计时，在他们离开之前最好要点算一下你的汤匙。

所有改革者，无论他们的社会良心如何一丝不苟，都是付得起多大的房就住多大的房。

理想主义者从他们的象牙塔上下来时，往往径直走入阴沟中。

立意低者调门高：纯粹为善而活者言辞骇人。

人在公众前，过的是一种他人心中想象的生活，随着在这面镜子中渐趋光鲜或越发黯淡，要么神气要么萎靡。

贤明的国王是逃避了职责的国王——为臣民活出了一个他们可望不可即的煌煌然不守本分的理想境界。

人类有些角色是如此固定，要是不按常理演出就太劳神费力了。做父亲的要专横跋扈，做儿子的要忘恩负义；做祖母的要挫

be tyrannical, and sons ungrateful; grandmothers ought to demoralize their children's children, and mothers-in-law make all the bad mischief they can.

Moralists who tell you that Envy is the only vice without a pleasure, have never known the pleasure of seeing bright reflections of themselves in the eyes of envy.

The Saints see men and women through the golden haze of their own goodness; and too nice a discrimination of the characters of others is a sign that you are not too nice a character yourself.

Only among people who think no evil can Evil flourish without fear.

Goodness is not enough; but what a lustre it gives and delicate glaze to people who are good as well as charming!

Uncultivated minds are not full of wild flowers, like uncultivated fields. Villainous weeds grow in them, and they are the haunt of toads.

How it infuriates a bigot, when he is forced to drag into the light his dark convictions!

Intolerable to us is the thought that people we detest must be delightful, if delightful people like them.

'Well, for my part,' they say, 'I cannot see the charm of Mrs.

掉她们儿女的儿女的锐气，当亲家母的要能生出多大的是非就生多大的是非。

要是有道德家告诉你羡慕是唯一不带快感的恶，那是根本不知道看见他们自己的身影亮闪闪地映在羡慕的眼睛里是一种什么样的快感。

圣人是透过他们自己仁善的金色烟雾来看世间男女的，对他人性格的优劣区分得太好是你自己人不太好的一个迹象。

只有在不思邪恶的人当中邪恶才能枝蔓横生无所忌惮。

心好还不够，但是心好把一种怎样的辉光、怎样一层蕴藉的色泽加给了那些心好人也好的人啊！

未经调教的心不是开满野花的，不像未经调理的田野。那样的心，里头长的是毒草，其间出没的是癞蛤蟆。

一个偏执的人会怎样火冒三丈啊，要是谁逼他把自己那些暗黑的信念拖出来见光！

让我们无法容忍的是想到自己讨厌的人必定讨人喜欢，要是讨人喜欢的人喜欢他们的话。

“嗯，就我而言，”他们说，“我看不出琼斯太太有什么吸引人

Jones.'

'Is it not just conceivable,' I feel inclined to answer, 'that Mrs. Jones hasn't tried to charm you?'

Charming people live up to the very edge of their charm, and behave just as outrageously as the world will let them.

Those who are contemptuous of everyone are more than anyone terrified of contempt.

Never be sorry when fine creatures snap at you; it is a sign that they hunt with another pack.

Don't tell your friends their social faults; they will cure the fault and never forgive you.

Dark and distorting are the minds of people who dislike us. When we meet them, we make dismal reflections.

I find a fascination, like the fascination for the moth of a star, in those who hold aloof and disdain me.

What a joy to find suddenly among strangers a fish from our little swarm of fishes, a bee from our hive!

We need new friends; some of us are cannibals who have eaten their old friends up: others must have ever-renewed audiences before whom to re-enact an ideal version of their lives.

之处。”

“这不恰恰可以想见，”我真想回一句，“琼斯太太并没想要吸引你吗？”

有魅力的人极尽其魅力之能事，世界会让他们多荒唐，他们的言行可就有多荒唐。

谁他们都看不起的人，比谁都更怕被人看不起。

好人向你张牙舞爪时千万不要难过，那是他们跟另外一群家伙一起狩猎的讯号。

不要告诉朋友他们社交上的错误，他们会改掉错误而绝不原谅你。

阴暗变形的是不喜欢我们的人的内心。遇见他们时，我们映出来的模样扭曲不堪。

我发现那些人有一种吸引力，如同一颗星星对蛾子的吸引力，那些高高在上看不起我的人。

多么令人开心啊，突然在陌生人当中发现一条从我们这小鱼群来的鱼，一只从我们的蜜蜂窝里来的蜂！

我们需要新朋友；我们有些人是食人族，吃光了老朋友：另外一些必须不断更新观众，好在他们面前再次演出自己生活的一个理想版本。

Don't give to lovers you will replace, irreplaceable presents.

All our lives we are putting pennies—our most golden pennies—into penny-in-the-slot machines that are almost always empty.

We live in a world of monkeys; and are victims for ever of the illusion which makes monkeys, at a distance, look like men.

But it is not always easy to treat men and women as apes, and not baboon oneself in the process.

It is a great mistake to talk to one set of people about another set they do not know. We should return as taciturn as cats from their nocturnal outings.

What impossible company we keep in the kind thought of those who think kindly of us!

A friend who loved perfection would be the perfect friend, if that love of his didn't shut his door on me.

'But we have the right,' people protest sometimes, 'of entertaining our friends!'

'But have you the right,' we are too polite to answer, 'of compelling us to meet them?'

If we treat people too long with that pretended liking called politeness, we shall find it hard not to like them in the end.

别给你将要换掉的情人不可替换的礼物。

我们一辈子都在把硬币——我们最金灿灿的硬币——一便士一便士投进那些几乎永远是空的自动售卖机里。

我们生活在一个猴子的世界里；还永远蒙蔽在幻觉中，让猴子，远远地，看着像人。

但这么做并不一定容易：一边把男男女女当猿猴看，一边又不把自己看成狒狒。

跟一拨人谈论他们不认识的另一拨人是大错特错。我们应该像猫夜游返家那样一声不响地回来。

我们结交的都是些什么人哪！那些对我们有好感的人好心地觉得。

一个热爱完美的朋友会是完美的朋友，假如他的那份热爱没把我拒之门外。

“可是我们有权，”人们有时抗议说，“有权招待自己的朋友！”

“可是你们有权，”我们太客气了没这么回答，“有权要我们非见他们不可吗？”

要是我们太长时间以称为礼貌的那种装出来的喜欢待人，到头来会发现很难不喜欢他们。

Since few things—as we know—more annoy other people, why do we delight in crabbing their friends?

Those who say everything is pleasant and everyone delightful, suffer the awful fate of believing what they say.

How many woes when you marry, how many ancient calamities you invite to the Wedding!

It is a matter of life and death for married people to try to tell each other's stories; if they didn't, they would burst.

If they lost the incredible conviction that they can change their wives or their husbands, marriage would collapse at once.

The act of flesh is an unsteady basis on which to build the house of life.

It is interesting to peep through most keyholes, but not into the bedrooms of married people.

Married women are kept women, and they are beginning to find it out.

Eunuchs are no longer procurable to guard the chastity of females; but there are gentlemen who can be absolutely trusted.

People have a right to be shocked; the mention of

既然没多少事情——就我们所知——更惹别人生气，那为什么我们还以数落他们的朋友为乐呢？

那些总说事事都好人人都好的人，命苦就苦在相信自己说的话。

你结婚时是把多少苦痛、多少古老的灾祸请到了婚礼上！

对于已婚之人，生死攸关的是使劲要把彼此的故事说出来；如果不说，他们会撑爆的。

夫妇间真要是失去那匪夷所思的信念，不再以为自己能把对方改变，婚姻马上就垮了。

肉体行为是建造生活之屋的一个不牢固的基础。

从锁孔偷窥，大都很有意思，只要不是往已婚夫妇的卧室里看。

女人结婚就是被包养，她们正开始发觉这一点。

再也寻觅不到阉人来守护女性的贞洁了，但有绅士可以绝对信任。

人有权大吃一惊，把不能说的事说出口便是参与其中的一种

unmentionable things is a kind of participation in them.

What are the Queens of Sodom to do when their sons come from school?

Statisticians tell us that in Russia before the war six Christs came to save St. Petersburg every year, and were every year seduced by six great ladies of that capital.

What is more disheartening to think of than the unremitting monogamy of grim couples?

How many human types have fallen out of fashion! Where can we find the Black Sheep, the Angel Child, and the Permanent Invalid on her sofa? Into what suburb or sad limbo have departed the dear Old Lady with her cap and laces, the Seducer, the Fop, the Aesthete and the Fallen Daughter?

Ⅳ. In the World

People not born on the top of the social tree must have climbed to get there.

The flavour of social success is delicious, though it is scorned by those to whose lips the cup has not been proffered.

You should wear in the Great World your heart on your sleeve, but it must be a sham one.

方式。

所多玛[88]的女王们在儿子从学校回来时要做的是什么呢?

统计学家告诉我们,战前在俄国每年有六位基督徒来拯救圣彼得堡,每年都给那座都城里六位了不起的女士勾引了。

有什么想来比这更令人沮丧的呢:两情相怨却严守一夫一妻?

有多少种类型的人都已经过时了!上哪儿去找有辱家门的败类、天使般的孩童、永远躺在她沙发上的病人?都去了哪处乡郊或者哪个化外伤心地呢,那戴着帽子和蕾丝的亲爱的老妇人、那偷香窃玉之人、那纨绔子弟、那唯美主义者和失足的女儿?

四、人世间

不是生在社会之树顶端的人必定是攀缘到那里去的。

功成名就的滋味是甜美的,尽管看它不起的是成功之杯没端给他们的那些人。

在这个大世界上你要喜怒形于色,但那必须是假喜假怒。

The romantic impulse of our nature to people the world with Gods seems to us pretty in lovers: in Snobs we dislike it.

The hallucinations of sex are not to be trusted, but we can count on our worldly illusions to keep us company to the grave.

And yet to be worldly, to hold to the world's simple creed and believe in its heaven, must surely stagger the faith of the firmest believer.

The spread of atheism among the young is something awful; I give no credit, however, to the report that some of them do not believe in Mammon.

It is the wretchedness of being rich that you have to live with rich people.

Eat with the Rich, but go to the play with the Poor, who are capable of Joy.

You cannot be both fashionable and first-rate.

All worldly goods are good; why otherwise should the world pursue them? And yet the old indictment stands; and garlands and vainglories are best as baubles for our thoughts to play with, like those crowns which drunken Kalenders take and give each other at the doors of Persian wine-shops, a brick beneath their heads, their feet resting on the Seven Stars.

我们天性中要让世界住满神仙的浪漫冲动，如果来自恋人似乎很可心，如果来自阿谀奉承的小人我们就不喜欢了。

性的幻觉不可信赖，但我们能指望我们世俗的幻梦空想做伴到坟墓。

然而做俗世中人，秉持人世简单的信条又信仰其天堂，肯定连最坚定的信仰者的信心也会动摇。

无神论在年轻人当中传播，这事很糟糕；然而，我一点也不相信所说的他们有的人不信财神。

为富之苦，是你不得不与富人同住。

同富人吃饭，但同穷人看戏，他们快活得起来。

你无法既跟时尚又成一流。

世上资财样样都好；否则世人为何孜孜以求？然而古训所言依然不虚；花环与虚荣再好也不过是供思想把弄的小玩意儿罢了，就像那些王冠，喝得醉醺醺的托钵僧们拿着在波斯的酒肆门前相互传来递去，他们头枕一块砖，脚搁七星上。

I love money; just to be in the room with a millionaire makes me less forlorn.

Wealth is a kind of leprosy, and wealthy people should be segregated like lepers to keep them from contaminating others.

To suppose, as we all suppose, that we could be rich and not behave as the rich behave, is like supposing that we could drink all day and keep absolutely sober.

Rich people would not enjoy their little meannesses so much, if they knew how much their friends enjoy them.

Every situation in life provides us ready-made with the outfit of thoughts and ways of behaving which perfectly fit it.

Quality-folk are seldom at their ease with intellectuals, among whom they make a great deal of mischief.

And when in their azure veins they dip their pens of gold, how vapid, and (but hush!) how vulgar are the books they write!

The ladies who try to keep their Beauty are the ladies who lose it.

There is a toad in every social dish, however well they cook it.

I rather like singing for my supper; what grates on my ears is the song of the other singers.

我爱钱；只要跟一个百万富翁同处一室，就令我不那么凄凉。

钱财是一种麻风病，有钱人要像麻风病人一样隔离起来，不让他们传染别人。

假设，我们都这么假设的，自己有钱了不会像有钱人那样行事，这就像假设自己可以整天饮酒而头脑绝对清醒一样。

富人不会因为自己的小气举动而乐成这样，要是他们知道这些举动让他们的朋友有多快乐。

生活中的每一个情境都为我们提供了现成的思想套路和行为方式，与之完美匹配。

大人物很少和知识分子处得舒服，在知识分子中他们生出许多是非。

当他们在自己蓝色的脉管中蘸着他们的黄金之笔时，写出来的书是多么了无趣味、多么（但是，嘘！）了无品味啊！

想着尽力保持美丽的女人便是美丽不再的女人。

社交场上每一道菜里都有只癞蛤蟆，无论他们烹调得有多高明。

我颇喜欢自食其力，为自己的晚餐自己唱歌，别人唱的硌我耳朵。

'I have eaten from the timbrel,' I chant. 'I have drunk from the cymbal, I have carried the sacred vessel, I have crept beneath the bridal chamber.'

More fascinating, at a party, than any other music is the rushing sound of fashionable voices; the vociferation of all those fairies, each faintly blowing its own trumpet.

There are people whose society I find delicious; but when I sit alone and think of them, I shudder.

Ladies there are who know too much of London, and stand petrified, like Lot's wife, when she looked back on Sodom.

'When people say they hate gossip, remember,' the son of a celebrated upholsterer once warned me, 'that some of them do really hate it.'

There are such astonishing things to be told about men and women, and hardly a man or a woman to whom one dares to tell them.

If you want to be thought a liar, always tell the truth.

To say what you think will certainly damage you in society; but—why should I refrain my mouth? —a free tongue is worth a thousand invitations.

When we find it amusing to shock people, we forget what shocking the experience it is.

“我用手鼓吃过饭，”我唱道，“我用铙钹饮过酒，我捧过圣瓶，我钻过新房的床底。”

聚会上，比任何其他音乐都更迷人的是时尚中人嘈嘈切切的说话声；听这些精灵夸夸其谈，看他们若明若暗自吹喇叭。

有些人，他们的社交圈我觉得很有滋有味；可等我独自坐着想起他们时，便不寒而栗。

是有些女士，她们对伦敦知道太多，便石化般立着，犹如罗得的妻子，回头看所多玛城便化成了石像。[89]

“当人们说他们讨厌流言蜚语时，记住，”一位有名的家具装饰商的儿子曾经告诫我，“他们中有些人是真的讨厌。”

关于男人女人，有如此令人吃惊的事要说，而几乎没有哪个男人或者女人你敢把这些事跟他们说。

如果你想让人觉得是个骗子，那就总说实话。

想什么就说什么，这肯定会让你在社会上倒霉；可是——我干吗要管自己的嘴呢？——一条自由的舌头抵得上一千份请柬。

发现吓人很好玩时，我们忘了吓人有多么吓人。

Hearts that are delicate and kind and tongues that are neither, —these make the finest company in the world.

Nice men are not nice-minded, but—with a few sublime exceptions—nice women are.

Those who talk on the razor-edge of double-meanings pluck the rarest blooms from the precipices on either side.

How full is the world of Fallen Angels!

Beware of the execrable talk to be heard in certain drawing-rooms of this stony-hearted city. You may when too late find that you cannot live without it.

How pleasant, with the impunity of years, to sip those cups of enchantment which would have poisoned our youth!

Friendship in the middle-classes is founded on respect; in the world of fashion they simply adore men and women whom not one of them would dream of trusting round the corner.

The fundamental distinction between the good and bad eggs of the world is one which people of the World find convenient to ignore.

The charitable attempt not to smell the smell of a bad egg only makes it worse.

To win a friend is success; but if you can snatch the friend

心细腻善良，舌不细腻不善良——这两样堪成世上绝配。

好男人没有好心肠，但是——几个极端者例外——好女人有。

那些踩在一语双关的刃脊上说话的人，从削壁两边或左或右采摘最珍稀的花朵。

世界充斥着多少堕落的天使啊！

当心那些恶言恶语，在这座心如铁石的城市中的某些客厅里会听得到的。你可能等到太迟才发觉自己生活缺不了这东西。

多快活啊，因年岁而免罚，可以来啜饮那些本会毒害我们青春的恣情欢乐之杯！

友谊在中产阶级中是建立在尊重的基础上；在时尚圈里，他们无非是崇拜些男男女女，这一众男女一转过街角他们谁做梦都不会去相信的。

世上好蛋坏蛋根本不同，世故的人觉得这是个不看更省心的区别。

与人为善地企图不去闻坏蛋之臭，只会让坏蛋更坏。

赢得一个朋友是成功；但如果能抢走一个朋友的朋友，那你

of a friend, then blow your trumpet!

We need two kinds of acquaintances, one to complain to, while we boast to the others.

One can be bored until boredom becomes a mystical experience.

When we talk politely of new books with a new acquaintance, what abysses may yawn in drawing-rooms between us!

But what festivals of unanimity we celebrate when meet what I call a 'Milver' —a fellow-fanatic whose thoughts chime in a sweet ecstasy of execration with our own!

Those who like the same thing find it the hardest thing in the world not to like one another.

'O Joy!' sings a bird in the heart, 'O Joy!' another bird answers; while the world, like a large, thoughtful cat, sits by and watches.

Words are not always mere words: a few almost inaudible articulations may fetter two people together for life.

就大吹大擂吧!

我们需要两种熟人,一种用来诉苦,一种用来夸口。

人可以觉得无聊,直到无聊成了一种神秘的体验。

当我们和一位新结识的人礼貌地谈起新书时,真不知道客厅里双方之间会裂开多大的深渊!

可我们庆祝的是怎样一种相见恨晚的欢乐啊——当逢着一位我称之为"觅尔"的人,一个同路狂人,与我们在同仇敌忾中甜蜜地忘乎所以,心心相印!

喜欢同样事物的人发现世界上最难的是让他们彼此不喜欢。

"啊,欢乐!"一只小鸟在心中唱着,"啊,欢乐!"另一只小鸟和着;而世界,像一头大大的、深思熟虑的猫,坐在一旁盯着。

话语并非永远只是话语而已:说几声几乎听不见的话可以把两个人锈在一起一辈子。

V. Art and Letters

The indefatigable pursuit of an unattainable Perfection, even though it consist in nothing more than in the pounding of an old piano, is what alone gives a meaning to our life on this unavailing star.

The test of a vocation is the love of the drudgery it involves.

Artists who do not love their art are more numerous, and more unhappy, than we think.

The Muses are vindictive virgins, and avenge themselves without mercy on those who weary of their charms.

We should nourish our souls on the dew of Poesy, and manure them as well.

Slavery and Infamy are the merited chastisements of Success.

Walk in the gutter if you can.

The great art of writing is the art of making people real to themselves with words.

Style is a magic wand, and turns everything to gold it touches.

五、艺术与文学

不懈地追求一种无可企及的完美，哪怕只是在一部老钢琴上敲琴键，单凭这个就给了我们在这无用的星球上的生活一种意义。

一项职业考验人之处在于是否喜欢其中包含的苦工琐事。

是艺术家又不爱自己的艺术，这种人比我们想象的更多，更不开心。

缪斯女神是报复心很强的处女，对那些厌倦了她们魅力的人出手毫不留情。

我们滋养灵魂要用诗的甘露，同样也要施以粪肥。

劳役和坏名声是成功应受的惩罚。

走在阴沟里，如果你行的话。

写作这一伟大的艺术，是以文字使人真实面对自我的艺术。

风格是一根魔棒，点到的一切都变成金子。

Poets' words have wings: they float up the stairs of palaces on them.

What a paradise for poets the great world would be, if any sort of discrimination were made in those palaces between fine gold and brass!

Fine writers should split hairs together, and sit side by side, like friendly apes, to pick the fleas from each other's fur.

Authors know that the age of miracles is not over; how otherwise explain the transfiguration of asses who praise their writings into exquisite arbiters of taste?

Desperate writers, who once, by their cries of agony wrung tears from tender-hearted readers, come to prefer the glittering smiles of hostesses with hearts as hard as the marble mantelpieces in their drawing-rooms.

A best-seller is the gilded tomb of a mediocre talent.

If you are losing your leisure, look out! You may be losing your soul.

Poverty and her sister Solitude, to whom princely talents used to look for their tuition—how these two shabby old Maids of Honour are now hooted at by the young!

Writers who write for money don't write for me.

诗人的语言有翅膀，他们借此扶摇飞上宫廷的阶梯。

偌大世界，会是诗人怎样的一处天堂啊，如果那些宫廷中人稍稍区别一下黄金和黄铜！

好作家应该在一起吹毛求疵，排排坐着，活像友好的猿猴，互相拨毛捉跳蚤。

写作人知道，奇迹的时代还没过去；要不然该怎么解释赞扬他们作品的傻瓜们会给美化成精妙的品位仲裁者呢？

绝望的作家，曾经以他们凄惨的哭喊赚取了软心肠读者的眼泪，转而看上心硬得像客厅大理石壁炉架的女主人们粲然的微笑。

一部畅销书是一个平庸之才的漆金坟墓。

如果你在失去自己的闲暇，当心！你可能在失去你的灵魂。

贫穷和她的妹妹孤独，旧时轻世傲物的才子多要向她们讨教——如今这两位寒酸的老侍女被年轻人怎样寒碜讥笑啊！

为钱写作的人不是为我而写。

The notion of making money by popular work, and then retiring to do good work on the proceeds, is the most familiar of all the devil's traps for artists.

What I like in a good author is not what he says, but what he whispers.

Nothing is perfect in this world; and in spite of the noise they make and their big incomes, the complacency of our full-blown authors is not untroubled at odd moments, I am told, by the thought of that little group, just round the corner, of unimpressed, jeering, sneering people.

How gay it would be to glitter, with no fellow-performers, alone in the limelight!

Every author, however modest, keeps a most outrageous vanity chained like a madman in the padded cell of his breast.

When we see what people we like will do for money, best it is to be sad and say nothing.

After all, a little good taste does no harm, and the fever of Perfection is not catching.

The most heart-breaking of all people are those who bow with us before our Gods, and then trip off to the shrines of false ones.

What humbugs we are, who pretend to live for Beauty, and

想着用通俗作品赚钱，再退而以所赚的钱弄出好作品，这是最为人熟悉的魔鬼给艺术家设下的圈套。

一个好作家让我喜欢的不是他说了什么，而是他悄悄说了什么。

这个世界上没有什么是完美的；尽管名噪一时，收入丰厚，我们的大作家们一想到左近有那不为所动、对他们冷嘲热讽的小小一群人，自得之余，我听说，偶尔也无法安之若素。

这该多惬意啊：无人同台表演，独自在舞台灯下闪光！

每一个作家，不管多谦虚，都怀有一种骄狂非常的虚荣心，就像锁疯子那样锁在他胸中的软垫密室里。

看到我们所喜欢的人要为了钱去做的事，这时最好是悲而不语。

毕竟，有一点好的品位无伤大雅，追求完美这一热病传不起来的。

所有人当中，最令人心碎的是那些人，他们与我们同在我们的神明面前鞠躬，接着又步履轻快地赶往假神灵跟前。

我们是怎样的一群骗子啊，假装为美而活，却从来没看到

never see the Dawn!

The vitality of a new movement in art or letters can be gauged by the fury it arouses.

If you try hard enough to seem to like pictures, you will like them in the end.

What sight in the world is sadder than the sight of a lady we admire admiring a nauseating picture?

If you are up to date to-day, how dismally out of date you will look to-morrow!

He who goes against the fashion is himself its slave.

All our affirmations are mere matters of chronology; and our bad taste nothing more than the bad taste of the age we live in.

If we are told that an odd piece of our china is worth a hundred pounds, how rare will be its beauty!

How amazing are those moments when we really possess our possessions!

We who travel thousands of miles to gaze on beauty, are rather put out by the flaming at home of unfashionable sunsets over fashionable shops.

黎明!

艺术或文学的一场新运动,其生命力可以用所激起的愤怒来度量。

如果你下足功夫要显得喜欢图画,最终会喜欢上的。

世界上,还有什么能比这情景更令人伤心的呢:看到一位我们所欣赏的女士在欣赏一幅令人作呕的画作?

假如你今天很入时,那么明天你的样子会过时得多么不堪!

与时尚对着干的人本身就是时尚的奴隶。

我们所秉持的一切不过是年代更迭使然,我们窳劣的品位无非是我们所处时代的窳劣品位而已。

如果我们听了谁说我们一件古怪的瓷器值一百英镑,那它该有什么样的稀世之美啊!

我们所拥有的真正为我们所拥有时,那样的时刻是多么奇妙啊!

我们这些不远千里出来一睹美景的人,看腻了家乡不时髦的落日火烧火燎地照耀在时髦的店铺上。

Ⅵ. Myself

The extreme oddness of existence is what reconciles me to it.

Our personal affairs are not really worthy, as Plato tells us, of our consideration; the fact that we are forced to take them seriously (as I was forced to run after my hat when it did blow off to-day), being, as he said, the ignoble part of our condition.

My life is a bubble; but how much solid cash it costs to keep that bubble floating!

I like to walk down Bond Street, thinking of all the things I don't desire.

Why should my Soul so rejoice in the crimes placarded by the evening papers, and never weary, in the streets of this cathedral city, of dallying with images of wrong?

'Let me cease,' I pray, 'O thou Perfectly Awakened, to remain as an ape in the great world-forest, perpetually ascending and descending in search of the fruits of folly.'

To count all things as vanity and yet nothing as vain; to wander through the show of things without illusion, or care, or desire, or disappointment; is not this the way (for why art thou proud O Dust and Ashes?) to walk the London streets?

How my reason totters in her contemplative tower, when

六、我本人

是存在那无以复加的怪诞令我与之和解。

我们个人私事真不值得，如柏拉图说的，我们去费心；至于被迫对一己私事隆而重之（就像我今天帽子吹跑了被迫跟在后面追），乃是，他说了，我们生活状况中不光彩的部分。

我的生活是个泡泡，但要多少实打实的钞票才能让那泡泡漂浮不坠！

我喜欢走在邦德街上，沿路想着所有我不想要的东西。

为什么我的灵魂要如此喜欢晚报上登出的种种罪案，乐此不疲地，在这教堂城市的街道上，与不端的形象吊儿郎当调笑一番？

“且让我消停吧，”我祈祷，“全知的主啊，让我别再是一头猿猴，在世界的大森林中，不停歇地爬上爬下找寻愚蠢结的果实。”

视一切为虚荣又不以一物为虚妄；徜徉穿过物的炫示而不存幻想，不费思量，不怀欲念，也不心生失望；这岂不是（问君何以得意，呜呼，这副尘与土的皮囊？）伦敦街头的行走之道？

当人们说他们见到我在街上时，我的理智在她沉思的高台上

people say that they have seen me in the street!

But how hard it is, as Pyrrho of Elis said, to discard our human nature!

I like my universe as immense, grim, icy and pitiless as possible.

When to the lady I met at luncheon I tried to explain that there is no enchantment in life like that of disenchantment with it, she looked at me as if I were a cloud, or a steeple on the horizon, and her answer was as cold as the moon.

When I look at those beautiful and mysterious apparitions we call people, I like to think of their adorations one for another; how they love to gaze in the mirrors of each other's eyes.

'O, for an axe!' my soul cries out in railway stations, 'to hew limb from limb all the fiends and Jezebels between me and the ticket-office!'

When I come in talk on a blank wall of stupidity facing me, why do I go and break my bald head against it?

'Isn't it odd,' I said, as we were looking at the roses with those ladies, 'to think that flowers are the reproductive organs of the plants they grow on?'

People who live among photographs of their friends are not friends for me.

晃荡得多厉害啊！

可是多么难啊，正如伊利斯的皮浪[90]所说，要我们丢弃人性！

我喜欢我的宇宙尽可能的广袤、严酷、冰冷、无情。

我力图要给午餐会上遇见的那位女士解释，说生活中任何迷人的魅力都不像其祛魅之后的醒悟那样迷人，这时她看着我，好像我是一片云，或是天边的一点塔尖，她的回答则冷得像月亮。

看着那些我们称之为人的既美丽又神秘的幽灵时，我便喜欢去想他们如何惺惺相惜；他们多么爱盯着彼此的眼睛当镜子照。

“啊，来一把斧头！”我的灵魂在火车站里呼喊，“一条胳膊一条腿地把那些男女恶棍全砍掉，别堵在我和售票处之间！”

我在讲话中碰到一堵空墙般的愚鲁正对着我，干吗我还要冲着它撞破我的秃脑袋？

“不觉得奇怪吗，”我说道，这时我们正与那些女士看玫瑰，“想想花是它们长在上面的那些植物的生殖器官？”

生活在朋友照片中间的人不是我要的朋友。

I might give my life for my friend, but he had better not ask me to do up a parcel.

Like other Moralists, I like to poke about in that dark cabinet, the human heart, and expose its shady corners.

And what pursuit is more elegant than that of collecting the ignominies of our nature and transfixing them for show, each on the bright pin of a polished phrase?

Aphorisms are salted and not sugared almonds at Reason's feast.

On scenes of worldly splendour I gaze with eyes more mild than those of Moses when, at the sight of the Golden Calf and the dancing, his heart waxed wroth within him.

And the tremendous enigma which so troubled King David—the prosperity of the Wicked, and the Righteous as withered grass—this moral paradox does not spoil my appetite in the least.

I like diaphanous illusions, with the shapes of things as they are showing not too faintly through them.

When people tinkle coronets in the conversation I am inordinately solaced.

I don't hate the Aristocracy; but I do wish they wouldn't publish slip-slop with their photographs in the penny papers.

我可能会为我的朋友献出生命，但他最好别叫我打包裹。

像别的道德家一样，我喜欢在那个暗匣子里探来探去，人心的暗匣子，再把它那些阴暗的角落亮出来。

有什么追求比这个更雅致呢——搜集我们本性的龌龊，刺穿了挂出来展示，每一样挂的别针亮闪闪的都是一枚琢磨过的词语？

格言警句是理性之筵席上的盐焗而非糖渍杏仁。

目睹一幕幕俗世荣华的盛景，我的眼神比摩西的温和，他一看到金牛犊[91]和拜神舞蹈，心中可是怒火万丈。

让大卫王[92]百思不得其解的大谜题——恶人兴盛，义人衰萎如草——这个道德悖论一丁点也坏不了我的胃口。

我喜欢透明的幻象，其中事物所显示的状貌透过来不至于太模糊。

看到人们谈话中把冠冕敲得叮当响，我满心欣慰难以言喻。

我不讨厌贵族，但的确希望他们别在小报上配着自己的照片吧嗒吧嗒说无聊话。

People say that life is the thing, but I prefer reading.

It is the misery of young people that they have to read each other's books.

I hate having new books forced upon me, but how I love cramming them down the throats of other people!

From the bright, unbookish constellations my thoughts float back to the dim-lit reading-room of this circulating library, the earth.

The world, as I know from my books, is full of abominable evil; even some of these books have never been returned.

Of all the themes of sentimental novels most of all I love a marriage, loveless in appearance, between a high-souled hero and heroine who really do adore each other, but are too proud—ah, far too proud! —to avow it;

Till suddenly,
After years of icily polite relations,
The flame of their mutual ardour blazes out,
And they fall at last
(While I almost swoon away with bliss),
Into the heaven of each other's arms.

I cannot claim to be a dainty feeder; I like to read of frantic passions, and am not at all reluctant to wade ankle-deep in blood.

人说过日子最实在，但我更喜欢读书。

年轻人苦就苦在不得不相互读对方的书。

我讨厌人家把新书强推给我，但自己又多么喜欢把新书往他人的喉咙里塞下去啊！

从那些明亮、没有书卷气的星座，我的思绪飘回这间灯光昏暗的阅览室，厕身这座巡回图书馆，这颗地球。

世界上，我从我的书中得知，充满了令人恨之入骨的恶；连这些书，有些给人借走了从来都不见还。

言情小说所有的主题中，我最爱终成眷属，表面上没有爱，其实两位心气高的男女主人公还真是两情相悦，但又太孤傲——啊，太太孤傲了！——就是不肯承认；

直到突然一刻，
经年冰冷的相待以礼之后，
两相爱慕之情如烈火喷涌，
他们终于扑进
(这无上福分差点让我晕倒)，
彼此怀中的天堂。

我不能声称自己口味优雅；我喜欢在书中读到癫狂的激情，一点也不会排拒蹚过深及脚踝的血泊。

Amid the mirrored corridors, the fountains and gardens of the Versailles within me, struts his bewigged majesty, my Soul.

I love to take a romantic view of my life, and I hate it.

How often my soul visits the National Gallery, and how seldom I go there myself!

Just as remorse at feeling no remorse is a form of the holiest contrition, so when beauty leaves me cold, I take my coldness as the proof of how warmly I love it.

I make no immoderate demands; my hopes for my declining years are not greedy. In January—like an old French unbeliever I have read of—I begin to think of the strawberry season; and I look forward, when that is over, to the ripening of peaches in August.

I shouldn't mind, though, living to my hundredth year, like Fontenelle, who never wept or laughed, never ran or interrupted anyone, and never lost his temper; to whom all the science of his day was known, but who all his life adored three things—music, painting and women—about which he said he understood absolutely nothing.

Or like Huet, that gay old Bishop of Avranches (*'flos Episcoporum'* a German scholar called him), who lived to be ninety-one, and read Theocritus every year in his favourite month of May.

那些镶着明镜的走廊、那些喷泉和花园，在我这座心中的凡尔赛宫里，信步穿行着头戴假发的国王陛下——我的灵魂。

我喜欢以浪漫的眼光看待我的生活，而我又讨厌这样做。

我的灵魂多么经常光顾国家美术馆，而我自身是多么难得前往啊！

正如因为没感到悔恨而悔恨是一种最神圣的忏悔，要是美丢下我令我浑身冰冷，我以这份冰冷为凭，证明我对美的爱是多么热切。

我没做出非分要求，暮年的希望也不贪求什么。一月份——像我读过的一位不信神的法国老人那样——我开始想着草莓成熟的季节；接着，这个季节过了，我便期盼桃子成熟的八月。

我不会介意的，话说回来，要是能活到一百岁，和丰特奈尔[93]一样，从来不哭也不笑，从来不差遣也不阻拦谁，还从来不发脾气；那个时代的科学他全知道，但是一辈子他心仪的只有三样——音乐、绘画和女人——关于这些，他说自己是一无所知。

或者和于埃[94]，那位法国阿夫朗什城快乐的老主教（“*flos Episcoporum*”，花主教，一位德国学者这么称呼他）一样，他活到九十一岁，每年在他最喜欢的五月里都读忒奥克里托斯的田园诗。

Or again I think with envy of the octogenarian Firdausi, who realized the dream he had dreamed in his childhood when, gazing into the irrigation canal which flowed by his father's garden, the Persian boy had reflected that it would be a fine thing to leave an image of himself in the world that passes.

Or the learned old Baron Walckenaer, who wrote important books on spiders, solitary bees and Madame de Sévigné; who established on a sound historical basis the chronology of Ninon de Lenclos' lovers, and published a romance called *'l'Ile de Wight,'* in which island he located his dream of bliss and his ideal habitation.

It would have been a disillusion for the Baron had he known how, standing on a little platform at the top of his house at Farringford, and gazing up through a telescope at the icy constellations which hung in a horror of bottomless space above that island, Tennyson would sometimes shiver, and, for a moment, almost doubt the existence of his benevolent Creator.

But most of all I envy the octogenarian poet who joined three words—

'Go, lovely Rose' —

so happily together, that he left his name to float down through Time on the wings of a phrase and a flower.

When I look at the Ocean, which seemed so inadequate an object of contemplation to Coleridge; —he and Wordsworth

或者我又怀着羡慕想起活了八十多岁的菲尔多西[95]，他实现了自己的童年梦想；那时候，看着从父亲花园边流过的水渠，这波斯男孩心想，人生好事一件，是把他自己的一个影像留在经眼而过的世界上。

或者那位博学的老男爵瓦尔肯耐尔[96]，他写了有关蜘蛛、失群蜜蜂和塞维涅夫人[97]的重要著作；在翔实的史料基础上确立了尼农·德·朗科洛[98]的情人年谱，还出版了一部传奇小说《怀特岛》，在这岛上他寄托了自己的幸福之梦，放置了自己的理想居所。

男爵要是知道了这件事会幻想破灭的——怀特岛上，站在他法令福德的房子一个小小的屋顶平台上，用望远镜眺望那些冷冰冰的星座，看它们惊恐万状地悬挂在岛上空无底的暗夜中，丁尼生[99]有时会不寒而栗，有一刻几乎还怀疑起他那仁慈的造物主的存在呢。

但我最羡慕的是那位八十多岁的诗人，他把三个词连在一起——

“走吧，可爱的玫瑰花”——

连得如此欢喜，让他的名字得以留下穿越时间乘着一句话和一朵花的翅膀飞扬。

在我眺望大海时，眺望这个对柯勒律治[100]来说似乎是不足以让他注目深思的物体；——他和华兹华斯 1798 年从雅茅斯乘汉

were sailing in 1798 on their memorable visit to Germany from Yarmouth in the Hamburg packet, and on Monday, the 17th of September, when the ship was out of sight of land and Coleridge came on deck and gazed at the objectless waters, he was exceedingly disappointed, he tells us, by the narrowness and nearness of the horizon; and was aware of none of that immensity which he had expected to find in such an unimpeded sea-prospect; —so poorly indeed can objects directly before our senses satisfy the Imagination, that 'awful Power,' as his fellow-tourist was afterwards to call it; —when, as I say, I look at the Ocean, I remedy the defect which Coleridge noted by contemplating it through the magnifying glass of our poetic vocabulary; and by calling it 'unpathed,' 'unfathomed,' 'insatiate,' and 'outrageous,' I arrive at a more adequate conception of the view of flat water before me.

There are great youths too, whose achievements one may envy; the boy David who slew Goliath and Bishop Berkeley who annihilated, at the age of twenty-five, the external world in an octavo volume; and the young David Hume, who by sweeping away all the props of the human understanding, destroyed for ever the possibility of knowledge.

To be an elegant and acrimonious scholar, and make emendations in Greek texts that shall fill the world with wonder;

Or an illustrious Egyptologist, with spectacles and a white beard;

堡邮船去德国的那次难忘的访问途中，在9月17日星期一那天，船行到看不见陆地时，柯勒律治到甲板上望着空无一物的一片水，大失所望，他告诉我们，没想到地平线如此之窄如此之近；他一点也意识不到面对这一览无余的水天一色本想要发现的那种恢宏；——的确是如此不济，物体直接展现在感官之前真难以满足人的想象力这一“可怕的力量”，正如他的旅伴后来会称呼的那样；——在我，如我所说，眺望大海时，对柯勒律治注意到的不尽人意处我的补救方法是通过我们的诗歌词汇这一放大镜来端详思量；称之为“无路可行”“无底可测”“聚敛无度”“汹汹然不可一世”，我便对眼前这平平一片水有了更充分的认识。

也有了不起的年轻人，他们的成就足以令人叹羡；少年大卫手刃巨人歌利亚，贝克莱主教呢，年方二十五，便以一部八开本巨著扫灭了外部世界；而年轻的大卫·休谟[101]，横扫人类理解力的一切支柱，一了百了地摧毁了知识的可能性。

做一名风度优雅、言辞辛辣的学者，对古希腊文本作的订正将让世人惊叹不已；

或者一个名闻遐迩的埃及学家，戴着眼镜蓄着白胡子；

Or a Lord of Thought, and sum up the universe in a single phrase;

And know all about it, whatever it is, and break the teeth of the young lions, break their great teeth in their mouths;

Or to lie in bed day after day like Joubert, in a pink dressing-gown, trying to think nothing and feel no emotion?

How hard it is for the good to go wrong! I seem to find all the pleasant paths of Transgression barricaded against me.

Round and around the world, on the storms that blow always about the Southern Pole, albatrosses float for ever; and only once a year they land to lay their eggs on some Antarctic island of the South Pacific. So from the circumgyrations of its skiey wheelings my soul descends to hatch once in a great while its Meditations.

How I should like to distil my disesteem of my contemporaries into prose so perfect that all of them would have to read it!

But good style depends, the Persian critics tell us, upon freedom from monetary troubles. Only thus, they say, can one arrive at perfect diction.

When by sips of champagne and a few oysters they can no longer keep me from fading away into the infinite azure, 'you cannot,' I shall whisper my last faint message to the world, 'be too fastidious.'

或者一位思想之主，将宇宙奥妙蔽之以一言；

一切全知，无论什么，敲掉少壮狮子的牙齿，敲碎它们口中的大牙[102]；

或者躺在床上，日复一日，像儒贝尔[103]那样，身着一袭粉红色睡衣，努力让自己什么念头都不想，什么感情都不动？

多难啊要好人去犯错！我似乎发觉所有能行差踏错的快活之路全给堵上了不让我走。

一圈又一圈地绕着世界，乘着南极不停歇的暴风，信天翁永远在翱翔；一年只降落一次，把卵产在南太平洋的某个极地岛屿上。也是这样，从它蓝天奋翼的盘旋中，我的灵魂久久地会降落一次，来孵化它的玄思。

我该有多喜欢把我对同代人的不敬与不屑提炼成文，词句完美得令他们一个个非读不可！

然而好的风格靠的是，波斯批评家告诉我们，摆脱了钱财困扰的自由。只有这样，他们说，一个人才能达致完美的言辞。

等到靠呷几口香槟啖几枚牡蛎他们已不再能阻止我隐入无尽的蓝天时，“你不能，”我要将我最后微弱的留言低声说给世界，“太挑剔。”

LAST WORDS

最后的话

Last Words

Growing old is no gradual decline, but a series of falls, full of sorrow, from one ledge to another. Yet when we pick ourselves up we find that our bones are not broken; while not unpleasing is the new terrace which lies unexplored before us.

And far below we may pluck from the Tree of Life its mellowest fruit, that joy of Survival, which can only ripen there.

'Yes,' I said one afternoon in the Park, as I looked rather contemptuously at the people of Fashion, moving slow and well-dressed in the sunshine, 'but how about the others, the Courtiers and Beauties and Dandies of the past? They wore fine costumes, and glittered for their hour in the summer air. What has become of them?' I somewhat rhetorically asked. They were all dead now. Their day was over. They were cold in their graves.

And I thought of those austere spirits who, in garrets far from the Park and Fashion, had scorned the fumes and tinsel of the loud World.

But, good Heavens! these severe spirits were, it occurred to me, all, as a matter of fact, quite as dead as the others.

If it didn't all depend on me; if I wasn't bound to vindicate the Truth on all occasions, and shout down every falsehood, standing alone in arms against a sea of Error, and holding desperately in place the hook from which Truth and

最后的话

年华渐老绝非渐渐衰弱，而是一连串的跌落，充满着哀伤，一级跌一级。然而当我们重新爬起，便发现自己的骨头并没有摔折；不无欢欣的是那片新的平台展现眼前，还等着去探索呢。

在很深的底下，我们可以采摘生命之树最甘美的果实，那生存的欢乐，只能在那里才能熟透。

“是的，”我有一天下午在公园里说道，一边颇为不屑地看着那些时髦人物，瞧他们衣着光鲜地在阳光中缓步而行，“但其他风流人物呢，旧时的那些大官、美女、公子哥儿？他们锦衣华服，在夏日暖风中闪亮一时。这些人又怎样了？”我有些明知故问。他们现在都死了。他们得意的日子过去了。他们冷冰冰地待在自己的坟墓里。

我想到那些克勤克俭的遗世精魂，他们住在远离公园和时尚的阁楼里，对人间纸醉金迷的烟华嗤之以鼻。

可是，天哪！这些严于律己的魂灵，我突然想起，一个个，说白了，死得跟其他人差不多。

要不是全仰赖我；要不是事无巨细我都得为真理辩护，高声压住每一句虚言假语，独自披挂上阵面对浩瀚如海的错误，拼着命把那钩子稳住，而钩子上挂着的真理、正义和优雅的品

Righteousness and Good Taste hang as by a thread and tremble over the unspeakable abyss; if but for a day or two; —it cannot be. I cannot let art and civilization go crashing into chaos. Suppose the skies should fall in while I was napping and the round world collapse into stardust again?

'What an intolerable young person!' I exclaimed, the moment he had left the room. 'How can one sit and listen to such folly? The arrogance and ignorance of these young men! And the things they write, and their pictures!'

'It's all pose and self-advertisement I tell you—'

'They have no reverence!' I gobbled.

Now why do I do it? I know it unhairs my head and makes my joints rigid; —why then do I go on talking myself into a toothless old fogey?

Shabby old waistcoat, what made the heart beat that you used to cover? Funny-shaped hat, where are the hopes that once nested beneath you? Old shoes, hurrying along what dim paths of the Past did I wear out your soles?

Oh dear, this living and eating and growing old; these doubts and aches in the back, and want of interest in Nightingales and Roses ....

Am I the person who used to wake in the middle of the night and laugh with the joy of living? Who worried about the existence of God, and danced with young ladies till long

味正颤巍巍千钧一发地悬在那无可名状的深渊上；哪怕只是一两天；——这可不行呀。我不能让艺术与文明崩坍，堕入混乱。想想要是天塌了而我在打盹，要是这圆圆的世界又崩溃成星尘了呢？

“真让人受不了的一个年轻人！”他一离开房间我便感叹道，“一个人怎么能安坐着听这等蠢话？听这些胸无点墨又目中无人的年轻人！还有他们写的东西，画的画！”

“全都是装腔作势自我吹嘘，我告诉你——”

“他们没有崇敬之心！”我嚷道。

而我为什么做这事呢？我知道这是让我掉头发腿脚僵硬的事；——那我为什么还讲个不停，讲得自己都成了个牙齿掉光的老古董？

破旧的马甲，有什么令人心跳的事情你过往屡屡遮掩？形状滑稽的帽子，如今在哪里呢，那些曾在你下面筑巢的希望？旧鞋子啊，匆匆行过哪些往日昏暗的小路，我磨穿了你们的鞋底？

天哪，这样活着、吃着、老着；这些个心中的疑窦和背上的疼痛，这种对夜莺与玫瑰的兴趣缺缺……

我是否仍是那个人，他曾经常常半夜醒来，为生的喜悦而欢笑？曾为上帝的存在而忧心，与年轻女郎跳舞直到晨光高照？曾

after daybreak? Who sang 'Auld Lang Syne' and howled with sentiment, and more than once gazed at the full moon through a blur of great, romantic tears?

Mind you, I don't say that their eyes aren't bigger than ours, their eyelashes longer, their faces more pink and plump; — and they can skip about with an agility of limb which we cannot equal. But all the same a great deal too much is made of these painted dolls.

Think of the thinness of their conversation!

Depicted in gaudy tints on the covers of paper novels they look well enough; and they make a better appearance, I daresay, in punts, than we do. But is that a reason why they should be allowed to disturb the decorum of tables, and interrupt with their anecdotes and giggles our grave consultations?

One Autumn, a good many years ago—I forget the exact date, but it was a considerable time before the War—I spent a few weeks in Venice in lodgings that looked out on an old Venetian garden. There was a rustic temple at the end of the garden, and on its pediment stood some naked, decayed, gesticulating statues—heathen gods and goddesses I vaguely thought them; — and above, among the yellowing trees, I could see the belfry of a small convent—a convent of Nuns vowed to contemplation, who were immured there for life, and never went outside the convent walls.

The belfry was so near that when, towards dusk, the

经唱着《友谊万岁》而动情号啕，不止一次凝望着高天满月，双眼模糊，噙着大颗大颗浪漫的泪珠？

请注意，我不是说这些人不比我们眼睛更大，睫毛更长，脸更圆润；——还能跳来蹦去呢，那伶俐劲我们比不上。但不管怎么说还是拿这些施脂着粉的娃娃太当回事儿了。

想想看这些人的言谈有多单薄！

用俗艳的色调彩印在平装小说的封面上，这些人看着够漂亮的；河上泛舟时，我敢说，模样也比我们耐看。但这是个理由吗，允许这些人扰乱餐桌礼仪，用逸闻和傻笑来打断我们事关重大的商讨咨询？

有一年秋天，很多很多年前——我忘了确切日期，但那是战前很久的时候——我在威尼斯待过几个星期，住处对着一个古老的威尼斯风格的花园。花园尽头有一座乡村庙宇，山墙上立着一些残破的、比着手势的裸体雕像——异教的男女神祇我依稀觉得它们是；——在这之上，秋色渐黄的树木间，我看得见一座小修道院的钟塔——修道院的修女们立志专心于冥想默祷，在这里幽居终身，从不踏出院墙一步。

塔离得很近，向晚时分，当塔钟衬着天色响起，我都看得见钟

convent bell began to ring against the sky, I could see its bell-rope and clapper moving; and sometimes, as I sat there at my window, I would think about the mysterious existence, so near me, of those life-renouncing virgins.

Very clearly it comes back to me, the look of that untidy garden, of those gesticulating statues, and of that convent bell swinging against the sky; but the thoughts that I thought about those Nuns I have completely forgotten. They were probably not of any especial interest.

It came back to me this rainy afternoon for no reason, the memory of an afternoon long ago alone in the country, when, at the end of an autumn day, I had stood at the rain-dashed window and gazed out at the dim landscape; and as I watched the yellowing leaves blown about the garden, I had seen a flock of birds rise above the half-denuded poplars and wheel in the darkening sky. I had felt there was a mysterious meaning in that moment, and in that flight of dim-seen birds an augury of ill-omen for my life. It was a mood of autumnal, minor-poet melancholy, a mood with which, it had occurred to me, I might fill out the rhymes of a lugubrious sonnet.

But my Sonnet about those birds—those Starlings, or whatever they were—will, I fear, never be written now. For how can I now recapture the sadness, the self-pity of youth?

Alas! What do the compensations of age after all amount to? What joy can the years bring half so sweet as the unhappiness

绳和钟锤的摆动；有的时候，我坐在窗前，不禁会思索她们神秘的存在，与我咫尺之间，那些遗世弃情的贞女。

历历在目重上心头的景象，是那座凌乱的花园，是那些摆着手势的雕像，是那个修道院的钟衬着天色在摆动；但是关于那些修女的思索，我已全然忘却。也许所想的并不特别有趣吧。

在这个雨中的下午无端端重上心头的，是久远的一个下午的记忆，孤身一人在那乡下，秋日将尽，我站在寒雨飒飒的窗前，望着眼前萧索的景致；花园四处风卷黄叶，这时，只见一群鸟雀从那些叶落近半的白杨树上飞起，盘旋在暮色渐浓的天空中。我感到了有一种神秘的意蕴藏于那一刹那间，群鸟若隐若现的飞翔透着关于我生命的不祥预兆。那是一种暮秋意绪、一种小诗人的凄清之情，此意此情，当时我突然心想，足以成韵，可以填出一阕哀声楚楚的商籁诗。

但是我关于那些飞鸟的商籁诗——那些白头翁，不管是什么鸟吧——到现在，我恐怕，是怎么也写不出来了。时至今日，我又怎么能捕捉回年少时的悲与愁呢？

啊！给年华老去的补偿到头来算什么呢？年岁带来的什么

they take away?

How the years pass and life changes, how all things float down the stream of Time and vanish; how friendships fade, and illusions crumble, and hopes dissolve, and piece after solid piece of soap melts away in our hands as we wash them!

Life, I often thought, would be so different if only I had one; but in the meantime I went on fastening scraps of paper together with pins.

Opalescent, infinitely desirable, in the window of a stationer's shop around the corner, gleamed the paste-pot of my day-dreams. Every day I passed it, but every day my thoughts were distracted by some hope, some disillusion, some metaphysical perplexity, or giant preoccupation with the world's Woe.

And then one morning my pins gave out. I met this crisis with manly resolution; putting on my hat, I went around the corner and bought three paste-pots and took them home. At last the spell was broken. But Oh, at what a cost!

Unnerved and disenchanted, I sat facing those pots of nauseating paste, with nothing now to wait for but death.

Like the Aztec Emperors of ancient Mexico who each year took a solemn oath to make the Sun pursue his wonted journey, I too have vowed to corroborate and help sustain the Solar System; vowed that by no vexed thoughts of mine, no attenuating doubts,

欢乐，能有它带走的愁滋味一半甜美？

情何以堪哪，岁月流逝人生变化，万事万物随时光漂流而湮灭；友情淡去，幻想破灭，希望瓦解；一块又一块，实实在在的肥皂一边洗一边就在我们手中消融！

生活，我常常以为，会很不一样的，只要让我来过就成；但这时我还是照样用别针把碎纸片别在一起。

乳白色的、让人无限向往的、摆在街头转角一家文具店橱窗中微微闪着光的，是我朝思暮想的那罐浆糊。每天我从那前面走过，可每天都有东西令我分心，某个希望、某个失望、某个形而上的困惑，或者因世界的悲苦而心忧如焚。

然后，有一天上午别针用光了。面对这个危机我拿出男子气概当机立断；戴上帽子，走过街角买下三罐浆糊带了回来。魔咒终于破了。但是啊，代价多大！

怅然若失如梦方醒地，我坐着面对那几罐令人反胃的浆糊，现在没什么好等了，只有死亡。

就像古代墨西哥的阿芝特克皇帝们每年都庄严许愿要让太阳一仍旧贯地运行那样，我也发誓鼎力帮助维持太阳系；发誓绝

nor malicious scepticism, nor hypercritical analysis, shall the great frame of things be compromised or shaken.

No one last month but myself seems to have seen it; there was apparently no notice taken of the unwonted, super-abundant flourish of the Blackthorn under the black skies of March all over England, when the hedges shone like walls of moonlight in the fields, and all those gnarled little miserly trees showed themselves off in their pale, silvery wealth.

In all our flower-coloured Poesy I find no mention of this aftershadow of the February snow, this forecast of the white splendour of May. Not one of our purblind poets seems ever to have gone afield to gaze at this ghost.

Like the late Dr. Johnson, when at the age of seventy-two he retired to that summer-house at Streatham to plan a life of greater diligence, I too sometimes go off by myself and resolve to spend eight hours of all my remaining days in some grave employment.

But with all that I know about life, all this cynical and sad knowledge of what happens and must happen, all the experience and caution and disillusion stored and packed in the uncanny grey matter of my cerebrum—with all this inside my bald head, how can I ever dream of banging it against the Stars?

How can they say my life is not a success? Have I not for more than sixty years got enough to eat and escaped being

不让我的恼怒、有损其严整的质疑，以及恶意的揣度、百般挑剔的分析，对这万物的伟大框架造成损害，令其动摇。

上个月，除了我自己似乎没有人见到这情景；看起来谁也没注意到黑刺李在英格兰全地三月的黑色天空下异乎寻常地怒放招展，一道道树篱亮闪闪的，犹如一面面月光之墙立在田野上，这些瘤瘿累累又贫气孤寒的小树一棵棵披上淡淡的银装炫耀着它们各自的繁盛。

在我们所有花色斑斓的诗歌里，我都没找到有哪处提及这二月雪踪的续影、这五月瑶光的先导。我们两眼蒙眬的诗人似乎从未有哪位踏足荒外来见识这野地幽灵。

像已故的约翰逊博士那样，年纪七十有二时退居那座位于斯特雷特姆的夏日别墅，计划过一种更为勤奋的生活，我有时也一个人抽身，决心在自己剩下的日子里每天将八个钟头派上什么大用场。

但是，以我对生活所知的一切，对发生和必定发生的大小事件抱持的所有这犬儒和悲哀的认识，在大脑那玄妙的灰质中存储包藏着的所有经验、审慎、省悟——有这一切囤在我的秃头里，我怎么可能会做梦拿脑袋去撞星星呢？

他们怎么能说我的生活不成功呢？难道六十多年来我不是

eaten?

The old know what they want; the young are sad and bewildered.

Don't let young people confide in you their aspirations; when they drop them they will drop you.

There is more felicity on the far side of baldness than young men can possibly imagine.

The denunciation of the young is a necessary part of the hygiene of older people, and greatly assists the circulation or their blood.

But what if we can find no freshly-kindled fires for our wet blankets to put out?

To deprive elderly people of their bogeys is as brutal as snatching from babies their big stuffed bears.

Moonshine is all moonshine to me.

Thank heavens, the sun has gone in, and I don't have to go out and enjoy it.

Give me a bed and a book and I am happy.

The mere process of growing old together will make the slightest acquaintance seem a bosom-friend.

有吃有喝，而且成功逃脱没被吃掉吗？

年长的知道他们想要什么，年轻的伤心又迷惘。

别让年轻人向你吐露他们的抱负，他们放弃抱负时你也会给放弃的。

谢顶之后福气之大，年轻人大概想都想不到。

数落年轻人是年长者的保健必备，大大有助于他们的血液循环。

但要是找不到刚点燃的新鲜火苗让我们的湿毛毯去扑灭，那又该怎么办？

夺走老人心中的暗鬼，跟抢走小孩的玩具熊一样残忍。

是蠢话，对于我就全是蠢话。

感谢上天，太阳进来了，我不用出去就享受得到了。

得床一张书一本，我心自喜。

光凭一道老去，就足以让最疏的交情似乎成了最亲的挚友。

What with its crude awakenings can youth know of the rich returns of awareness to old people from their afternoon naps; of their ironic thoughts and long retrospections, and the sweetness they taste of not being dead?

When elderly invalids meet with fellow-victims of their own ailments! then at last real conversation begins, and life is delicious.

Because once, in the unbelievable past, they underwent that amazing mutation, there are old people who will tell you that they know what Love is.

The follies we could not see through in our youth are what make us play the fool when we are old.

Unrequited affections are in youth unmitigated woes; only later on in life do we learn to appreciate the charm of these bogus heart-breaks.

'Go to the ruins,' whispers the excavated voice of Babylonian disillusion, 'and behold the skulls of the former and the latter; who was the evil-doer, and who the benefactor?'

All my life, as down an abyss without a bottom, I have been pouring van-loads of information into that vacancy of oblivion I call my mind.

Pins, penknives, spectacles, scissors, great paper-cutters,

凭那粗豪的说醒就醒，年纪轻轻能知道什么老年人午间睡醒意识回归的那种丰足呢？能知道多少他们心中的反讽和久久的追忆反省，还有那种此身未殁的甘甜呢？

老人同病相遇！这时候，真正的交谈终于开始，生活也有滋有味了。

因为曾经，在难以相信的从前，他们经历过那场奇妙的蜕变，所以有老人会告诉你，他们懂得爱是什么。

是年轻时看不透的傻事，令我们在年老时装傻。

钟情而不得回报是年轻时不能消减的痛；只有在往后的生命里我们才学会欣赏这些虚矫的心碎具有的魅力。

“去废墟吧，”巴比伦人的醒悟之声出得土来轻轻说道，“看看前人及其后人的头骨吧；谁是作恶之人，谁又是行善之人？”

我这一辈子，就像对着一个无底深渊似的，把整车整车的信息不断倒入那个遗忘的虚空，我把它叫作头脑。

别针、铅笔刀、眼镜、剪刀、大裁纸刀、雨伞，还有一个个大活

umbrellas, and friends as large as life—the things I lose grow bigger and bigger every day; and one day soon I shall lose the big world itself.

The Universe is becoming a bore.

'Since you're going straight back to Chelsea, would you mind taking these plovers' eggs to poor Gertrude? She's so ill; but she eats plovers' eggs, and these have just come up fresh from Norfolk.'

'Of course, you won't do it,' whispered a voice in my ear, as I carried that little mossy basket of eggs on the Underground; 'You won't do it; you're too white-livered a milksop. But a real Lord of Life with a zest for experience, who wanted to know what it feels like to snap his fingers at decent behaviour, would take those eggs home and eat them himself. But you,' from his realm underground Satan sneered, 'haven't the guts to do it.'

When hope fades away and belief and craving, and we come to contemplate in temporal things only their eternal meanings, then our life ceases at last to be a sham and a failure; and when we die, dainty will be our death.

I got up with Stoic fortitude of mind in the cold this morning; but afterwards, in my hot bath, I joined the school of Epicurus. I was a Materialist at breakfast; after it an Idealist, as I smoked my first cigarette and turned the world to transcendental

人朋友——我失去的东西一天天越来越大；不久会有一天，我将失去这一大个世界本身。

宇宙正变得无聊。

“既然你是直接回切尔西，能不能麻烦你把这些鸻鸟蛋带给可怜的格特鲁德？她病得这么重；但吃得了鸻鸟蛋，这些蛋很新鲜，刚从诺福克送过来。”

“当然，你不会干的，”我拎着那个苔渍斑斑的装蛋小篮子坐在地下列车上时，有一个声音悄悄在我耳边说，“你不会干的；你是个胆子太小的胆小鬼。但真正的生活之主有着经历新体验的热忱，他想知道对体面的举止打响指是个什么感觉，会把那些蛋拿回家自己吃了。但是你，”撒旦自他的地下幽界冷笑道，“没这个胆干这个事。”

当希望逝去，信仰和渴想也淡漠了，我们便开始只思考眼前事物的永恒意义，到那时我们的人生终于不再是一场假戏、一次挫败；死，也将死得雅致。

今早，我怀着斯多葛学派坚忍的禁欲之心冒着寒冷起床；但过后，泡在热水浴缸中，我加入了伊壁鸠鲁的享乐派。吃早餐时我是个唯物主义者；吃过了是个唯心主义者，一边抽着一天的第一支香烟一边把世界转化为超逸的水汽。但是，我一开始读《泰

vapour. But when I began to read the *Times* I had no doubt of the existence of an external world.

So all the morning and all the afternoon opinions kept flowing into and out of the receptacle of my mind; till by the time the enormous day was over, it had been filled by most of the widely-known Theories of Existence, and emptied of them.

This long speculation of life, this thinking and syllogizing that always goes on inside me, this running over and over of hypothesis and surmise and supposition—one day this infinite Argument will have ended, the debate will be for ever over, I shall have come to an indisputable conclusion, and my brain will be at rest.

晤士报》便毫不怀疑存在着一个外部世界。

就这样整个上午整个下午各种见解不停地在我内心这个容器里进进出出；等到这沸沸扬扬的一天过完，那里便满满地填过大部分耳熟能详的存在理论，又清得空空如也。

这经年累月的生命思考，这永在我心中持续的思索和推理，这种对假设、揣测、假定一遍遍的推敲沉吟——将来有一天这个无尽的争论就结束了，辩论彻底了结，我将会达致一个无可辩驳的结论，我的大脑将从此安息。

EPILOGUE

Quale nei plenilunii sereni
Trivia ride tra le ninfe eterne—

IL PARADISO.

跋

犹如夜空清澈月轮正满，

特丽维亚微笑于永恒的林泽仙女间——

《神曲·天堂篇》第二十三首

Epilogue

'What funny coats you wear, dear Readers! And your hats! The thought of your hats does make me laugh, and I think your sex-theories quite horrid.'

Thus across the great gulf of Time I send, with a wave of my hand, a greeting to that quaint people we call Posterity, whom I, like other great writers, claim as my readers, —urging them to hurry up and get born, that they may have the pleasure of reading TRIVIA.

跋

“你们穿的大衣多滑稽啊，亲爱的读者！还有戴的帽子！一想到你们的帽子我真就忍不住要笑，另外我觉得你们的各种性爱理论很是吓人。”

就这样，跨越时间的巨大鸿沟我挥一挥手，送去一声问候，给那些古怪的人，我们称之为后人的那些人；我，一如其他大作家，认他们为我的读者——催他们快点，快点出生，好有幸读读这琐事琐思，这闪现于巷陌间的特丽维亚。

注释

1 巨石阵是英格兰南部索尔兹伯里平原 (Salisbury Plain) 上一处史前巨石建筑遗址，现为著名的旅游景点。

2 东方三博士指耶稣降生时从东方来朝见的三博士。

3 古希腊神话中，猎人亚克托安因为偷看女神阿尔忒弥斯 (Artemis) 洗澡而受到惩罚变为牡鹿，最终被自己的狗群撕为碎片。在古希腊古罗马神话的发展中，阿尔忒弥斯最终和原文中所称的狄安娜演变为同一个神祇。

4 在伦敦南部有一座"柏莱大楼" (Bligh House)，但建于1794年，第一任主人是威廉·柏莱船长，1789年他任船长的"邦蒂"号 (*Bounty*) 船员哗变事件之后，一家人在那里住了十来年，直至1805年他被任命为新南威尔士总督为止。而英国内战时期有名的围城之战攻的是位于伦敦东南方汉普郡的贝辛城堡 (Basing House)，该战事发生于1642年至1645年之间。因此，本文所写的柏莱大楼具体所指，还有待考证。

5 卢顿是英格兰东部一个城镇，位于伦敦以北五十一公里处。

6 此处所指应该是曾任牛津大学牧师的学者罗伯特·伯顿 (Robert Burton, 1577—1640) 的巨著《忧郁之解剖》(*The Anatomy of Melancholy*) 一书。该书1621年初版时有近九百页，后有多次修订、扩充和再版，1932年的版本于2001年重印再版。本篇所述典故，多出自该书"嫉妒的解药" (Cure of Jealousy) 一节。其中既有古罗马的著名统帅和政治家恺撒大帝 (公元前100—前44) 和庞贝 (公元前106—前48)、罗马帝国的开国君主奥古斯都（公元前63—公元14），也有与神话相关的特洛伊战争中阿开奥斯联军统帅阿伽门农、阿伽门农之弟和海伦之夫斯巴达国王墨涅拉俄斯、罗马帝国有“哲学家皇帝”之称的马尔库斯·奥勒利乌斯（121—180）。另外提到的腓力是马其顿国王腓力二世（Philip II of Macedon，公元前382—前336），而伯丁那克斯（126—193）又是在生命最后三个月在位的罗马皇帝，伊拉斯谟（约1466—1536）则是荷兰神学家、人文主义思想家，其于1511年出版的拉丁文讽刺作品《愚人颂》（*In Praise of Folly*）是文艺复兴时期最著名的作品之一。

7 约伯，《圣经》人物，以受苦和坚忍著称，历经磨难却坚信上帝。

8 典出荷马史诗《奥德赛》（*Odyssey*，11.14），其中描述了辛梅里安人一族，他们居住于世界边缘冥界之门的黑暗之地。

9 语出古罗马诗人贺拉斯的《本达希尔姆之泉》（“Spring of Bandusium”，《颂歌》，3.13），诗人在诗中承诺以自己的诗让这泉水不朽。

10 爱德华·吉本（Edward Gibbon，1737—1794），英国历史学家和作家，著有《罗马帝国衰亡史》（*The History of the Decline and Fall of the Roman Empire*）。

11 埃德蒙·伯克（Edmund Burke，1729—1797），英国政治家、作家、政治理论家和哲学家，反对英王乔治三世和英国政府，支持美国殖民地和美国革命，对法国大革命持批判态度。

12 即查塔姆第一伯爵老威廉·皮特（William Pitt，1708—1778），1766年到1768年的英国首相。作为七年战争（1756—1763）时期英国的政治领袖，他对战胜法国贡献良多，这一胜利奠定了英国此后作为世界大国的地位。他反对政府中的腐败，鼓吹英帝国的扩张主义。

13 原文Mammon（玛门），本义为“财富”，《圣经·新约》中用其来描绘物质财富或贪婪，也即七宗罪中的贪婪。

14 乔治·贝克莱 (George Berkeley, 1685—1753)，爱尔兰唯心主义哲学家，英国近代经验主义哲学家代表人物之一，圣公会驻爱尔兰科克郡克洛因镇的主教，于1709年出版第一部巨作《视觉新论》(*An Essay Towards a New Theory of Vision*)，其最重要的哲学著作《人类知识原理》(*A Treatise Concerning the Principles of Human Knowledge*) 于1710年问世。他认为存在即被感知。

15 贾拉鲁丁·穆罕默德·鲁米 (Jalāl ad-Dīn Muḥammad Rūmī, 1207—1273)，波斯伊斯兰教苏非派诗人，出生于巴尔赫 (今阿富汗境内)，其主要著作《玛斯纳维》(*Masnavi*) 即《训言诗》为二行诗体，包含约两万六千个对句。

16 《仙后》(*The Faerie Queene*) 为斯宾塞 (Edmund Spenser, 约1552—1599) 所写的英语长诗，完成之后为六卷本的宗教、道德、政治寓言诗，描述代表美德的各位骑士如何效忠代表女王的"仙后"的故事。

17 乔治·斯蒂芬孙 (George Stephenson, 1781—1848)，英国机械工程师、发明家，被称为"铁道之父"，于1814年设计了第一个火车头。

18 詹姆斯·瓦特 (James Watt, 1736—1819)，英国皇家学会院士，爱丁堡皇家学会院士，是苏格兰著名的发明家和机械工程师，他改良了蒸汽机，从而奠定了工业革命的重要基础，是工业革命时期的重要人物。

19 克娄巴特拉方尖碑 (Cleopatra's Needle) 共有两块，一块立在伦敦泰晤士河畔，另一块在纽约中央公园。

20 亨里克·易卜生 (Henrik Ibsen, 1828—1906)，挪威戏剧家、诗人，将道德教育的话剧改造为揭露社会问题的问题剧，影响深远，被认为是现代现实主义戏剧的创始人。

21 索福克勒斯 (Sophocles, 约公元前496—前406)，古希腊三大悲剧诗人之一。

22 斯宾诺莎 (Spinoza, 1632—1677) ,荷兰哲学家。

23 艾娣夫人 (Mrs. Mary Baker Eddy, 1821—1910) , 认为基督能治病的美国基督教科学派创始人,于1908年创办《基督教科学箴言报》。

24 弗兰西斯·培根 (Francis Bacon, 1561—1626) ,著名英国哲学家、政治家、科学家、法学家和散文作家,是古典经验论的始祖,十九世纪中期有人提出莎士比亚的部分甚至全部戏剧其实是培根写的这一推测。

25 老皮特 (William Pitt the Elder, 1708—1778) 即查塔姆第一伯爵。见注12。

26 很可能指奥利弗·克伦威尔 (Oliver Cromwell, 1599—1658) , 英国历史上最重要的军人和政治家之一, 内战时率军打败王党军队, 处死国王查理一世,建立共和国。

27 原文Pentecost是五旬节, 即基督教的圣灵降临节, 在复活节后第五十天和耶稣升天节后第十天。

28 梅非尔是伦敦上流社会顶级住宅区和商业区, 西邻海德公园 (Hyde Park) ,北到牛津街 (Oxford Street) ,南到皮卡迪利大街 (Piccadilly) 和格林公园 (即绿园, Green Park) ,东到摄政街 (Regent Street) 。

29 圣赫勒拿岛是南大西洋上一个小岛, 拿破仑兵败之后流放于此, 1821年死后也葬于此岛。

30 约翰·弥尔顿 (John Milton, 1608—1674) , 英国诗人, 思想家, 著有史诗《失乐园》和反对书报审查制的政治学著作《论出版自由》。

31 荣福直观是一个基督教神学概念, 指的是人对神最终的直接的自我沟通,因此而达到完全的天国救恩。

32 爱德华七世 (Edward VII, 1841—1910) , 英国国王, 讲究穿着, 性喜交际, 讲求风度和气派。

33 本文第一段提及的几个地方都是伦敦市区中的豪华住宅区,包括白金汉宫所在的皮姆利科区，与下一段提及的郊区形成对比。

34 典出《圣经·马太福音》第五章到第七章，指耶稣基督在山上对门徒的训话。

35 此处指的是英国诗人和版画家威廉·布莱克（William Blake, 1757—1827）。其作品有诗集《天真之歌》和《理想之歌》等。

36 第欧根尼（Diogenes，约公元前404—前323），古希腊哲学家，犬儒学派的代表人物。活跃于公元前四世纪。据说他住在一个木桶里，所有财产只包括这个木桶、一件斗篷、一支棍子和一个面包袋。

37 典出《圣经·诗篇》（39: 6）。

38 典出《圣经·约伯》（4: 19）。

39 出自莎士比亚十四行诗第八十五首。杨熙龄的译文是"满是被各位缪斯润色过的锦绣字眼"。

40 低教会派是圣公会基督教的一个教派，思想偏向新教团体，主张简化教会礼拜仪式。

41 典出《圣经·创世记》（37: 7）。

42 典出《圣经·士师记》（5: 1,7）。

43 典出《圣经·撒母耳记上》（17: 37）。

44 滑铁卢是伦敦市中心的一个区，区内有滑铁卢火车站，该站与同名的地铁站相连，邻近另一个火车站滑铁卢东站。

45 简·奥斯丁（Jane Austen, 1775—1817），英国小说家，代表作有《傲慢与偏见》（*Pride and Prejudice*, 1813），作品多涉及十八世纪末英国地主乡绅的生活。

46 伊伯利街是一条位于伦敦上流社区的大街。

47 保尔·魏尔伦 (Paul Verlaine, 1844—1896) ,法国的象征派诗人。

48 塞缪尔·约翰逊 (Samuel Johnson, 1709—1784) ,英国诗人、散文家,花了九年独力编出《英语词典》(*A Dictionary of the English Language*) ,成为历史上最有名的学者之一。

49 斯隆街是伦敦繁华地带一条南北走向的著名购物街。

50 圣约翰树林是伦敦的一个区,史上为古老的林地米德尔塞克斯森林 (Forest of Middlesex) 的一部分。根据地名翻译惯例,通常称作圣约翰伍德区。该区位于伦敦西北部威斯敏斯特市,摄政公园西北边,绿树成荫,是个非常富裕的居民区。

51 约翰·布赖特 (John Bright, 1811—1889) ,英国激进自由派政治家,主张自由贸易。

52 威廉·尤尔特·格莱斯顿 (William Ewart Gladstone, 1809—1898) ,英国自由党政治家,曾任四届英国首相,任期长达十二年至1894年。

53 书中不止一次提到的黄金时代,典出古希腊神话。在古希腊神话中,人类的历史演化经历了五个时代,即从最早、最高贵和最美好的"黄金时代"依次堕落为"白银时代""青铜时代""英雄时代""黑铁时代"。在黄金时代,人、神和谐相处,因为得神护佑,人不用劳作,无疾患之苦而丰衣足食。

54 琐罗亚斯德 (Zoroaster, 约公元前628—前551) ,出生于今为伊朗北部的米底王国 (Medes) ,创琐罗亚斯德教,是该教派经典《阿维斯塔》(即"波斯古经") 中《伽泰》(十七章赞歌) 的作者;该教信奉阿胡拉·玛兹达 (Ahura Mazda) 为创造一切的至高善神,故在古经中自称"阿胡拉教""玛兹达教";中文称之为祆教、拜火教、火祆教或白头教;据说该教对犹太教以及后来的基督教和伊斯兰教影响深远。

55 毗斯迦山位于约旦河东岸摩押平原上。据《圣经·旧约》记载,耶和华命摩西登上毗斯迦山山顶，看那所应许的流奶和蜜的迦南美地，但他不得进入。

56 昔勒尼的亚里斯提卜 (约公元前435—前360)，古希腊哲学家，昔勒尼学派的创始人，倡导享乐主义，主张通过自身适应环境来获得快乐。

57 贝德福德广场是英国伦敦一个花园广场，建于1775年至1783年间，有保存很好的乔治亚式建筑，为中上阶级居住区，曾有许多名人居住于此。

58 此处提及的几位都是波兰历史上的重要诗人，亚当·密茨凯维奇 (Adam Mickiewicz, 1798—1855) 是波兰浪漫主义的代表；尤利乌什·斯沃瓦茨基 (Juliusz Slowacki, 1809—1849) 也是位波兰浪漫主义诗人，还被认为是波兰现代戏剧之父；斯基蒙·斯基莫诺维兹 (Szymon Szymonowicz, 1558—1629) 是文艺复兴时期的波兰诗人；伊格纳齐·克拉西茨基 (Ignacy Krasicki, 1735—1801) 是波兰启蒙诗人的代表，也是波兰第一部小说的作者；扬·科哈诺夫斯基 (Jan Kochanowski, 1530—1584) 是文艺复兴时期的波兰诗人和剧作家。

59 卡多根花园也称卡多根广场 (Cadogan Square)，建于1877年至1888年间，为伦敦西区骑士桥一处高档住宅区。

60 “金苹果圣园”典出古希腊神话，也称赫斯珀里得斯圣园，是世界西方尽头的花园，住着赫斯珀里得斯 (Hesperides) 三姊妹等一众“夜晚的女儿”或“西方的仙女”；那里是地球上的天堂所在，太阳神车一天之旅结束的居停之地，长满奇花异草，仙女们欢歌曼舞，与一条百头巨龙一道守护天后赫拉的那棵金苹果树。

61 弗雷德里克·威廉·法拉尔 (Frederic William Farrar, 1831—1903)，英国教会牧师、教师和作家，著述颇丰，涵盖小说、语文学和宗教著作，并将达尔文的一些思想应用于对语言关系的描述。

62 费利克斯·门德尔松 (Felix Mendelssohn, 1809—1847)，德国浪漫乐派最具代表性的人物之一。

63 摩尔人是欧洲人对中世纪伊比利亚半岛(今西班牙和葡萄牙)和西西里岛等地穆斯林的称呼,带有贬义。

64 骑士桥是伦敦西区一处富人区,毗邻海德公园,有众多维多利亚式豪宅和花园广场。

65 布卢姆茨伯里是伦敦西区一个人文荟萃的地区和时尚住宅区,除了有众多花园广场之外,更是大英博物馆和伦敦大学以及其他高等教育和文化设施的所在地;当时活跃于这一文化艺术中心的有众多作家、批评家和艺术家,形成一个"布卢姆茨伯里派",成员有伦敦文学界的核心人物弗吉尼亚·伍尔夫(Virginia Woolf,1882—1941)。

66 巴勒姆地区在南伦敦,中心地带有许多酒吧、餐厅和店铺,有繁华的夜生活包括喜剧歌舞表演等。

67 切尔西位处泰晤士河北岸,为一著名的高级住宅区,除了豪华商店和餐馆之外也有始自十九世纪的文化和艺术传统,曾有不少作家居于此地,如奥斯卡·王尔德等。

68 杰里米·边沁(Jeremy Bentham,1748—1832),英国哲学家、法学家和社会改革家,功利主义和动物权利最早的倡导者之一,注重效益原则,政治上反对君主专制,提倡普选。

69 勒内·笛卡儿(René Descartes,1596—1650),法国哲学家、数学家、物理学家,解析几何创始人,也是西方现代哲学思想的奠基人之一。

70 伯沙撒是新巴比伦王国的最后一位统治者,据《圣经·但以理书》第五章记述,在伯沙撒举行的一次千人大宴上,有手指在墙上写字,他看了心慌意乱但无人能解,而后召但以理解读,知是上帝对他的审判,说他的国将亡。

71 语出英国作家托马斯·布朗爵士(Sir Thomas Browne,1605—1682)出版于1658年的《瓮葬》(*Hydriotaphia*,或*Urn Burial*)一书第五章。

72 亚他那修信经，又称得救经，是基督教三大信经之一，提出了圣灵双出说，即圣灵出自圣父与圣子；此信经的教义为天主教和基督新教所共同接受。

73 查令十字是伦敦威斯敏斯特一个繁忙的交会路口，传统意义上的伦敦中心点，也是英国习惯上的铁路、公路里程零基准点。

74 梯利·怀姆采石洞位于英格兰南部波白克（半）岛（Isle of Purbeck）上斯沃尼奇以南一英里的多尔斯顿郊野公园（Durlston Country Park），由三个古采石场组成。

75 原文Arcady（阿卡狄亚）是古希腊一个山地牧区，神话中牧神潘（Pan）的家乡，在艺术作品中是一个淳朴宁静的乡野，过着田园生活的居民与外面世界甚少来往，类似中文所称的世外桃源。

76 威廉·华兹华斯（William Wordsworth，1770—1850），英国浪漫主义诗人，湖畔诗人的代表，于1843年获任桂冠诗人。其《水仙》（*The Daffodils*）一诗清新自然优美，广为流传。

77 高派教会亦称高教会派，是基督新教里的一个派别，注重仪式，偏向天主教传统。

78 维吉尔（Virgil，公元前70—前19），古罗马最伟大的一位诗人，作品有《牧歌集》《农事诗》《埃涅阿斯纪》等，对后世诗人作家如贺拉斯、但丁和莎士比亚等有很大影响。

79 忒奥克里托斯（Theocritus，约公元前310—前250），古希腊著名诗人、学者，为西方文学田园诗派的创始人。

80 典出以十四世纪法国哲学家布里丹（Jean Buridan）的名字命名的悖论“布里丹之驴”（Buridan's ass），说的是一只具有完全理性的驴在两堆完全相同的干草之间，因为无法决定该吃哪一堆草而最终饿死。

81 让-安托万·华托（Jean-Antoine Watteau，1684—1721），为法国洛可可时

代的代表画家,作品多描绘田园牧歌的场景。

82 击桌通灵是一种通灵做法,几个人围坐桌边,灵媒不借助可见物体而敲击桌子发出声音,以此与死者魂灵交通。

83 伊曼努尔·康德 (Immanuel Kant, 1724—1804) ,启蒙时代著名德意志哲学家,德国古典哲学创始人,对德国唯心主义和浪漫主义以及后世哲学思想影响深远。

84 克塞诺芬尼 (Xenophanes of Colophon, 约公元前565—前473) ,古希腊哲学家、神学家、诗人,以及社会宗教评论家。

85 语出英国人类学家詹姆斯·乔治·弗雷泽爵士 (Sir James George Frazer, 1854—1941) 所著的《金枝: 巫术与宗教之研究》(*The Golden Bough: A Study in Magic and Religion*) 1894年麦克米伦版二卷本的第一卷第五十四页。

86 欧内斯特·威廉·布朗 (Ernest William Brown, 1866—1938) ,生于英国后入籍美国的一位数学家和天文学家,毕生研究月球运动,编制了非常精确的月球表。

87 乔治·威廉·希尔 (George William Hill, 1838—1914) ,美国天文学家和数学家,对天体力学颇有贡献。

88 所多玛是《圣经·创世记》中所说的罪恶之城。

89 典出《圣经·创世记》第十九章。上帝在摧毁所多玛城之前通知好人罗得携家小往山上避灾,不能回头看也不能中途站住,但罗得的妻子回头看了,马上变成了石头 (圣经中是变成一根盐柱) 。

90 伊利斯的皮浪 (Pyrrho of Elis, 约公元前 365—前 275) 是古希腊一位怀疑派哲学家,被认为是怀疑论鼻祖,有学派名为皮浪主义。皮浪一个很重要的观点是悬搁判断,认为人无法认识事物本身,人的意见永远是主观的,因此对待一切事物的正确态度是将判断搁置。伊利斯是古希腊的一个城邦。

91 典出《圣经·出埃及记》第三十二章。带犹太人出埃及的摩西在西奈山上见上帝的时候，犹太人制造了一尊神像金牛犊，犯戒拜偶像；摩西得知之后下山见到人们跳舞祭拜，极为愤怒，将写有十诫的两块法版摔碎，用火烧毁了金牛犊。

92 大卫王是公元前十世纪犹太以色列国的国王，事迹大多见于《圣经·撒母耳记上、下》，《圣经》中的赞美诗多是他写的。

93 贝尔纳·勒·布耶·德·丰特奈尔 (Bernard Le Bovier de Fontenelle, 1657—1757)，法国散文作家，对科学主题很感兴趣，曾任法兰西皇家科学院秘书达四十二年之久，是欧洲启蒙时代一位重要人物。

94 皮埃尔·丹尼尔·于埃 (Pierre Daniel Huet, 1630—1721)，法国学者，曾任苏瓦松 (Soissons) 和阿夫朗什 (Avranches) 两地的主教。

95 阿波尔-卡西姆·菲尔多西·杜西 (Abul-Qâsem Firdausi Tusi, 约940—1019/1025)，波斯诗人，很重要且广受尊重，最重要的作品是民族史诗《列王纪》(*Book of Kings*)。他出身贵族，父亲是富裕的地主。

96 查尔斯·亚瑟耐斯·瓦尔肯耐尔 (Charles Athanase Walckenaer, 1771—1852)，法国博物学家，曾就读于牛津大学和格拉斯哥大学，1791年回到法国并担任公职，1823年获封为男爵。

97 塞维涅夫人 (Madame de Sévigné, 1626—1696)，为法国书信作家代表，著有《书简集》(*Lettres*, 1725年初版，1862年至1867年出全本)。其风格生动、风趣，为十七世纪法国古典主义散文的代表作，内容反映了路易十四时代法国的社会风貌，当时宫廷和上层贵族的生活，被奉为法国文学的瑰宝。

98 尼农·德·朗科洛 (Ninon de Lenclos, 1620—1705)，法国作家，巴黎名交际花和艺术赞助人。

99 阿佛烈·丁尼生 (Alfred Tennyson, 1809—1892)，英国著名诗人，深受维多利亚女王的赏识，于1850年获得了桂冠诗人的称号，后来又在1884年获封为男爵；1853年之后大部分时间在自己位于怀特岛法令福德的庄园中生活。

100 塞缪尔·泰勒·柯勒律治 (Samuel Taylor Coleridge, 1772—1834)，英国诗人、文学评论家，英国浪漫主义文学的奠基人之一。作品包括名诗《古舟子咏》(*The Rime of the Ancient Mariner*)。

101 大卫·休谟 (David Hume, 1711—1776)，苏格兰哲学家、经济学家和历史学家，与乔治·贝克莱和约翰·洛克 (John Locke, 1632—1704) 同为英国近代经验主义哲学家中的三大代表人物。其最重要的著作《人性论》(*A Treatise of Human Nature*) 于二十六岁时完成，这也是哲学史上最重要的著作之一。

102 典出《圣经·诗篇》第五十八篇，大卫求耶和华敲掉恶人和少壮狮子口中的大牙。

103 约瑟夫·儒贝尔 (Joseph Joubert, 1754—1824)，法国文人，身体羸弱，一生未有著述，身后由好友整理结集出版的《随思录》(*Pensées*) 令其闻名。